I0825160

THE GREAT HOUSES OF PILL HILL

THE GREAT HOUSES OF PILL HILL

DIANE JOSEFOWICZ

Published by
Soho Press
227 W 17th Street
New York, NY 10011
www.sohopress.com

Library of Congress Cataloging-in-Publication Data

Names: Josefowicz, Diane Greco author
Title: The great houses of Pill Hill / Diane Josefowicz.
Description: New York, NY : Soho Crime, 2026.
Identifiers: LCCN 2025050427

ISBN 978-1-64129-808-7
eISBN 978-1-64129-809-4

Subjects: LCGFT: Detective and mystery fiction | Novels | Fiction
Classification: LCC PS3610.O66567 G74 2026
LC record available at https://lccn.loc.gov/2025050427

Interior design by Janine Agro

Printed in the United States of America

10 9 8 7 6 5 4 3 2 1

EU Responsible Person (for authorities only)
eucomply OÜ
Pärnu mnt 139b-14
11317 Tallinn, Estonia
hello@eucompliancepartner.com
www.eucompliancepartner.com

for Linda Josefowicz

1

My real name is Hannah Cooke, but no one ever calls me that. New Preston's druggist gummed me to my nickname, murmuring *Cookie, Cookie, Cookie Cooke* while my mother signed for her tranquilizer refill and I faked an interest in the paperbacks on the spinner rack. I was a lousy actress and a ruinous blusher, a child unused to attention.

It could have been worse. He could have called me Hard Tack or Sour Pickle, both accurate assessments of my personality in those days. But he chose a sweet name, and like all sugary things, it stuck. Occasionally he slipped me an old-time candy—a licorice, a horehound drop. Accepting these gifts, I discovered myself: a body with a sweet tooth and an appetite for nostalgia. Like the houses I restore, I'm built for a more extravagant era, when architects made allowances for the sweep of a woman's hip. As an interior designer, I believe all curb appeal is relative, specific to a time and place; as a person who values appetites, I am unmoved by appeals to curb mine.

If that sounds harsh, blame New Preston. We use things up; we wear them out. If there's a wound, we salt it. Isn't that what wounds are for? Sometimes I wonder if I'd be happier elsewhere, away from this small town with its elaborate historic houses and the secrets they conceal. It's not that my doubts take me by surprise. Not much, at this point, takes me by surprise. But I do find it strange how the question keeps coming up, like an upholstery tack I don't know I've lost until it lodges in the callus of my heel.

Cross my heart, hope to die: That first time in Chuck Halsey's bedroom, all I took were measurements. I paced them off the old-fashioned way, heel-to-toe, no tape. With its top-nailed floor and fireplace of marble veined delicately as flesh, the room set me to dreaming as soon as I laid eyes on it. Okay, fine—on him.

Chuck had many requirements for the room in which he failed to sleep. Chief among them was that he should not have to share it with his wife. To that problem I had my own solution but as it was not décor-related, I kept my mouth shut and my options open. I once asked Chuck to describe his ideal bedroom. He said: Give me an oblivion of light.

He was a neurosurgeon, and in expansive moods he talked like one—imperious, boastful of his smarts. I gave him what he wanted: I painted the bedroom a clinical white and finished the trim in the same shade, maximum gloss. I installed a skylight, modern up-lights, a galaxy of spots. Bright enough during the day, the room at night frankly blazed, in deference to Chuck, who preferred to work through his sleeplessness rather than spinning in his bed like a pig on a spit—which, in terms of char, is more or less what he became. The authorities say they're better equipped to judge such matters, having seen all manner of human destruction, but they don't know him the way I do. Did.

Better to remember what was beautiful: the sailcloth blinds in pale straw, the kantha quilt of sun-bleached silk, the snowy flokati I set adrift beside the bed. Whenever I touch the replica, a tiny manufacturer's swatch, I remember the spring of the original against the bare soles of my feet.

The deadbolt was Chuck's addition. I suppose he felt safer with the door locked against all comers, including those inside the house. But could I be blamed for providing what his wife would not? I stepped in; I stepped up. There was a need; I met it. Just as I am doing now, after hours in the basement forensics lab of New Preston's finest, attempting to complete this absurd commission.

Reproducing a crime scene in miniature should, in theory, be no different from making a mock-up of any other room. But this time, I'm working for the police, and the project is extremely personal. Detective Bill Phelps, who has commissioned similar items from me in the past, joked that I might even find the gig therapeutic, given my prior involvement.

The deadbolt wasn't the only oddity. There was a fresh gouge in the window casement, and a dusting of powder revealed a handprint on the pane. After a UV beam lit up bloodstains on the flokati, I opened a vein for verisimilitude's sake and allowed my blood to pool on the swatch. To reproduce the smoke stain over the mantel, I used a custard torch. The stain matched the one in the evidence photos only after I'd folded Chuck in half—the doll-sized version, I mean—and tucked him up the chimney. Whereupon my torch died, and I was forced to resort to oven matches. The fire burned differently around his bulk, a detail that had escaped me until I burned my own hands reconstructing the catastrophe.

You can learn a lot from a miniature. I kept the scale of mine conventional, one inch to the foot.

2

We met for the first time just over a year ago, one morning in autumn on the shabby side of Pill Hill. The day broke clear and cold with a kicking wind. The house, a brick pile on a narrow lot, was sandwiched between a peeling pair of Queen Annes, each topped with a witch's cap. Numb-fingered on the sidewalk, I fiddled with my camera. I needed just a handful of shots, images of *before* to be saved for redemption in some TBD *after*.

My heart beat fast. The job wasn't mine, not yet—but I wanted it.

For one thing, the house oozed history. Built in 1880, it was the pet project of architect Russell Warren, extravagant golden boy of New Preston's otherwise staid and truncated Gilded Age. For another, it was gorgeous. Warren liked his houses high, wide, and crusted with baroque details—intricately patterned slate roofs, stained glass fanlights, hand-carved trim. Confected from an immense quantity of mustard brick, this particular Warren manse had been a showstopper, once upon a time.

I nabbed clear shots of the gapped slate roof, a rotting soffit, and copper gutters hanging skew, the work of some local rip-off artist, a type with which the neighborhood abounded despite its genteel façade. That's Pill Hill for you. The name suggests the story: a once-fashionable neighborhood filled with doctors. When they decamped for greener pastures—private practices in the suburbs—the place filled up with weeds and needles. The hospital hung on, though, and easy mortgage terms have recently struck the first sparks of an upswing, although on most days it all still feels like hype. For one thing, everyone has a prescription for the new painkillers, and business is brisk at the methadone clinic, though no one has yet been so bold as to posit a link. At any rate, my would-be clients, the Halseys, had bought in. Either they were completely ignorant of what they had signed up for, or else they were extremely rich. I knew which option I preferred.

I ducked under the portico and tapped my office number into my phone. The line connected with a crash.

Fuckity fuck, shouted my assistant.

Organized and detail-oriented, Fiona Dunne is a godsend when it comes to the practicalities of running a small business, but night school has taken its toll, and no one would mistake her for a morning person.

Fiona, it's me. Is everything okay?

Goddamn, Cookie. Your dumb library stool just came between me and my coffee.

In my mind's eye, I staged the room: Fiona sprawled on the floor amid my sample books and blueprints and the scrambled contents of her school bag, broken Conté crayons and lumps of graphite everywhere, the coffee machine glugging as the library stool rolled toward the sunny corner by the worktable. My twin brindle mutts would be stretched beside the radiator, oblivious as always. Perhaps one would lift its head. They were hard to shock, those two.

Are you bleeding?

Please hold, she said. I am applying direct pressure.

You're bleeding!

Never mind, Cookie. It's just a flesh wound. What's the deal with the Halsey house?

I've renovated some dumps, I said, but nothing like this. The owners are going to need about a thousand permits. Electrical, plumbing, exterior—the works.

What do you figure for the upside? she asked.

The only people who buy into these disasters are romantics with money to burn, I said.

A black sports car slipped beneath the porte-cochère. Behind the wheel, buttoned into a luxe trench coat, sat a dark-haired man—the driver, I assumed, from his detached clock-puncher's expression. He had one gloved hand on the steering wheel; with the other, he cradled a flip phone away from his face. The car rolled to a stop. A statuesque blond draped in a whiskey mink emerged from the passenger side, her white shirt open at the neck to show off tanned collarbones. She hooked a cream leather tote over one elbow and strode up the steps. Summiting, she turned and, unsmiling, raised her hand. There was something peremptory in the gesture.

Bye, Fiona. The client's here.

I am manifesting richness, Fiona said. Please let them be rich.

IN THE shadowy foyer, an immense chandelier hung down, its cut-glass facets furred with dust, every socket empty. Some people take everything, even the light bulbs, when they leave.

Lana said her own name, and I took the buttery gloved hand she extended.

So you're Hannah Cooke.

Call me Cookie.

A flicker of irritation unsettled her features, breaking their expensive symmetry.

Cookie, she said. Right.

There was a silence. I let it unfold. Her gaze swept over me.

I know this place doesn't look like much, she purred. Everyone says we're crazy. But I bet you of all people must know what it's like.

Like what's like?

Her face rearranged itself again, and she vouchsafed a tiny smile.

Oh, well—what it's like to fall in love with something that doesn't exist yet.

Of course, I replied.

Of course, she repeated, touching my arm in a gesture that was supposed to be warm but wasn't.

I followed her through the grand rooms while she ran her mouth, telling me all about how she and her husband had lucked into this pile. The sellers had telegraphed every move. By the closing, she practically had them eating out of her French-manicured hands.

I nodded at the right junctures and made admiring noises.

In the hallway Lana yanked back some loose carpet. Underneath was original parquetry, thin strips of pale oak inlaid with mahogany, each strip bitten at intervals by a pair of tiny nails.

I bet this whole floor's like this, I breathed. It was, in fact, breathtaking.

That's the bet we made, too.

Here was common ground, a moment on which to capitalize. I brushed my fingers over a figured brass doorknob with an agreeable patina.

You've acquired something truly special, I said.

She looked hard at me, but once again, I held my tongue, and after a moment she softened.

I hope so, she said. She gestured at a chipped molding: Can that be repaired?

It's all very doable. Nothing here's so broken it can't be fixed.

The wind rose, rattling the windows, and a creak issued from the direction of the damaged soffit. Oh, it was all doable, but this project was going to require patience, fortitude, and plenty of TLC—tender loving cash. Not that Lana couldn't secure it. Although she looked every inch the New Preston matron—socially adroit, charming in a way that didn't invite inconvenient intimacies—she was the driving force behind Lana Pura, a line of home textiles that routinely sold out of the better department stores from New York to Boston.

How's business? I asked, to change the subject.

We have our ups and downs. It beats Junior League.

Junior League? You hardly seem the type.

Correct, she snapped. I am not the type.

There was the boundary: She would tell me what reality was, and I would agree. My fee increased by fifteen percent, the diva premium.

Downstairs, Lana led me through a glassed-in music room that gave onto a crumbling veranda. It was easy to imagine the scions of New Preston gathered here, sipping champagne from glittering flutes even as the jimsonweed shot up through the decking, sending its noxious shoots everywhere. I started to cough and found I could not stop.

Are you all right? Lana asked, alarmed.

I could use some water, I wheezed. This place does have an energy.

Lana beckoned me down a narrow, uncarpeted passage. I recognized it from other nearby houses of the same vintage:

This was the servants' corridor. It led to the kitchen, a small galley that was striking in its modesty after all those grandly proportioned rooms. She rummaged in a cupboard until she found a glass. She filled it from the tap and handed it to me. As I drank, she ran her fingertips along the battered laminate countertop and scowled at what she found there.

I can hook you up with a housekeeping service, I said, my voice still thick with whatever I'd inhaled in the music room. Landscaping, too, I added, if you want.

It's not that, she replied. Or not *just* that. This kitchen, I don't know. It's so dinky.

I looked away, suppressing a smile. I couldn't imagine Lana had time most nights to do more than dress an avocado, but here she was, dreaming of a magazine kitchen.

It doesn't match the rest of the house at all, she continued.

It's probably a late addition. Built for someone who needed something stripped down. Manageable.

Lana rinsed her fingers and shook them dry, spattering droplets on the tiny electric stovetop, the narrow refrigerator.

I couldn't manage anything in this kitchen!

It's giving *Semi-Homemade*, for sure, I said.

She laughed, a big open-mouthed *haw-haw*, but she kept her eyes trained on mine. I still hadn't passed her test.

You're thinking what, Lana—cherry, granite, stainless?

Rift-sawn white oak, she corrected me. And a farmhouse sink.

From her bag she extracted a folded sheet of creamy paper and handed it to me.

Here's my list, she said. Some are wishes. Others are proper to-dos. Note the fridge specs, please and thank you. I need every last one of those cold cubic feet.

I said: You must entertain a lot.

Oh, she replied airily, what I keep in my fridge is quite entertaining.

Having nothing to say to this mystifying remark, I focused on her list. I was just getting to the end when her driver, he of the sharp trench and gloves, strolled in and set his coffee cup on the counter. Without looking up, Lana shifted her handbag out of the spill zone. He smiled as if her fastidiousness were a charming quirk and pecked her cheek.

Either this was no driver, or he and Lana had a very unorthodox employment arrangement.

Hannah Cooke, I introduced myself.

Dr. Chuck Halsey, he replied, grasping my cold hand in his two warm ones. His hands were sinewy, long-fingered, with nails that were squared-off and immaculate: a surgeon's hands. He was older than Lana—closer to forty, I guessed, with lined olive skin and gingerbread eyes. Bright pennies shone in the slits of his polished loafers.

It's nice to meet you, Hannah.

Everyone calls me Cookie, I told him.

Oh, he said. That's cute.

I smiled as if I didn't have a single thought in my head.

Don't get me wrong. I *did* have thoughts, plenty of them. But putting on the ditz is part of my approach. No one likes a bossy decorator. He and Lana would have plenty of time to appreciate my talents once the job was mine.

I winched that smile up another notch. *Work it, girl.*

Lana's purse squealed. She extracted her phone and stalked, frowning, from the room. Chuck motioned for me to join him at the window. The view gave onto the circular driveway, and I felt the old, familiar pang. Here was contentment—doing the washing up, waiting for someone to come home. I've never had much luck in the domesticity department.

He was so close, I could smell his antiseptic hospital odor, his bitter coffee breath. A warm hand pressed softly on my lower back. I felt myself stiffen.

What do you make of the dream house? he asked.

Sweet view, I said, a sick heat coursing through me. *A licorice, a horehound drop.*

Lana whirled into the room, her heels clattering on the hardwoods, her whole being lasered onto Chuck. We sprang apart, and he shot me a look that rang all my bells.

I moved the meeting along as best I could, elaborating on different ways to enlarge the kitchen. I even made sure to mention the farmhouse sink. Lana was having none of it. I flailed on anyway, toward an ending that I still hoped might also be a start.

It's going to be a complex project, I said. I promise, it will all be worth it in the end.

It will be a relief to get to the end, Lana said.

Sweetheart. Chuck reached to brush a stray hair from her face, saying: This is supposed to be fun.

She pushed his hand away.

Please, she snapped. Don't smarm me.

They weren't going to make it easy, these two. But then all relationships have problems. Why should theirs be different?

Near the front door, an orange blotch of mildew glowed faintly just south of the crown molding. I made a mental note to add damp remediation to the to-do list.

Lana trained dead eyes on Chuck, saying: Thank you for your time today, Hannah.

Thank you, Chuck repeated. Thank you, *Cookie.*

Outside, the sky was an ominous gray. As Lana folded herself into their car's low front seat, Chuck reached to cradle her elbow, and her face contorted so grotesquely I thought she might spit. The engine turned over, and Lana's window slid down. She smiled with just the lower half of her face, showing an incisor smeared with lipstick, gummy pink.

Brainstorm! she cried. I want to throw a *party* when we're done.

Great idea, I said hollowly. I'd spent just an hour with the Halseys, and already I was worn out.

Well, but the party has to give people something to *talk* about. Can we get an oven large enough to roast a whole pig?

I opened my mouth to answer, but the glint in her eye made me self-conscious.

I suppose it depends on the pig, I said.

3

Here's the secret to New Preston's building boom: The real estate's cheap, and the housing stock's phenomenal. Neglected, yes. But phenomenal. Our slim-porticoed Federals and rambling Queen Annes find a ready market among aspiring homeowners priced out of New York and Boston.

Keen to renovate, these new arrivals have time travel on the brain. They're looking for historical accuracy, renovation as conservation. That's where I come in. I've been helming my own business, the Ministry of the Interior, for a few years now, and in that time I've earned a reputation as the one person who can always source the period-appropriate stuff they want: reclaimed hardwoods, hand-forged brass doorknobs, vintage wallpapers depicting tropical plantations, aristo deer hunts, and hair-raising scenes out of myth. Think Judith and Holofernes. The Rape of Europa. As it turned out, Chuck and Lana wanted these things, too—all of it, including the grim mythology, as if they knew, on some level, about the grim scenes that were already on the way.

But I'm getting ahead of myself.

I began in that cramped, impossible kitchen. My mood-words were *lavish*, *glam*. Channeling my inner Russell Warren,

I spec'd an extra-wide fridge, a restaurant-grade cooktop, a double oven, marble countertops, faucets in solid brass. I designed what appeared to be a chef's kitchen, but my brief was to account for the realities beyond appearances. For example: Apart from whatever experiments she might undertake—perhaps in sourdough or cider, and probably with a camera crew on hand—Lana did not cook. That was reality. So those countertops had to be extra deep to accommodate catering trays. Installing them would be challenging since the square footage of the whole kitchen was approximately equivalent to six full-size sheet pans. One architectural element was in my favor: The kitchen shared a wall with a rear parlor. Eliminating that wall would free up the needed space.

The only sticking point was an inconvenient chimney. To comply with the historic district's preservation code, I had to find a way to keep it. That was my first compromise.

Things only got more compromising from there. Sounding the wall, I discovered several large uprights where none should have been, concealed behind the sheetrock. In a house like this, the chimney usually supports the roof. Here, obviously, the story was different. How could I get rid of those uprights without causing the place to collapse?

I called my engineer, a flexibly minded guy who'd just rehabbed his own mid-century split-level. Designing his basement rec room, I accepted every cut corner he demanded, even the ones that put me at odds with the permit office. Now it was his turn to risk his professional neck, by figuring out how to get rid of that wall without bringing down the house.

We met on-site to check out the problem. My preliminary investigations had left dust and drywall everywhere. The engineer stood by the half-demolished wall fiddling with the little pencil he kept tucked behind one ear. I inhaled plaster and exhaled anxiety. What I felt was not fear, I told myself, but excitement.

I'm positive it's not serious, I said. The problem, I mean.

If you're so positive, Cookie, why call me?

I need an expert opinion. Just like you needed mine, not so long ago.

He grinned, showing me a rakish mouthful of expensively squared-off teeth. He might do me a favor, but he wanted something for it. I willed the cold tentacles of my silence right through those Chiclet choppers. His grin collapsed.

Not what you were expecting?

All right, Cookie. Don't get your panties in a bunch.

Not for nothing, I said, but the state of my underwear is not any of your business.

While he stood there smirking, I flicked on my flashlight and pointed it toward the blackened beams.

See these uprights?

I see what's holding up the second floor.

Is there any way to rebalance the load?

You'd be crazy to touch that, he said, stepping back.

Could I file for an exception?

He flicked dust from his shoulders.

You might *possibly* get away with eliminating the uprights closest to the chimney and letting the chimney take the weight. But it's a risk. If this house falls down, you won't be filing for anything but bankruptcy. Think of the lawsuit, Cookie.

He had a point. What I had was a problem. I arranged a meeting with the Halseys to show them what I'd found.

4

Demolition often reveals hidden flaws—rotting beams, jerry-rigged plumbing, an electrical system so outdated the house is exactly one fried rodent away from a smoking pile of dreams and a seven-figure insurance claim, which I suppose has its appeal. I was accustomed to snafus at this stage. But I had my doubts about the Halseys. For all their sophistication, they'd never taken a house back to the studs. If I couldn't project confidence, they'd spook.

We met the next day. The weather was overcast and raw, and the road to the house was deserted. I stepped beneath the porte-cochère, touching off a frantic scrabble along the roofline. A slate tile tumbled, inches from my face, and shattered on the paving.

Looking back, I'd say the Halsey disaster had its roots here, in the first near-miss of demolition. For what it's worth: Chuck and I weren't sleeping together. Yet.

THEY MET me inside, where the problem was. Chuck twanged with pent-up energy, hands nipping in and out of pockets, his beeper twittering at his waist. Lana was subdued—pale, thin-lipped, her face nearly swallowed by her mink's upturned collar. At the back, where the collar met the coat, a tiny tear marred the seam.

I set a cardboard tube of blueprints on the counter and pointed my laser at the problematic wall, into the ragged hole.

Quite a few studs back here, I said. More than you'd expect for an interior wall, and they're in strange places, too.

Lana leaned in, following the laser. Her cream handbag swung from her bent elbow.

These beams are so black! Is that normal?

I reached to touch an upright. It was bone-dry except for a knot that left something dark and sticky on my fingers. I brought them to my face.

It's pitch, I said. There's no mistaking that stink. Anyone have a tissue?

Pitch? Chuck asked. Isn't that incredibly flammable?

Their gazes met in a shared, worldly-wise glance. They'd come to know the world's cheapness, suffered it together. For better, for worse. They were prickly with each other, but I could see, even then, that theirs was a substantial relationship. Maybe Chuck was just a warm person, demonstrative. That hand on my back, last time—it might have been innocent.

Lana muttered: Flammable, is it? That was not disclosed.

Chuck offered me his handkerchief—pressed and folded, worn soft.

Old houses have a lot of problems, I said as I wiped. It didn't help much. Handing the cloth back to him, my fingers touched his, electric. He tucked the cloth away with a fleeting smile that revealed just a glint of tooth.

Oh my, oh my. That hand on my back? Definitely not innocent.

I retrieved the tube of blueprints and herded the Halseys out of the kitchen through the servants' corridor. In the narrow passage, I bumped into Lana's cream handbag. She clicked her tongue, irritated, as she pulled it toward herself. There wasn't enough room in that house for both of us, at least not with all of Lana's accessories. Maybe I was one of them, too, a pricey nuisance.

Sorry for the collision, I said when we reached the parlor. Tight quarters. You know, that small kitchen might have been a pantry back in the day. That's how these old houses were usually arranged. But something about the interior wall doesn't make sense.

Chuck hooted: A lot about this house doesn't make sense!

Make it make sense, Cookie. That's why you're here, isn't it? Lana sniffed.

Holding steady through discomfort is one of those unsung talents that sustain the world's tilt and spin, and so I smiled as I sought my internal level. *Eyes on the prize.*

I explained my engineer's plan. We would spare the chimney, I told them, by removing the nearest beams and reinforcing the remaining load-bearing ones.

You'll get extra space, I said. And we'll find out what's behind that wall.

What in the world might be behind the wall? asked Lana.

Probably nothing, I said. Though now and then, we do find items of historical significance. House plans. Wills. A friend of mine found a girl's diary between two uprights—

Lana pressed: But how did that kitchen get there in the first place? Would the earliest plans for the site be archived somewhere? City Hall?

An archival expedition's not likely to turn up much, I said. The homeowners of yore were not in the habit of documenting their upgrades.

Chuck, pensive, interjected: Why isn't a modern kitchen,

with a mostly open plan, good enough for you, Lana? After all, it's what you *said* you wanted.

I don't remember saying anything like that. I want to keep everything that's original.

That wall is *not* original. Whatever it is, it's not Warren's.

Lana's pout hardened. It was clear from Chuck's tone that this was an ancient battle, and the terms of the peace still had yet to be decided.

It was an honor, I knew, to be trusted with this scene. If they were willing to let me see this much, I had this job. How could I not? I was already part of the family.

Chuck turned to me. Penny for your thoughts?

A warmth spread beneath my collar.

Every renovation has its setbacks, I said. The question is how we deal with them.

Chuck narrowed his eyes. I was pressing him into a more collaborative posture, and he didn't like that.

I don't want to steamroller you, I said. But take it from me, a partial removal of that wall will solve ninety-five percent of your problem. We'll need a good-sized fan to ventilate the kitchen, but we were always going to need that. By the looks of things, there's not much space for a new duct. We might have to vent your kitchen through the chimney.

Chuck, aghast: Through the *chimney*?

It's not as complex as it sounds. These things are doable.

Well, Chuck said, *if* we go ahead with this plan, and that's a *big* if—because if I'm not mistaken, those uprights are what's holding up this part of the house—I want someone reliable.

Knowing reliable guys is part of my job, Chuck, and I would say Harry Deluca's the right guy for this one.

Who's Harry Deluca?

The right guy for the job.

Haw-haw, said Lana, from the shadows.

Chuck scowled, but I sensed hesitation. For all his confidence about the studs and what they supported, he was out of his depth. A specialist himself, he wasn't about to start a fight in someone else's wheelhouse.

I had my own reasons for being less than forthright. But neither Chuck nor Lana had any need to know about my history with Harry, never mind his dodgy impulse control and his mandated anger management sessions, his run-ins with the tax collector and the police. Plenty of people would judge Harry, especially since he did his time. I know the names they called him. I've called him a few of those names myself.

He's reliable? Chuck pressed.

He's a genius, I said. Especially when a historic chimney is involved.

I uncapped the tube of blueprints and shook out a large rolled sheet. I talked them through the elevation, showing them the engineer's proposal for the back parlor, pointing out the load-bearing beams we could see and those we could only guess at.

Chuck had questions about everything. I had a sense of him stretching, learning—perhaps my praise of Harry made him feel like he needed to get up to speed; or maybe it was just the abstraction that appealed, the blueprint reminding him of skills he already had, another map he could read like an X-ray or an MRI. Meanwhile Lana picked at her nails, then stepped out to make a call. Leaning in to examine the blueprints, Chuck reached to point out a detail, and his forearm crossed mine and rested there. His stillness surprised me, his pulse strong and deep.

Claiming another appointment, I rolled up the blueprint and left, my windshield wipers pounding through a sudden sleet. Honesty: Part of me had been spooked by that arm laid across mine, but another part, at once familiar and strange, was not spooked at all.

The job was mine. What else might be?

5

I returned home to find Edgar and Ethan sacked out by the radiator. Hearing me enter, they lifted their heads in tandem and regarded me with expressions of mild canine sympathy.

Boys, I said, it's been *a day*.

In the gray light of my kitchenette, I closed a mug of milk inside the microwave and rummaged in the cupboard until I found a packet of cocoa. But when I opened it, the wizened marshmallows put me right off my Swiss Miss. *Ding!* I pulled the mug from the microwave and poured its contents down the drain. Who was I kidding? I did not need a milky drink. I needed to get on the right side with the Halseys, and for *that*, I needed a solution to their kitchen ventilation problem.

A shimmer in my peripheral vision drew me to the window over the sink, where I watched a woodchuck lumber across the parking lot. Thanks to a mast year's bounty of acorns, these pests were now overrunning New Preston. The woodchuck lifted its nose, scenting the air. I banged on the window until it disappeared into the culvert on the lot's far side.

I should have dialed animal control. Instead I called Harry.

You got a minute?

For Cookie Cooke, I have all the minutes.

I just need five minutes of your time.

All business now, are we?

He laughed, and when I didn't join him, he laughed harder.

Well, well. What can I do you for, Ms. All-Biz?

I told him about the Halseys' kitchen conundrum.

They hardly have room to turn around in there right now, I said, but the wife wants a restaurant-grade kitchen. Six-burner cooktop, double-decker oven, the works.

That'll be a lot of BTUs when it's all up and running, he replied. Forty thousand *easy*.

And I can't touch the chimney! How do I *vent* it?

You vent it *through* the chimney.

That chimney is more than a hundred years old, I said.

And it will be there for another century. That I can promise you, Cookie. We'll duct it, adding a restaurant-grade hood with a fan that'll clear the kitchen in under a minute if things get smoky.

Those fans look too modern. The wife wants to keep the historic vibe.

So you'll design a cover. Make the fan invisible. Out of sight, out of mind. Denial, he teased, is not just a river in Egypt.

You'll have to do better than that, I told him, if you want a reaction from me.

Someday, he said, you'll rise to my hook.

Someday, I replied, you'll bait it properly.

He laughed again, a thunderclap. I thanked him for his advice, keeping things cool between us. It was one thing to know that Harry was the right guy for this job. It was another having to work with him again—to risk being alone in tight spaces, reviving the old familiarity he had not forgotten.

~

I SUPPOSE I keep my vulnerabilities well concealed, Harry chief among them. My go-to chimney guy is a little tall, a little dark, more than a little handsome—and we go way back. In fifth grade, Harry howled with laughter when, having finally connected my foot to a rolling kickball, I landed it precisely on a sharp prong of the playground's chain-link fence. The next day, he chased me with the dead ball's plump replacement while singing that 1980s song about a girl who's a man-eater.

I wasn't anything like that, and I see now that his teasing had nothing to do with me. It was just his way of experimenting with calling himself a man. But I was easy to tease, being short, awkward, and distinctly unlucky on the playground.

Still, he needed me. With my help, Harry weathered World History and English Lit. In return, he taught me to change my own oil. Senior year, we both had roles in the school play, a gender-swapped version of Ibsen's *A Doll's House.* In a yearbook photograph, he's chasing me again, the kickball replaced by a garden spade reshaped with muslin into a huge spoon. In the photo, he's tied into a frilled kitchen apron, and I'm buttoned into a three-piece suit and moving so fast I'm blurry. That was the effect of the gender swap: Domestic misery returned as domestic farce.

With a soupçon of terror.

There was a real spade, a heavy one, inside that prop. Harry would have felt the weight of it, a suggestion of the damage he might do. Not that I thought much about it. My mind was on other things. There were always boys, forgettable types. I tended toward the wispy and distracted, who were plugged into their own worlds—video games, academic study. Their distraction left me free to get lost in cut-and-paste worlds of my own.

Harry saw through my pretenses, including the mask I adopted later, in art school, of the isolated *artiste.* I'll say this about Harry: He paid attention. He knew what I wanted, what I liked, sometimes better than I did. Every year he showed up on my doorstep holding out a clutch of peonies, my favorite, for my birthday. He drove me down the coast whenever I needed a hit of ocean. He didn't care if I took days to call him back. He knew I would, sooner or later. Our relationship has taken many forms over the years, but somehow, we've always managed to keep going, as friends and collaborators and occasionally something more, so dense is the weave of New Preston.

RIGHT AFTER I graduated, Harry and I took a road trip to Nevada. On the day we left, he pulled up in an enormous silver sedan. I can see him now, grinning out the open window, his arm resting in the gap. He'd outfitted the car with keyhole covers shaped like *Playboy* bunnies, and the same bunnies were silhouetted on the mud flaps. The ignition cylinder was gone, though I did not immediately link its absence with Harry's other interventions.

Harry was in an uncomfortable position: His father planned to give him the family masonry business, but he wanted impossible concessions, including a promise never to leave New Preston. In exchange, he'd always have a trade. Harry found the prospect stultifying, but he was clear-eyed enough to know his father's offer was as good as he was likely to get without going back to school, which he despised.

There aren't too many guys like Harry, masons who know their way around historic chimneys. Harry learned from his father, who learned from his father, the magic traveling down the family line along with the know-how and the tools. But Harry's father had a way of undermining him, throwing him off a job as soon as he made even a small mistake.

As we sped out of town, I spotted an aglet, one of those plastic sheaths that terminate a shoelace, on the floor mat. He was hard on shoes, Harry was. That was another of his father's grievances, the great expense of shoe leather. The man had many grievances and found much to criticize in his son.

The miles slipped by. *Talk about giving me the business*, Harry muttered, abstractedly spinning the radio dial. *Why do I have to suck so much?*

But something more than mere parental undermining was bothering Harry. When he wasn't cursing his dad, or himself, he discoursed about the pointlessness of restraining orders, punctuating his soliloquies with anxious glances in the rearview mirror.

Unnerved, I focused on the ribbon of road unwinding the country as it went by: Cleveland, Omaha, Denver.

Perhaps he felt bad about his inattention, or maybe he was simply bored, but on that trip, Harry found ways to teach me small mechanical things, like how to start the car by jiggling a screwdriver in the slot left where the ignition cylinder was supposed to be. Of course the car was stolen, I see that now, but then I was still young enough to push such hard-nosed considerations to a Vaseline-smeared corner of my mind.

WE WERE four hours past Reno and running short on cash. We stopped so Harry could make a call, and he returned with good news—there was an opening for a pit mechanic at the Bonneville track. I'd be on my own for a few days while he went out there. No problem, I said. I was happy to hold the fort while he earned enough to fund the next leg of our trip, wherever that took us.

Harry's situation was tough, but mine was not much better. Having failed to specialize in art school, I'd hardly covered myself with glory, and now that I'd graduated, I was in a jobless funk, jealous of the students I'd previously scorned, who majored in practical things like graphic design. Even worse were the ones who graduated into immediate acclaim, with solo shows in Boston and Philadelphia if not New York. My closest friend, a spitfire named Erica Subiaco, had majored in sculpture, which was not practical, either, and she had already left New Preston to chase work as a scenery painter in Hollywood. She sent breezy letters, keeping me up to date, including a photograph of herself sprawled in front of a batik wall hanging, looking relaxed and confident, a Left Coast creative in the perpetual sunshine, making rent while chasing down gallerists in the off hours. Harry's road trip felt like an escape from being left behind—though we do still keep in touch, me and Erica.

Harry found a motel with a vacancy, an efficiency room with a kitchenette. There was a gas station nearby, attached to a diner. The dust-and-brush landscape slipped toward the dark line of the horizon; over it all, a blue cup of sky. I shut the door on Harry's receding back and stretched out on the pilled coverlet, powder-blue wool-poly washed thin. Harry would be gone for a week at least. I hugged myself. A huge chunk of time stretched in front of me, completely free and mine, all mine.

There was a ritual in art school: At the beginning of every term, the teachers would have us all perform the same task. Starting from the nearest corner and working clockwise, we were to name every single thing in the room, right down to the wall scuffs and the busy forelegs of the wolf spider nesting in the window lock. The point was not just to look, but to figure out exactly what you were looking at—in other words, to *see*. I found the assignment meditative, calming. It cleared the mind. Alone in the motel room, I was no longer a student. But surely the magic of the exercise did not depend on that.

The dim room was a collage of blues: the pale-blue door with its deadbolt; the low-pile carpet, beige with thin stripes of blueprint-blue; the long, foxed mirror, in which I observed my own reflection, my tanned legs sticking out from my cutoff shorts as I lounged atop the powder-blue coverlet. Over the bed, a brightly painted pair of Nevada mountain bluebirds popped from an expanse of deep-blue velvet set in a rough-hewn wooden frame. The kitchenette was on the far side. Beyond that, a door opened onto the bathroom, though all was blue darkness from where I lay. On the nightstand was a fake Tiffany table lamp and a bowl of cobalt glass containing two deep-red apples, and beside that a pile of advertisements for local attractions. The racetrack schedule rested on top.

Hunger stole over me: class dismissed. Disappointingly the apples were plastic. I gathered my wallet and room key. The diner was thirty yards away, and my stomach was rumbling. The hot air seemed to split as I pressed through it. As I entered the diner, a bell rang, summoning an older woman in an apron. Her name tag said DOOCIE.

I took a seat at the counter. Doocie gave me a laminated menu and disappeared through swinging kitchen doors. A moment later, while I was studying the menu, Doocie returned with a phone clapped to her ear and staked a position by the coffee pots, the curling cord stretched taut.

I told them everything I saw and heard, she said loudly. Is that not what you wanted me to do?

There was a silence as she listened. Then, cursing, she hurled the phone away. It flew over the swinging doors and landed with a clatter somewhere beyond. A man roared: DOOCIE!

She pulled an order pad from her apron: What can I get you?

I ordered a soda and buttered toast. She fitted the slip to the slide, tapped the little bell. Order up!

Slip and slide: A summer day in New Preston, my mother

stemming chrysanthemums and setting them to float in a crystal bowl. *Order up*, she said, pushing a flower toward me.

Doocie slapped a tumbler of soda and ice on the counter.

The desert sun, the long drive, my gnawing hunger—everything had made me feral. Bold.

Doocie, I said. You told them what you saw. But what did you see? What did you hear?

I guess you're new in town, she said. Buckle up.

Some months back, she began, there'd been a death. A man had been shot in one of the rooms. All signs pointed to suicide: The long rifle had been rigged so he could pull the trigger from the bed. But Doocie had seen the man with a woman that same afternoon. They were out by the pumps, and he was gassing up their car.

He was drunk, Doocie said. I had smelled booze on him when he came in to order a coffee. He went out, and I followed. It was my break, and I had to smoke outside, because of one of those new regulations. Anyway, he was out there pumping, but he kept knocking things around as if he couldn't see straight, which he probably couldn't. He just couldn't insert the nozzle into the tank. The woman got out of the car and told him to cut the shit. He waved the nozzle at her, yelling. *You cut the shit*, he said. *You're the one who should cut the shit.*

Suit yourself, she told him. *I made myself clear, and whatever happens next is up to you.*

I said: And then what happened, Doocie?

He turned to me, she said, dropping her voice to a whisper. *To me*—who was just standing there. And he starts to shout, *Put that goddamned cigarette out before you kill us all.* I did just what I was told, which was a damned good thing because he immediately started pouring gas around, on the asphalt, all over the rear tire, and finally he splashed her, just a little at first, wetting her tennis shoes. Then in one jerk, he splashed her to her knees, soaking her legs and the hem of her skirt. Now she was yelling, what a loser he was, she'd always known it, and what the hell did he think he was doing, things of that nature.

He had a book of matches, and he started lighting them. He threw the lit matches in her direction. They fell to the ground, only just missing her. She unbuttoned her top and took it off, started blotting her legs with it. She was still telling him off, but I didn't hear the words.

He replaced the nozzle. The girl looked at him, and he must have told her to get in the car, because that's what she did, and he calmed right down, and they drove off. That night I didn't see them come back, but I heard the shot. She came flying out of the room, shouting, *Call the cops!* A few weeks later, I was summoned to testify. The guy on the phone just now—that was my brother, he's a lawyer. I told him what I told them, what I'm telling you. I don't know if she killed him. If she did, though, it wasn't less than what he deserved.

I chewed my toast. I accepted a refill. You think they'll convict? I wondered.

I don't know, Doocie said. Her shoes were recovered from the scene. I could smell the gas from the witness box.

A month later, I was home again in New Preston, but part of me remained at the diner, Doocie's voice still quick in my ear. That was when I realized I could make my own version—and perhaps, by doing so, defang it, clear it from my system.

I cut openings out of plywood sheets and hammered them together to make a room. I turned a metal hinge into a door and slotted in a rectangle of glass for a window. While walking around the neighborhood, I found a powder-blue scrap of wool washed to felt, just large enough to fit a miniature queen-size mattress. I wired a tiny Tiffany lamp and set it on a dollhouse night table. At a rummage sale, I found a toy soldier's rifle and a pair of doll-sized tennis shoes. I took a jointed balsa-wood mannequin, one of those that's in every art supply store, and stuck it in the little bed beneath the coverlet, pressing the head into a miniature pillow crusted with dark-red nail polish. I used more nail polish to create a blood spatter. The next time I filled my tank, I let gas spill into a container along with the tiny tennis shoes. Once they'd dried, I set them on the replica carpet, wondering where they might have been found at the real scene of the crime.

As I worked, possibilities presented themselves. So many different things might have gone down in that room. A lot depended on the shape of the spatter and the position of the gun as it went off. I tangled the gun in string, to suggest what the girlfriend had said—that he'd killed himself—and set it on the floor where it might have fallen if her story were true. Then I shifted it again, to account for the possibility that his girlfriend had pulled the trigger and merely set things up to suggest a suicide. I repositioned that gun again and again.

I added things, too, bits and pieces that weren't in the room I'd shared with Harry but had personal meaning: Instead of the velvet bluebirds, I created a replica of a touristy painting of an attraction near New Preston, a rocky outcropping shaped like a man's face in profile. In place of the tourist brochures for Bonneville, I made advertisements for Quarry Lake, a chasm filled with water as cold as it was deep, where kids from all over the region drowned every year, and even so, no one closed the place. Harry and I used to swim there sometimes, on August nights when New Preston's heat became truly unbearable.

A librarian helped me find newspaper accounts of the crime and the trial. As it turned out, the judge had ruled on a technicality—someone at the police station had lost track of the woman's shoes, rupturing the chain of custody. Without the shoes, there was no case; the woman on trial could not be definitively placed at the scene. Case dismissed.

I didn't so much finish the diorama as set it aside. It remained in my studio for a long time, the glow of that tiny Tiffany lamp brightening a dark corner. Something about the piece felt too intimate, like I'd violated a taboo by mixing art so closely with the stuff of life and death. But I recently had reason to revisit that decision, and so I brought the box to Bobby, an art school friend who runs a gallery called the Roach. In the main room, I set *The Blue Bedroom* on an empty plinth, so the diorama was at eye level. Bobby paced around, peering in from every angle, and I told him the story from start to finish, including what Erica had written after I emailed her a photograph and an update about the work: *Heaven in a wild flower, paradise in a grain of sand.*

Bobby pulled the little string I'd attached to the miniature blinds and gasped when they lifted. He looked through the clear plate-glass window and met my gaze on the other side.

Make me a few more, he said, and you'll finally have your solo show.

6

The Halseys called with their decision: We would knock down the odd wall, sparing the chimney and the most important supports, and excavate further if necessary, to ensure that no historically significant items were hidden behind the sheetrock.

We: As if the Halseys' home were mine to make, all its corners mine to cut.

I donned my work boots and went about my business, ordering supplies, rotating crews. It's assertive work, and my subs always find me insufferable at this stage—insufficiently feminine, too much like a boss. Bitch is the term of art, though no one was dumb enough to say it to my face.

To keep the project on track, Chuck and Lana agreed to meet me at the house on Fridays after work. On the day of the first meeting, I arrived early with my push broom, wanting to make sure the place at least looked tidy after the demolition crew had removed the wall.

In the cold foyer, sheets of red rosin paper were taped neatly to the floor, protecting it. I wished the crew had also tarped the staircase, or at least the fancy newel post, whose crevices were fuzzy with dust. Making my way toward the kitchen, I felt a surge of expansion—the light was different, better, brighter. The wall was just a memory now, already ancient history.

But something was off. On one side of the newly created void, there was another empty space, about three by five. It reminded me of a lean-to. I couldn't recall seeing it on any blueprint. I turned my flashlight toward the mystery and hit the switch.

Inside the space, the walls were peeling, and the floor was made of wide, scarred planks. The little secret room had seen some use, and then many years, perhaps a century, of disuse.

A cold draft and the creak of a hinge sent me hustling toward the foyer. My investigation would have to wait. Draped in her whiskey mink, Lana stood in the doorway, peering into a compact mirror, angling it to catch the scant light from the open door.

Sorry for the lights. The electrical's cut, I said. We're keeping the demolition crew safe. Watch your step as you come in. There's grit all underfoot—

Chuck's right behind me, she interrupted, snapping the clamshell closed. Neither of us can stay long. He's got something this afternoon, and I've scheduled a call in five.

I'll keep it short, I said. But there's something you need to see.

I led her into the kitchen where the wall once stood. Pleased, Lana cooed: It's already brighter!

There's a void here, I said. It's older than the rest of the house. Look at these floorboards.

She said: Those planks are so wide. How big were the trees?

They must have come from an old-growth forest. Either they were recycled from another dwelling, or this place was constructed over another, older property. Trees of this width could not be found locally when Warren built this house. There was no just-in-time global shipping in those days, I said.

Lana laughed. Just-in-time global shipping! Take it from me, that's a fairy tale.

But I thought all your textiles were locally sourced.

You're right, Lana replied, her voice edged suddenly with ice. They are.

Never mind, I said quickly. I'm sure I'm misinformed.

I stepped farther into the gap, flicking my flashlight toward the corners. Stylized images danced in the shadows—a falcon, an ibis, a seated figure wearing a *deshret* crown, shaped like a honeybee's tongue and known as a symbol of fertile Lower Egypt. Another part of the wall bore traces of a long-limbed female form: Nut, the sky goddess, whose limbs embraced the heavens.

Lana ran her fingers lightly along the curved edge of a cartouche.

Hieroglyphs?

Or a good imitation, I replied. Frescoed walls were popular in Warren's day. But the Egyptian theme is unusual.

Chuck murmured, *Spooky*.

I spun around. Lana laughed again: He's like a damned cat! I should put a bell on you, Chuck.

Go ahead, he said. I dare you.

He was in a bubbly mood, teasing and joking. He moved to grab Lana in a hug, but she stepped out of his reach, and a bunch of business cards slipped from the depths of her coat. She rushed to collect them, bending awkwardly in her heels. When I moved to help, she shooed me.

I flashed my little light around, to shift their attention back to the job. Their marriage was like their house: full of secret passageways lined with signals that were indecipherable, at least to me. Never mind. I still had other things to show them. Demolition had revealed the chimney's true extent and dimensions—there was much more brickwork here. And there was something else—a small hearth at the very far end, with a little door to one side.

Oh, my God, Lana cried. Is that a beehive oven?

I was surprised she knew what it was. Most people have never heard of beehive ovens. People used to install these little brick-lined, dome-shaped ovens to one side of the hearth, creating a hot cavity for baking. This one was crumbling. Chunks of mortar had fallen to the floor. The loosened grit crunched softly beneath my shoes.

Cookie, you said the room might be from an older property on the site. Could this room be *colonial*? Lana asked. Aren't beehive ovens colonial?

They can be. It's possible. New Preston's an old place.

Chuck! she cried. We have to keep it. *All* of it. We have to retain as much of the original as we absolutely can.

We definitely *can* keep it, I said. It adds character. But what about the fresco? The New Preston Heritage Society might be willing to underwrite a removal to their museum if you wanted to get rid of it. At least then it would be preserved somewhere.

Not on your life, said Lana. We'll put a plexiglass cover on it, and it will be just as nice as any museum.

Ha, Chuck scoffed.

What?

I thought you said a mausoleum.

Lana's phone rang, and she bustled out to take the call. Chuck followed behind, and I heard the distant door bang shut. In the gloom I noticed a bright rectangle on the floor. It was one of Lana's business cards, a funny one made on the cheap, a clip-art pepper stretched contentedly on an ice cube. *Gimme that chilly! Cold chain logistics at a very chill price.*

7

Chuck took the next meeting by himself. Lana was attending to business elsewhere—something about a warehouse in New Hampshire, Chuck explained as we made our way up the front walk. She was planning something in Italy, too, he went on. I didn't catch the details, didn't try to. He was talking just to talk, filling time as he touched all of his pockets, searching for his keys. I played my part, pretending to be impressed, but I didn't buy it. At least not the Italian part. Lana's stuff was good, but not that good.

Cat's away, Chuck murmured, unlocking the door. He looked at me, and I felt him come into focus, a force gathering. Would we touch again? I wanted those arms around me. I wanted to feel that pulse again, slow and steady.

That day he found reasons to draw close, resting a hand on my arm while we reviewed blueprints, brushing against me when we ducked inside the hidden room to stare at the odd fresco. I did know better. I knew I was being put to his purpose, whatever it might have been; and that purpose was surely part of a larger picture, a system that turned women into handmaidens of more powerful men, available to soothe and tend and reassure, to replenish their nerve as their own sources seeped away.

But knowledge was nothing compared to what he stirred up. Our secret meetings continued: On days when he was available, he simply texted a time. At the house, he grew bolder: He cupped a breast, a buttock. He caught my earlobe between his teeth. He sucked a hot blotch onto my neck, my first hickey since high school.

My habits now included noting the arrivals of the Halseys' emails and calls, which gave me a sense of their schedules. In addition to fielding Chuck's texts, I proposed additional unnecessary on-sites whenever I thought Lana might be out of town—anything to keep the ball rolling, until it landed in my bed, or his. Then I went further; I googled their property records and tax assessments. I ruminated about the health of their marriage. I was, I admit, a little preoccupied. Okay, fine—I was obsessed.

The feeling gripped me tighter, forked me like an old tree. Outwardly I was professional, competent, all-business. So was Chuck. I've heard that doctors are great compartmentalizers, able to set aside their work, with its horrors and losses, to secure the tranquility of their time off the clock. Maybe that's why, during our Friday night threesomes, the liaison felt distant and unreal, as if covered in a tarp of discretion so thick, our involvement did not leave so much as a ripple. But when Lana was absent, I became another version of myself, wolfish and stupid. To all these mistakes, I added a tactical error: I found Chuck's photograph online and sent Fiona the link.

That day Fiona was stretched on my sofa, her laptop propped on the step stool. The light streaming in through the tall windows was electric with motes of dust and filaments of dog hair. My place was on the top floor, in a L-shaped space lined with windows. The front door opened into a galley kitchen with a pass-through, a living area just big enough for a sofa and coffee table, and a bed tucked into an alcove. Around the corner was my office—a big worktable, a file cabinet. Beyond that was my studio—another worktable, a rolling chair. The building had once been a pencil factory, and ancient powdered graphite still sifted from the floorboards.

You're going to have to vacuum in here one of these days, Fiona said as she waved her hands in front of her face. And seal these revolting bricks.

Even amid the dust and debris, Fiona looked smart, decked out in post-punk vintage-plus: frayed T-shirt, studded belt, and a faded black voile skirt with a handkerchief hem that brushed the tops of her Doc Martens. Her school bag sat plumply on the other end of the sofa, a can of graphite fixative peeking out the top.

Perhaps Fiona had plans after work. Once upon a time, I did, too.

The bricks have been fine for two hundred years, I told her. They'll be fine for a minute longer. The floorboards bug me more.

I'll bet they bug you, Fiona said as she leaned over to scratch a nearby head-of-mutt. She burbled on in doggy-ese: They bug you, too, don't they? This place is truly buggy, isn't it?

You're spoiling them, Fiona.

It's bugnuts Bananagrams, she went on, and that's a fact, Jack.

The bug business was a little joke. When Bobby first bought the pencil mill, its nearest neighbor was an out-of-business pesticide company. The owner, who dabbled in metalworking, had bolted together a huge metal cockroach, poison blue, and stored it in the basement. One day, perhaps sensing a kindred spirit in Bobby, he showed Bobby the big metal bug. Bobby bought it on the spot and installed it on his roof beside a neon sign announcing THE ROACH. I'd had my doubts, but Bobby knew his stuff: Overnight, the pencil mill became a landmark, and Bobby with his bugnuts scheme transformed himself into an impresario—and made me part of it, carving out a live-work space for me. I could see the Big Blue Bug from my kitchen.

Fiona clicked a few keys, and Chuck's face filled her screen.

This guy, Cookie? I don't know. He is no golden god.

Wait until you meet him, I said, my heart sinking. You can't judge anything from a photograph.

Then why'd you send it?

Why indeed. How stupid to involve Fiona.

I can't believe he spends all his time opening people's heads, she said as she closed the tab. I wouldn't trust him to open a door.

DEMOLITION GAVE way to framing; once the walls were in place, I brought in the electrician and the plumber. I didn't find any more secret rooms. But I still had plenty to distract myself, especially after the Halseys began to lubricate our Friday on-sites with nice Napa vintages supplemented with take-out Chinese.

They were practiced hosts. Chuck brimmed with anecdotes about his patients, their close calls and false alarms. Every story had the same moral: He was needed, his work was life and death. One night, speaking of his patients, his voice softened, and in the depths of his talking, I felt myself relax. So this is how he does it, I thought. He had a nice bedside manner.

Lana smiled at me, and then she rolled her eyes. She'd heard Chuck's war stories before.

Isn't he darling? she said. Their mutual gaze was warm, embracing. Never mind what Chuck and I got up to in her absence. Even if I was covered in his love bites, I was still the interloper here.

It was not all sugar. There was another night when Lana interrupted Chuck as he was telling one of his just-so stories from the clinic, sighing: We all *know* you do vital work, darling.

No need to bang on about it, then, eh?

A mild response—but also mildly dismissive. He didn't take her seriously. He didn't take me seriously, either. Though he would never have said as much to our faces, on some level he found us both to be lightweights, lacking some vital seriousness, some *depth*. I suppose the point was basic: We need our bodies far more than our houses or the things we fill them with. My designs, for instance. Lana's textiles. Tables and chairs, beds and mirrors. These were life's surfaces; he lived within its depths.

I sipped my wine, then drained the glass. How could I blame Chuck for his superior attitude? After all, he was only accepting me on my own terms. What he thought was just what everyone thought about decorators, and as a matter of professional survival, I did sometimes cultivate a lightweight, people-pleasing impression.

LANA HAD her stories, too, and like Chuck's, they were mostly about work. She styled herself a chronically underestimated small businesswoman who just wanted to be credited with the same killer instinct as her male competitors. I heard exactly zero about her purported Italian triumph, but there was a kernel of truth to the New Hampshire scuttlebutt. She was in the midst of moving Lana Pura's manufacturing to a larger site north of Boston, over the state line, and the relocation was not going well.

The cooler weather must make it easier, I said, thinking of

gimme the chilly. It's got to be hard to keep moths out of all that wool.

She looked hard at me. The warehouse, she sniffed, is strictly climate-controlled.

Whenever I tried to connect with her on a business level, I had a way of getting things wrong. First I'd made that dumb remark about her local sourcing of materials; now I'd failed to understand what her materials required.

Of course, I said, backtracking. What do I know about wool?

If only I weren't such a cream puff! she cried suddenly. If only I could master the Art of No!

I wouldn't say that's your problem, Chuck teased.

Their eyes met, and I had to look away.

Still, no matter how carefully a façade is maintained, sooner or later, cracks will appear. That's simply how façades work. Just as Lana was impatient with Chuck's war stories, Chuck could be impatient with her jokey self-effacement. He would check his watch or respond a beat too slowly, as if dragging himself to enjoy her storytelling.

One night he took an emergency call, leaving me and Lana alone with the take-out containers and the empties. We regarded each other in silence as the votives burned out one by one. We were sharing the same man, and I couldn't tell if she wanted to kill me or to ask me to move in. It occurred to me that my role might be different than I thought—perhaps I was keeping Chuck busy while she chased her dreams of world domination via luxe woolens.

Chuck returned tight-lipped. Lana touched his arm.

What is it?

Problems with a colleague. I try to help. You know what a mistake that is.

Chuck leaned against an upright and loosened his tie. How

safe he felt, having me and Lana around to take care of trivialities, creating the pretty backdrop for his important life. When he moved to refill my glass, I waved him off.

Thanks, no. Headache.

Concern—if that's what it was—deepened the lines around his eyes.

It's nothing, I said. I've just been breathing sawdust all day.

Shall we call it a night? I can zip you home.

I don't want to put you out of your way.

Lana slapped irritably at her sleeves, raising dust. She'd had enough of something—the reno, my presence, her husband's.

Go on, she said to both of us. I'll tidy up.

WE TOOK the long way back, across town and down the Chepinoxet. We were cresting a hill, going at a nice clip, when Chuck stomped hard on the gas and the road fell away. For some reason, he'd switched off the headlights. We arced through darkness, and my heart clutched. A moment later I was soaring: Now I was the one in the fast car, and Lana was at home doing dishes! To hell with contentment, the happy domestic scene. Real life was out here, racing along the banks of the Chepinoxet.

When we reached the Roach, Chuck turned into the lot, pulled up near the rear entryway, and jolted the transmission into *park*. All the movement tripped a sensor, and a floodlight clicked on above the car, cutting his face into irregular segments of light and shadow. He squeezed my thigh.

There was never any danger, you know.

I passed a hand over my hot face.

Mr. Toad, I said, I did not consent to this wild ride.

Oh, but you liked it, he replied. You like flying in the dark.

INSIDE THE fluorescents hummed, and I led him down the corridor, trying not to notice as he, grimacing, took in the grimy floorboards, the incompletely sheet-rocked walls pocked with divots. As we reached my door, the dogs were barking, their nails scrabbling at the weather-stripping down low. I threw the bolt, and the door swung open. Chuck's breath warmed the nape of my neck.

Sorry about the mess, I said, cranking open the window over the kitchen sink. Coffee?

The dogs sniffed and wagged around Chuck, tails swinging, ears at guilty half-mast. What had these rascals done in my absence? The sofa sagged, and there were telltale twin dents in the cushions. Chuck crouched down and rolled one of the dogs on his side. The other followed suit, tongue lolling. I'd never seen them take to a stranger so quickly.

Sorry, I said. My dogs are rude. We don't have to sit on the doggy sofa.

What do you mean, Cookie? I come all the way here, just to miss the doggy sofa? But you must introduce me properly to these gentlemen.

You're well past formalities. The gentleman who's presently drooling on your slacks is Ethan. Ethan Allen to be exact, as in the patriot and the furniture store. The one on his back who's covertly eyeing the sofa is Edgar Allan, as in Poe.

Good old Poe, said Chuck as he dropped to the floor, risking a face-licking.

Poe liked a functional room without too much ornament, I said. He thought that rooms should be composed like paintings, with the same care. He had a whole philosophy of furniture, you know.

I didn't, Chuck wheezed. But I always suspected he was interested in more than just birds. You know, this sofa doesn't look half bad. But I could really use that coffee, Cookie. Either that or a Sudafed.

I didn't realize you were allergic to pets.

I'm not. But my immune system's been wacky lately.

While the coffee maker glugged away, I located two mugs, a Job Lot set with a stained crackle glaze, and set them out. How weird, to hear a doctor being so cavalier about his own health, like he'd never heard of bone cancer or fulminant leukemia.

Maybe you should get checked?

Unnecessary. I'm just—never mind. It's not worth getting into.

When the coffee was done, Chuck accepted his mug with a gratitude so sincere it surprised me. His prissiness wasn't actually part of his character, as I'd thought, but something he slipped on and off like his white coat. He gestured toward a mess across the room, on the worktable where a crime scene in miniature was developing, a work in progress.

Tell me about that, he said.

That. Oh God. I'd left everything out, not expecting to bring anyone home tonight, and now I'd have to explain myself. I wasn't used to talking about my work—my private work, my real work—with anyone except Bobby, who after all had a financial interest.

You're looking, I said, at the *Acorn Studies of Unexplained Death.*

I didn't know you had a sideline making interiors more comfortable for criminals.

The crimes have already happened. These are the acorns. The crimes are the oaks.

Chuck's expression shifted from open curiosity to something more ambiguous, and I fell silent, regretting my decision to spill my guts.

Who commissions stuff like this?

Almost no one, I said. Have you heard of Frances Glessner

Lee? She was a Chicago socialite who, feeling hemmed in by the society pages, found an outlet for her talent in making tiny crime scenes for the police. Even though her dioramas are decades old, I said, they're still used to train detectives.

Sometimes, I added quietly, I help with those kinds of things, too.

I rooted beneath the coffee table until I found a large volume covered in black cloth. I handed it to him.

Look at this, I said. It's the closest thing we have to a catalog of her work.

Turning the pages, Chuck lingered over details—a toppled lamp, a thumbnail-sized volume of *Sherlock Holmes* splayed face down on a blood-soaked carpet. The room cooled, and on the breeze, I smelled the river, algal and metallic.

Settling deeper into the sofa, Chuck stretched his arm behind my shoulders. I leaned into him, feeling the slow *lub-dub* of his heart.

You actually like doing this?

I love it, I blurted, surprised to discover I was telling the truth.

You love working for the cops?

Not the cop stuff, I said. That work just pays. I've only spent a handful of nights at the lab.

I'm surprised they have so much for you to do, he said. New Preston's not what I'd call an underworld hotspot.

It isn't. But they hired a new guy, Bill Phelps, who's keen on forensics.

I saw something in the paper about him, Chuck said. Isn't he the guy who pissed off the Historic District Commission by demanding an exception to install solar panels on the roof of his historic house?

And destroy the roofline, yes. The very same. That's how I met him, at that meeting.

In person Phelps is unprepossessing, small of frame and badly near-sighted, with large wet eyes and a froggy mouth. The newspaper article had run with a headshot of Phelps looking alarmingly young and unproven in his dress blues.

He seems like a real move-fast-and-break-things type, Chuck said.

He has a complete inability to keep a low profile, I replied. Lately he's been opening up cold cases all over New England. I've done three dioramas for him, and he's solved two cases already.

Chuck's eyebrows shot up.

I sifted papers on the coffee table, glad to shift my face out of Chuck's line of sight.

You're surprised?

Don't you aspire to the big commissions? Solo shows?

Ha, I said. Such things are not for mere mortals like myself.

Chuck, frowning: You do aspire to them.

Stop, you'll blow my cover. I've done fictive dioramas, too, like a mock-up of a *Sherlock Holmes* story, complete with a secret room, a postage-stamp-sized faked will, and a tiny fingerprint pressed onto a wax seal.

"The Adventure of the Norwood Builder"!

The very same. I had a lot of fun with that one. But you're right, no one's throwing money at me. You'd need to be a special sort of connoisseur to want a crime scene in your drawing room.

When it's not a crime scene already, he said darkly.

Happy wife, happy life?

Bite your tongue, he said, returning his attention to the book of photographs. Busy lady, this Glessner Lee.

Beats Junior League.

From the moment I met you, Cookie, I knew Junior League was not your scene.

From the moment he met me. In the dinky kitchen with the pretty view, his hand on the small of my back.

He stood and made his way to the worktable. I followed, switching on the task lamp. My latest diorama was a New England saltbox house with the lid lifted and, beside it, a kidney-shaped piece of plexiglass that would eventually become a skating pond.

Which cold case am I looking at?

Lizzie Borden's.

Of the famed forty whacks?

She's a bit of a *cause célèbre* around here.

Isn't the Borden homestead just up the road?

It sure is. You can still see bloodstains in the floor.

Chuck gave me a quizzical look, one that told me I was probably too excited. But I do like those unsettling things, the unnoticed parts of ourselves we leave in our most private spaces.

He wandered to my one piece of real furniture, a large glass-fronted cabinet that I was holding for my mother who, on her way to finalize the papers for the sale of the family home, had stumbled on the steps to the realtor's office and shattered her kneecap. Now she was in rehab at a place called Tomlins Manor, relearning how to walk so she could move into her new place, a one-bedroom apartment in an assisted living facility. We put most of her belongings in storage, but she asked me to keep this piece and its contents, the most valuable things she owned.

As Chuck peered in, I came up behind him, pleased by the view of the two of us reflected in the glass. If it weren't for his marriage, I'd say we were in a real relationship. It's easy to forget that a mirage is an image, too, just trickier.

Chuck gestured toward the cluttered shelves, pointing to a human-shaped figurine in blue faience, and asked: What's this?

A shabti, I replied. From ancient Egypt. They were buried

with the deceased person to ensure that someone else would do the deceased's work in the afterlife. Because the number one thing a dead person needs is an assistant to take care of all the little details that go with being dead. Cooking, cleaning, picking crops—

Decorating palaces, performing surgeries—

Exactly. Everything here belongs to my mother. She had a degree in art history. Specialized in ancient art. She loved these little objects—they're all grave goods. Eventually she opened a shop, and things came her way.

I'll bet they did. Who would question an antiquities dealer in this backwater?

I flashed on a memory of my mother puttering in her spare-room office, methodical as a spider sounding the threads of her web.

I don't ask too many questions, I said. New Preston's estate sales are really something to behold. You know how it is, we're fighting forever wars, and in the course of all the destruction, so much goes missing, only to turn up elsewhere in cupboards and drawers—

He said, No wonder you like small things.

Two steps, and he had closed the space between us. I leaned into his warmth.

Cricket song rose and sharpened; farther off, heavy engines droned down the freeway. I licked my lips and tasted the Chepinoxet.

His eyes grazed mine, held them.

You don't scare me, Cookie Cooke.

We shouldn't, I said weakly. It won't end well.

I don't care, he said, becoming forceful. I don't care how anything ends.

8

Looking back, I see that I missed a key sign: That sneezing fit, which Chuck had dismissed as evidence of an immune system gone temporarily haywire, was not some one-off episode. There was more to that story, a suggestion of Lana's malfeasance and Chuck's complicity. But I couldn't see it, certainly not in the haze of that first morning after, when I woke to the purr of an expensive engine. No loiterer over dawn coffee, Chuck. But his warmth lingered on the far side of the bed, and I still felt the press of his mouth on mine.

I padded to the kitchenette, the dogs slinking around my ankles. I threw on a sweatshirt and a pair of shoes. Outside, they yanked me down the cracked path that led to the river. I struggled with them, wanting to take my time. That morning every leaf was distinct, the air soft and rinsed. The dogs seemed distracted. Was it me? I was in such an unaccustomed mood.

FIONA ARRIVED and shrugged out of her cardigan, a junk shop find, mid-brown and threadbare at the elbows. Underneath she wore a cantaloupe-colored halter top over a pair of wrinkled salmon chinos stitched with tiny bees. She was whey-faced, and her makeup looked slept-in.

Did you even bother to go home last night, Fi?

You're just jealous. Never mind where *I* spent the night. Where did *you*? Don't pretend you don't know what I'm talking about. You have *the glow of good sex*.

And you have the glow of weird colorways. Melon over salmon? You look like a catered app.

Is Chuck Halsey responsible? she pressed. Your cheeks are pink as my pants.

Shoe's on the other foot, I said. Now who's jealous.

She flopped onto the sofa: *Too-shay.*

We need to talk, I said.

Where I spent the night is none of your business.

We need to talk *about paint*.

Fiona regarded me blearily. I spread my paint chips on the coffee table, a range of whites from whipped cream to titanium. I had chosen a huge white flokati, ten feet by fourteen, for Chuck's bedroom. The heavy rug would dampen sound, and its light color would play up the fireplace, which I planned to have sealed and painted in the glossiest white I could lay my hands on. Fiona swept up the chips and moved to the window, where she turned them, one after the other, in the light.

Aren't you overthinking this? They all look pretty much the same.

Several are actually very yellow. They might dry down to mummy—or cadaver. And with my luck, I won't see the nasty pallor until the second coat. Or the third.

Yecch. I know you have your little macabre sideline, but must you talk this way between nine and five? It's just paint. *White* paint.

Just paint is what we get paid for. The decision's got to be right. And until we make it, I can't finalize anything else. The drapes still have to be ordered, and they're custom—they'll take weeks. And the kitchen's still just blueprints—

Cookie, she intoned. This job is not till-death-do-us-part. If you want it to go on forever, you're in the wrong role. You're stringing it out, and your justifications could stuff a Chesterfield.

Aren't you overstating the problem, just a little?

All I'm saying, Cookie, is that it would be easy to take things too far.

I SHOULD have heeded Fiona's warning. Something about the previous evening bothered me. Not just what we'd done, which felt like the natural culmination of all that had gone before, but the way Chuck seemed to know my most secret self. I kept coming back to Chuck's question about my work or, more precisely, my ambition. Didn't I aspire to a big commission, a solo show?

The only other person who ever had a clue about this part of me was my art school friend, Erica. I'm proud to say I knew her when. She was petite, built spare as a Nevada bluebird, with a mass of black hair that flew out behind her as she rumbled around campus on a skateboard stickered with slogans celebrating peace and love and the perfection of anarchy. She knew the complete discography of Janis Joplin, and she loved working big. Her canvases covered walls; her installations filled rooms. She was from Reno, and I can see now that this slender fact was one pretext for my trip out West with Harry. I was hoping some of her desert fairy dust would rub off on me.

We shared an apartment during our thesis year, and she had made a habit of calling me out on my banked ambitions, what she called my *cheap façade*. But as much as she tried to insult me, I wasn't offended. How could I be? Erica was just being herself. I have a picture of her, squaring off before a cow-sized block of plaster, a ratty Janis T-shirt knotted around her head to keep that great hair from her eyes. She looks authentic. Present. Fierce.

Not like me. I had grown up lost, deep in a shell I carried with me everywhere like a makeshift home. My parents weren't bad people; probably it had something to do with New Preston, a once-prosperous city in decline. At any rate I wasn't ready to leave my hiding place. I pretended to be like everyone else. Art school is great for this. Anywhere everyone is trying to seem cool and different is the easiest place in the world to disappear. No one was looking at me anyway—except Erica. But her interest only went so far. The person behind my mask was not Erica's concern. What enchanted her was the mask. The illusion. Which, I admit, I found convenient.

Erica's thesis project was explicitly and intentionally disgusting. In the last term of senior year, she chewed a week's worth of meals, spit them into jars, sealed the lids, and arranged the results chronologically on racks. Installed in the school's gallery, the contents of the jars began to decay except for a deep-red lollipop she had sucked down to a sticky nugget and sealed in a jar on its own. According to her artist statement, this was life itself—a cheap confection, promising at first but grown tacky and disappointing, even as its bright industrial coloring remained weirdly unchanged.

The installation provoked headshaking among the faculty, and the other art students—who might have been more sympathetic, out of solidarity—responded with detached politesse. Once, over tea with Bobby—young Bobby, with an untrammeled waistline and a headful of curls—in that same cruddy kitchen, I confessed I didn't see the point.

That day, Bobby had just closed a mortgage on the derelict mill building that would eventually become the Roach. He was already making a name for himself, running pop-up shows in vacant strip malls and monster raves in empty lots along the waterfront. But he was making a start at something even bigger, full of talk of live-work spaces and creative communities, marketing plans and financing.

The kettle whistled. I poured out the water and watched my tea bag rise. I'd used it once already, at breakfast. To Bobby I'd given my last fresh one.

I don't understand Erica's project, I said. I don't get it.

Of course you don't, Bobby said, dunking his tea bag. You wouldn't understand the dark impulse.

What dark impulse?

To undermine cherished beliefs.

Like that food is for eating?

Like that *life* is worth *living*.

I was finishing my own senior project, a collage series centered on historical advertising of domestic technologies like washboards and wooden clothespins. Even in those days, my interests aligned with the operations of practical domesticity, the need for handles that turned, valves that opened and shut. We use things up, we wear them out. I was reusing tea bags. What were these so-called dark impulses to me?

Her point, Bobby insisted, is that she doesn't have to swallow. None of us do.

Bobby had been right, in his way. Banks, businesses, governments—everyone passes costs onto those least able to object. Maybe the best you could do, sometimes, was to spit your meals into jars, or plead your case on an anonymous website, which seems to be the way these days. Protest, in other words.

My mother had her own take, naturally. When I told her about Erica's senior project, we were in my student kitchen. She was making one of her lunchtime visits. Tucked neatly into her deep-pocketed work jacket, she perched on a small stepladder that doubled as a stool.

Brilliance is beside the point, she said when I told her about Erica's project.

What Erica has, she went on, is an instinct for publicity.

Cold comfort, I replied.

Is there any other kind? She grinned. Put the kettle on, will you? I'm in the mood for a cup of your pauper's tea.

My mother was busy in those days, as if she'd sensed the first shadows of age falling across her path. And it *had* taken her weeks to finish her latest engagement, cataloging a cache of ancient things—papyrus scrolls, scarabs, shabti, the remnants of a very rich and reclusive man's collection. She'd angled for the job, strategizing over the phone with friends for weeks, but now that she had it, she'd grown uncertain and fussy, repeatedly going over the provenance of each piece, filling index cards with her cramped handwriting as if she might forget some crucial detail, and all would be lost.

What you need is a change of scene, she said, glancing at me over her pince-nez. Go someplace warm. Bring a friend. A real one. *Not* this Erica, who competes with you.

She does not.

She does so. Don't look at me that way. I know she's your friend. She might not be perfect, though. Since when can't you afford to see all around a person? Oh, never mind, what do I know? I'm only your mother! Listen to me, now. You need to get out of town. Loosen up. Cut a rug. Now's the time.

Now's the time. I'm sure she meant well, but over the years, after so many *nows* that were never somehow quite *the time*, the meaning of those three syllables has taken on a dark weight. She had discovered ancient history in college, but then she'd fallen pregnant with me. She was too kind to say so, but my birth had derailed her, changed the arc of her life in a way she had not anticipated.

She patted her pockets, puzzled.

What is it, Mom?

She put me off with an impatient shake of her head. A moment later she exhaled in relief as she lifted up a silver coin, about a millimeter thick and satined with age.

I thought I'd lost it, she murmured. For a moment, I was sure I had.

What is it?

A gift.

For me?

Who else? I have no idea where it's from, so don't ask. It was plundered, no doubt, from some Greek who had the misfortune to die far from home, probably in Alexandria, where it fell into an ancient oil lamp that I just purchased for a song from my Boston dealer.

One side of the coin showed three flag-like figures she called netchers, which I already knew to be ancient Egyptian symbols of divinity. On the coin's reverse side was a bee.

Technically it's called an obol, she said. And, well—let me put it this way, its provenance was not disclosed.

I slipped the coin into a pocket, felt the chill of it there against my skin. Later, I learned what an obol really was—a token pushed into a dead person's mouth and buried with the body as advance payment for the soul's journey in the afterlife. It was a strange gift for a daughter on the occasion of finishing a degree. I reminded myself of all the sacrifices my mother had made—the study she'd been unable to pursue, the books she didn't have time to write because she was going around with a laundry basket, picking up socks instead of resurrecting lost worlds of emperors and pharaohs. Maybe the obol was her way of preparing me—as when I learned to drive, she always gave me cash for gas and tolls. As if to make sure I could pay my way, even in death. Perhaps especially in death.

9

My dalliance with Chuck took a familiar, sad shape. As I heated, he cooled—grew distant, controlling. Several times he promised to call and didn't. If I pinged his beeper, or left a message with his service, he never seemed to get the notification. I responded as if these loser moves were erotic catnip. He made me angry, he hurt my feelings, and that was it: I had to have him.

I know, I *know*: Acting like a thermostat in order to regulate another person's behavior is a standard weapon in the arsenal of control freakery. Let me say plainly, I failed here. I got greedy. Me—with my life, my projects, my interests, the business I was on the verge of ruining. Apart from common sense, I didn't need more of anything, certainly not from him. Yet, in my insecurity, I did want more. More information, more reassurance.

Was Lana not good in bed? Wasn't I better? What did I have that Lana did not, what made me special?

My insecurity was running the show. I can hardly bear to think of it—but recent events demand an accounting. So: I laid traps, hoping to push him to disclose the source of his dissatisfaction with his marriage. Chuck responded defensively, which fueled my hurt. Spackling cracks in my ego, I did everything I wasn't supposed to: I tried to unlock his phone while he showered. I rifled through his wallet. I eavesdropped on his calls.

We bickered. We blew up and broke up, again and again. A few days later, he'd call, or I would, and we'd arrange to meet at the house, where I found him with his arms full of flowers, a bottle of my favorite California white nesting in a stone cooler on the newly refinished parquet floor.

Not that we needed much loosening up. The spark between us always caught, desire being its own augment. Spooned against him on an air mattress I'd installed in his bedroom, I felt flush with happiness, at peace in the renovation's atmosphere of fresh-cut lumber and his own smells, so distinctive, of laundry starch and hospital soap.

THE RENOVATION had reached a delicate stage. I was ahead on some aspects and falling behind on others. Those rift-sawn kitchen cabinets remained elusive, and the new chimney duct needed a final inspection, but in the paint department at least, I was moving things along. In Chuck's bedroom, I switched on the site lamp and arranged paint chips on the floor. I set the flokati swatch beside the chips and shrugged out of my blazer. Underneath I wore only a camisole. That night my wardrobe was the only thing I had thought through.

Leaning against the wall by the window, Chuck replaced his cell phone in its holster. His smile reflected brightly in the dark glass.

We have too many options, I said.

I see only one option, he said, and that is to remove your shirt.

Stop it. Paint is important. What do you think of Cotton Balls?

I reached up, offering him the relevant chip. He nudged it under one strap of my camisole, slipping it off my shoulder.

The name is unsuitable, he said.

There's also Angel Food. Sugar High. Snow Day.

He selected a card. Wite-Out, he read. Without the aitch.

It's not really white, I said helplessly as his teeth grazed my neck. More like beige.

We tumbled onto the mattress, shucking our clothes. I couldn't undress him fast enough.

I woke later to the sound of his beeper, which he silenced with extreme prejudice.

Who was that?

Just my loony colleague. She likes to ruin my nights with made-up catastrophes. But, funnily enough, she only does this when Lana's out of town.

Funnily enough, I repeated. There were many things that only happened when Lana was out of town.

He went on: I don't know why the damned beeper went off. Her calls are supposed to go straight to voicemail.

The site lamp popped. An arc of electricity crossed the room, and everything went dark. I felt my way to the window. Chuck padded up behind me. Below us, a car screeched to a stop beneath the porte-cochère. I recognized the driver. *Lana*, I whispered. She's here.

Chuck hissed: *Quiet*.

Lana flew out of the car, her face contorted with rage. I felt my eyes saucer. She looked so scary, I almost missed the elderly man who was with her, folded stork-like into the passenger seat, his knees pulled nearly to his chest.

Who's the guy? I asked, reaching for my panties, which were balled up by the radiator.

He sighed. That would be Benno.

Benno?

My therapist.

I sped across the room and started throwing on my clothes. Like everyone in Chuck's life, including me, even his therapist was at his wife's beck and call.

Cookie—

Since when is driving around at night with the patient's wife part of someone's medical treatment? That's supposed to happen in a *room*, on a *couch*—

It's not like that. Cookie, please listen. I hate to tell you this, it feels like a betrayal. But Lana wants marriage counseling.

Oh, does she? I sputtered as I zipped my skirt. Well, I see how you might not want to tell me that.

I wanted him to say that he was leaving her, that counseling wasn't going to save their marriage, that their marriage was beyond saving. And maybe it was. What he said next surprised me.

I told her I'd try individual therapy first. That's when I found Benno, who told me I needed a psychoanalysis. Fine, I said. Whatever it takes. I just need her off my back.

She might divorce you?

Lana will never divorce me.

I thrust my feet into my shoes. Chuck shifted the curtain and peeked out. On the doorstep Lana was rooting in the depths of her satchel, presumably looking for her keys. My heart hammered in my chest, and my mouth was bitter with adrenaline. Gripping my arm, Chuck steered me toward the threshold.

My eyes pricked; something was lodged in my throat.

You better go, Cookie. Use the back stairs.

10

Around this time Harry became a nuisance.

On the job I have a few rules. First of all, my subs talk to me, not to the client. The Halseys were no exception. So when Harry started arranging on-site tête-à-têtes with Lana, I wanted to slit his throat with the site key. Not only that: He started to act like he was the general contractor, in charge of everything from roof to cellar, coming at me with questions way outside his lane: Wouldn't Lana need an extra water line for an ice-maker in the fridge? Was I sure that I had obtained the correct permit to repair the creaking soffit?

Once I caught them in the kitchen giggling over one of my blueprints. They fell silent as soon as they saw me. My indignation went down like a mouthful of acid. I took Harry aside. In the corridor, Lana's perfume lingered on him, a pricey floral that set up an itch deep in my throat.

You're not running this job, I fumed. If she wants to seal her beehive oven with nail polish and mortar it with honey mustard, the news has to come through me.

He slammed his tool kit onto the parquet and laughed when I glared, his teeth bright against his Florida-prison-yard tan.

So that's how it is, Cookie? Well, it's your party, princess. I'm just the hired gun.

I should have fired him there and then, and I still wish I had. But the plain fact was, I needed him.

Listen, I said. I heard from the chimney inspector. The news is not good.

Ventilation? he asked. A smug smile played on his lips.

That was your job, I hissed. You said you'd manage it.

Relax, he replied. We can parlay this and that.

This is the biggest job of my career, for New Preston's most prominent doctor, and you want me to relax?

Harry smirked.

Don't you huff at me, he said. The whole town knows his reputation's in the shitter. Turns out your fancy boy's not all that, now, is he.

CHUCK'S PUBLIC relations were none of my business. But his insufficient kitchen ventilation was my responsibility. I'd promised him a venting solution, for one thing. But I had skin in the game, too: If their kitchen went up, I'd be doing nothing but powder room retiles for the foreseeable future. I called an emergency meeting. On the appointed day, I found Harry by the shrub border kicking at the hollow boulder that hid the site key.

Hey, I called out, keeping my voice absolutely neutral to hide the fact that I was absolutely pissed. He wasn't supposed to know about the key. But then he seemed to know about everything.

Harry tipped the fake rock back into place. A trail of dark fluid snaked down his forearm.

For security's sake, I had asked the gardener to plant a perimeter of dragon-lady holly. The fierce thorns encouraged strangers to keep their distance. Most of them, anyway. I wasn't so sure about Harry.

Those thorn bushes you put in don't do shit, he said.

Your epidermis begs to differ.

A scratch like this? Ain't gonna stop anyone from boosting the TV.

He wiped his arm on his shirt, leaving a dark smear.

The idea is to discourage, I said, as discouragingly as I could. The Halseys will be here any minute. Why don't you go home and take care of that scratch? The last thing I want is to make a scene.

You never change, do you? Always burnishing that good-girl image.

Well, I had nothing to say to that. He smiled, pleased to have talked me into a corner.

I'll tell you this. All play and no work makes your Harry a broke-ass boy. How's that for reality, eh? You know I found that mattress you left upstairs. You're not exactly an all-work type, are you?

Can't say as I am, I replied, willing my jaw to unclench. Can't say it's your business.

Well, pardon me, Mizz Cookie Cooke. I didn't know we were still on a *formal* basis.

Ignoring him, I marched up the front steps. The front door was freshly painted in shiny black, and my key turned smoothly in the lock. Behind me Harry huffed and puffed, too close. I sensed him switching gears. Next would come the sweet-talking.

You're a good egg, Cookie.

I spun around and grabbed his bad arm. Wincing, he pulled away, and I gave him my kindest dragon-lady smile.

It's been over between us for a while, I said. Let's let bygones *be* gone.

He stomped inside and up the stairs, making a racket with

his tools. Gravel crunched in the driveway, and I heard a motor cut out. Moments later Chuck appeared in the kitchen wiping the day's grime from his glasses, and the gesture's sheer ordinariness stung me with longing. Couldn't he be mine, couldn't we share this kitchen, this house, this life?

Always burnishing that good-girl image.

Where's Lana? I asked.

Busy, Chuck said with a shrug. You know how she gets.

I tugged his elbow: Let me show you what we found.

Not another problem with the chimney?

The very same, only worse. We have to figure out another way to vent it. Harry's here, I added. He's going to take measurements.

More demolition? Jesus. We were almost done!

Upstairs Harry had been pacing and muttering on the landing. Now he called down.

The corridor's short, Cookie. I counted off thirty feet downstairs, but only twenty up here. That downstairs room, the secret one we found? It continues up here. It *has* to.

Chuck and I met Harry upstairs, where he was banging his palm against different parts of the wall. Sure enough, there was a hollow-sounding zone just where the room would have extended to the second floor.

Harry hoisted his sledgehammer; a vein bulged over his bicep. He moved so fast I couldn't even scream *Wait*.

A moment later, it was all wrecked—the new sheetrock, the fresh paint.

Chuck shouted, *What are you doing?*

Sorry about the mess, Dr. H, said Harry, with a deference that surprised me.

My throat burned. The air was thick with plaster. I wheezed through the dust: *Respirator.*

Harry crouched, searching in his bag. He came up with a handful of masks and handed them around. Then he pointed to a dark smudge on the bricks at the rear of the new void. The chimney was crumbling. It would need to be inspected, most likely repaired, and sealed from top to bottom so it wouldn't leak fumes, or worse, channel a fire into the walls—which, if the dark marks I saw rising upward were any indication, seemed to have happened once already. I remembered the blackened uprights in the kitchen. So there really had been a fire, long ago.

There was another surprise, too. Chuck noticed it first.

Is there a hole in the roof? he asked. That gap looks daylit.

Harry whistled low. Get a load of this, Cookie.

I peeked in. Sure enough, the void went up to the roof. Sunshine edged through a glass roundel at the top.

An oculus, I said as I backed carefully away. Once upon a time this house must have had a dumbwaiter. This was the shaft, and it must have gone straight down to the kitchen.

Before someone made an Egyptian temple in the middle of it, Chuck said, adding: Don't forget the frescoes.

I stuck my hand in the void and ran my fingers along the interior wall.

What is it? Chuck asked. You look like you've just touched something revolting.

The interior here feels *furry*.

It's probably lint, Harry said.

I peered in again. Sure enough, the walls and floor were lined thickly with it. Tilting my head, I could just make out a shadow in the corner of the far wall.

You see that mouse hole in the corner? Harry asked.

Chuck said: Don't tell me that's the dryer vent.

Good guess, Harry replied. The laundry room is on the other side of the wall.

The dryer vents *here*? Into this little room? But that stuff's flammable.

Well, it ain't insulation, that's for sure. The dryer needs to vent *out*.

I said: Give me your flashlight, Harry.

I focused the beam with one hand, reaching into the void with another. I brushed at the dusty surface. Beneath the dust, something had been etched into the wood. Three stylized letters—JVM—set within a circle.

Chuck leaned in, following the beam. What the hell's that?

It looks like some kind of builder's mark, I said. Whoever built this part of the house—whatever it is, or *was*—left a calling card.

Builders are all the same, Harry offered. Territorial as dogs. Sniff and piss.

I tugged at a loose piece of sheetrock.

Chuck murmured, That's friable.

You bet it's friable, Harry said as he leaned over and brusquely yanked the fragment free. That's why people put their fists through it.

Harry, I warned. He was getting worked up.

Amazing what people don't know about their own homes, Harry said.

I stared at him, thinking of his time in the big house. He'd learned something there, for sure, about menace. Or maybe it was something he'd always known, but kept hidden, tucked behind some inner sheetrock. He'd chased me on the playground, he'd chased me across the stage with that dolled-up shovel—

That's enough for today, Chuck said wearily. Close up that gap, and let's forget about it. This floor's in fine shape as it is. We don't need to start moving more walls around.

But we have to vent the dryer, I reminded him.

Chuck was shaking his head as if to dislodge some horrible thought.

The home inspector found nothing. Your demolition crew, also nothing. Yet now that we're almost done—

We can handle it, I said quietly. Harry huffed, a soft skeptical noise.

For God's sake, what is the actual problem here, Harry? Tell me quick. My patience is expiring.

Venting *anything* through this space is going to take some doing. Maybe *a lot* of doing. We need to extend the duct, for one thing. I got the beehive oven to vent through the chimney, but it's not going to draw diddly with the condition those bricks are in, and the first time Lana decides to do an Easy-Bake, all the heat will collect in this combustible rathole.

Could you rebuild the chimney?

I could repair it. We could install supplemental fans and route them through the roundel, so no matter what happens, everything just blows up and out.

Good grief, I said. That beehive oven may be more trouble than it's worth.

New construction's what I always recommend, said Harry. Not that anyone ever asks me.

Chuck rubbed the toe of one shoe on the opposite leg, leaving a dry white smear on his scrubs. We were all dusted with plaster. His beeper whirred again.

I have to take this. It won't stop until I do.

What won't stop, Chuck?

He waved me away, already talking to the person on the phone: Hello. Benno, *yes*. What?

Harry and I followed Chuck out. As we left, I peeked into Chuck's bedroom. The air mattress was flattened against the floor, slashed from one end to the other.

I lunged toward the wreckage. Snickering, Harry tugged me away.

11

I off-loaded the venting problem to Harry. The problem was chimney-related, and I needed him to focus on something besides enlarging his control over the renovation. My nerves were frayed, alternatives were thin on the ground, and to top it all, the Halsey project had hit yet another snag. Lana's rift-sawn oak cabinets were so delayed, I feared the supplier was still growing the trees.

I placed this order weeks ago, I reminded my carpenter.

It's not like you can get rift-sawn white oak at Home Depot, he said. In the background I heard the staccato bursts of a nail gun.

A few days later, he forwarded photographs of the work in progress. The Halseys' new kitchen seemed designed by Dr. Seuss. Panicked, I called again: Whose project is *this*? He insisted he'd understood my design. Why was I changing my mind on him, and so on.

I made an appointment to explain my requirements in person. The first Boston train left New Preston at six A.M., and Fiona would join me a few stops down the line, where there was a station closer to her house.

I sat down in a three-seater. To avoid company, I slapped my sunglasses on my face, pressed my headphones in my ears, and opened my laptop, pulling up some articles on Lizzie Borden that I'd saved for just this sort of extremity. No one in their right mind would bother me. The train heaved out of the station.

My Lizzie B. files were open and waiting. But Facebook had other plans. I got an alert: Erica had tagged me in a posting chain, one of those dumb questionnaires people liked to pass on, a new take on an old-fashioned chain letter. She'd filled it out and reposted it, tagging me along with twenty-four of her closest Facebook friends, and now my feed was blowing up with replies, dozens of them, rippling down the screen. Erica's computer would be pinging with responses all day. So would mine. Maybe that was the point: to make a disturbance in one place that became a disturbance everywhere.

Getting to Know Me
If you're reading this, you have the honor of copying all these goofy questions, writing your own responses, and posting them while tagging twenty-five other victims. If you don't do this, you'll have bad luck for a year.

1. What time did you get up today?
i didn't

2. How do you like your eggs?
broken

3. What did you have for breakfast?
coffee & Certs

4. What is your favorite cuisine?
home cookin'

5. What foods do you dislike?
filter organs

6. Cup 1/2 empty or 1/2 full?
i resent this math assignment

7. Favorite color?
field's orange

8. Who do you think will not tag you back?
Cookie

9. Person you expect to tag you back first?
Cookie

10. Whose responses are you most curious about?
[whistles]

I sent her a message right away. *Ugh, Erica! Can't believe you called me out on Facebook. No harm done, of course. But I don't want to tell the whole world my business. Let's catch up by phone or email instead. Good to know you're still eating the Breakfast of Champions. Never change, friend of my youth!*

I typed fast, but once I had the sentences, I dithered over the message, switching up the punctuation, trying to hit the right note—breezy and welcoming, not dismissive. For all her laid-back, California cool, Erica might have been—must have been—lonely. Only lonely people got mixed up with dumb chain letters on Facebook. In her way, she was hailing me, asking for interaction. But I didn't want to say too much, to burden her with my loneliness when she may have already been contending with her own.

The train reached Fiona's stop. I gave up and hit send.

Fiona was waiting on the platform, an oversized bag depending from her shoulder and all the buckles on her moto jacket fashionably undone. I stashed my laptop and slid toward the window, making room. The doors thumped. The conductor shouted. Fiona jangled down the aisle and sank into the seat beside me.

Oof, she said. Why did you schedule a meeting at this ungodly hour?

The conductor swaggered down the aisle, calling for tickets. When he reached our seats, Fiona dug in her bag.

I swear it was just in my hand, she fluttered.

The conductor's gaze softened.

You'd lose your head if it weren't attached, isn't that right?

You can say that again.

Naturally he did say that again, and I had to suppress a wince as Fiona obliged him with a laugh. She still couldn't find her ticket, though.

Not to worry, he said, punching her a freebie.

My hero, she trilled as she pocketed the scrap. He winked at us both and headed off with a distinct bounce in his step.

I can't believe what I just saw, I said.

A girl's gotta eat. Plus I am about to be more broke than ever. We really have to talk, Cookie.

Fiona had picked quite a moment to renegotiate her salary. I began to regret agreeing to this trip. What I paid Fiona was part of what was lousy about her situation, but I didn't have so much margin myself.

What's happening? I asked, to be polite.

Fiona's story was long and involved. Most of it I already knew: Her mother had disappeared a few years after her father, leaving Fiona alone with her kid brother, Owen, whom she adored. As busy as she was with her classes, she wouldn't let Owen lift a finger around the house; she lived and breathed for his happiness. Now Owen had decided on an occupation, and it was distinctly not remunerative.

He wants to become a funeral aesthetician. He's even landed an internship at the morgue.

Unpaid?

Naturally, she said.

I was trying hard not to scowl. The effort must have told on my face because Fiona sighed sadly and stared out the window.

Look on the bright side, I offered. Nothing important will change. He'll be around even less than he is already, and you'll still foot all the bills.

Are you kidding me?

Sorry. You know my limits when it comes to Owen.

He might do very well for himself, she insisted.

She wanted badly to believe this, I could tell from her face. Her devotion was something beyond sisterly, or else I didn't know that much about siblings, which was also possible.

A narrow bank of cloud shadowed the train as we passed Chepinoxet Pond, the whole scene—train, clouds—reflected in the surface like a painting.

Incredible fishing in that pond, I said to change the subject, trying not to notice the blackened railroad ties piled on the far shore, the flicker of memory that place evoked.

You'd hardly know from looking at it, Fiona said.

I used to fish there with my dad. He caught a pike once. Teeth like a mouthful of needles.

Your dad, she said. She fell silent, and I sensed my error: At least I had a dad.

We fished on weekends, I said. He was a loom mechanic. A relic, really. By the time I arrived, there wasn't much left to fix.

She flicked her gaze away.

What about your mom?

Ginny Cooke, antiquarian? Specialist in the knickknacks of death? He never had much time for her.

Maybe you have a thing for these guys. For that type.

Which type?

Pikes. Harry. Chuck. Guys with teeth.

Wow, I said. That's frank.

What about your mother's knickknacks of death? Fiona pressed. Do I hear an echo of Lizzie B.?

The apple didn't fall far, did it? I guess I inherited things from both of them, I said.

Massachusetts sped by, dun hills beneath white sky.

Where's your father now? Fiona asked.

He died five years ago. Pancreatic cancer. He was gone before we could put the final round of chemo in the calendar.

I'm sorry, she said, with an automaticity that suggested she'd had her fill of lost fathers, terminal diagnoses, all of the sad apparatus of adulthood. Fair enough: I'd had my fill of Owens, their dreams, and the debts they ran up chasing them.

She pulled her laptop from her bag, flipped the lid, and opened a web browser.

I almost forgot. I've been doing some digging. Online, I mean. Chuck Halsey may not be the paragon you think he is.

Did someone give him a bad rating on MDReportCard.com?

It's called MedGrade. But—yes.

How much "digging" did you do?

Just a Google search. This site was the top hit.

What does it say?

Who let this guy out of medical school? she read. *He can't tell his cerebellum from his*—oh Lord—*cerebelbow?*

That's a good one, I said. The pun sounded like one of Harry's.

She continued: *He's always late, he doesn't answer his phone.*

People expect a lot from their doctors. It's only natural to feel disappointed by them.

One person was so upset, she left fifteen one-star reviews!

That can't be good for his average.

He's a quack and a fraud. Fiona kept reading. *Think twice before putting your life in his hands.*

12

Boston was a bust. The carpenter spent the meeting flirting with Fiona, putting off my increasingly pointed questions about his ability to read a floor plan. In the end, he agreed only to a fresh deadline, which meant that I had once again allowed the ball to land in his court. But I didn't want to fire him. Burning bridges is a bad habit, expensive. All I could do was wait.

And so there I was, the lady in waiting. The position was familiar, but I felt strangely uncomfortable. Cramped. Stuck. I wasn't thinking only of the cabinets. I was thinking of the pikes. Harry. Chuck. The guys with teeth.

I returned to my *Acorn Studies*. It was my way of reverting to form, finding nothing to do but work. It was a bit of zoning out, if I am honest. More than a bit, in fact. Shaping a tricky cornice, I sent an awl flying into the meat of my right palm. I crouched in a corner of the bathroom, struggling with one hand to wrap a bandage around the torn flesh of the other. Shit *and* shinola. Effectively left-handed, I was going to be laid up for a while, with plenty of time to rue the wages of mindlessness.

~

A NOTE arrived from Erica: *Fine, don't play my questionnaire game. You'll just be cursed with a year of bad luck. Don't say I didn't warn you!*

Along with this note was the invitation to her next gallery show. It bore an address somewhere in LA. I imagined a cool boutique tucked somewhere unexpected, like in a warehouse of old movie props stashed behind the Glendale Galleria. On one side of the postcard was a photograph of an envelope that someone, probably Erica, had used as a place mat. There was a thick coffee ring, and below that a gorgeous pencil sketch, of a branch and leaves, that transformed the stain into a strange flower. Beneath that, in a scrawl I recognized as Erica's: *Behold, the magic of juxtaposition!*

A gallery show. She hadn't put me on the mailing list—she was still protective of me to at least that extent—but it was only a matter of time before she'd be too famous to reach out personally with this kind of news. Good for her. But oh, why couldn't this be me?

Indeed, why couldn't it? Bobby liked my *Acorn Studies*; he might be persuaded to exhibit them. And if the show was in New Preston and not Los Angeles, so what? I had to start somewhere, and that would certainly count as a start. I had only to make it. Which meant going back to basics: What did I really know about the Borden murders? What had I missed about that crime scene? I downloaded another trove of documents from the internet. One of them, by a historian who'd studied the Borden family and the sources of their hoard, contained a reference to an archive held by the New Bedford Historical Society, which was just up the road.

The time seemed right for an archival expedition. So long as Harry was occupied, I doubted fresh Halsey-related trouble would find me perspiring politely over ancient documents in a stuffy archive. Where I caught an unexpected break. In the household ledger of Borden *père*, on neatly ruled pages, Lizzie's father had tracked staples—flour, sugar, and cordwood—weighing quantities purchased against quantities consumed. He made a careful inventory of heavy wool, so many yards apportioned to Lizzie, so many to his wife. It added up to a lot of fabric—so much that, at first, I was surprised. Then I remembered: Those were the days of fireplaces and stoves. Fuel was expensive and scarce. The Borden house was a warren of tiny rooms for a reason: They could be shut up to save fuel. Woolen clothes would help with that economizing, too.

But rooms weren't the only things that could be shut up in the interests of economy. Old Borden had many mouths to feed—and stuff, and clamp, and worse.

It was just here, where the structure of the house met the ledgers of the household, that I sensed a clue to the curdling of Lizzie's psychology. How awful to be a young woman of that time and place, packed into corsets, stifling under heavy wool dresses and restricted to such cramped quarters, day after hot, itchy day.

Another mystery in the ledger: *$15 to Vinnicum, Way-Farer, for his Help*.

Feeling watched, I looked up. The archivist, with arms crossed, glared from behind his desk as he pointed at my injured hand. Bright-red blood was seeping through the bandage. Not a good look for a visitor to an archive. I was endangering the documents, and he didn't seem the type to keep a first aid kit around, unless it was for the books. But dustcloths and book tape weren't going to help me. I grabbed my stuff and fled.

DRIVING BACK to New Preston, I stopped at the Halseys' place. The street was a gritty mess, halfway prepped for a fresh coat of asphalt. I parked in the driveway, behind a truck that belonged to my flooring crew. In the front parlor I found another mess: Two guys wearing knee pads, dusty pants, and sheepish expressions were attempting to reinstall a sconce they had just knocked off the wall. Electrical matters not being their forte, the wall's fresh paint was now scuffed, and the formerly pristine sconce housing bore a deep dent. I shouted and waved my bloody fist. The guys vamoosed, and I slumped against the fireplace, listening to the gravel fly as they hightailed it down the mangled road.

Reckon you won't see them again, someone said.

An older man, sixty if he was a day, stood before me in a pool of sunlight. He was about as tall as Chuck, with the same bantam build. His gray suit had thinned at the elbows and taken on a sheen.

Who the hell are you, and how did you get the site key?

He tilted his head, a listening posture, his pupils tiny as pencil points.

This is a worksite, you know. Where people work?

He mumbled something that sounded apologetic. Lana swept into the room, heels clacking. Her eyes flicked over me.

There you are, Cookie.

Is Chuck on the way, Lana?

He usually is, she said bitterly, when you're here.

The strange man extended a bony, solicitous hand.

So you're the famous Cookie Cooke. I'm Dr. Benno Sanger.

This was Chuck's shrink, the guy I'd seen in Lana's car. I wheeled on Lana.

He's a psychiatrist, she said, as if that explained anything. An *analyst.*

Whatever he is, Lana, I don't think he can vent your chimney.

The stranger chuckled as he leaned toward me: Never mind

the semantics. I'm here to look after the spiritual dimension. Shall I take a look at that wound?

Are you going to ask me how I feel about it?

Lana smirked. I saw myself out.

THAT NIGHT, I went over my accounts. Everyone was past due with everything, including the Halseys. I called Chuck to let him know.

You never heard of net thirty? he asked.

What I resent is how you assume I can't count. You're way past thirty days, Chuck. You've skipped two payments in a row.

Meet me at the house.

You can't just send a check?

It's complicated.

Fine, I told him. I'm on my way.

New Preston's road repair crew had worked fast. The Halseys' street was so freshly paved, the asphalt was still setting. The day had been warm, and as I made my way up the walk, I felt my soles grow sticky. I'd have to be careful to avoid tracking in the mess. Inside, I left my gross shoes by the door. Chuck led me up to the bedroom, which was finally almost finished. I'd replaced the air mattress with a proper bed made up with the best materials to be found anywhere—Egyptian cotton, Indian silk, Canadian goose down. He'd been working in that bed, his laptop still open on the coverlet. I recognized the MedGrade logo.

Catching up on your fan mail?

The customer is always right, he said tightly, assuming they survive whatever brings them to me in the first place. You'd think survival would be sufficiently gratifying, he went on. I suppose I should be glad they're functional enough to slander me.

I extracted his overdue bill from my bag.

You know I'm good for it, he said, snatching up the slip of paper.

If you really cared about my trust, I said, you'd have handed me a check already.

Why would I do that? I know you won't push.

You don't know that.

He shrugged: When have you ever been different?

I read your profile on MedGrade, I said recklessly. Are your patients unhappy?

Those sites are chock-full of nutters.

Lana was here today, I pressed. With that gray dude, Benno.

He groaned. We're doing this again? You know I don't take time to see you just so I can talk about my wife.

Doesn't it seem the least bit strange to you that your wife is spending so much time in private consultation with your therapist?

We like unorthodox practitioners. That's one reason we hired *you.* Why can't you let this go?

I knew what I should do: Hold faith with our familiar things. Stop falling prey to petty doubts. Our moments together were special because they were ours, wrested from lives that otherwise mostly owned us.

I need you to stop treating me like an emotional forklift, Cookie. You want me to knock Lana down so you'll feel better. *But he who truly loves the world*, he reminded me, *shapes himself to please it.*

I suppressed a sigh. The portentous "He who truly loves the world" line came from an old novel I'd never heard of—*Confessions of Felix Krull*, by Thomas Mann, the same one who wrote *Death in Venice*. It was the one novel Chuck admired, and possibly the only one he ever read. At its center was the con artist who gave the book its title. Chuck repeated the line whenever he wanted to prompt my self-reflection without criticizing me outright, which was irritating.

But he wasn't entirely wrong, either—which was also irritating.

He moved to the window, delicately loosening one shirt button after another. We were thoughtful with each other that night. Subdued. Afterward he asked: Can I give you a lift home?

Heading out, he was pink-cheeked and whistling. His embrace under the porte-cochère was tender. But as soon as he shut me into the car, the charm vanished. When I reached to reposition the passenger seat, he snapped: *Don't touch that.*

Lana was a tall woman. I was not.

Leave no trace, he warned. The reminder kicked me in the chest.

He took the long way to the Roach. He didn't want to be with me, that much was abundantly clear, but he wasn't in any hurry to return to his laptop, either. Some unpleasantness awaited him there, perhaps, though for once his beepers had been silent.

It was a clear night lit by a full moon, with a breeze that smelled of the river. He parked, and I reapplied my lipstick, knowing he wouldn't try to kiss me.

Don't forget about my bill, okay?

Sure thing, Cookie.

Getting out of the car, I noticed I'd left tar marks on the floor mats. I stepped away, careful to leave the seat in position, and shut the door on the mess.

The realization only hit me later. With his threadbare literary quotations, Chuck was actually giving me what I wanted, or thought I did: an explanation of what he found unattractive about Lana—her dominance, her pushiness. As for me: I had definitely shaped myself to please him. My passivity was precisely what he *liked* about me. Shame coursed through me, reaching even into the distant corner of my being where once upon a time I'd stashed my self-respect. It would be nice to have that back.

Later that week a check arrived signed by Chuck and made out to me for an amount that covered about half of what he and Lana owed. That was his way—to give some but not all, and so keep me around, unsatisfied, waiting. But the partial payment was better than nothing, and anyway I was hardly in a position to object. I made trips to the hardware store where, shivering in the aggressive air conditioning, I bought the supplies I needed to speed the job to its conclusion.

The remaining work wasn't hard. The kitchen cabinets had finally arrived, planks of gorgeous rift-sawn pine, stained light and buff-waxed to a luster, along with their installer: The cabinetmaker, feeling guilty about the delay, supervised the installation himself. I worked alongside him, ignoring his increasingly pointed questions about Fiona's relationship status as I tweaked the faucet on Lana's farmhouse sink. I also installed the remaining fixtures in the powder room, replaced blown bulbs throughout the house, and cleared leftover construction debris in preparation for the Halseys' official move-in, on the fifteenth of October, after the rugs were down. Lana's pig party was scheduled for later in the fall, between Thanksgiving and Christmas. I'd received an invitation in the mail, a jokey mondegreen lettered in gilt on heavy cream paper: *Beans don't burn in this kitchen, we don't fry no fish on this grill, took a whole lot of CRY-Y-INN, just to get up Pill Hill . . .*

Laugh or cry, I thought. In any event, the joke was on me. I hadn't imagined Lana had a comic bone in her body. I'd underestimated her, or maybe just her sparkling clavicles. That was one thing about Lana: She could be surprising. If only I'd known then just how surprising she could be. I returned the card with my regrets.

I didn't see much of Chuck, but I kept an eye on his MedGrade page, which was being regularly trolled. The allegations included charlatanism, quackery, and every version of malpractice, including wire fraud, now that we'd entered the age of telemedicine. How many of the complaints were legitimate, and how many just women whom he'd seduced and abandoned, who slammed him online for revenge? That many of the entries used similar phrases and vocabulary raised a third possibility: It was all the work of one busy nemesis.

Once I overheard him as he took a call on his way up the front walk. He was incensed, shouting about an operation that had gone wrong. I slipped out of earshot as I waited for him to finish, pretending to investigate a dinged toe molding. The fight seemed connected to the news stories I kept hearing about faulty painkillers. How was Chuck mixed up in that mess? With his caller he used strange words: *Hysteria. Liability. Taint.*

THE SEASON turned like breakfast butter on a tray. A rancid odor suffused New Preston. At the Halsey site, the radio kept me company as I continued to complete the punch-list items for which Lana and Chuck had no time. The news was full of stories from the hospital where an outbreak of pharmaceutical incompetence had led to patients being sickened by their post-op painkillers, an entire lot ruined by a lapse in the cold chain that kept the hospital supplied with the particular stuff they needed. It was a chemical story, nothing I could understand. Listening to the news, I felt like an eavesdropper—the reports gave a glimpse into Chuck's other life, the one he lived when I wasn't there. And yet the sickened people were all around me, my neighbors in New Preston.

I removed the sticky labels from the front of the dishwasher and brushed a spill of yellow leaves from the front walk. I even managed several white-glove installations of large pieces of furniture—a dining room table made from a long, wide plank of waxed black oak, a tufted sofa in deep-green leather. This was the fun part, or it should have been. But nothing about the project pleased me anymore.

Privately, after hours, I was clinging to illusions, paging through catalogs of flawless rooms, populating them with equally idealized daydreams of myself and Chuck: cuddling fireside beneath a blanket, while outside, a thick snow fell; gazing at each other over mugs of mulled wine garnished with fair-trade cinnamon sticks that cost a dollar apiece. As if I actually *wanted* the boring catalog dream, right down to the high-narrative cinnamon sticks. What I really wanted was unavailable for purchase anywhere: a buffer against the reality of Chuck's situation—his failing marriage, his crazy colleagues, the inexplicable rash of illness that had broken out at the hospital and his involvement in that, whatever its nature.

I wasn't the only one who'd fallen prey to catalog fantasies. Even Lana had succumbed, piling pimpled squashes on the steps and hooking a sheaf of bruise-colored corncobs to the grand front door. When I met Chuck on-site, dried cornstalks whispered near my face as I followed him inside. He was just off a hospital shift—cheeky, quippy, bouncy with adrenaline, and trailing an odor of yuzu shampoo.

This was to be our last official meeting, to prepare the installation of draperies in his bedroom. But something seemed off. I cast a glance around. The source of my unease wasn't hard to spot. Someone had fitted the door with a deadbolt, set at eye level. I fiddled with the mechanism. It was heavy, well-made, expensive.

Chuck shut the door and shot the bolt. I fought a wave of mischief, pushing back scenes of what we might yet do together.

An unauthorized change, he said. I won't bullshit you, Cookie. I installed the lock without your input. But it's a quality object, I think you'll agree—and let me be clear, it is *not* a comment on your design.

You're talking too much for someone who's confident in his choices, I said.

You don't like the lock?

In fact, the lock was fine—solid, functional, not cheap. I just didn't like the fact of it. I flashed on a scene from one of my in-progress *Acorn Studies*, a case that had turned on the disposition of locks and doors.

I said: I don't care if the lock is a museum piece or some junk you picked up at the Job Lot. What I want to know is, why in the world do you *need* it? Is this about Lana?

Let's not fight, he murmured, reaching around in his coat. A moment later, he opened his hand to reveal a tiny potbellied figurine glazed in the particular bright blue known as faience. It was a shabti, a real one—or else an excellent fake. He pressed it into my palm.

A gift, he said.

But a shabti stands in for someone, I said. It makes up for an absence.

It's a *parting* gift. Please don't be upset, Cookie. We had a good run.

I wasn't expecting this, I said—even though I had been expecting it, for weeks.

It really is the perfect gift, I said.

He touched my cheek.

No hard feelings? Please say there are no hard feelings.

It's just having them that's hard, I sniffled.

He kissed me, and I stumbled back, banged my head on the deadbolt. Everything I'd been holding back—grief, rage, frustration—spurted out, along with hot, humiliating tears.

Why did you install this stupid lock, anyway? I wailed.

Hold still, Cookie. You took a heck of a bump.

His fingers were in my hair, parting it. He palpated a tender spot at the back of my head.

Ouch!

Have you ever noticed, he said, how whenever we're both in the same room, Harry becomes a number one jackass?

You're worried about Harry? You don't need to worry about him. Sure, he can be controlling. But you have to be a bit of a control freak to do what he does.

Don't tell me I should put up with it just because he's excellent.

I stifled a laugh. I had often put up with Harry for precisely that reason.

He's jealous, Chuck insisted. That makes him pliable, don't you see? And here you are, covering for him because he's your friend.

The air conditioner whined, cycling loudly. Chuck tipped my face toward his. But this time I pulled back, for once unwilling to make myself complicit in my own humiliation, which now included an insinuation that I was blind to Harry's faults—which, as I knew all too well, were many. But Harry wasn't the one sneaking around with Chuck's psychiatrist—the one person who might actually be privy to whatever fear had caused him to install that lock. Chuck gripped my arm—*Cookie, listen*—but that just made me madder. I was squirming away when I noticed the nodule on Chuck's forearm. A dark line extended from it, marking the pale skin like a hairline crack in a porcelain cup. When I touched the spot, he winced.

AU TRAVAIL was just one of my mantras. I had others, and I was using them on the daily. Heartbreak is no piece of cake, no cakewalk, no walk in the park; not easy peasy, nor as pie.

Sorting fabric samples at the worktable, Fiona gave a Hollywood groan.

Oh, trah-vai, aye-yai-yai.

She sounded like Maurice Chevalier mainlining Red Bull. I laughed so hard I popped a button. The dogs rolled around on their beds, all paws and tails and tongues.

MIGHT AS well laugh, I thought. Anything to relieve the gloom that had fallen over the town as the darkening days were mirrored by yet more disquieting news from the hospital—what started as a rash of illness now had a rising body count—and patients were sent scurrying elsewhere. It was only a matter of time before someone left a comment on Chuck's MedGrade page; in a place this small, his involvement, whatever its nature, would not stay secret for long.

I was up early most days, working at the edges of my Lizzie diorama when I was not checking the web for new slander against Chuck or hoping for a message from Erica, who had gone quiet. I had plenty to be glad for, and I tried to be sensible of this, grateful. The Halsey job was all but done.

One flaw marred the renovation's topcoat: Lana hated the sailcloth draperies I'd installed in Chuck's bedroom. What really chapped her ass, of course, was the person who installed them. But for obvious reasons—I needed to draw the project to an end, finish the punch list, send the final bill—I had to play along, let her imagine the fault was design-related.

I met Lana at the house on a day when the sky was white with impending snow; in Chuck's room the desaturated light bounced off the white walls and played on the folds of Lana's suit, also white. The effect was dazzling, as I had hoped.

Lana plucked at the draperies, frowning.

What were you thinking, putting these on the windows? This is a *man's* room.

I waited. No point in interrupting her when she was on a roll.

I want a house I can bear to live in, Cookie. I cannot bear these *skirts*.

The next day, she dropped off an envelope filled with fabric samples—all pale, with little texture but substantial heft—from an Italian mill she favored. They were not especially different from the sailcloth I'd installed, but still, to placate her, I chose one and placed the order. Then Lana said she wanted fabric from a different mill. Then there was a strike. The labor problem seemed to involve her personally, or at least Lana Pura. The order was delayed; then it was canceled. Chuck called, fuming. He wanted the sailcloth back. He called me from work, between patients.

I imagined him at his clinic, hunched over a dull Formica counter on an old-style phone, the cord wrapped and tightening around his wrist. How the blood would pulse against the pressure, how it would throb around that dark nodule of flesh.

With a venom that surprised me, he said: Get these curtains in, Cookie. Just in case you have forgotten, I have to undress in that room.

I said: I have not forgotten.

So many things I had not forgotten, would not forget.

IN THE end I sourced the drapes locally. As soon as I heard from the supplier, I called Lana with the news.

I'll need to go back to the house once more, I said. To measure.

You've done nothing but measure! Surely you've got the measurements by this point.

She was correct, I did have them. What I wanted was one more trip to the house, one final pass through Chuck's room, to be closed one last time within those four bright walls—maybe then I'd find peace.

I just want to get this right, Lana.

Oh, *fine*. Go ahead, make double sure.

As soon as I reached the driveway's edge, the smell of roast pig lodged deep in my nostrils. Right: Today was the day. Lana had made good on her original taunt. She'd gotten her party. She'd roasted her pig.

Heading up the steps, I pushed past a holly hedge, and I caught my hand on a thorn.

Best to move quickly, to get in and out before Lana could brain me with a fireplace iron.

I detoured through the dining room, which Fiona had done herself in a palette of inky blues. I'd suspended three milk-glass globe chandeliers down the room's center, their roundness relieving the room's squared-off shape while their light, partially absorbed by flocked indigo wallpaper, softened the room's edges. A set of mid-century chairs upholstered in cornflower leather surrounded the wooden dining table, which Lana had set with the china I'd selected. It was edged in my signature color, the blue of Egyptian faience, my secret mash note to Chuck.

The scratch on my hand was going to need attention. I beelined to the kitchen where a wave of mail had crashed against the espresso maker. Greasy pans cluttered the countertop. When I stumbled over a pair of work boots someone had dropped by the door, a woman in a white caterer's uniform looked up, startled, her forearms plunged in the steaming sink.

You're bleeding, she informed me, glancing at my hand.

Just a flesh wound, I joked, toeing the boots aside. They were decrepit, the ends of the laces no more than tufts. Which of my subs was cretin enough to leave a job in his stocking feet?

Suit yourself, she said.

I'll grab a paper towel and be on my way, I said.

A phone rang from elsewhere in the house, beyond the foyer. Shaking water from her hands, she hurried to answer it. I tore a towel from the roll and dabbed at my cut. The bleeding had stopped. It was just my pride that needed a Band-Aid.

In the oven, the pig sizzled. It was small, not much more than a suckling, and it had been traditionally prepared—scraped, plucked, stretched, glazed, and gagged with an apple, tiny white teeth just visible where they pierced the skin. Some monitor was tripped; the oven beeped, and I heard the whoosh of the oven's gas ignition. As if in sympathy, the refrigerator—a side-by-side, stainless-finished as wide as a pickup truck—was issuing distress calls. Opening the door, I spotted among the champagne bottles and sheaves of cut flowers a pale-yellow shopping bag bearing the logo of a pastry shop in town.

There was no way I'd help myself to so much as a truffle. But there was no harm in peeking.

Instead of pastry, the bag contained tiny flat-topped glass ampoules filled with a clear fluid. Each was marked with a paper label that said PREPARATION UNSTABLE—KEEP COLD.

As I reached for the bag, someone grabbed my arm. I spun around, and there was Benno, creepy Benno, in the nickel-toned flesh.

Pardon me, he said, maneuvering me out of his way.

With his other hand—spotted with scabs I'd only seen while

visiting my mother at the rehab facility, on restless patients who couldn't stop picking—he plucked the sallow bag from its niche and hurried toward the door. As he left, he turned and, with a strange formality, inclined his head in a gesture that acknowledged *something*—perhaps just our common status as lackeys on the Halsey estate. He left with the bag tucked under his gray arm, the vents of his jacket flapping.

My mind whirred. It's not exactly professional for a physician to leave injectables in someone else's personal stainless double-wide. But then again, this is New Preston, where rules exist to be interpreted, and interpretations must serve the needs of the moment. See no evil, and all that. I still needed to take those measurements. I escaped down the servants' corridor.

At the threshold to Chuck's room, I waved away a line of spider silk. *Au travail*, I told the spider, hidden somewhere in the brilliant room, and wished that I could hide there, too.

At least one thing had turned out right. I'd made the most of Chuck's directive, his demand for an *oblivion of light*. The effect had been expensive and difficult to attain, but I'd done it. The white I'd finally selected for the walls was perfect—brilliant but not blinding. The flokati had settled beautifully on the floor. I'd sealed the fireplace, bleached the hardwoods. If only I could have handled Chuck with the same élan. The room succeeded where the relationship had not. I would have to content myself with that.

I crossed the room, unspooling a length of measuring tape. Someone had submerged a clutch of blue tulips—not my blue, but a different one, darker—in a thick-sided rectangular vase and set it on the white fireplace mantel. The assemblage reminded me of the glass coffin in which Snow White's dwarves had laid her out, dead from the poison she'd been tricked into eating, the poison that turned her lips that same bruised hue.

My measuring tape retracted with a snap. Those flowers. Only a dolt could fail to get the message. Here was Lana, asserting her rights.

IN THE kitchen, the mess had vanished. Sunset pinked the shining marble countertop. Waiters soft-shoed around caterers who were basting, chopping, and stirring with fierce concentration. Sleeked into another of her wide-lapeled ivory satin suits, her décolleté ornamented by a wide gold choker, Lana towered at the center of it all. Thanks to the shameful Google alert that I had not yet disabled, I suspected that her grandiose mood stemmed from recent good fortune: Her line of home textiles, Lana Pura, had been picked up by Martha Stewart and was about to debut in department stores from coast to coast. Lana had made a pile from the initial licensing, with more to come as the celebrity-branded product line expanded into new territories.

She called to me as I scuttled toward the back door. From her arm depended the familiar cream-colored purse, the same one she'd had that day, early on, when I'd brushed against her with my pitch-sticky fingers in the corridor. Was that a shadow on the bag's exterior?

Cookie!

We're all set in the upstairs bedroom, I chirped. Don't let me distract you from your prep, Lana. I can find my own way out.

Oh, but you can't leave now, Cookie. We're just getting started! Let me introduce you around, she purred, laying a hand on my arm, a heavy controlling grip. For a few minutes, she piloted me through the room, introducing me to the caterers and the cleaning staff. Her staffers were polite, but it was the bare minimum; they hardly looked up. I supposed they were used to her, the way I was. Her patronizing couldn't be separated from her patronage. Putting up with it was just part of the job.

Chuck arrived on a burst of chilly air. He pecked Lana on the cheek and glanced at me, smiling awkwardly. I tucked my bad hand, wadded into a paper towel, behind my back. With my good one, I adjusted a petit four that was misaligned on a tray.

Chuck cried out: So you've decided to join the party after all! I hadn't imagined you'd grace us with your presence.

He picked up the petit four I'd adjusted and popped it into his mouth.

Or is it not your scene? he continued, talking around the food. I suppose you're more comfortable at the Roach.

I shrugged, saying: I'm only here on business.

Oh, please, Cookie. All work and no play! Let me pour you some wine, for old time's sake.

He winked and grinned, and I felt the same familiar heat. Some liaisons just don't go quietly. A shared glass of wine wouldn't hurt me, wouldn't change anything at this point.

I said: All right. It's been a long day.

Guests began to arrive, each of them with the pinked-up look of the well-exercised rich, as if they had all just spent the afternoon on the squash court. I accepted the full wineglass Chuck offered and took quick inobtrusive sips, wincing at its sourness. I could see myself as their guests did, a working stiff nervously pushing her wrinkled shirt into her waistband with one hand, a bloody wad of paper towel stuck to the other. My phone buzzed. I recognized the number: It was the night clerk from Tomlins Manor. I silenced the call. Whatever it was could wait until I finished this glass of wine and perhaps another one. My long day was just getting longer.

Benno sidled up to Chuck, who whispered something that puckered the older man's expression. From an inside pocket, Benno withdrew a manila envelope and offered it to Chuck, who waved him away. Benno spoke sharply. I caught his tone, but not his words. He sounded like a person who had been pushed beyond some important limit.

Chuck caught my eye, as if he still expected to share a secret wink or nod. When I failed to respond, he looked away, disconcerted, and I felt a new, cold power. An insight can break over a body all at once, sunlight pouring into a shut-up room. Here was enlightenment: The fancy party with all these fancy friends was as substantial as a stage set. Even Lana seemed unreal, doll-like.

Chuck, though, was never one to go quietly. At once he was at my side, all innocence, snaking an arm around my waist.

Cookie, he murmured. It's been a minute, hasn't it?

I pulled away. I'd had enough of his buying my interest with crumbs.

A round-faced woman pressed toward us, apologizing as she pushed others aside. She was stout with blunt-cut, bleach-burnt hair, and dressed in a thick wool suit the color of asphalt.

Here comes trouble, Chuck muttered, his master-of-the-universe façade collapsing.

You must be Hannah Cooke, she hollered. Chuck! Is this not the famous Hannah Cooke?

Resentfully, like a child pushed to behave as an adult, Chuck swung himself into making introductions.

Dr. Martha Benton, please meet our decorator, Hannah Cooke, whose reputation has preceded her. Deservedly, I'd add.

He smiled at me. I smiled back, barely, and set down my glass.

Call me Cookie, I told her, offering my undamaged hand to shake.

I've heard all about this renovation, the secret room with the hieroglyphs on the walls—

Yes, I said vaguely, you can see them still, over there.

I gestured to the butler's pantry, where the fresco shimmered behind a plate of museum glass. Lana must have ordered some additional work: The colors were brighter; the long-limbed sky goddess had been rather obviously touched up.

As Martha exclaimed over the Egyptological kitsch, Chuck slipped away down the same corridor I'd used to make my own escape earlier. His curls, still damp from his post-work shower, grazed his collar—another of those details I was so keen to avoid, tiny reminders that clutched my gut.

Martha wanted to know all about the fresco, the chimney, the system of fans and ducts, the whole adventure of the renovation; chattering around a wad of pink gum—cinnamon, I guessed, from the humid holiday odor she exuded—she pressed me for every detail. I answered tersely. I disliked the way she'd homed in on me. Her behavior seemed to conceal a dangerous intention—but then, who was I to judge? Her gaze caught on the beehive oven, the hardware on its tiny door.

That thing looks just like . . . She paused, working her jaw thoughtfully.

Like what?

She shrieked: *Like a peewee crematorium!*

The room did feel warm. I took a step back, feeling for the wall.

We worked hard to keep the hearth, I said, remembering the early meetings. It was trapped beneath a crappy piece of drywall which was definitely not original. We had some discussions about that, for sure.

Oh, she cried, originality is so overrated! What I mean is, any project's always a team effort, even if not everyone gets the credit—

She turned and shouted down the corridor where Chuck had just slipped away: *Am I right*, Chuck?

She gestured with both arms, taking in the room, the guests, the party, then gripped my arm, whispering conspiratorially: *They're all fakes!* Phony-baloney, all of them, such *cronies*.

Excuse me, I said, disentangling myself. I need some air.

I drifted toward the foyer where the crowd was thinner. A huge bouquet of lilies had been set on the central table, giving off a heavy fragrance. This really was a work party. The hospital seemed the only topic of conversation. I overheard snatches—stories of the summer's chaos, the heat and the blackouts, patients in pain but afraid to take the pills they'd been prescribed. Emergency evacuations to other facilities. Sudden overdose deaths. A pharmacist stabbed, the painkillers burgled. An epidemic, someone said.

But that's impossible, came the reply. They're not addictive.

My phone buzzed again in my bag. Someone was trying hard to reach me. But before I could pick up, Martha's cinnamon breath once more invaded my nostrils. I spun around. She had followed me into the foyer. I curled my lip, about to snarl, but Chuck rushed up and took her by the elbow. She flicked her hand at him, a gesture of dispersal. A waiter pulled up short behind them, nearly dropping a tray of champagne flutes. Gliding around the traffic jam, Lana took two of those brimming flutes and offered one to me.

To homewrecking! Lana raised her glass, her smile tight as the feeling in my chest.

Those drowned blue tulips—of course she knew about me

and Chuck, and now I knew she knew. Smiling through the ache of my clenched jaw, I clinked my glass against hers.

The tulips upstairs are a knockout, I said.

Lana cawed with laughter, New Preston's answer to Elaine Stritch.

The room had gone from warm to unbearable. Smoke prickled my nostrils, and the air was full of the stench of burning pork. Whatever Harry had done was worse than useless. Rather than clearing smoke, the system was sending it back into the room. The wall by the oven had darkened, the stain spreading like the shadow of some large and ancient animal.

Lana excused herself to see to the problem, and I rushed after her. Someone was shouting, and then everyone was shouting. The smoke alarm shrieked. I joined the crowd rushing out the back door, scarves stretched over faces, fingers plugged in ears. Lana caught up with me in the driveway.

That wasn't supposed to happen, she snapped. I don't know if you noticed, Cookie, but the fire started in that damned void over the oven.

A woman said: It could be a squirrel's nest. Oh, the damage those glorified rats can do.

Lana replied, The infestation is in his practice, actually.

Rumors, said the woman in the shadows. In the near-dark, I couldn't see her face, but I could smell her disgusting gum.

The fire was now threatening the roof.

What a mess. What a fucking mess! Lana shouted.

I'll take care of it, I said. We'll replace the fan. It can all be fixed.

Lana, coldly: Can it?

I slipped through knots of guests who stood, drinks in hand, gawking at the spectacle of that grand house burning. It had gone up fast—very fast. Had Harry failed to remove the flammable dryer lint from the upstairs chamber? Or were those dry, time-blackened beams to blame?

My phone buzzed—Tomlins Manor, for the third time. I accepted the call, but it wasn't easy to hear over the howling of the fire engines. From what I could gather through the hubbub, my mother had a reaction to her pain medication and in her confusion wound up socking a nurse. Now she could not be calmed, and they were considering chemical restraint. Could I swing by? Of course I could. The evening had started manageably enough, but at this point, a complete change of plans was exactly what I required—anything to get myself out of this hot mess, which was clearly only getting hotter and messier. Reversing out of the driveway, I stopped short to avoid a woodchuck. As it hurried behind the hedge, I caught a glimpse of Benno beating the same retreat, riffling the dragon-lady holly.

13

The night clerk directed me to the conference room, a grim affair lit by spotty windows and crammed with office furniture. I maneuvered myself into a wobbly chair, one of several positioned around a crumb-strewn conference table, and rested my head on my arms. My breath smelled of Lana Halsey's bad wine; my hair, the smoke of her ruined house.

Behind me, the door creaked. A nurse hustled in and landed heavily opposite me. Her face was creased as if she'd slept with it folded up in her glove compartment. Her faded scrubs were printed with Hello Kitty in various attitudes of melancholic people-pleasing.

We're afraid she might become aggressive, the woman said.

She seemed to be speaking to someone just behind my right ear.

More than she already is? I asked.

It could be an indication of a deeper problem.

She's not dead yet, I said.

The aggression—

Is she on a new pill? When you changed her meds last month, she pushed a lunch trolley into another resident who'd offended her by creeping too slowly down the hall. Remember that?

The nurse frowned.

I'm not *blaming* you, I said.

She opened her mouth to speak, thought better of it. Like all my meetings with the nursing home staff, this one was edged all around by potential lawsuits.

I said: Mom felt terrible after that. Anxious and guilty. She told me, over and over. *I'm not that person*. And you know what? She isn't. She isn't!

The truth—

The truth! She was *poisoned*.

She was not poisoned.

We all make mistakes, I said.

Hannah.

Can I see her?

The nurse consulted her watch. Hello Kitty waved her arms around the clockface.

The nurse said: It's after hours.

It wasn't when I got here.

She sighed: Fine. Go ahead. I'm sure you know the way.

I slunk down the corridor, trying not to stare at the people sitting motionless along the hallway. Their eyes followed me, and I felt guilty, judged.

I should get my mother out of here and into a condo, I thought. Surely she could manage with temporary help. Surely there was a way to bring a physical therapist into the mix, someone who could see her in her own home, while there was still time. Surely, surely there would be time.

I walked faster, breathed deeper—so as not to go to pieces. The last thing she needed was me in pieces.

She was slumped in an armchair, with her bum leg up on the bed. I sat carefully on the edge, trying not to jostle her, not bothering to remove my coat.

Eventually she opened her eyes. From my woolen redoubt, I called quietly: Mom.

She turned her head away.

I needed to stay calm. Then she might feel safe enough to surface, to grace me with lucidity, to clue me into just what the hell was going on. It was a long shot, but they were all long shots now. No one could feel secure in a place like this, full of frowning Hello Kitty fans hiding loaded syringes.

Mom, I repeated. I'm sorry.

I'm sorry, she mocked me, her eyes popping open like a doll's.

Mom!

You're always sorry, she went on. We're all sorry. Never met such a sorry lot as we have here on Planet Puree. Planet Pap. What about Planet Pap-n-Smear, how do you like that one?

This was a running joke. When they were short-staffed at Tomlins Manor, all the meals were basically thick liquids, to cut down on time spent observing who was chewing and who was not.

I still have all my teeth, my mother said. But you wouldn't guess from the sludge they serve me. It's good to see you once in a blue moon, Hannah. How are you faring with the pharaohs of Pill Hill?

Another little joke. In ancient Egyptian, "pharaoh" could refer to the king, but it could also refer to his house—the great house, the greatest in the land.

Funny you should ask, I said, aware of the smoke clinging to my hair and clothes.

I withdrew the potbellied shabti—Chuck's gift—from the pocket of my coat. My mother straightened in her chair and raised her arms above her head, a stretch that was supple as a cat.

Hello, she said. Hello Kitty!

Mom?

Oh, Cookie. Now don't you go looking at me like I've lost *all* my marbles. At last inventory it was determined—I'm only missing a few. But I still know enough to tell my ass from my elbow, and I can also tell you that your little *objet*—she pointed to the shabti—is none other than Old Pataikos!

She grinned.

Pad thai a-what?

She repeated the name slowly, as if to a small child: *Pah-thai-ah-kos.*

He has nothing to do with whatever you're having for dinner, she went on, though I wish you'd invite me along now and then. We've already discussed the so-called food in this place. I don't know if you've noticed, but it's also deader than a hanged man on a Wednesday.

Why a Wednesday?

Woden's day, when he takes the dead out with the trash. Worst day of the week here on Planet Papillary Granola. Granuloma. Aren't you going to let me take a closer look at that?

I handed her the object. She rolled it in her fingers, which were steady. Even her tremor was gone. She grinned. Eyes bright, cheeks pink. There she was, back again. My mother.

Who's Pataikos, Mom?

A protector. Like Saint Anthony. He usually takes the form of an amulet. But this is a shabti. You remember those?

I nodded.

Egyptians were such realists! They understood that even in the afterlife, chores weren't just going to take care of themselves. You know those signs that hang in people's kitchens: *Your mother doesn't live here.* Well, your mother doesn't live in the afterlife, either.

She paused, watching me intently.

I get it, Mom.

So you say, but I'm the one who has to live here. Oh, don't mind me. I'm only talking about ancient history. In the afterlife, Egyptians had shabtis to do their work.

She turned the shabti in the weak institutional light.

It even has an inscription, she said. Now, it's been years since I could read these things. But this looks like a standard incantation, excusing the owner from a task and summoning the shabti to work in his place.

She gave me a sharp look.

Where did you find this little *objet*, anyway? It's not one of mine, is it?

Yours are all still on the shelf, Mom. That's what we agreed, remember?

Oh, agreements, she said.

Maybe you don't remember.

She slumped in the chair, casting her gaze out the window. Her shoulder had slipped out of her nightgown, and her upper arm was bruised, her bicep ringed with dark spots like fingerprints. Someone had held her down.

A soft snore broke my reverie. So they'd sedated her, too. What the clerk had called it: *chemical restraint.* Had no one simply tried to speak with her?

Exhausted, I slipped away, too. Fatigue had burrowed deep within me, and all I wanted was to follow it, to hunker down, to become wise in the way of small animals who avoided the day and its hard light.

14

They blame me! They're lawyered up the wazoo, and they intend to put me out of work!

Harry was shouting. I had to pull the phone from my ear. I was in the office with the dogs, just back from our walk, and they were tussling by the doormat.

Boys, I hissed. To Harry I said: Calm down.

Out of *work*! Do you even *know* what that means?

Belittling me isn't going to help, Harry.

Who's belittling? I'm just *telling it like it is*, Cookie.

Let's stay calm. Let's stick to facts. A fire broke out in a chimney you repaired.

That's right, he said. Them's the calm and stuck-to facts.

What he didn't say: In a mess, only shouting reassured him, made him feel at home. He was loud and angry outside, to match what was within. And so to vent it, like a chimney.

I did know him and his ways.

Of course you're upset, I said. I'm upset, too. You take pride in your work. We all do. So why don't you tell me what happened. From your perspective.

From my *perspective*?

I'm on your side, Harry. Really, I am.

And yet you're antagonizing me right off the bat. As if I can't see the obvious. As if I don't have the brainpower to understand your precious *reality*. *Of course* the story will have many sides. And I don't need any reminders from you, thank you very much.

You're right, Harry. I'm sorry, I said.

Damn straight, I'm right. Now you listen, Cookie, and I'll tell you what happened *from my perspective*.

He paused, knowing the mockery would echo in the space that had long ago opened between us, when I went to college and he did not, when I got out of New Preston and he did not. Until lately, anyway.

The wife called, he said. Had a real bee in her bonnet.

I withheld my response: *I'll bet she did.*

I mean, seriously, Cookie! Something went up in her wall, so what? Electricity came into that house in the goddamned nineteenth century when wire insulation was just some kind of nice-to-have. Those places are full of mice, and they get roasted all the time in those firetraps. Seen the headline many times: RODENT BARBEQUE BURNS DOWN THE HOUSE. Doesn't mean the chimney guy's responsible.

I get it, Harry.

Do you, now? Really?

I sensed him expanding, blowing up full of hot and crazy air. He said: That chimney was completely shot behind the plaster. I don't know why people don't bulldoze these old houses and start fresh. This shit never happens in new construction, dammit!

Calm down, Harry. Let's stay calm enough to actually think.

Think! *Think?* Isn't that your job, you who went to school? Aren't you the one who *thinks*?

Harry, listen. The insurance will pay the claim, you'll do the repair, and in the end, you'll get paid twice.

I heard the snap of a lighter and his familiar exhale.

I still have to *do the job* twice, let's not forget that.

Okay, Harry.

Done's done, he concluded. From *my perspective*.

He paused.

Now will you let me buy you a drink, as the winner of this little skirmish, or are you too good for that now?

You've chosen an epically bad time to flirt.

So flattery doesn't do it for you anymore, Cookie Cooke?

He paused, and the silence was like a furled whip.

Well, he continued, you know what would really flatter you? A decent suit. Bet you'd look great in one of Lana Halsey's, he pressed. That woman has whole closets full of fancy clothes.

Leave her closet alone, Harry.

She's probably got six versions of that white suit she likes so much. You know the one.

I did know it, but I hadn't known that *he* knew it. Those off-piste meetings, those whispered conversations—he and Lana had grown intimate.

Women like that, he went on, they never take an inventory. Something slips away, they upgrade.

Harry.

He adopted a falsetto: "Oh, I lost it," they say.

Harry, please.

Bet you never noticed you and Lana are the same size. How about a new coat?

I don't need a new coat. We're *not* the same size, either. And may I remind you, even if a client doesn't *know* what she has in her closet, stealing from her is still illegal.

Illegal! That's rich coming from *you*, Cookie-Puss. You've changed a lot, haven't you? But I'm sure you remember what it was like, once upon a time. When we were partners in crimes. Very small ones, of course. But crimes, nonetheless.

After a pause, Harry said: We were friends once, you and me.

The line went dead. I held the receiver, listening—for what, I hardly knew.

The irony—that I was unwilling to let Harry steal from Lana, yet I was perfectly willing to abuse Lana's trust in a different way, with Chuck—was not lost on me. But there was no time to wonder about whatever Harry hoped to accomplish by pointing out the blank spots on my moral map. Besides, I had other problems. By the door the dogs were whining in plaintive stereo just in case I was too thick to get the hint.

I leashed them and let them yank me outside. We took the rutted path toward the narrow park that ran along New Preston's side of the Chepinoxet. The route looped around a defunct textile mill that had been snapped up by a developer who turned it into loft apartments and pop-up shops. On the ground floor, a neon-lit bar offered a wall of craft beers on tap and, Fiona had told me, some decent live music. All the brick had been repointed. It looked fantastic—but one of the new windows was already broken, leaving a dark gap that marred the hopeful tableau like a shiner on a bride, a reminder of values more entrenched than property, values without which property would not exist. The values of patriarchy, not to put too fine a point on it. I sighed, feeling defeated. I could see how I'd been doing the work of patriarchy, too, undermining Lana at home while she made moves in the wider world, making space for herself as CEO of Lana Pura.

The mill abutted a shallow waterfall, where I let the dogs sniff and ramble. There was a little hill, not more than a mound. I clambered up, and from this vantage I had a wide-angle view of the landscape, the hills bright with the season's turning leaves, the pink-tinged cranberry bogs, and, in the middle distance, the electrical substation, which was not classically picturesque but appealed to me as a reminder of real dependencies. The hospital needed power, as did the nursing home, not to mention the streetlights and the traffic signals. My site lamp. My soldering iron.

But there were so many reminders of this. The river, for one. Chepinoxet was a Narragansett word meaning "little place of departed spirits," and the ancient name was still apt. Sadness washed over me. I flashed on a memory of fishing with my father on Chepinoxet Pond. Often there was a couple who liked to bring an entire living room in the back of their pickup truck and set up everything, right down to floor lamps fitted to run off the truck's battery, on the shore.

Hermit crabs, my father called them.

I could see the appeal. I wanted to effect a similar escape, to close the books on the Halsey job and with it, my dalliance with Chuck, the shame and cheapness of it, and its failure. I was ready for a change, but where would the impetus come from? I suppose this is why divorced people so often leave their homes: A fresh start demands a fresh carapace. I made a mental note to look into the asking price for one of those new lofts. *Values, schmalues*. Why not buy in?

I called the dogs, and we headed back the way we came. As they snuffled around their favorite stumps and hydrants, their busy intensity set my mind again to whirring. Had I been out of my depth with the Halsey project? Or just with Chuck? I had wanted to do justice to the job, to make myself part of the grand history of the house. Was my pride justified or just plain arrogance?

In my mind's ear, I heard the hiss of sand draining from an

ancient beehive-oven mold, the modest clamor of a job well done.

Pride, then. For all my flaws, I was all right, and Harry had done well, too, or so I hoped. His masonry had always been fantastic, made to measure, exact. Whatever caused the fire, it could not have been Harry's negligence. He'd earned my trust with the work of his mind and hands, and that, for me, defined him. I didn't like to think about the turns his life had taken. The jail term was probably the least of it.

My phone buzzed with a text from Fiona. *Do you need me tomorrow? Owen's in a mess. I've got to make him another set of keys.*

In the short time I'd known Fiona, I'd learned that Owen's misfortunes were numerous—he always had some questionable deal in the works. Something about him seemed wavering to me, uncertain, as if he'd never had anyone to show him the ropes. I doubted Owen would manage to do anything so practical as to get keys made on his own, but I couldn't bring myself even to hint as much to Fiona. She had enough to worry about.

Take care of Owen, I texted Fiona. *See you next week.*

15

The driveway had been cordoned off with yellow police tape, and squad cars lined the road. I couldn't see anything from the far side, so I slipped beneath the tape.

Slate fragments scraped and crunched beneath my feet. That was all that remained of a passel of slate roof tiles—the heat must have popped them right off the roof.

I looked up and my breath caught in my throat. On the side of the house where Chuck's bedroom was, the roof had collapsed completely. That was where Harry had done all that work on the chimney. My heart sank.

A hand came down heavily on my shoulder. I turned to find Norman Sawyer, the medical examiner, standing in the drive. A tall, lean-faced man, he hadn't changed since the days he ran varsity track. As I slipped out from his zombie grip, he lifted his baseball cap and ran his hand through what remained of his hair.

I might as well be the one to tell you, he said. He was dead when they found him, Cookie.

Who? Who was dead?

The homeowner. Chuck Halsey. I'm sorry, Cookie. I know you were close.

I spluttered, trying to control my ragged breathing. Where—where did they find him?

In his bedroom. Sort of.

Sort of?

I must have looked confused because he went on to explain: Chuck had been attacked. Knocked out, rolled up in that damned flokati. Someone doused him with accelerant and set him on fire, Norman muttered. Stuffed him up the chimney and cooked him like a pig in a goddamn blanket.

I remembered the moving blankets, the site tarps, everything we'd ever wrapped ourselves in.

So that was the source of the fire?

Well, Norman said. He wasn't the only thing to have gone up the chimney. Seems there were several fires. Hot ones. Fast.

I swallowed. Did he—

A howling from somewhere far off. Norman held me by my shoulders, his face warped with concern. I shoved my fist in my mouth, recognizing the noise for what it was, whose it was.

A television truck turned into the driveway, one tire lifting over the curb to roll straight through a flowerbed, flattening a clutch of late marigolds. Atop the truck, the satellite dish was already spinning, a mechanical flower seeking the sun.

An oblivion of light.

I shuddered. Norman slung an arm around me and steered me toward the road.

I'm sorry, he said. But I have to ask. Do you have any idea why his bedroom door was locked from the inside?

What would I know about his bedroom habits?

Norm stared hard at me.

I'm going to give you a bit of advice, Cookie. Lay low for a while. Whatever you do, don't leave town.

Oh, come on. You don't think—

The police will be in touch, he replied. This is no joke. You should expect to be questioned.

The air smelled thickly, oppressively, of burnt plaster.

Norm, I said, fighting back a wave of nausea. I'm five two and all I lift on a regular basis is a fork. How could I stuff a grown man into a chimney?

Go home, Cookie. Get some rest.

He gave me a nudge, enough to send me back the way I came. I don't remember the drive home or how I got inside. I locked the door, cranked the heat, and huddled beneath the duvet. Norman was right: Being home was comforting. My house seemed reassuringly small and manageable compared to the violence that swarmed inside the estates of the lunatic rich.

16

I kept Ministry closed for a few days, and then a few days more. I ignored the phone. I let the mail pile up. Out of respect for the dead, I would have said, had anyone asked. For the bodies that were on the ground, or in them, or wherever they were. Out of respect for the truth, too, but no one asked about that, either, even though the truth was clearly something that needed telling. I could do my part there, at least.

So, the truth: Whoever had killed Chuck had an intimate knowledge of how heat would move through that chimney, how to kindle that heat and make it hotter, how to direct it. I had some of that knowledge; Harry certainly had the rest. I should go to the police, tell them everything I knew.

But I wasn't going anywhere. I stuck my hand in the pocket of my bathrobe, rooting until I found Chuck's shabti. Pataikos, the protector. It rested cool in my palm, its carved face twisted into an expression I could no more read than the hieroglyphic inscription on its back. My grief would be similar—a private matter, necessarily obscure, inscrutable to outsiders.

As a mistress, I understood my lot. That understanding did not change the facts. The house was now a crime scene, and that was the province of crime scene investigators. Which decidedly I was not. Whatever Lana was doing with Benno and those syringes, not to mention her weird dallying in cold chain logistics—what could she need that for, in the business of sweaters and blankets? Was she getting into the lamb chop business? Testing her wares on human beings under controlled refrigerated conditions?—it was none of my business. As for Chuck, there was no bringing him back. Dead was dead. Ways and means were not my concern.

FIONA TURNED up on the third day of my confinement. She buzzed at the door, and I glimpsed her through the camera feed, dwarfed by her big army surplus coat, a leather satchel hitched over her shoulder, a casserole dish canted off one hip. She was shouting through the intercom, the wind high in the background. *Let me in! I will only stay a minute.*

The day was cold, and that wind sounded bad. I buzzed her in, reluctantly. She burst through the doorway trailing a cold smell of leaf mold, the perfume of approaching winter. From her satchel she extracted a foil-covered casserole that gave off a rich odor of tomatoes and cheese. She set the casserole on the counter.

Enough with the moping, she said.

You brought a lasagna?

A traditional condolence meal. You need to eat.

The New Preston media's having a field day, I said miserably. I can't turn on the radio without hearing about the big reno that went all wrong. I'll never work again in New Preston. Food is the last thing I want.

Pride goeth, sighed Fiona. I heard there was evidence of a struggle at the scene—overturned furniture, a smeared footprint on the wall. The police established a tip line.

I doubt they'll get much, I said. Next thing you know, there'll be fears of a general crime wave.

Not good for business. But you not eating, letting everything go to hell—that's also not good for business, Cookie.

I guess I have no choice, I said.

You've made plenty of choices. You can still make them.

We looked at each other. She was so young. All she had were choices.

Ministry won't be closed for long, I said. I promise. I have no other work. A girl has to eat.

Which is why the lasagna, Fiona said. Think about what I'm saying, will you?

AFTER FIONA left, I got a frantic call from Bobby. He'd been blindsided by a client who'd failed to produce enough work for a show that Bobby had been promoting nonstop for the last month. His sunk costs were significant.

It's a *catastrophe*, he breathed.

He wanted to know: Did I have enough material to mount that show we'd been talking about—in a week?

You know I'm always glad for an opportunity, Bobby. But one week is not a lot of time.

Listen to you! I hardly recognize the voice I'm hearing. Is this really Cookie Cooke?

I've had a hard go of it lately—

Because let me tell you, Bobby continued, Cookie Cooke does not need a lot of time!

I don't have much new, I said. Will you take my Lizzie dioramas?

Yes. They're just the thing. But I'll need a couple of others to completely fill the space. That one called *The Blue Bedroom*—you still have that one, right?

I do, I said. There's also the Sherlock Holmes one, about the Norwood builder—that makes three. But—

But what, Cookie?

Never mind, I sniveled, miserably fingering my shabti.

I wouldn't have asked if I didn't have complete confidence in your ability to deliver.

I wouldn't say it's a piece of cake, Bobby. I wouldn't say it's a walk in the park.

The exercise wouldn't do you any harm, though. And as for the cake, well—

Well?

Well, I wouldn't say you needed that, either.

And there it was, the flip side of Bobby. The support he doles out with one hand, he snatches back with the other.

17

Alone in my studio, I poured myself into the Lizzie Borden dioramas. How does a place shape those who live there? How misshapen are we, the products of New Preston? That was how I put it to Bobby in my artist's statement. I'll admit the question had a fresh urgency now that Chuck was in the morgue, or what was left of him anyway, the burnt-up bits I could not stop thinking of despite the new commission, the loss that dogged me as I shuddered and paced and finally retched up Fiona's lasagna.

Au travail. Retching or not, I had to prep this show. I'd planned three separate Lizzie-related miniatures: of the house, in cutaway view, transformed into a crime scene; another of the backyard where Vinnicum Morse—Lizzie's maternal uncle, the guy whose name had shown up in the household ledger—perched in the crotch of the old pear tree, calmly eating pears while police swarmed the yard; and a third of a cranberry bog where Lizzie liked to skate in winter.

I raised the light and swung the loupe, illuminating the cutaway dollhouse where the father rested, darkly bloodied and quite dead, on a tiny tufted sofa, while the mother sat in the parlor, absorbed in her needlework. Nearby was a tiny porcelain doll, one of Lizzie's, with a hairline fracture near the right elbow and a fingertip-sized cobweb woven from strands of my own hair. I finished this part first. The work went easily. The domestic space felt safe and familiar, even with all the blood. Or maybe because of it—but I pushed that thought from my mind.

Beyond those four stifling walls, I struggled to imagine Lizzie. I felt overwhelmed by deadness, as if I were sounding my own depths and hearing only silence or the dull thud of an axe on bone. Unless the feeling belonged as much to Lizzie as to me, something we had in common. Maybe this deadness was exactly what she was trying to master or perhaps just escape. At least she had an idea of freedom. But where, in her closed world of locked doors and pulled-tight whalebone stays, had she managed to find it?

I REPOSITION my chair, I raise my brush. And here is Lizzie, gliding into my inward view, bundled into her good wool coat, his precious gift—the signet ring with which he'd joined his fate to hers—depending from a chain around her neck. Rehearsing a rite of New England girlhood, she skates across the frozen cranberry bog, figuring her eights.

It's not a bog, of course—it's a sheet of plexiglass that I've sanded to opacity and scored to show her path, each turn marked by a burst of pink ice. Circling a crimson-tipped brush in a pool of thinned white paint, I try to get that pink just right. Proportions matter. So does timing.

And force, always force.

Her skates leave traces, contrails I have not scored deeply enough into the plastic. Leaning harder on the knife, I will Lizzie more fully into the world, imagining her gaining speed as she pushes across the ice. My furnace roars, and she darts away. I work a different corner, waiting for the dream to reassert itself.

For now, Lizzie's in a state of innocence. She has not yet hacked her way to her fate—axe-wielding parricide, unmaker of homes. She's still everyone's best girl, compliantly buttoned into her heavy coat, still asleep in the long dream of adolescence.

She will shatter awake, her girlhood falling away in shards that prick her cheeks like snow. No secret endures in this world. Someone will tattle. Visits will be forbidden. She will find her way to the New Bedford rooming house, spend the night without expecting to, and stumble into the next frozen morning, still dizzy from the rye fizz he bought her, dazed by the sun glinting off the harbor sea. There's a prickly rash on her neck where he'd nuzzled her, where the chain now rests heavy with the weight of a secret. Hers. Theirs.

He would offer kindnesses: another drink, a lift upward into the dark cab.

Kindnesses? Okay, lures. But they would have felt like kindnesses to Lizzie, as they would to anyone in her situation, of having been judged and found wanting, set aside.

You'll not amount to much will be her mother's assessment. I hear it now, in my mind's ear, a hard voice mingling with the rasp of my palette knife. I adjust Mrs. Borden's doll body, seated fireside with her sewing. I've roughened her plastic knuckles with sandpaper, and on a nearby table, I've arranged a tiny candle so her needles, attached to her hands with dabs of Krazy Glue, seem to be moving in a cone of tallow light. Before the murders, Lizzie's father had even killed her pet pigeons, saying he couldn't stand their noise, the feathers everywhere, dusting his lapels, drifting into the soup. Perhaps because he then sensed trouble, he installed locks on all the interior doors.

Chuck. Oh, Chuck.

How Lizzie must have roared—but quietly, inside herself—with every thrown bolt.

From the newspaper: *The blood fouled the ceiling and the walls.*

I flick a brush loaded with crimson, spattering the living room. Another swipe, vicious, and Mrs. Borden wears a red mask. All my wounds are useful. Of course they are. We use things up, we wear them out. That's just what we do here, in New England.

The blood pinked the water in the mop-up bucket.

I stir a drop of paint into a thimble I've repurposed.

The smell of an abattoir hung in the air.

Out on the frozen bog, Lizzie's not killing anyone. She's just slow-figuring her eights. With hands clasped in her muff—a repurposed rabbit's foot—she dreams of existence beyond that warren of locked rooms, the oppression of that house.

Around the Borden homestead, a stone wall snakes. It's half-built, to be finished in the spring. Resting on it is a tiny trowel, belonging to the mason who will be questioned after the murders. In the dooryard, the wind whips the branches of the ancient tree where the mason says he saw a man, high up, eating pears on the day of the crime.

It's gone midnight. The evening's flown. An image lingers as I douse the lights: Lizzie turning circles on the bog, light with her hopes, free in her unknowing. I still see her there.

18

Norman was right: I did get a call from the police—a real old-fashioned cop social, the kind that starts with a loud knock and zero advance warning. As I made my way to the door, the dogs circled my legs, whining; they'd need a walk soon. On the doorstep stood Detective Bill Phelps, the latest addition to New Preston's finest and my erstwhile commissioner of official crime scene replicas. I opened the door and the wintry day pushed in, a sudden icy slap in the face. Phelps took my disheveled measure in a two-beat sweep and flashed his badge.

So this is an official visit, I said. Here you are in your business blues. Maybe I should fix my hair.

It's not as official as it looks. I'm sorry, Cookie.

Behind his thick lenses, his gaze was lugubrious, *caring*. Ugh.

Save it, I said. Your pity.

You're in shock. Of course you are. It's only natural, a first stage of grief. Jesus, but it's freezing out. May I come in?

Did I have a choice? I did not. That remark about grief threw me off my game. He'd insinuated that my losses were more than professional, as if he already knew all about me and

Chuck. How else to explain his solicitude, this all-too-personal business about stages of grief? There was only one way to find out. I stepped aside, to let him in. Frigid air trailed him as he passed, and I caught a whiff of soapy cologne.

Right away, Phelps's eyes were all over the place. He followed me into the studio, taking in every last chaotic detail.

Bless this mess, I muttered. I've got a show soon at Bobby French's gallery.

Someone commissioned you to do another diorama? Who?

No one. It's art for art's sake.

Phelps made himself at home, lifting the curtains on the miniature Borden residence and peering into the tiny rooms. Coffee gurgled in the pot. I slid the carafe from its niche and poured out mugs for the two of us. Phelps sipped his appreciatively, smacking his lips.

That's real good, he said with a wide smile, a man accustomed to being seen as a spigot of delight.

It's only coffee.

It gets to you, the lack of sleep, he said. As I suspect you know, from the suitcases holding up your eyeballs. That's some dollhouse you've got there, by the way. But that's not the only thing keeping you up nights, is it?

I could see myself as he did—exhausted, unwashed, half-mad from the grief I was determined not to feel. Surely he'd inferred the obvious: My life was one crime scene after another.

He set a tape recorder on the table and pressed the button.

Everything's on record, he said.

I nodded.

I know it's hard to talk right now, but nonverbals won't cut it. Use your words.

I spoke through what felt like a mouthful of cotton wool: Everything I say can and will be used against me.

You're not under arrest. You're not even under suspicion. Not yet, anyway. Just take your time and tell me what you know. What can you tell me about the Halseys' financial situation?

They paid their bills. More or less. Once or twice they fell behind. Nothing unusual about that.

What about the mortgage? How heavily they were leveraged? You'd be surprised how creative people can be when it comes to subsidizing large mortgages, he added.

I was sure I *wouldn't* be surprised, having been in this business for more than a decade, but I nodded anyway.

Your words, he reminded me, tapping the recorder.

The renovation *was* expensive, I said. Sometimes even rich folks struggle to assemble that much cash.

Were they rich?

I imagined they were. But really, I have no idea. As you can see—I gestured at my cramped linoleum-and-laminate kitchen—big-ticket expenditures aren't really my thing.

His glasses had slipped down his nose; he pushed them up.

What about their marriage?

They seemed happy enough, I said.

Happy enough?

I could not control my voice. It kept pitching a half-octave upward.

They weren't any less happy than any other couple I've worked for. Renovations are hard on relationships. Tempers flare. It's normal.

Any odd habits, strange friends?

There were always people around—housekeepers, gardeners. Staff.

Did anyone have a grievance against either of them?

They were successful professionals. Many would find plenty to resent.

He drummed his index finger on the tape recorder case: A direct answer, if you please, Cookie.

What would I resent? They respected my expertise and paid me for it.

Phelps eyed me with a mixture of curiosity and suspicion. Perhaps he'd found the nastygrams Chuck's patients had left online. My gaze snagged on the tape recorder. I stared at the turning wheels.

Any lawsuits? Malpractice?

How would I know? I only do interiors.

I thought you might know why he needed a deadbolt for his bedroom door. Most of us get by with an ordinary lock.

I shrugged.

The subject shrugs, he told the recorder, and continues not to use her words as directed.

I stared at the tabletop, remembering the online complaints and Chuck's bragging, contrasting those images of Chuck, the bumbler tussling with the proud professional. But whatever leads Phelps needed on this score, he could find for himself online. He didn't need to know about my extracurricular interest in Chuck's life.

I got nothing, I said.

Phelps pushed a button and the recording ceased. He rose, mug in hand, and set it in the sink. He placed his spoon inside the mug and briefly ran the water. The dogs circled, casting anxious glances in my direction. Their need for a walk was becoming urgent.

Before we meet again, Phelps said, I want you to send me a list of your subs, anyone who knew the house well. And I need the name of someone who can vouch for your whereabouts after the party.

I was checking on my mother at Tomlins Manor—

He raised one fastidious hand.

Say no more. Someone will call you.

Reaching for the leashes, I asked: This interview's not enough?

The forensics team isn't nearly finished, he said. This meeting's just preliminary.

I BUNDLED up and walked the dogs, and then I spent the rest of the day huddled beneath the duvet, piecing together all the possible consequences of Phelps's visit and fighting with the dogs for the business side of the hot water bottle.

Lana's "homewrecking" toast left little doubt about her knowledge of what had transpired between me and Chuck, and Phelps's probing into the state of their marriage suggested that she was not the only one who knew. But if Lana talked, she talked—there was nothing I could do about that. As for myself, I intended to keep my mouth shut. I had nothing to say that was not esoteric specialist bullshit, interior design woo—or, what was much the same thing, a recapitulation of my *Acorn Studies* artist's statement. Not that any of this would convince anyone after the news got around about me and Chuck. To be known as Chuck's mistress was hardly going to enhance my reputation among the house-proud of New Preston, who were hiring me to redecorate their homes, not wreck them.

And then there was the fire, which had started behind the chimney, in that linty, combustible little void. Norman had suggested they'd found Chuck there, which made me reluctant to remember the ventilation structure in any detail—that is, in the sort of detail that I'd then be obliged to relay to Phelps. The only people who knew about the void were me, Chuck, and Harry. Perhaps Lana, if Chuck had shown it to her. Had he? I never asked.

How had the fire started, and when? Had Harry, my legendary mason, my go-to chimney guy, made a mistake? If he had, he'd lose his livelihood. And how liable was I? After all, I'd hired him. More: I'd insisted, over Chuck's doubts, that Harry was the right guy for the job.

As much as I dreaded it, I was going to have to speak with Harry. I placed call after call, leaving increasingly terse and irritated messages. After a few days of this, I gave up. He'd call me back eventually, or he wouldn't. I could not lift the phone for him, place his fingers on the buttons. His silence might well be protective. If he'd gone to ground somewhere, he couldn't call me back without implicating me in whatever stupid scheme he'd gotten himself wrapped up in. I'd just have to wait. Trust and wait. This was never my favorite position to be stuck in, and certainly not when Harry was the only one who could help me out of it.

Huddled in my bedroom, I mourned what I could. The ruined flokati was on my mind, standing in, of course, for everything else that I was refusing to imagine, let alone feel, as I inched toward matters more immediately pressing, like shoring up my accounts. Everyone in my line of work knows a stalled renovation poses urgent problems on the financial side, but one that ends with the client's violent death catapults a decorator into a whole new universe of difficulty. And I was not just his decorator. Not to engage in obnoxious special pleading, but it's seldom acknowledged that mistresses don't have the privilege of public grief. We are not invited to funerals; we do not receive condolence cards or deliveries of food and flowers. No one sits with us through the first days and nights of an existence made wild and strange by loss. I was clear-eyed enough to know the risk of being thrust into this unusual isolation was always part of the deal, but Chuck was young and vigorous. I never expected to lose him this way.

Grief held me, but not for long. I grew restless. Bored, I began to plan my return to the daily round, crafting responses to questions I was sure to be asked by the nosy and the insensitive, selecting the right words to spackle over awkward moments: how sorry I was to lose such a client, and under such terrible circumstances, too. This clucking would sound as false as it was. I had no illusions about that. Conventionalities would do nothing to assuage my private grief, either, and in any event, grieving could not substitute for payment of the Halseys' final bill.

Grief does tend to unbalance one's books. Since my father died, I do my duty to his memory and keep my feelings to myself. Grove Point, where he's buried, invoices me monthly for maintaining his grave, while my mother persists in this life, declining at her own mysterious pace. This year it was the crisis with her knee, next year who knew? I'll tell you this: She didn't have a shabti to pay her bills; or it might be more accurate to say that, in this case, her shabti was me. In addition to everything else, Chuck's death had put me behind on all these rents.

The Halseys' bill came back marked: *Return to sender, no such addressee.* So Lana had skipped town, exacting a last revenge that amplified the distasteful rumors—of insurance payouts, mainly—already buzzing in my ears. In any other place, the thought would be uncharitable—but here in New Preston, we keep an eye on the bottom line. Hoping someone else might have more success with the collection of Lana Halsey's outstanding balance, I finally called in a local, shall we say, dunning service. The man I spoke with assured me I could expect results "soon."

How soon?

Why push?

I'm running a business here.

All due respect, Ms. Cooke. But if pushing ever did you any good, you'd already have your money.

19

My *Acorn Studies* show opened on time, and that's the best thing I can say about it. My lack of enthusiasm was in direct proportion to my pain. Beneath my frozen surface lurked hidden pockets of steam under high pressure. I was a TV dinner of grief. One little fork-hole in the tinfoil of my self-presentation and I would blow like a square of overheated strudel.

The day of the opening, I carted my dioramas down to the gallery, making a series of trips with a large dolly. While I went back and forth, Bobby paced outside on the sidewalk, taking aggravated puffs from a cigarette while poking at his phone. It wasn't hard to find the source of his irritation: The gallery's glass door had fractured in a spiderweb centered on a jagged hole about the size of an Oreo.

When Bobby finally noticed my presence, he greeted me with a testy nod and slipped the phone into the pocket of his pricey jeans, which he'd cuffed over a pair of chukka boots. A thick wool scarf in a smart holiday plaid—Bobby's concession to the season—completed the ensemble.

Did a bird fly through your front window? I asked. A plane? Superman?

He snapped: You don't even want to know.

I'd made a joke to lighten the mood, but the damage was serious. Whatever caused it—a rock, a bullet, the shabti in my pocket, or the cold nugget lodged in my own chest, which felt edged all around with freezer burn—might have been casual vandalism, a passerby seeing a chance for mischief and taking it. But it might have been premeditated, too. It's said that artists are the shock troops of gentrification, can-do types who improve a neighborhood and in so doing, raise its profile and its rents. Not everyone's pleased with those developments, and they have ways of making their displeasure known. I felt for Bobby, as one small business owner to another. No matter what it was, it would be a while before he recouped the cost of that shattered door.

My show was unlikely to help. I didn't have much to sell apart from the main pieces, relatively large and priced to match, that I'd brought down on the dolly. I didn't expect they'd move; my stuff rarely did unless I kept the price low, something Bobby refused to do. Knowing that, I'd also brought a box of salable tchotchkes—mugs and photographs of the dioramas taken from different angles—for the folks who weren't in the market for the big-ticket items but still wanted a memento. As I lugged the box inside, Bobby held the broken door for me, giving my cheap wares a baleful once-over.

He ushered me into a small, chilly office off the narrow foyer. I set my box on the floor and took a seat in a metal folding chair. The cold went right through my slacks. Loosening his scarf, Bobby settled into his own perch, a wheeled stool that was Bobby all over—maximal mobility, maximal slouch. His desk, a dinged-up green steel affair from the 1950s, was topped with a faded leather blotter. He opened his laptop and fired off a volley of keystrokes.

You know we could get a crowd tonight, he said without looking up. A bunch of websites ran the listing.

You seem pleased, I said, though he seemed nothing of the sort.

I see you've brought your tchotchke box, he sneered. Is everything else inside? We'll need to set up right away. Showtime's at six P.M. I'd help you install the pieces myself but, well, you won't believe this: I've come up in the world. I have a kid to do my fetch-and-carry.

As if on cue, a lanky six-footer appeared in the doorway. This "kid" was thirty if he was a day. He flashed a smile, deepening the creases at the corners of his eyes, which were cornflower blue and matched his sweater.

Come in, Bobby said to his protégé. You need to meet Cookie, the star of the show.

The assistant smiled, revealing two highly organized rows of white teeth.

How do you do, he said.

I'm exhausted, I said. And I hate parties—

Don't mind her, Bobby interrupted. She's mouthy, but she won't bite.

He smiled again, and I tried not to stare at his hypnotic teeth.

I ferried my materials into the gallery and the assistant arranged them on smart-looking plinths and platforms that Bobby had assembled from scrap wood and drywall screws and painted a flat white. He'd lit the room forensically, with overhead fluorescents evocative of hospitals and morgues. In the antiseptic light, the assistant's dental work fairly glowed. The dioramas didn't look so bad, either. I switched on the little Tiffany lamp in *The Blue Bedroom*. In Sherlock's study, I lit the fireplace. The tiny light gave off enough heat to set the tissue-paper flames waving back and forth. It was cheesy, but then that piece was the one I liked least. I'd told Bobby to underprice it.

Bobby had set up a simple bar with artist wine, the cheap vintages everyone could appreciate. Somewhere in the bowels of the building an ancient boiler roared to life. As the room warmed, I poured myself a glass of Bobby's wine and tried to relax. The assistant set out a basket of single-serve bags of potato chips and pretzels, plus a pile of sharp-looking postcards advertising the show. On one wall, Bobby had hung a framed poster of a quote I'd sent him, something Glessner Lee had once said about her work. In black letters rendered large and stark against a white background was Glessner Lee's own explanation for why her miniatures existed in the first place: "to convict the guilty, to clear the innocent, and to find the truth in a nutshell."

It was a nice touch. Feeling hopeful, I refilled my glass.

Bobby's friends arrived first, fashionable types dressed in thin T-shirts draped to advantage, just-dorky-enough eyeglasses through which they cast polite glances at my stuff. It was useless to engage them in small talk. They weren't here for me; they were here to improve Bobby's scene.

Which, all things considered, was a good one. The controlled atmosphere of the gallery was a world away from my own. My show would seem frou-frou to my workday collaborators—to guys like Harry, I mean—a distraction from the real business of life, getting and spending. But Bobby's bright space tempted me to think about the bigger picture, whether I might still fit within the art world's frame.

I smelled Phelps before I saw him. He floated into the gallery on a cloud of his usual soapsuds cologne. That night he was in civilian mufti, khakis and an ugly sweater patterned with reindeer on the march. He offered me a damp hand to shake, then crouched beside the diorama of the Borden residence and inclined his head to peer inside a window.

How's it going, Cookie? I remember this one. It looked good

when I saw it, but now—well, the detail's incredible. Just look at those tiny family portraits on the credenza.

His compliment sounded sincere. He switched position and peered through a different window.

And those pots! Real copper? So meticulous!

I aim to please, I said.

In fact, Harry had made those pots, but no one needed to know about that.

He leaned over the central diorama and lifted a corner of a tiny curtain, one of the ginghams, in Lizzie Borden's bedroom. I touched his arm.

Hey, I said. You break it, you buy it.

He drew back and turned his sudsy gaze on me.

Not on a public servant's salary, he said. But you know how I like to have these models for investigative purposes.

Find a forensics specialist. Up in Boston, that's what they want anyway.

Those guys have too many preconceived ideas about the architecture of a crime scene. I want someone who knows how the beams run together, who knows how the bones of the house developed. Glessner Lee made dozens for the city of Chicago. You couldn't manage one more for old New Preston?

So that's why he was here: to flatter me. The show of support was aimed at getting me to do more work for him—to make a scale model of the Halsey disaster. My vision swam. I set my glass down and set my sights on the back wall's EXIT sign. It offered a message I appreciated.

Besides, Phelps said, you know the property inside and out.

You already have my take on the Halsey case, I said. I don't see what more you need.

I want your take on the *crime scene*. Give it a think. If you're in need of cash, say—

Yes? I asked, for once managing a degree of *hauteur*.

I know it's not easy to lose your sugar daddy, he said, smiling through shining wet lips, his tone so snide, I wanted to slap him.

He slipped away. I watched him go. He had a knack for moving through a crowd. A detective's slipperiness, I decided, an expert's appreciation for the possibilities of ambiguity. I was feeling slippery myself, my head floating further and further from my body, the effect of the cheap wine augmented, now, by a fresh anxiety. If Phelps didn't intend to name me as a suspect outright, his snideness suggested he wasn't going to just let me off the hook, either.

Fiona shimmied over in her fringed coat, her hair piled on top of her head and a pair of big gold hoops swinging from her earlobes. On her arm was a smiling young person with a cycling enthusiast's whippet build, set off by black stovepipe jeans that enjoyed only the most casual relationship with the hips.

Cookie! This is Owen!

Owen! I cried.

They did look similar. Owen was smaller than I expected, like Fiona almost delicate. But his handshake was firm. The webby part of his hand was pierced with something round and shiny. I let go quickly, hoping I had not pressed too hard. The spot looked tender.

I've heard so much about you, I said.

Thanks for looking out for Fiona. Lord knows someone's got to.

Owen turned away to grab a drink, and I saw, embroidered in gold and green on the back of Owen's jacket, a New Agey symbol—a wedjat eye, the ancient Egyptian symbol of protection.

THAT NIGHT I did my smiling best, distributing business cards and encouraging people to call if they were interested in bespoke work. Sometimes one piece can generate demand for ten similar ones, though I had my doubts about my *Acorn Studies*. They're not the sort of things you might find at the Pottery Barn, except maybe around Halloween.

The evening wore on. Hanging out by the crudités and trying not to look at my watch, I found myself cornered by a petite brunette wearing a tailored black suit cinched at the waist by a broad belt. A Mondrian-print scarf was knotted at her throat.

I'd seen that scarf before, at the Met gift shop. It was a budget-buster, real silk.

Hannah Cooke, she murmured, snagging my gaze on hers, which was surprisingly intense. Yet she spoke in baby-talk tones, contradicting her all-business presentation.

Cookie, I corrected her.

The gallery's harsh light spilled over her face, revealing the flaws in her makeup: too much powder, mascara in clumps. I cleared my throat and gestured toward the nearest diorama, Lizzie on the cranberry ice.

I can do one of these for you, to your specifications. I'm not too proud to repeat myself.

This is all *fine*, she said, making a gesture that encompassed the good-enough diorama, the pared-down space, the cheap wine, the desiccating crudités. I knew what she meant: This was not really her scene. She probably liked the Providence Art Club.

What I need, she went on, is your *help*. What I *need* is an *interior decorator*.

She grasped my arm. I smelled breath mints. She didn't want a work of art or even a postcard. What she wanted was free advice. I twisted my arm to remind her of who owned it, and she dug her fingers in.

My husband can't keep clients. The office needs something. A woman's touch.

You can't touch it?

He won't let me touch a thing.

From her blazer's inside pocket, she extracted a business card.

She said: Call me.

I tucked the card into my wallet. A moment later, a tall man rushed up. With his khaki pants and gold-buttoned navy jacket, he gave off a distinct whiff of prep. His shoes were unfortunate, the graceless offspring of a loafer and a sneaker, and his khakis flapped a good inch above the laces.

Uh, hey. Hey, Wendy, he was saying, at a volume more suggestive of prayer than any communication that might be effected between human beings. *Hey. Hey, Wen.*

So this was the husband. He didn't need a decorator so much as a stiff drink and a wardrobe consultant.

They left in a hurry, both attempting to push through the doorway at once. He stepped aside to let her pass, which would have been gallant had he not made a big show of his yielding, pulling her closer with one arm while holding the door open with the other. She stumbled, bumping him again, and said something that must have been fairly derogatory, because he rolled his eyes. She sped out; he followed.

Maybe it was just Bobby's plonk, but something about his bony ankles moved me.

THE NIGHT had pressed in, and I was not succeeding in small talk, so I took my leave the sneaky way, without even saying goodbye to Bobby. To clear my head, I took a long drive alone—in retrospect, not the wisest decision. A giant white truck roared up behind me and rushed past on my right, too close. I honked long and hard, and the truck swerved, cutting me off. I stamped on the accelerator, hot to my scalp with stunned rage. Through the driver's side window emerged a strong, tanned hand, raised in an obscene gesture. The truck sped away, easily outpacing my old Volvo. But I knew that hand, I knew that driver: It was Harry, gleeful as a naughty kid, at the wheel of a new truck, which looked just like his old one.

Unbelievable. The bastard wouldn't return my calls, but he felt free to run me down at midnight in New Preston.

20

I reopened Ministry the following Monday, starting the coffee at eight sharp. There was an alert from the bank: My business affairs were in a bad way. For the next few hours, I played spreadsheet jockey, trying out different near-term scenarios: *if* I was careful about heat, *if* I rationed Fiona's hours, *if* I kept away from shops and restaurants. *If, if, if.*

Phelps's commission would give me a cushion, but I wasn't that desperate—yet. For one thing, I was still hopeful about the show. People did sometimes call afterward, to inquire about something they'd seen that they could not evict from the mind in the usual ways. So much of commercial success was just a matter of getting past that particular landlord.

I downed my coffee, cup after cup. My receivables danced across the screen in a manner suggestive of an imminent hard drive failure. When I refreshed the page, the application froze. I rebooted the computer and stood up. Fiona regarded me from the worktable, her eyes wary slits.

Is there any more coffee? I asked.

Aren't you wired enough? Why don't you ever check your messages? You missed a bunch of calls.

One call was from Harry—at last. He'd left a long message,

transcribed by Fiona, that I would have to look at carefully. The other two messages were from someone named Martha Benton. It took me a moment to place the name. She was the crazy woman from Lana's party, the one in the asphalt dress.

I'll deal with Harry, I told Fiona. Tell Martha Benton I'll call her back soon.

Fiona snorted: Everyone in this business knows what *soon* means.

Harry's message was barely coherent, interspersed with Fiona's question marks and exclamation points—she clearly had tried her best to make sense of it. There was much ado about the insurance adjuster—who evidently was going through a divorce, the details of which were numerous, complex, and utterly irrelevant. So much circumstantial richness had only one purpose: to convince me to return to the Halsey house with him on any pretext he could gin up. No matter that the Halsey residence was a burnt-out ruin, not to mention an active crime scene. Of course, Harry was not the sort of guy for whom police tape constituted much of an obstacle. I didn't want to think about what he'd done with his truck last night, either.

The phone rang.

You can't hide forever, Fiona said. Take the call.

She was right. Of course she was. I picked up the phone, cleared my throat.

You've reached the Ministry of the Interior.

Oh, hello, Cookie! I bet you don't remember me. We met at your show?

Wendy! I effused.

I was sucking up, as befit an impecunious artisan. Of course I remembered her. Her rapid-fire baby talk was seared in my brain, and her card was still taking up space in my wallet. As she talked, I pulled out the card. She worked for the hospital. Her official title was "Director of Communications."

Do you also remember the trouble with my husband?

Not exactly. Remind me?

Simon is not very good at his job.

I'm not sure an interior designer can help with that. What did you say he did?

He's a psychiatrist.

An analyst? A therapist? Or just a pill doctor?

Semantics. What difference does it make? The point is, he can't retain patients. They show up once or twice, and then they disappear. Meanwhile he sits for hours in his office chair, running up bills. He's paying a commercial rent—and for what? It's outrageous. He works all the time, and he's made exactly no money. He needs to decide if he wants a real business or an expensive *cos*play.

The course of true love never did run smooth, I said. Nor the *cos* of it, either.

She fell silent, and I felt her scowl.

Do you really believe décor is what's keeping patients away, Wendy? There are worse things than having bad taste in knick-knacks.

She heaved a sigh.

His taste, she sighed. Oh God. I don't know. It's weird.

She paused, and I sensed what went unsaid: *Weird. You know, like him.*

Wendy knew what she wanted, and it had nothing to do with design. While renovating her husband's office, my real task—the subtext of the official one—would be to bolster her implicit conviction that, despite having married her, her husband was a tasteless oaf.

It's not that I don't think décor matters in a doctor's office,

I said. But I have misgivings about imposing a renovation on an unsuspecting spouse.

Through the receiver came an irritated *tch.* I was having thoughts of my own, and Wendy was unaccustomed to those. Well, I, too, was unaccustomed to certain things—to a job turning into a crime scene, to losing a lover to an excessively hot fire that had started mysteriously inside an otherwise normal wall, to being considered a suspect in that lover's death.

I just want to be sure we're not setting ourselves up to fail, I said.

You'd be surprised what goes on in a marriage, she said.

Maybe, I said, though I doubted I'd be surprised by what went on in hers.

Once you see the office, she went on, you'll have enough to worry about without troubling yourself with setups. Or failures.

Failures. That single word nearly finished me. The Halsey fiasco was still so fresh.

But I had other reasons to be flexible. As the Halsey news spread, so would the damage to Ministry. I could take this job, use it to rebuild my reputation.

I wasn't proud. I could be Wendy Teller's factotum.

She recited an address at the edge of Pill Hill.

I'll require an advance deposit to secure my commitment, I told her. The fee is nonrefundable.

Whatever, she said.

Because, of course, she had money.

I made my usual inquiries: Did she want any specific say in the proceedings? Any special preferences for finishes—paint versus wallpaper, hardwood versus wall-to-wall?

None whatsoever, she said. I want him to make all of those decisions. *That* is my preference.

She hung up, leaving me to suffer the conversation's subsidence.

But if her terms were clear, so were mine. She'd definitely earned the diva premium.

The phone rang, startling me out of my payola daydream.

Well, if it isn't Cookie Cooke! Harry boomed, prompting a headache that clawed down to my jaw.

There's something you need to see, he insisted, and only I can show it to you.

21

The pantry door was clinging to its last hinge. Residue from the extinguishers slicked the floor. One entire wall was black with soot, and another, near the oven, had collapsed into a pile of rubble.

I ran a hand over what remained of the wall. It wasn't much. The soaked plaster had begun to swell. We might as well have busted down this wall, too. We probably should have.

I called out: Harry? *Harry!*

His voice slithered from the darkness: Easy does it, Cookie. You don't want to go messing with the evidence. This is still a *crime scene*, you know.

I spun around to find him standing there, legs spread wide beneath his loaded tool belt, his mouth twisted into a cynical leer.

The bastard had crept up on me. What's more, he'd seen me jump.

Behind him, through the window, I saw a gray sedan roll into the driveway. Shiny new, with tinted windows, no license plates—a cop car. Phelps? The car turned slowly around the drive.

Limping to the window, Harry slipped in the foam. He had to use the wall, what remained of it, to steady himself.

Did you hurt your foot?

New shoes, he grunted.

I looked down. Sure enough, the raw-looking suede was stiff and thick.

It's agony, he said from the shadows. Breaking them in.

I shifted position, wincing at the glass crunching beneath the soles of my boots. Virtually all the windows had shattered from the fire's intense heat. So had the glass-fronted cabinets. All that work, not to mention all that waiting—what a shame.

Heading for the remains of the fireplace, Harry raised the sledgehammer. It shone in the dim light.

Harry! Harry, there's a car out front—

A slam, and my mouth filled with dust. As I spat and coughed, Harry enlarged the hole until a small person could fit through it. He trained his flashlight's beam onto the gap.

Look, he said.

I had to bite my own tongue. His chimney fan installation was the shoddiest I'd ever seen—the brickwork was crumbling, and wires were looped and tangled everywhere. Cords were even wrapped around the big beams supporting the second floor and ran right up into a gap in the chimney bricks—a gap that had been plugged with some kind of orange putty. It was smeared all over, like someone had been messy with the Whitman's Orange Creams.

What the hell is that?

Semtex, Harry said. Putty explosive. I'm surprised you don't recognize it.

Of course I recognized it. The sight sent me right back to our salad days, when I was still a baby designer and he was just a junior mason with a weird sideline in combustions. But I wasn't going to give him the satisfaction of knowing I still carried those memories, and I was certainly not going to admit any knowledge on this score when ignorance might serve me better on any eventual witness stand.

I looped my bag across my chest and took a cautious step backward: I have not seen a thing, Harry. Not one blessed thing.

It's just property crime, he said, and you and I both know the real crime is the existence of property in the first place. Isn't that right?

He shook his finger in my face. I'm asking you, Cookie: *Isn't that right?*

You're getting wound up, Harry.

Didn't they owe you money?

You got paid.

But you didn't.

I can take care of myself.

Methinks the lady protests too much. You haven't been exactly what I'd call on time with your payments to me lately. It's not like I'd press you for it, Cookie. But I do wonder what's going on, and I'm not as dumb as I look.

In my bag, my phone buzzed. I ignored it. I had my hands full with Harry.

I saw the writing on the wall, he said proudly, and I don't just mean the hieroglyphics in that little closet you found.

What do you mean?

I got myself another gig, at the Academy Club.

The AC was members-only, an old New Preston institution where wealthy people played squash and lunched with their brokers. It was the last place I'd expect to find Harry. It was also the last place where Lana had been seen in public, in the hours before the fire.

Were you working the night Chuck Halsey bought it?

I was there, he said. And so was Lana, and that's just what I told the police.

So he had his alibi. What Lana had, I wasn't sure.

I saw them there a few times, Harry went on. They weren't popular with the staff—they never tipped. Nor were they well-liked by the management.

He said: I heard they were about to get booted for not paying dues. The rumor was, he was out of dough, and his business partner was suing him.

Suing him? What for?

Do I look like a lawyer to you? Whatever it was, the wife was *pissed*. Women like that, Harry opined, are not so overjoyed when the money dries up.

Women like that. Women "like that" milked their husbands for cash, designer clothes, expensive club memberships, and of course, renovations.

Not only that, Lana was yet another impossible thing—beyond Harry's reach socially. As a working girl myself, I couldn't blame Harry for feeling this way. Not that I needed Harry's reasons to resent Lana. I had plenty of my own.

Harry gestured toward the explosion-in-waiting.

All I'm saying, Cookie, is that you could still get what you're owed. This kind of thing, well, it's what insurance companies are for. These folks are insured to their Hollywood teeth. Their policies cover everything you can think of, including vandalism.

You call that vandalism? It looks more like terrorism to me.

Picky-picky! You don't get to play Miss Innocent with me, Cookie Cooke.

Again, my phone buzzed. I pulled it out and glanced at the screen: Tomlins Manor.

I have to take this, I said.

Harry shrugged. Be my guest.

On the phone, the receptionist connected me with my mother's floor nurse, who said: She's running a fever. She won't eat, won't drink. Her doctor suspects an infection, but we can't locate the source.

C. diff again?

She's agitated. Is she ever. It's the fever, you see. We're trying to bring it down. But we don't want to medicate her any more than we have to.

Again with the threats, I said. Chemical restraint, isn't that what you call it?

The nurse sighed. She's awake, she's alert, and she's asking for you.

Story of my life, I said, hanging up. I've always been my mother's favorite tranquilizer.

Harry called out as I was leaving: Tell the old lady I said hi.

22

I found my mother sitting up in her bed, staring at a talk show. The cast on her leg had finally come off, replaced with a light brace. My mother had been making good progress with the physical therapist, getting up and down, taking a few steps without help. Now she'd had a setback. How long would it take her to regain that lost ground?

Someone had left her lunch on a low table beside her armchair: creamed corn, mashed peas, and a viscous smear that might once have been chicken. I opened the window a crack, then settled into the armchair and waved a sporkful of creamed corn in her direction.

Mom?

She lifted her hand and let it fall back to the bed with just a touch more drama than creamed corn required, strictly speaking.

This food *stinks*, she said.

She wasn't wrong about that. I felt nauseated myself. I set down the loaded spork and took the tray out into the corridor. A tall cart was stacked full of dirty trays. I slid Mom's in with the others—all, like hers, barely touched.

When I returned she was sitting up straight, fumbling with

the remote. The television snapped off. The air in the room smelled fresher.

Any news from Old Pataikos? she asked.

Funny you should mention him.

Oh?

I told her about the Egyptian room, the hidden one, at the Halsey residence. It was a relief to talk, to lay it all out. I didn't think she'd make anything of it.

Who found it? she asked.

Does it matter, Ma?

She reached for her brush and began to push it through her hair. Someone had taken the trouble to wash it. Strands flew out in all directions, staticky. When she struggled to reach the back, I took over.

Of course it matters, Cookie. How old was the house? Or are you keeping that a secret, too? Never mind, let me guess. Late Victorian? Gilded Age?

More or less, I said.

Just as I thought! The colonials had no Egyptological interests.

So it's not colonial?

Ouch, she said.

I'm trying to be gentle. There's a knot.

Just cut it out, she said. There are scissors in the drawer.

They don't let you have scissors, I reminded her.

More's the pity, she said.

I smoothed her hair as best I could, set down the brush, and repositioned myself on the edge of the bed.

This secret closet, Mom—or whatever it is—could it be colonial?

I doubt it. My guess is Gilded Age. This region was a hotbed of theosophy, you know.

Theosophy?

I looked into it once, when you were small. I was writing a paper on the early history of the reception of ancient Egyptian ideas in New England. It was as if Egypt didn't exist here until the late nineteenth century, when the whole place erupted with holly rollers.

Holy, I murmured.

Holly, she repeated. As if it were a joke. Which it might have been. Unless her language skills were deteriorating now, too.

If you roll in the holly, Mom, you'll get a nasty scratch.

That Harry, she mused, still smiling. Then her voice took on an edge: *Is he still shooting up?*

I flashed on an image of Chuck's forearm—the tender white flesh, the dark nodule there.

Harry's problems aren't any of my business, I said.

Not anymore, she cackled. But you're better off.

Harry has nothing to do with this, Mom.

Of course not, Cookie.

I could see the nurses' station from where I was sitting. No one was behind the desk.

Someone always shoots the heroine, she said, patting my hand. Her palm was hot, her cheeks flushed. My heart, for some reason, was pounding.

You're feverish, Mom. That's why you're saying crazy things. See you soon, I told her.

Sure you will, she replied. If you don't completely lose the plot.

I hustled out. As I turned the key in the car's lock, there was a metallic screech. I looked up to see my mother leaning out her open window, holding her robe closed with one pale arm. The other she raised in a vague gesture—of warning perhaps, or benediction. She caught my eye and shook her fist.

23

In her eerie way, my mother with her chatter was on point: The plot in question was not funerary, as those matters had always been her concern, but marital—more precisely, what was at issue was an idea of marriage, a marriage plot. Is that too tidy? Perhaps it is. I would consider it recompense.

Nothing about my marriage to Harry was tidy. It was a month-long dream verging constantly on nightmare. We tied our strange knot on our long trip west, a few miles outside Reno. For twenty dollars, a young man with a posture stiff as his pressed jeans performed the ceremony in a Florida room where immense plastic ferns swayed in the air conditioning. We promised to love, honor, and cherish one another until death did part us, and then we signed ourselves over to each other on documents that looked about as authentic as the ferns. Harry seemed only waveringly present, coming in and out like a weak radio signal. The only warmth I felt was the obol, my mother's gift, which burned where I'd tucked it into my bra. Something old, something new: I was killing two birds with one obol. Or three birds, if you believed my mother's story about provenance and were willing to squint a bit. Take intentions out of the equation, and a plundered object is just like a borrowed one: something you haven't given back yet.

We'd left New Preston in such a hurry, I'd failed to see some important things. It wasn't just the stolen car. Harry's fiercest passion had nothing to do with me. He'd gone completely goggle-eyed for a homemade hot rod. It even had a name. BLAST FROM THE PAST! was one of those Spirit-of-America scrapyard miracles that enthusiasts liked to assemble in their backyards, recycling spare parts into formidably engineered machines. The stolen sedan was just the leading edge of his mania, merely the means to another end, one that traveled like a rocket, hundreds of miles an hour across the desert. The speed trials were coming up.

Nothing on Earth travels as fast! he crowed, slapping his hand on the steering wheel so hard, the car swerved across the center line. I quelled the urge to shout him back to the realities of speed limits and oncoming traffic.

Nothing on *this stupid Earth*, anyway, he continued, righting the wheel.

Something massive, transformative, would happen to him, he thought, if only he could get close enough to that car, that energy.

I just have to feel it, he insisted later, over gas station sandwiches. It was an intensity I should have known better than to accept without question. But I hadn't yet fully understood Harry's need for experiences that defied symbolization, experiences that could only be felt, like a beating.

To know these things, he liked to say, *I have to feel them in my bones.*

After he left me at the motel outside Reno, he'd gone on to Bonneville where he was working on the pit crew of BLAST FROM THE PAST!, doing something related to ensuring the optimum flow of oxygen through the engine, feeding the heat that fueled the car's miraculous travel—*at speed*, as he liked to murmur, whenever we were together on those desert nights, *at speed*.

What I'm doing, he had told me, is like building an oven. I make it burn hotter. The brainiacs were supposed to figure out how to turn the extra energy into speed. They couldn't. Those guys can't tell a crack screw from a cracker.

Neither could I, but I had other talents. I tidied our room. I did our laundry. I kept the kitchenette clean and the small fridge stocked with ice, beer, and fancy salamis, little comforts Harry could enjoy when he returned from work. Meanwhile I drank sodas with Doocie, performed my art rituals, and dreamed of unremitting and unquestionable success, a life of big commissions and solo shows. I would make a home—and I would make art. I had not yet imagined how I might combine the two, or even that I might; I did not yet see myself as a decorator, someone who could treat a room as a work of art.

Visually, the desert was a paradise. The rust-red landscape was pressed against a gemstone sky and dotted with ragtag homes assembled from strangely abundant cast-off materials—sheets of corrugated iron, odd lengths of wood and wire. Discarded electronics took the place of lawn ornaments and had their own strange beauty. All of it might have become a body of work, in time.

But there was no time. The marriage fell apart as quickly as it came together. One weekend, I was trying to convince Harry to accompany me to some caves. According to the brochure, the cave walls still showed traces of ancient painting. We took our discussion to the grocery store. I was craving chocolates, and the proprietor kept boxes of them, plain and fancy, in the cold case. As Harry and I bickered over the trip to the caves, another man—fresh-faced, medium build, nondescript is how I'd fill in the blanks of a police report—loitered near the register. We weren't exactly fighting, but I was feeling some urgency about these caves, and Harry wanted just as badly to return to the speed trials. The stranger offered to take me to the caves in Harry's stead. Harry left us—to make arrangements, I thought—and returned with a Whitman's Sampler tucked under one arm. I'll never forget Harry's face, twisted with rage, literally twisted, like a cartoon character's. He paid for the candy and skulked off, his raveled shoelace dragging like a part of himself he might just as soon leave behind.

I caught up with Harry in the parking lot, where he was scraping dead bugs from the windshield. Grasshoppers mostly, though there was no grass for miles.

Are you angry?

Why should I be angry?

The ride back was completely silent apart from the irregular splat of bugs on glass. For some reason that afternoon the carnage was immense, biblical. I thought of my mother, her Egyptian preoccupations; I wondered what she'd make of this new locust plague. There was an accident; the traffic was bad; by the time we returned, Harry was so far behind schedule, he had to call his boss to say that he would have to miss the first heat. When I tried to apologize, Harry shrugged.

No big whoop, he said. I don't expect she'll even place.

Harry put the chocolates in the fridge. All night, I dreamed of hell. The following day, he took the chocolates out again, removed the lid, and pushed them at me.

Who wants to go to the caves?

I didn't like his crazy eyes but, thrown off-balance by my nightmares and not wanting to seem churlish, I agreed to the excursion and fortified myself with an Orange Cream. It was too sweet, too cold, and it brought on a migraine that blurred my vision. We parked at the trailhead, where I vomited quietly behind the car and then followed Harry into the brush. A half-mile later, I tripped over a loose rock and went sprawling. Blood streamed down my leg.

It's nothing, I told the dust. To the high white sun I said: Just a flesh wound.

When I looked up, Harry was yards away, wearing the same crazed look as the day before, and the distance to the next town took on a fresh relevance. I changed my mind about needing to see the caves, and I changed my mind about Harry, too. We drove back to the flats in silence, blood oozing through my sock.

We left soon afterward, rushing east, staying in cheap rooms that ate the last of our cash. I didn't want to be in the desert anymore, not on my own and certainly not with him. Better to go home to New Preston, where there were lots of other people around. At least then someone could hear you scream. The signs blinked all night: VACANCY, VACANCY.

At these motels, I noticed, all day long men in shiny shoes came and went, meeting women who exchanged favors for whatever they needed to nurse their private addictions through the hazy afternoons. I date my interest in Lizzie Borden from this trip. She might have become one of these women, in her nineteenth-century fashion—but unlike them, she had an axe and a talent for seeing things through.

As we were driving to our final motel room, somewhere outside Philadelphia, I told Harry about my idea for my first diorama, the shooting in the blue bedroom and the scene that had led up to it, the woman who had pitched the tent of her life on the precipice of catastrophe.

I did not consider that I might be talking about myself.

I was interested, I said, in women like that.

Harry laughed hard, snot flying.

Everyone is interested in women like that, he said, when he recovered.

Peeved, I fiddled with the radio until I found a soft rock station I knew Harry would detest. He deserved to be irritated, for having ruined everything with his possessive rage. I turned the volume up, and he laughed maniacally, showing all his teeth. And then something amazing happened: BLAST FROM THE PAST! roared up alongside us and who was behind the wheel but Erica Subiaco, her great hair flying out behind her like a banner, a lollipop stuffed in one cheek. She took out the lolly and waved it, bright red. She lingered for a moment before vanishing far down the road in a cloud of russet dust that settled in my memory as a question: Now who's the sucker?

My married life was over, apart from the paperwork. I don't want to blame Harry. He had always been my friend. But in the desert, I saw another side of him, the one that I had failed to imagine despite all the encouragement he gave me, which in retrospect was quite a lot. As soon as we got back to New Preston, I insisted on having the marriage annulled. The decision, so unilateral, surprised us both. Acting independently on impulse, dark or otherwise, is exactly what reliable pleasers like me *don't* do.

I never saw the obol again, either.

I suppose I should explain one last detail, about Harry and the dogs. Edgar and Ethan were gifts from Harry. When he got into his trouble, he left me the dogs, an intermittently functional Florida phone number, and the address of a PO box in Tampa, so we could at least write while he laid low.

The dogs were just puppies. Since I'd agreed to keep them, Harry said I could give them names. At first, I called them Ethan and Allen, except for the times when I slipped and called them Edgar and Allan. Soon they became, simply, the Allens—except that I also called them the Allans.

They didn't mind, and neither did I, but the vet put her foot down. She had a business to run, a database to manage. I had to choose.

When I finally got him on the phone, Harry didn't understand: the Allans and the Allens sounded the same to him, and besides, he grouched, what did it matter since no one could tell them apart anyway? I wrote a letter, spelling out the problem. When he didn't reply, I felt sure that I'd alienated him with this ridiculous concern. Then Harry sent a note introducing me to the *schwa*, the character that looks like an upside-down *e* and makes an "uh" sound. It sounded sufficiently indeterminate, he explained, to work as the second vowel in both Allen and Allan.

The scheme did work, if you weren't too fussy about your vowels in the first place—as we are not, here in New Preston. So the Allәns were named, though I rarely make the spelling explicit. In that way it remains our secret, between me and Harry. And ever since then, I've been careful about assuming I have the market cornered on smarts in our relationship.

Which is one reason why Harry's revelation—of the value that could still be extracted from the Halsey wreckage—unsettled me. Why the insistence on showing me the Semtex arrangement? Why return to the scene of the crime in the first place, unless he had committed it? Was he signaling that he was in cahoots with Lana, the same way he'd signaled his alliance with Erica, through the explosive intermediary called the BLAST FROM THE PAST!?

He was too smart not to be up to something.

In the kitchen, Ethan Allan rested his head in my lap, his leash hanging between his jaws. As I worked the folds on his forehead, Edgar rushed up, also carrying a leash. Edgar Allen, Ethan

Allan: Leave it to Harry to figure out how to name them. How in the world had he known about the *schwa*?

Allons-y, boys, I said, fastening their leashes.

I WALKED the dogs, then went to see my mom. When I arrived, the clerk told me she was out, attending a physical therapy appointment across town. The day, already half-wasted, threatened to unravel. Returning from Tomlins Manor, I got stuck in traffic on the Chepinoxet Bridge. The cause of the slowdown was peak New Preston: The accident itself was just a fender-bender, but everyone had to take a good look. Waiting for the traffic to clear, I got a message from Martha Benton—Chuck's weird colleague, she of the asphalt dress—and called her back.

I'm between patients, she snapped.

You called *me*, I reminded her. Beyond the whir of my engine, I heard her shut the door. I spoke into the expanded silence: What do you want, Martha?

How much did you know about Chuck?

You're the one who worked with him every day.

Didn't *you* also, she asked nastily, *work* with him every day? Your boyfriend was hiding a lot more from his wife than just a mistress—

What are you trying to say?

Don't you know?

The connection died with a loud, hard beep.

Had Chuck conveyed me to this stranger? Or had she followed him to the worksite and seen us together?

At home I searched the web for any dirt I could dig up about Martha Benton.

Like Chuck, she had a profile on the website that rated doctors; and, like Chuck, she also had a troll. A busy one. I scrolled through the entries. Many of the complaints were familiar.

She was accused of having a brusque manner, of coldness and incompetence. *No good deed*, remarked one correspondent, who had apparently gone out of his way on Martha's behalf. *Nutty*, proclaimed another. Toward the bottom, many entries were marked *Removed by site administrators for violation of community norms.* The admins had been thorough, but their system had a glitch. Although the comments had been removed, the author's name had not. I counted fifty redacted entries, each one signed *FIONA DUNNE*.

24

On the phone Phelps hadn't said why he needed to see me. He didn't need to. He told me he'd seen my car at the Halseys' place, and I made the obvious inference. For this new trouble, I had only myself to blame. What was I thinking? I should never have let Harry persuade me to return to the house.

Phelps and I arranged to meet on the river path. The day was damp, with heavy clouds that covered the town like a lid. My watch read half past two, and I reminded myself to keep an eye on the time—I had a meeting scheduled for later in the day with the shrink, Simon Teller.

I fingered Chuck's shabti, still in my pocket. In the distance, the substation dominated the landscape, pressing dark points into the white sky. The dogs rushed past me, barking.

Hannah Cooke, for the love of God, *call off your dogs*!

Phelps was thirty yards away and upwind. No wonder the dogs had missed his approach. I whistled them back and leashed them. Phelps sauntered up, scowling over his popped collar. His leather bomber jacket had seen better days.

Leash laws not your thing?

You know they're friendly. Worst case, you'll get whapped with a muddy tail.

Phelps wiped his nose with the back of one hand before pushing both deep into his pockets. He looked at me warily, his wetly pink nostrils almost translucent in the chilly air.

They're *nice* dogs, Bill.

I'm sure even the Hound of the Baskervilles had his Kodak moments, he replied.

We turned onto the path toward the river, scuffing the deadfall of last year's leaves. Phelps turned to face me.

Look, you shouldn't be at the Halsey house, not for any reason, he said. I'm telling you for your own good.

I get that a lot, I said. Advice for my own good.

You were breaching a crime scene, he continued patiently, which as everyone knows—except you, apparently—is against the law. I could drag you down to the station in a heartbeat. But you've been here a lot longer than I have. You know things I don't. Instead of hauling you in on trespassing charges, I'm asking you to reconsider my proposal. You know I like your work. And I think you're onto something with those dioramas. I saw the Borden case differently after your show.

He was flattering me, a carrot to follow the stick of his threat: a trespassing charge to start, followed perhaps by others. I didn't want to go to jail, or get hauled down to the police station where I'd be obliged to explain what I was doing on the Halsey property with Harry.

It's your choice, he said. The work would remain in your name. It would be yours to sell or keep, and you can have it back right after it's no longer needed for the investigation. If it becomes some kind of *cause célèbre*, which don't get me wrong, I hope it doesn't, but—

You're saying the piece could be worth even more, thanks to its association with the case.

I'm not saying anything, he said. But I'm also not *not* saying.

Knowing I had practical reasons to cooperate, Phelps had pressed on an obvious sore spot—my thwarted artistic ambitions. But Chuck's death struck me as a poor means of career advancement, and I didn't want to let Phelps manipulate me with his carrots and sticks. After all he, too, might be playing a game, baiting one trap with the threat of punishment and another with the promise of fame and fortune. Sounding my fear, my greed.

Not for nothing, I began, but I don't think an obscure death in this backwater has Hollywood written all over it. But let's say I agree to this proposal. Then what?

To get your model right, you'll need to know about a discovery we made at the crime scene. Can you keep a secret?

I was keeping quite a few secrets. What was one more?

Sure, I said. What did you find?

It's not easy for me to say this, Cookie. But the fact is, no one can tell who anyone is after a fire like that. All you have are dental records, if you're lucky. But there was evidence of a lot of blood, even after the fire.

I must have flinched, because Phelps, looking surprised, murmured, I wouldn't have pegged you for squeamish.

I'm not squeamish, I said.

That's good, because it was all over the rug.

What was?

He stared at me: The blood, Cookie.

I thought: *On the flokati.*

Where—where did the fire start?

Downstairs, he said. In the weird little oven.

Right, I thought. The weird little oven that Harry had

preserved, that vented into a secret chamber, lined with extremely flammable lint, in which Harry had stashed some other hot stuff.

One thing's for sure. Halsey didn't die of smoke inhalation. Or at least not just that.

If he didn't die of smoke, then what did he die of?

Blunt trauma. A lot of it. To the head.

A darting breeze swirled the leaves at my feet.

That's horrible, I managed.

I appreciate your taking this on.

It's not like I have a choice.

With me, he said, you always have choices.

He paused again, and I suppressed a wave of irritation. His discretion was getting on my nerves. Finally he said: You know there's been some talk about Harry Deluca. Did you have any reason to think Harry might have been unhappy with the Halseys?

All the accounts were in order, I lied, still unwilling to reveal the Halseys' half-paid bill.

Harry had done the chimney, right? And the oven?

I nodded.

Couldn't have been easy, Phelps said. All the demolition, and so much to preserve.

It was a big job, but Harry was up to it.

He hadn't felt slighted by, or resentful of, your clients in some way?

Lana had a way of making everyone feel resentful. But don't tell me you're going to pin this disaster on a disgruntled contractor.

He shot me a hard look. Your contractor had both means and motive, he said. All I need now is to find out whether or not he might have seized an opportunity.

My phone buzzed: *Teller*. I was late.

Sorry, Bill. I have another appointment, I said. I suppose there'll be a funeral?

How the hell would I know? Phelps snapped. Seeing me wince, he softened: If there is, it'll be after the medical examiner releases the body.

I'll get started, I said. On that job.

If anything comes to mind—

Of course. I'll call.

I watched him go. He had a rolling gait, almost a waddle. It was hard to imagine him in quick pursuit of anything, let alone a homicidal maniac who'd beaten a man to an unrecognizable pulp, rolled him in a carpet, and set him on fire in the chimney of his own historic house, knowing all the while the ventilation wasn't good. Especially if the homicidal maniac in question had been Harry. There was another possibility as well. Harry had been my sub. But had he also been Lana's hired gun?

25

I talked a good game, but so much about Chuck's death mystified me. I didn't know what to make of the details Phelps had shared, nor did I understand Martha Benton's interest in me, though I suspected I could count on Fiona's help on that score. And then there was Phelps. Hiring a decorator to make crime scene miniatures was not a rookie detective's most straightforward path to job security. Did he hope I could provide details only the killer could know?

Best not to spin the wheels, I thought, sliding the key into the ignition. I needed to stay focused, make the right moves. It was a relief to have a new project, a reason to set everything else aside.

I piloted my car downtown, the radio tuned to news of gyrating financial markets and a temblor near Santa Monica, not far from where Erica lived. Closer to home, the city council had been busy with New Preston's annual holiday glow-up, decking the streetlamps with oversized snowflakes and threading twinkle lights through the shrubbery. But the overall effect was subdued. The hydrangeas by the bus stop were almost bare, the last dry blossoms nodding off, their russet heads weighting the branches. Just as well, I thought as I listened to the newscast. Seismic or economic, all that movement could only mean one thing: The big one was already on the way.

Teller's place was just as Wendy had described it—a triple-decker rezoned for mixed use and layered like a pousse-café, two floors of offices topped by an apartment. The cedar shingling was so new, I could smell it from the front walk, and the yard was freshly landscaped, lined with green rectangles of thriving sod ringed by a neat privet hedge. This place was looking good—but the rest of the neighborhood was rooted in a different reality. Porches sagged, and weeds invaded the sidewalks. Despite recent improvements, the area remained a haven for landlords accustomed to the old ways of getting things done, to greased palms and averted eyes.

In the lobby I scanned the register, sifting the alphabet soup of credentials: MD, PhD, EdD, LICSW. Teller had only the MD, but of course, that was all he needed. If I'd learned anything from Chuck, it was that this degree put a medical professional at the top of the heap.

His office was on the second floor. Making my way up the steep, narrow staircase, I noticed that the original woodwork had been preserved, and the window hardware, also original, had a desirable patina.

On the landing, a door bore a brass placard: WAITING ROOM. I opened it and was assailed by the smell of rubbing alcohol. An odd choice for a shrink—how much antisepsis could the job require? A cloche-shaped noise machine silvered with dust sat silently on a low bookcase containing shelves of banged-up textbooks and a hardcover set of the complete works of Sigmund Freud, the corners only slightly bumped. More books, mostly paperbacks of pop psychology, littered the coffee table. I was quelling an urge to tidy the mess when I tripped on the rug.

The offender was a threadbare kilim. Underneath was a lovely hardwood floor, the original parquetry still intact. What a shame to cover it—but, of course, the dubious kilim would minimize wear and tear. To the floor, anyway. My ankle told a different story.

Simon Teller appeared in the doorway. He was just as I remembered from the gallery—a tall brunette with strong features, like an off-brand Gregory Peck. His navy blazer was slightly too large, his khaki slacks slightly too short. Minor flaws, eminently remediable. In real estate terms, he was a fixer-upper.

Hannah Cooke, he said. A pleasure to see you again.

Call me Cookie, I said, sticking out my hand for him to shake. He took it reluctantly, weighing and discarding it. As he led me into the consulting room, we bumped at the threshold. I could barely contain my laughter—the guy actually flinched.

Au travail, I reminded myself. If I couldn't get a handle on my snark, our engagement was likely to be a short one.

Painted in beige, the consulting room was long and narrow, the result of partitioning the original large parlor into offices, a common landlord's trick. A tatty pressboard desk occupied the long side of one wall. Dominating the far end was a boxy sofa and armchair, both upholstered in sage-green velour that had seen better days. Angled off each other, they formed the two legs of an L, and were flanked by a fragile-looking lotus chair covered in a threadbare cream-colored linen. A vinyl recliner, shiny as a poblano pepper and exactly the same color, completed the picture.

He settled into the poblano recliner, and I squished myself into the lotus chair. From there I could inspect the framed items hanging on the opposite wall: diplomas from impressive schools, certificates from the American Psychiatric Association, New Preston's Better Business Bureau.

Sunlight poured in through a bay window, which had been propped open with a banged-up Rolodex.

We haven't gotten off to the best start, I said.

I'm afraid I'm the one who should apologize, he said. For allowing my wife to shanghai you.

Shanghai: He spoke like an old-time antihero, James Cagney by way of Harvard Yard.

Please don't take this the wrong way. I abhor this project, he said.

Maybe your wife just values a nice environment. She certainly has opinions. But couples counseling is your department. If you don't agree with her about the need for a refresh, I'm not sure how I can help.

Your uncertainty appeals to me, he said, smiling. I could use more of it. In fact it was our marriage "counselor"—he made quotation marks with his fingers—who advised us to undertake this project. Advised us with great certainty, in fact. The idea is that I should accept some "influence"—he made finger quotes again—from my wife.

He paused, considering, then thundered: It's preposterous! Would *you* recommend a renovation to a couple looking to save their marriage?

I don't know about marriages, I said quietly.

And how long have *you* been divorced? he snapped.

I felt my expression harden.

Half of all marriages end in divorce. That's decent odds for guesswork, I said.

He grunted, and I thought: my point. Wendy had warned me that he was withholding.

To my right, intruding on my field of vision, was an

enormous ceramic lamp, bell-beaker style. I shifted position, unwilling to sit there peeking out at him from behind its expansive linen lampshade.

So how do you spend your days, Dr. Teller? I suppose you mostly just prescribe?

Mostly I listen, he said. I'm not a pill doctor.

He didn't like that I might see him that way, as a pill doctor.

I said: Let's start again. If you could change anything about this place, what would it be?

He leveled me a strange look. Perhaps he'd expected more of me, a better opening gambit.

Maybe I should explain what I *don't* want, he said. Let me tell you about the most disappointing shrink's office I ever saw.

Knock-off Eames? Matisse prints? Tufted leather chaise?

I was always afraid I'd slide off that damned daybed.

We can avoid slick fabrics, I said.

That's a practical point of view.

I'm a practical person.

I suppose I found him impervious.

Who?

My therapist. Analyst.

The difference?

I used the couch. Benno sat out of sight and listened.

Right, I said, retreating behind the lampshade so he could not see my face. *Benno!* This guy was the bad penny of psychiatry in New Preston. Or in his gray case, the bad nickel.

That's how you know you're in analysis, he went on. When you talk to the ceiling. Or the wall. Though it seems right now, I'm speaking to the lampshade. Why are you hiding behind it?

I peered out: Everyone's so hung up on who's an analyst and who isn't, I said.

Simon grunted again. That's my bread and butter, he said. Hang-ups.

I did have a therapist once, I said. As a client. She wasn't an analyst, just someone who listened. When I finished her place, she covered the walls with photographs of ancient ruins she saw on her vacations. She'd been all over Italy and Greece. She'd even visited some ruins in Turkey. She'd photographed every single standard view. It was like being inside a brochure.

Not a style cognate with your own, then?

Cognate. How this guy talked. I was developing a serious aversion to him. But then our eyes met, and he smiled warmly. Beneath the surface prickliness, he was actually sweet, one of those hedgehog-like people whose spiky exterior concealed a surprising vulnerability. The contrast had its charms. I could see how he made his living.

Now was the time to pry a little more out of him.

Are you still in touch with that analyst of yours, I ventured, this Benno—

Before I could finish, the Rolodex slipped, the window crashed down, and the door to his office blew open with a *whoosh.* He rose, shut the door, shot the bolt.

Excuse me. There's a wind from the hallway.

These old houses, I said as airily as I could. It wasn't easy, given the lump in my throat.

Penny for your thoughts?

Your furniture's dated, I choked. The rug's worn. That kilim in the waiting room—at the very least, it needs a pad. You could use modern lighting. These 1980s cans aren't cutting it.

He shifted in his chair, which emitted squeaks of protest.

And you'll need a new recliner. I hope you're not attached to that one. It's terrible for your back.

You'll find I'm not attached to much. I suppose that's a good quality in a client, Ms. Cooke?

Cookie, I corrected him.

He held my gaze a beat too long.

No doubt you've had your own experiences with disappointing clients, he said.

Au travail. Au travail.

These are easy fixes, I said. But let's start with the floor plan, get a sense of the big picture. I'll take a few photos today, but I want to make a proper sketch. And for that, I'm afraid I'll need to come back. I know it's an intrusion. I'm sorry for that. I want to get everything right.

He opened his calendar, a huge AT-A-GLANCE.

So come back, he replied, readying his pen. Get everything right.

26

On the day of Chuck's funeral, I made my way to Grove Point. Being in the cemetery chafed lingering rawnesses, my memories of Chuck mingling painfully with those of my father. The last time I'd been here, it was to bury him.

I turned the usual corner, where a huge split beech marked the path toward our family plot. Chuck's grave loomed just beyond, a dark hole before a stand of leafless trees. Cars were parked along the road.

What awful luck, that the two graves should be so close together. Or was it kismet, a sign? In a very short period, I'd lost my father and my lover—who was also another married man. I didn't need a therapist *or* an analyst to recognize the oedipal resonance. I just didn't know what to do with it. I never knew what to do with my father, either. But then again, New Preston's a small town. There are only so many possibilities for romance. There's only so much space in the graveyard. No need to posit anything supernatural.

The weather was fine, the air crisp. As the group gathered, I kept my distance, staying in the shadow of the giant beech. I didn't see Lana, but then I wasn't keen to. I didn't see Martha Benton, either. From the looks of the mourners—well dressed and not overly broken up—I deduced that these were mostly friends from the hospital or former patients, people Chuck had helped.

Because he *did* do that. He did help people. All those stories—he couldn't have made them *all* up.

The bare trees broke the river into glittering segments. Peeking out from behind the beech, I looked everywhere except at the hole in the ground. I read lines on a tombstone: *Be near me when my light is low, and all the wheels of Being slow.*

I came to the edge of the group, skirted it. My breathing grew ragged.

At last I caught a glimpse of Lana in the crowd, her face nearly hidden behind a netted veil. She lifted it to confer with a distinguished-looking man sporting the expensive overcoat and bright shoeshine characteristic of those whose business is the disposition of assets.

Hollowed out with the grief I still couldn't process, I flipped my collar up and watched a hawk ride a thermal over the main road.

Be near me when my light is low.

I'd wasted so much of our limited time. Chuck had never told me outright that things with Lana weren't good. Now I understood why he didn't need to. They weren't even sleeping in the same room. And then there was the lock he'd installed on the door. He may have been afraid of her. Maybe she and Harry were in cahoots over more than the chimney.

I was expecting a proper burial, but now the group was inching toward the part of the cemetery devoted to inurnments. I hung back as they formed a semicircle around a shaded spot where urns were displayed in niches in a long wall.

Phelps picked up on the second ring.

I'm at Chuck Halsey's funeral, I sputtered. Except there's

no casket. He arrived in a fucking jar. Is there something you need to tell me, Phelps? Anything else I should know before I get started on your little crime scene?

You better come down to the precinct, he said.

27

Out past the city limits, New Preston's historic built environment lapses into seedy suburban gothic—buckled sidewalks, blighted trees, top-heavy utility poles leaning at alarming angles suggestive of outages to come. Usually that transition, from town to suburb, tugged at me. For so long virtually my whole existence has been oriented toward finding possibilities in neglect. Today it just got me down. Driving with the windows open and the sea breeze smacking grit into my face, I saw only more of the same.

The police station was a low-slung, cement-block structure fronted by a parking lot and bordered by a chain-link fence overgrown with Virginia creeper. The strip mall next door was also overgrown, but I'd heard about recent changes afoot, rumors of new management. The Sleeping Dog, a longtime cop diner, had recently branched out into fancy Sunday brunches—bespoke waffles, omelets made with eggs from local chickens, maple syrup sourced from a nearby farm. As I got out of the car, the air was thick with the smell of tomatoes and garlic wafting from the vented roof of Pizzeria D'You Know. Beyond that was a novelties shop, Haute Topic, where Owen was moonlighting from his internship at the morgue. Owen's bike, recognizable from the orange prayer flags flapping from a tall pole attached to the rear, was locked to a rack outside.

Inside the station, I announced myself at the front desk, and the clerk buzzed me through the heavy double doors. Elevator's on the fritz, he said, motioning me through. You better take the stairs.

The staircase was walled in cinder block painted institutional greige. My footsteps echoed dully as I made my way down to the forensic lab, where Phelps did his macabre business.

My sadness was still there, but it had receded a bit, replaced by the embers of an unfamiliar desire: *to know*. What had actually happened in that rebuilt chimney? What had been done to Chuck, and who had done it?

I found Phelps bent over a lab table, paging through the contents of a file folder. Emotions flitted over his face—surprise, dread.

You screwed up this time, I said.

Well, to be fair, *we* screwed up. Me and my team.

Evasion doesn't help your cause, Bill. Surely you'd keep the body, or what was left of it, intact for forensic purposes?

You need to watch less television.

What happened to the body?

We release remains to the family as soon as we have everything we need. After that, the family—well, they do what they want.

Decent of you.

He toed a rolling stool toward me. I kicked it away.

Please calm down. There's only so much I can tell you. A person actually has to go to school to do—*all this*.

He waved his arms, taking in the lab bench, the empty stretcher, a wall's worth of refrigerator drawers, a tile floor pocked with drains.

So the investigation did at least *begin* with a body?

Of course. Now, if you'll excuse me—

You said you screwed up. You never said *how*.

He removed his glasses, located a handkerchief, and set to polishing the lenses.

Well, he said finally. If you must know. Someone made a mistake with the tags.

The tags?

After the forensics are taken care of, the job is basically all bureaucracy. We tag 'em—

I winced.

We tag 'em, he repeated, and then we bag 'em, and then we send 'em on their way. I'm sorry if it sounds crude. It's like filing a document. Now and then someone will make an error. Tag fails to match bag, hilarity ensues.

I don't find this funny, Bill. You mean to tell me, no one double-checks? Getting it right seems, oh, I don't know, kind of important?

The party responsible did not check in this case, Phelps said stiffly. And his supervisor was not in the habit of encouraging diligence in the first place.

Chuck Halsey was cremated *by accident*?

By the time the funeral home discovered the mistake, it was too late.

Someone at the funeral home must have gotten quite a shock, opening up the body bag expecting to find Chuck Halsey and instead finding—well, someone else.

They've been dealt with.

Who?

The parties responsible for the snafu.

You fired Norman Sawyer?

He was *let go*. Along with his assistant, the new kid, I forget his name. He should never have been doing what he did.

The new kid. It could only have been Owen. Fiona would be devastated.

If you really want me to get this miniature right, I said, I'll need to know more about the disposition of the body. How you found him.

Phelps looked away. I willed my jaw to unclench.

We've got a line on something strange in the victim's work environment, he said after a moment. Do you know anything about it? Maybe you overheard something at the job site?

You know what it's like to have a stressful job, Bill. He knew enough not to take the work home with him, even to a home he was renovating.

Phelps hesitated, taking that in, and handed me the file folder. Fair enough, he said.

I paged through the file, focusing on my breathing: *Keep it together, Cookie.*

One photograph showed the body, what was left of it, from the neck down, burned beyond recognition. Some circumstantial details I could bear to look at: a dusty handprint on the window, the half-obscured impression of a work boot on the wall. Beside it, a feathered dark smear.

What's that?

Blood on the wall. A very bloody job can soak all the way to your shoelaces. If they're loose or long, they'll fly around, and the blood spatters in a particular way. You see the edges?

I nodded, remembering the ratty work boots I'd kicked out of the way in the Halseys' kitchen on the night of the fire.

The spatter has that pattern, he continued, because the aglet's missing.

Clever, I thought.

The shoes were old.

Or the laces were.

Another photograph showed a close-up of what appeared to be a forearm. It had escaped the worst of the burning.

Was it tucked beneath the body somehow?

He shrugged.

Make of it what you will. Norman already noted the puncture wounds.

Puncture wounds?

I looked again, and this time I had to catch my breath. These were the marks Chuck didn't want to talk about, and it occurred to me that the contents of the ampoules I'd glimpsed in the fridge may have been destined for Chuck's bloodstream. Perhaps not with his consent, either—he had installed that deadbolt, after all. But it would be hard to attest to these intimate details without having to explain how I came to possess that knowledge.

Needle tracks, most likely, Phelps explained.

I nodded. *Right.*

Anything else? I don't see dental records in here.

Again with the Hollywood protocols. Who said anything about dental records?

You did!

I said it was the sort of job that *might* require them. We don't have 'em yet, he concluded, rolling the stool, the one I'd kicked, back into its niche beneath the desk.

28

Wendy's check had cleared. Given the state of my finances, I should have been relieved. But the project continued to trouble me. It was as if I'd been hired to renovate not Simon's office, but Simon himself. That was one job I didn't need any piece of. A conversation unfurled in my mind, all the things I could not say to Wendy: *Sure, I'm a decorator. Improvement's my job. But Simon can't be. Isn't it his office? Shouldn't he decide?*

But this inner monologue was not solving my problem, and I had too much on my plate to add yet another ruminative side dish. All I could do was the professional thing. I had to let Wendy know.

She picked up after a ring and a half. The preliminaries were pleasant enough. But as I thanked her for the check, I sensed a meter running on the conversation.

Simon's office is a disaster, I said, getting straight to the point. But I think that's just how he likes it.

Don't you go all balky on me, too, she sniffed. I could hear her pout through the line.

Behind me, my dogs erupted in furious barking.

Sorry, I said when they quieted. There's a woodchuck in the yard. Drives them crazy.

I know the feeling, she replied.

Simon has to want this change, Wendy. He doesn't.

Now you see my problem. Whenever I have an idea, a wall goes up. But you know how to get things done.

She was a brazen bullshitter, praising me for qualities I didn't have in the hopes that I might develop them. If I didn't want to become her creature, I would have to watch my step.

What I don't see, Wendy, is how I can help.

He acts like a wall, but he isn't one. Not at his best.

It might be easier if he were. A wall, I mean. I could cover him in flocked wallpaper, hang a mirror, and tell you the job was done.

She laughed, and then, with surprising warmth, invited me to their place for a drink.

Just come for cocktails. You can see what we did last year, updating our kitchen. Not that you have to reuse the design, of course. You'll do something even better. But you might get some ideas. Humor me. Please.

The invitation seemed so openhearted, and her distress so plainly urgent, it would have been churlish to refuse.

Come tonight, she said. Bring your dogs.

My dogs?

He'll trust you more if he knows you're a dog lover, she explained. He's a dog lover himself, and he's got some psychological theory about it that I don't pretend to understand. But we can make it work in our favor.

Our favor. I'd called to wriggle out of the job, and I'd only dug myself in deeper. For all her flaws, Wendy could be persuasive when she wanted to be. No wonder Simon felt outgunned.

29

The Tellers lived on one of Pill Hill's more crowded tree-lined streets, where the houses were packed so closely together that a body could pass a cup of sugar to the neighbor just by reaching through a kitchen window. Their house, a well-preserved Queen Anne, was set back on a picket-fenced lot and painted in the same pale neutrals I remembered from Teller's office, the familiar hues of sage and cream that never hurt anyone's resale value, the colors of a fresh dollar bill.

The wind picked up, swirling dry leaves down the driveway. A navy minivan was parked at the far end, bearing a license plate pleading TELL HER. The incongruity made me smile. A psychiatrist with an ugly office loves cheap puns and favors utility over ostentation, yet he will express those modest values on a vanity plate if doing so amuses him. So much bad décor is just mild-mannered incoherence. I had come to the right place.

I settled the dogs, fluffed my hair, rang the bell.

The door swung open. The petite brunette from my Lizzie Borden show appeared in the doorway with sleeves rolled and hair scraped back, thin strings of a kitchen apron knotted at her waist. Beneath the apron she wore office clothes: a white blouse with wide lapels, neat black slacks, sensible flats. A thin line of soapsuds clung to one side of her face.

I hope I'm not early.

Come in, come in, Wendy urged me in her high-speed baby talk. Stepping into the foyer, I felt my face harden.

Admire, admire, I reminded myself as I yanked the dogs along, hurrying after her as she receded down the corridor. Disheveled as she was, Wendy had flair. Her ponytail was high and tight, like a 1960s ingenue's, and wrapped with the same Mondrian-patterned scarf she'd worn to my gallery show.

Like the house's exterior, its interior was unobjectionable. The previous decorator had taken no risks. Everything was familiar, right down to the corridor's classic wallpaper, pale-green vines on a cream background, the warm white semigloss on the trim, and framed posters advertising CINZANO and FERNET. Even the mail piled messily on the console table did little to mar the cleanly upmarket vibe. The only discordant detail was the line of framed family photographs on the wall, a row of stern old-world faces set in thick black frames. Here were the ancestors, looking on and finding nothing to judge about the safely neutral and expectable décor.

Wendy led me into her large, bright kitchen. Machines for making bread, espresso, toast, and rice stood in formation on the granite counter, lit by tiny under-cabinet lights. Dinner smelled promising. Braised lamb, I guessed, from the rich aroma. My stomach growled. The Allәns scrambled around the central island. Wendy smiled tightly. She wasn't a dog person, but she was trying.

Should I set out some water for your pups? And what about you, would you like a drink?

Water's fine for all of us, thanks.

I settled onto a stool, one I recognized from a high-end

catalog that advertised "credible distressing," mechanical daubs and scratches that rendered the advertising true enough.

From deep in a cabinet, Wendy extracted a plastic punchbowl, which she filled with water and set on the floor.

Adorables, she said, in the French way: They are simply *ah-door-ahhb*.

You don't have pets?

Too much trouble. Selfish, I know.

She slid a glass into a niche on the fridge door, prompting a mechanical whir followed by a spill of water and crushed ice. She handed me the brimming glass, and I set it on the counter, nearly overcome by déjà vu. I didn't want to repeat my adventure with the Halseys, and yet here I was, in danger of doing just that.

She gestured at her spotless kitchen: Sorry for the chaos. You wouldn't believe the day I've had. Even I can't believe it.

Just as it had been with Lana, my first task with Wendy was to believe. Oh? I said. Some days can be awful, I added as I lifted the glass to my lips. The water dribbled down my front. I swore under my breath. Wendy handed me a paper towel, and I did my best to blot the stain.

She said: I envy you, running your own shop, making your own hours. They've actually called me back to work.

Some days are just too awful, I said. Should we reschedule?

Not on your life. I need you to take this job.

Few life circumstances require the urgent attentions of a decorator, I said.

She set her mouth in a thin line.

Wendy, I told you I can't work with someone who doesn't want to work with me. What if Simon doesn't *want* to renovate his office?

A door slammed somewhere in the house.

What he wants is irrelevant, she said.

Simon burst into the kitchen looking like he'd just woken up from a nap—rumpled chinos and puffy tube socks, a fawn-colored Mister Rogers cardigan buttoned over a matching polo with a fraying collar. He pecked Wendy on the cheek she offered. She flicked her gaze over him.

Busy day? he asked.

Like you wouldn't believe. And it's not over yet. A patient had an acute reaction to a medication. One of those new pain-killers. Heard of them, Cookie?

No, I lied. In fact Chuck had mentioned them, but I wasn't getting into that with Wendy.

You're better off, she said. Stick with ibuprofen. To Simon, she said: They need me back at the office to draft a statement ahead of the late news.

That's twice in—what's it been, Wendy—two months? It is sheer hysteria.

But think of the liability if it isn't!

Edgar emerged from beneath the counter to cadge a belly rub from Simon, and Ethan nudged between them, wanting a turn. Simon obliged with an enthusiasm that surprised me. Wendy hadn't lied about that: He really did love dogs.

As usual they have to alert the supplier. Not that *they* care, they'll cut their stuff with any old crap just to keep costs down. I keep telling people, you get what you pay for.

Simon turned to me. Can they have treats? he asked, meaning the dogs.

Does anyone ever listen? Wendy persisted, her voice rising.

Wendy, Simon interrupted, we must have a treat in this house somewhere.

An icy expression wisped over Wendy's face.

Simon, why don't you help Cookie with her coat?

I followed Simon into the hallway, where he lifted my coat from my shoulders with an easy motion. He smelled homey, like ironing starch and parsley. I sighed.

Yes?

Sorry. I don't know what's gotten into me.

Never mind. We'll talk. Maybe even eat. Though that part depends on Wendy.

I'm just here for drinks. It sounds like drinks are all she has time for anyway.

Wendy has time to eat. So do you.

Back in the kitchen, Wendy was twisting a corkscrew into a bottle of wine. I stole a glance at the clock. An hour would be enough for a glass. Just one, to be polite, before making my getaway.

Is red okay with you, Cookie? We're not big fans of the white.

Red's fine, I said.

Wendy struggled to extract the cork, making little gasps of effort, then handed it off to Simon, who smiled as if he found it all too cute and finished the job with an efficient twist. The exchange wasn't exactly warm, but it was close enough to make their marriage seem plausible. Maybe this job would work out after all.

Simon filled two wineglasses and gave me one. I took a sip and choked: The stuff was nearly vinegar. Simon's eyes were merry.

Two Buck Chuck not your speed?

Chuck, Chuck . . . I willed my expression to be blank.

Wendy sloshed an impressive quantity into her own glass, leaving a damp handprint on the bottle.

I like these cheap vintages, Simon said, how they push the limits of drinkability, how they insist on their rights—

Salut, Wendy interrupted, glass high. After the first one, even this rotgut is fine, just fine.

Isn't marriage just like that? Simon pressed. The question seemed directed at no one in particular. Perhaps he'd been at the wine already. A spider slid down from the ceiling on a silver thread and scuttled across the countertop. I looked up. Sure enough, the can lights were strung with spider silk, thick in places where, I knew, eggs were about to hatch. I felt my gorge rise. Wendy noticed. *Tch*, she said. Who has time to dust?

I see it all the time, he continued, as if she had not spoken. Lower your standards, I say. Learn to enjoy Two Buck Chuck. Practicality has to trump exquisiteness once in a while. Wouldn't you say so, Cookie?

I aim to please, I replied. My taste shouldn't be my client's problem.

Vive la résistance! Simon cried, lifting his glass. He barreled on: To your taste!

I had to lift my own glass, to hide my blush. An appliance pinged.

Timer, Wendy snapped. She donned a pair of thick mitts and wrestled a cast-iron pot from the oven. As she pinched salt over the pot's contents, I noticed the take-out container sitting open on the counter. She really was headed back to work, leaving Simon to eat his dinner in this strange kitchen where nothing was beyond the reach of that Cinzano cheer, yet no one looked closely at anything or anyone, and so the spiders nested in the ceiling lights and laid their eggs there unobserved and likely also unimagined.

Behind Wendy, through the window, I watched as the second-floor neighbor, a woman about my age, reached to fill a bird feeder. A dark line of shingles had lifted from her roof. She couldn't see them, but I could. In my mind's eye, I could also see the stained interior ceiling, the sodden plaster. Everyone's always so surprised when the roof falls in.

Clearing her throat, Wendy nudged me out of my daydream: So here you are, Cookie, in our newly renovated kitchen. And here we are, Simon—entertaining in it! You see? It's not so bad.

Not so bad? It's a miracle! The oven heats to four hundred degrees in less than five minutes, and the fridge has a sensor so it texts me when we're out of milk.

It most certainly does not, Wendy said mildly, though her eyes had narrowed.

What an idea, I said. You should work in Silicon Valley, Simon.

Please don't encourage him, Cookie.

Simon slapped the countertop, making a big show of being encouraged anyway.

Once I tried to program it so it would send this news to the grocery store via a weekly shopping list. I lost enthusiasm for the project when I realized I was trying to engineer a perfect system of communication from my unconscious to my mother—

No need to bring *her* into it, Wendy said, tilting the bottle to gauge the remaining *vin de payless*. Your mother's been dead for years.

We should talk about your office, I said, hoping to change the subject.

I should tell you, Cookie, that Simon really doesn't mind renovations. We actually had a *fabulous* time renovating this kitchen, despite the jokes he feels compelled to make.

Simon snorted: And *why* would I behave so childishly, Wendy?

Wendy slammed a cupboard shut: Don't patronize me.

We do what we can, he patronized her further, *and what we must.*

Wendy picked up a knife and grimly began to debride the lamb. Slices plopped into the to-go container.

You'll be going, then, Wendy? You and your doggie bag?

One cannot live by words alone, she replied. You gotta have someone to say them at the press conference.

Oh, but we all know it's a systemic problem that won't be fixed overnight no matter how you spin the story to the good people of New Preston. Surely you can stay for dinner.

She paused from her slicing and looked hard at him.

How I *spin* the story? So I'm a liar now? That's a new low.

We could go lower.

Don't, she warned. The sharp syllable rebounded against the floor, the countertops, the stainless appliances—all the hard surfaces of this slick kitchen. Wendy shut the container's lid and wiped the edges with a paper towel.

All I want, Simon, is for you to see your office from another person's point of view. Surely you're not so far gone as to be incapable of that.

Surely not, said Simon. He refilled his glass and Wendy's, then slopped the lees of the bottle into mine, spattering my hand. A dark stain appeared on my cuff. Wendy stared at him, her face all reproach.

What? he said.

Never mind, she said as she glanced at her watch. I thought we'd have time to talk about his office before I went back to work. Bad planning on my part, mea culpa, so sue me.

As she spoke, she extracted two plates from the dishwasher.

I cut in: No. Don't. I'm just here for drinks, really—

Wendy shot me a look that brooked no argument. Even the dogs went to ground, both of them flat on their bellies and whimpering by my feet. Simon and I sat in silence as she plated the lamb. But when a parsnip escaped her ladling and landed limply on the counter, Simon broke out in wild laughter, the kind that leads to fainting or throwing up. In the moment I felt capable of either.

Wendy swept the parsnip into the trash, exchanged her apron for an overcoat that was hanging by the back door, and tottered out, unbalanced from the argument and, I feared, too much wine.

Shouldn't we stop her—

There is no stopping her.

I looked around for my bag, the dogs' leashes.

Simon, quieting, said: No. Stay.

He picked up his fork, and I did the same, to be polite, despite my nausea. The lamb tasted metallic.

When I'm in this room, he said, I feel like Wendy and I might be the last two people on the planet.

Sound does bounce around, I said. All this stone and glass.

Well, maybe not the last two people. I suppose I'd have to include necrophiliac Norman, too.

Do you mean Norman Sawyer? The medical examiner?

The very same. He's the one getting the benefit of Wendy's company tonight, along with her home cooking.

I thought there was an emergency at the hospital.

And there may well be, Simon said.

I don't need to get in the middle of this, whatever it is. I'm only here for a job.

A *job*! This was no *job*.

Simon set down his fork and touched my wrist, gripping it for long enough to let me feel his power.

This was a setup from soup to nuts, he said. From nose to tail.

It was only supposed to be drinks!

She really put on a show, didn't she.

Domestic scenes, I said, thinking of Lizzie B., her gruesome theater. But had I also come here for the same reason, to make another Halsey-style mess? My fork scraped my plate.

Seconds?

No, thanks. I've had enough.

I leashed the Allǝns and made my way to the vestibule. Simon trailed behind, muttering apologies. I was making apologetic noises of my own when he cupped my chin, angling my face toward his.

The blood fizzed in my veins. He backed away, receding into a shadow that seemed to stretch down the entire corridor.

30

To say I was nervous about seeing Simon again would be like saying Benjamin Moore runs one heck of a mom-and-pop. The first meeting in Simon's office had been a shit show, and Wendy's cocktail hour had only reprised my first flop. I had no illusions about the difficulty I was in—this particular uphill climb was tending toward the vertical.

When I arrived in the WAITING ROOM, someone else was waiting, too. In the corner nearest Simon's door, crouched under her heavy coat, was none other than Dr. Martha Benton.

If she recognized me, she gave no sign. But she was hard to miss with her strange vibe, sitting there imitating a pile of cast-off clothes. Not that Simon's waiting room provided any incentive to better self-presentation. He could do worse than invest in a coat rack, or even just a row of hooks.

I settled into the farthest chair and texted Fiona: *I'm sitting here with Martha Benton.*

Fiona texted back: *Who dat?*

That was odd. I typed: *Don't you know?*

The door opened, and Simon appeared in the doorway. He stiffened as he took in the tableau.

Why, hel-*lo*! he boomed at Martha. How *are* you?

Better all the time, she simpered, her expression darkening. She'd caught the fakery in his bonhomie. I hate to disappoint, she continued, but I'm on Lou's calendar today.

Lou was Louise Deuso, a name I recognized from the foyer register. She was an EdD with an office next door.

Simon's face collapsed like a valance falling from a snapped rod. Either he was surprisingly rejection sensitive or a damned fine actor.

Simon motioned for me to follow him, then disappeared down the hallway.

Nice to see you again, Martha, I hissed as I stood. I owe you a call. Don't think I don't have your number.

She stared at me open-mouthed. I felt her eyes on me as I left the room.

IN THE consulting room, Simon turned to shut the door. The bolt slid home with a decisive *thunk*. Turning back to me, he asked: What was *that* about?

I could ask you the same question, I croaked as I sank into the depths of the lotus chair.

The poblano recliner received him with a wheeze.

We need to talk about that near-miss in your vestibule, I said.

You have expectations, he replied.

I went to your house to do a job, I snapped. I still expect to.

You really don't get it, do you? I have *terrible* decorating anxiety.

You have interior design *trauma*, but instead of leveling with Wendy and letting me get on with *my* life, you catch me in a clinch in your vestibule?

Don't say it didn't turn you on.

I won't, I said.

He laughed. *Ha!* It did.

He wasn't wrong, but his easy assumption pissed me right off.

A handful of little objects were arranged on the coffee table: a whale carved from honey-colored wood, a basket holding a trio of wooden eggs painted in geometric patterns. Pysanky, I remembered, turning one of them in my hand. Ukrainian. Something to do with Easter, resurrection, spring. The egg was heavier than I expected. Something you could raise a good lump with, if you aimed it right.

You like those? he asked. Go ahead, poke around. You may as well get comfortable, he said. I've budgeted an hour.

I returned the egg to its nest. I said: I suppose you should tell me about this "trauma."

Shoe's on the other foot, eh? Does it pinch? Maybe just a little?

He wanted to talk, but he still wasn't sure of me. It was a state I knew well. He would settle if I kept quiet. I looked at my hands.

Early in our relationship, he began, Wendy and I had a fight about furnishing our apartment. I was a resident, working thirty hours at a stretch, my free time all but gone. On my rare days off, Wendy wanted neither to fuck nor to sleep, which were my priorities, if you don't mind me saying.

I said: I'm listening.

All she wanted to do was *shop*. For *sofas*. She had conceived a particular affection for an overstuffed "Slocum" model, and she would not be called off the chase. Needless to say, my free-time plans did not involve upholstery—or curtains, or oriental carpets, or framed photos of evocative beach scenes, or oversized posters advertising European liqueurs. I made myself absolutely clear, Simon said.

Transparency is *everything*, I said.

He paused, uncertain. I'd been too emphatic. He took a breath, exhaled, relaunched.

Our "discussion" of this small matter, the disposal of my free time, took place over an elaborate breakfast. Most of the crockery finished on the floor.

I guess that's clarity.

That's marriage. Wendy did get her sofa in the end. It wasn't such a bad investment. We retired it to the basement, where it now relinquishes its stuffing in ill-tempered huffs and puffs, as narcissists do when you sit on them. Not that I would ever recommend such a treatment modality.

He glanced at me, smiling slyly.

Au travail, I reminded myself. What work could I do?

In the far corner, the molding fit poorly, leaving a gap between its lower edge and the floorboards. Rain had leaked in through the window, the same one Simon liked to prop with his Rolodex. I could see why: The window had been indifferently installed in the casement. Of course it would close on its own, unpredictably; and it was leaky, too. The floor below it was pitted from the damp. Above it, the wall paint had alligatored—evidence of moisture collecting beneath the paint.

We can replace that damaged molding, I said. That wall only needs a scrape and a lick of paint. I could do the prep myself over a weekend.

I pulled my deck of paint chips from my bag and fanned it out before him: All you need to do is pick a color.

He drew back, and I remembered: Wendy had warned me about this. A hesitation at the moment of decision.

You're the decorator. Shouldn't you choose?

I did choose. Before I came today, I made a selection of colors, as you can see here. What happens next is up to you.

I'm wary, he began, because these decisions aren't *just* about me. You should be aware of the risks you pose. I have actual patients, you know. I see them right here, in this actual room.

We're talking about paint! There's no risk in paint. You choose the wrong color, you don't go to the loony bin. You just paint again. Look, Simon. What do you think of these?

I indicated chips with colors similar to those in the Halseys' dining room—Fiona's blues.

Blue is what all my clients are, he said. They've had enough blue.

Fair, I said as I flipped the deck. Color names slipped by: Butterball, Thin Mint.

You make it look so *easy*, he said bitterly. Have you ever, even for one minute, considered how hair-raising it is, this business of laying a hand on another human being?

I flashed on an image of Chuck in surgery, lifting some unspeakable object in his gloved, bloody fingers. Simon must have noticed because he asked: Sore subject?

You don't miss a thing, do you?

Occupational hazard. Sorry.

Do you admire any of your colleagues' offices?

They all remind me of high-end hotels—anonymous, cold, exclusive. Some spend a great deal on decorators just to produce this off-putting effect. I like idiosyncratic offices better. Down the hall, one of my colleagues knits while she listens. She smoked pretty heavily, back in the day. Still does, I guess. Though she knows better. Anyway, at termination, she would offer her patient the sweater she'd made during their conversations, perfumed by her Marlboro Lights. Once upon a time, he mused, I thought I could imagine an entire psyche from these tiny behaviors, as if I could see a whole world in these details—the proverbial universe in a tobacco flake.

Tobacco, I repeated, riffling the deck in search of something suitable. A nice color. Warm and light.

We called it "depth psychology." Now I think my colleagues are tempted to just call it bullshit.

It's a loss, I said, handing him a pale card labeled *Oaken*.

Yes, he nodded as he set the card aside. An unmourned loss.

Let's choose a color, I tried again.

We all have these unacceptable but entirely recognizable impulses, he continued. It's my job to be aware of them, careful of what my environment evokes.

I remembered Erica spitting into jars.

He said: I envy you. As an artist, at least you're able to channel them. Turn an ordinary room into something wonderful. Sensuality is a marvelous ego strength.

We locked eyes. A heat rose up my neck. Blushing, I had to look away. I didn't like his power, the way he could push himself right up against me just by talking.

I strive to make myself nonreactive, he said.

Nonreactive, I replied stiffly, is not a color in the deck.

I wear the psychological equivalent of gloves, gown, and mask.

You wear chinos and a navy blazer.

Please understand. I have a professional commitment to neutrality.

Let's choose neutrals, then. Which do you prefer? Taupe, greige?

Murk, he spat, his patience exhausted. Nebula, static, blank. A rainy day.

Rainy-day gray?

Well, gray-*ish*.

Ish, I repeated, making a note: That one might even be in the deck.

ON MY way out, as I passed by Lou Deuso's open door, I couldn't help peeking into her office. The room, cluttered with books and papers, was anchored by two sagging armchairs on the far side. Lou had flopped into one of them, languorously lighting a fresh cigarette from the end of the one she'd just finished. The walls were stained yellow from her smoking.

In the lobby, the last of the day's weak light filtered through the windows. I imagined that, for Simon, there couldn't be much to closing up: a bill to send, another to pay, a few calls to return. Above me, the floor creaked as someone—it must have been, it could only have been Simon—came onto the landing and stopped at Lou's threshold.

I ought to leave right now, I told myself, even though I was already creeping back up. Just one step. Okay, two. By the time I'd reached the third, my heart was pounding.

Lou's voice was tight with rage: He denigrated her work at every opportunity, Simon! She got passed over for promotions, she hasn't had a raise in years. It's amazing she didn't have a breakdown long before. And so, to appease him and improve her prospects in the clinic, she started helping out. Every time *he* screwed up, *she* covered for him! He would criticize her, and she'd do even more. Now he's gone, and she's complicit.

I heard the snap of a lighter. The sharp smoke of the cigarette made my nose itch. I pinched the bridge to stifle a sneeze.

I can't believe she still *cares*, Simon. Not about him. About his patients.

She does care, though. Never mind what you can or can't believe. That's *reality*.

She worries, Lou said. Had those patients been *poisoned*? Did she—unwittingly—help?

So she told me, Lou, during her intake interview. But she's not sure she's right, and that's a healthy-enough doubt, given the circumstances. I don't think she's completely round the bend.

But sometimes she feels really crazy, out-of-control crazy.

Which brings her to our doorstep.

To mine. Where she continues to arrive, week after week, and I continue to fail her.

This comment brought me up short. The story was the same one Martha had been telling me about Chuck. It was consistent with the comments on that website, too.

When are you going to stop smoking, Lou? You'll kill yourself, you know.

My death wish is not your problem. My *problem* is your problem. Which you turfed to me, by the way.

I did do that, Simon said. I admit it.

And you bear some responsibility. Now don't look at me that way, it's true. So here is what I do. She comes, she frets, she ties herself in knots. At minute thirty-one, I tell her, stop catastrophizing. His patients are dying—so what? Dying is something patients do. At minute forty-five, I throw her out, saying, see you in a week.

You sound angry.

Isn't that the point of everything she does, to shift the anger? Because it's too much for her to bear? The question, though, is what to do.

What do you do?

A lighter clicked.

Damn it all, I say. Damn it all to hell.

Simon said: I see we have reached the damn-it-all portion of the consultation.

After a silence, she said: Never mind. What have you heard from Benno?

Benno! He was everywhere.

I tried to call him, Simon said. I left a message with his answering service. That was three weeks ago. Since then, nothing. But I know he didn't send that case history as a roundabout way to request a meeting. He was too straightforward for that.

The conversation faded to pleasantries. I hurried away, through the foyer, making sure to be out of sight before Simon reached the landing.

31

I had a fresh gig, with money coming in—and Phelps had sweetened his offer, too, with a budget to cover all the specialty supplies my heart desired. He even sent a New Preston police ID, complete with the photo from my driver's license. I could go to the station anytime, grind away all night if I wanted to. I had plenty of work, if I wanted it.

If only I wanted it.

Everything about the Teller job made me uneasy. Martha Benton was seeing Lou, but Martha had also been seeing Simon. Since both Lou and Simon knew quite a bit about the problem between Martha and Chuck, they might have light to shed on the circumstances of his death. I could have gone to Phelps with this connection, and I wondered if I should. Still I resisted taking any action that might endanger my hold on this job that I nevertheless did not want. Simon's office—that place was in a bad way. Could I leave him to stew in it, when I could so easily fix it up? No, I could not. And yet, and yet—

I stowed my bags in my car and took off for the river path. A walk might clear my head.

Along the riverbank, the farmers market was in full swing. Attractive young people stood behind tables hawking artisanal pickles and homemade biscotti. Everything reminded me of those night picnics with the Halseys. When a rosy-cheeked woman in a Santa hat convinced me to fork over twenty dollars for a container of bluefish pâté, I realized I was not in my right mind. At all. Overwhelmed, I headed for the exit.

Outside, the low sun was almost fully banked behind a thick layer of cloud. When I reached the river's edge, I stuffed my hands in my pockets. My fingers closed around Chuck's shabti, small and cold. My grief was similar—another small, cold thing tucked deep inside. Until I lost control of it, and it became something else, one dark impulse or another. To scream, to spit, to scratch, to cut. Unless, of course, I just let it go.

I heaved the shabti as far as I could. It landed near the middle of the expanse of water and disappeared with a little splash. Perhaps the river was a better pocket for this impossible object that, ripped from its original context, made no sense anywhere, anymore, anyhow.

On my way home, I drove past Simon's house. I didn't want the job, but I certainly wanted *something*—a peek into his life, a bit of privileged information, some deflating little tidbit that would let me pull him from my mind like a splinter.

I turned into the cul-de-sac. The house loomed ahead. A cold wave of fear washed over me. What the hell was I doing? It was too late to turn around. If either of the Tellers saw me, I'd have to brazen it out, pretend my presence in the neighborhood was purely accidental, just one of those coincidences that happens all the time in a small town.

Worse, the Tellers had company—serious company, the kind no one wants. The medical examiner's truck was parked in the driveway beside Simon's minivan with its silly TELL HER license plate. A squad car down the road flashed its lights. A police woman hustled over and motioned at me: Go back.

I reversed in a neighbor's driveway and parked across the street, in the shadow of a hedge. The bushes gave me cover as I made my way toward the knot of people congregating at the end of the front walk. Another cop stood in the front doorway, his bulky frame silhouetted by the glare from the entry. As I neared, he raised his hand.

Unless you're with the family?

Behind him, the corridor was dark as a mummy's mouth, opened by main force to abet the soul's escape. But no souls were escaping. Instead there was just my old friend, Norman Sawyer, pushing past the big cop, and stumbling drunk from the look of it, too. I slipped behind a tree.

He'd always boomed, and he was booming now, as Simon, his eyes glazed and unseeing, hustled him down the steps. *I'm sorry*, Norman cried. *I'm sorry!*

A SLEET storm caught me on the way back. I warmed myself in the kitchen, standing in the wall of heat from the open oven, Norman's shout still ringing in my ears. Fiona turned up later, catching me by the sink eating the fancy market bluefish pâté directly from the container while scrolling MedGrade on my laptop. She was wearing yoga pants and a tank top, and her hair was coming out of her ponytail.

Just back from the gym?

Self-defense class. Owen insisted. After he got fired from the morgue, he's been splitting his time between Haute Topic and dog-sitting for the police chief. Now he's worried about my safety.

She pulled up a stool at the counter, turned serious eyes toward me.

It's understandable, I said. Now that he knows all about what's possible, in terms of criminality in New Preston, he's thinking more about security.

But it's not like anything's changed. Owen just knows more.

I sighed.

Did you find the reviews I told you about? Fiona asked.

I also found some you wrote.

I turned my laptop toward her. The web page loaded in my browser. I scrolled until her name appeared, repeating down the page in comment after comment.

But this isn't me! I've never posted anything online.

Not one comment? Not one review?

She pulled the laptop over and peered at the screen. Her gum went around in her mouth.

Someone's borrowed my name. To take this Martha Benton down! No wonder Owen's worried. He must have seen this and imagined the worst.

While she chewed her thumbnail, I extracted the folder from the teetering pile at my elbow.

I need a favor, I said. Now that Lana Halsey is nowhere to be found, the renovation plans might be the only evidence left.

Evidence of what? They're blueprints, not fingerprints.

The detective in charge of the investigation is a fan of Glessner Lee.

Oh no, she said.

He thinks scale models are useful tools for investigation, and he believes blueprints might be similarly useful. The Halsey blueprints might encode something about their marriage, or provide some other clue about who killed Chuck.

Fiona scoffed: That sounds like the sort of kooky thing I'd find on the bookshelf at Haute Topic. Besides, we already have an idea of who might want to kill Halsey. Any one of his patients, for instance. That's clear as day from the reviews on MedGrade. Since when did you give up on your project of making still-lifes of heinous crimes, something you are at least somewhat trained to do, in favor of actual crime-fighting, which you emphatically are not?

I can't argue with your logic, I said. And I'm sure I'll drop the idea as soon as I realize how kooky it is. For now, though, I have to give Bill Phelps a chance. If he's right that the key to the murder could be hidden in the renovation, a clue could be somewhere in the original plans. Do you think you could head over to the Preservation Society and ask around?

But you're always saying research trips are useless, that the past doesn't give a hoot about posterity.

And it doesn't. But remember how, during demolition, we found a blocked-up Egyptian room on the property? There might be other secrets, passages we don't know about.

You'd get to take a walk, I added. Get some air.

All right. Since you asked. But don't think I don't know what you're doing, sitting here watching your bricks fall out of the wall. If you're really keen to get the historical lowdown on this place, or maybe even if you just want a break from feeling sorry for yourself—

Ouch.

Yeah, well. The truth hurts sometimes. You might also want to check in with the city archivists. They might have kept records relating to the property.

I'll be better tomorrow, I promise. I'm in no shape for anything today.

Creatives, she huffed, winking. Want to see Owen's new tat?

Not really.

But you do, she said. I insist.

She swiped through the images on her phone.

Here, she said. Look.

She showed me a photo of an upper arm, apparently Owen's, inflamed and covered in translucent orange goo partially masking a freshly inked cartouche containing hieroglyphic signs. I recognized one of them, a prayer flag that stood for a netcher. There'd been a set of three on the flip side of that obol I'd lost, long ago, with Harry out West.

He brought a little bit of ancient Egypt right into New Preston!

I thought you'd appreciate it.

I know someone else who'd like it even more. Send me that picture so I can show it to my mother.

Sure thing, she said.

You know he asked for more hours at Haute Topic.

Ah, yes. Cultural appropriation for fun and profit.

The kids like it, Fiona said.

The tattoo will help, I told her, glad for the change of subject.

As soon as Fiona left, my phone whirred. *Simon.*

There's been an accident, he said, with an audible gulp. It's Wendy.

Wendy? What happened?

In a tight voice, Simon sketched the details. Perhaps those unvarnished facts were all he had. Wendy had been hit driving over the Chepinoxet Bridge. According to the taxi driver who was the accident's lone eyewitness, a large white truck had raced up and struck her from behind. Her car had jumped the central barrier, skidded across the opposite lane, and crashed through the railing on the other side.

Where is she now?

He inhaled sharply. *She's dead, Cookie.*

My God, Simon. I'm so sorry—

His voice hardened: The police suspect foul play. You may hear from them. They'll want you to confirm that we'd had a meeting at the time of the accident. If it was an accident.

Wasn't it?

No one knows. The damage to the truck won't be easy to hide, and a surveillance camera may have caught something.

He rang off, and I stared at my neglected work, a twist of sandpaper gripped in one hand, the miniature Halsey house scattered in pieces on the table. Despite my angry jettisoning of the shabti, I was still fighting to free myself from the botched Halsey job, and here was a new and wrenching development, another dead client for my list.

32

At the hardware store, I scored a handful of paint chips in a taupe that seemed close to that indeterminate *ish* Simon liked, the kind that took no risks. The whole day was a study in dull monochrome: black river, white landscape, gray sky. *Grisaille*, as the Parisians call it, referring to a white-sky, pressed-in sort of day. I made a mental note: Perhaps *grisaille* was in the deck.

A driverless shopping cart connected with my hip. I spun around and there was Harry, grinning, at the far end of the aisle.

Can't a girl have a moment to herself?

I made a gesture he was sure to understand, and he burst out laughing, and then so did I.

We don't do this enough, Hannah Cooke.

Do what, Harry Deluca?

He regarded me, his smile fading.

He said: For a moment it was like you almost remembered who you are.

And who might that be?

Don't you know? You're the same homegirl as ever. The one with big ole daddy issues.

—

DADDY ISSUES. *Well, I'll be a monkey's uncle*, I heard my father say, as if he were still around to bend my ear. He was still bending it, internally anyway, all the more often now that Chuck was dead. Maybe that's what having daddy issues meant, but I was finding it hard to distinguish that from simply having a daddy.

At Simon's office, TELL HER was parked in the lot. I found this promising: The doctor was in, stilling his grief with work, that great salve. But what could I *tell him*? My thoughts were wild: Daddies and their issues, monkeys and their uncles.

I flashed on a memory: My father, his last day in the hospital, blinking awake in the cold room, feeling for my mother with his pale hand. My mother beside him, stony-faced. I wanted to run out of there. I had to force myself to stay. I was all they had.

Think, I told myself. What can you actually do for this man?

I could tell him what I told all my other clients: Let's fix everything up so at least one place in your life is nice. Everybody needs a refuge. Let me make you one.

The stairway smelled of Lou's cigarettes, the waiting room of rubbing alcohol and the dust of ages. I picked up a couple of the piled paperbacks; they were moldering, the pages jaundiced and sliding from the spines. It was like a library in a tomb.

The door to Simon's consulting room was open. I stood at the threshold, watching as he did something on his computer. Absorbed, he didn't hear me approach. I cleared my throat. When he looked up, his face was pale and drawn.

Got a minute?

He shrugged like the person he was, caught up in a bad situation—a dead wife, an investigation ongoing, and no choice but to wait for whatever would happen next. Sure, he had time. He had all the time, he had nothing but time.

I fanned the chips. He said: You've got to be kidding.

We can use a lighter shade in the waiting room, and a deeper one in here. Your patients will feel invited more deeply into the treatment space, where you'll lead them more deeply into themselves.

He regarded me balefully. Frankly I wasn't convinced of my off-the-cuffing either, but the proof would be on the walls.

He sighed.

Cookie, I'm in crisis. At home she's everywhere. I hear her footsteps, like she's just down the hall.

As he talked, I felt a chasm within me, a crevasse opening violently along a fault. Simon was putting on a brave face by coming to work, but his bereavement was seismic.

I haven't been this exhausted since residency, he said. And while you're here experimenting with chromotherapy, I'm seeing patients in Lou's office and trying not to claw the nicotine off the walls.

Maybe we should do this another time, I ventured. You have a lot on your mind right now.

I am in hell right now, he snapped. But that doesn't mean I'm unemployed.

I'm still employed, too, I said. Do you mind if I make the call for you?

I'd be relieved if you did, to be honest.

Okay, I replied—reluctantly. I was remembering Wendy: *I want him to make all the decisions.*

He surprised me, then, by closing his hand around my arm. His gaze was intense.

I don't want to talk about the heat between us, Cookie. Not today. But I'm not going to pretend it isn't there.

~

THAT TOUCH sent me reeling, but in the end I dismissed it—after all, I had a job to do. On opening day, I thumped up the stairs in my work boots, the handles of two cans of primer digging into my palms. This time around, it seemed prudent to make a deep *all-business* impression.

Lou waved from her armchair as I passed, and then I heard the door shut. I shoved furniture out of the way; I rolled the rugs, starting with the treacherous kilim; I boxed the sofa cushions, the books, the mysterious pysanky; I stashed the framed diplomas in the closet. Simon would not allow me to touch his desk—he'd been very clear about that—so I draped a tarp over the mess and taped the edges down. I worked like this, doing nothing but prep, for two days, over the weekend when the office was empty.

After that, my painters took the lead. They had quite a bit to do, but because it was the slow week between Christmas and New Year's, they could work without interruption. I didn't see Simon often, but whenever I did, he praised the crew's progress and seemed otherwise pleased, if a little absent. The "heat" he mentioned seemed to have dissipated, if it had ever been there in the first place. Grief makes you crazy; maybe that was the explanation.

I made myself useful, checking in at the site, helping out as I could. It was better than staying home, worrying about the bodies piling up and what I might have to do with them. Meanwhile patients scooted in and out with eyes averted. Most didn't even bother to remove their coats, not that they had a place to hang them. Yet. The coat hooks were on order.

I was crouched in a corner in the waiting room, scraping flaked paint from the windowsill, when someone tapped my shoulder. I turned to find Martha right up against my face, waving a printout of Chuck's MedGrade profile in front of my nose. Her eyes were small and shiny, like raisins in a bun.

It's all true, she hissed. *All of it!*

Lou called: *Ready, Martha?*

And that was the end of that. She came and went, always raging, but she didn't approach me again.

I fell into the habit of hanging around after hours, cleaning brushes and collecting residual paint from the spent cans, smelly work that left its traces in my nose and throat. I didn't mind. I liked the rawness, the way my insides matched my mood, irritated and inflamed. Newly sensitized to fire risk, or perhaps just because I sensed my own combustibility, I even replaced the decayed fire extinguisher I found under the kitchen sink.

Simon's desk drawers were locked, of course. The mystery was why I kept playing with them, why I couldn't seem to resist lifting the tarp and giving each handle a tug. I lifted the lids on the banker's boxes in which I'd stored his books, scanning the spines for Benno's name. I fingered Simon's special objects—the heavy carved whale and the pysanky in their wicker basket. That set of three eggs might represent anything, but I liked to imagine it stood for the smallest unit that could be called family.

Unless they stood for other, less innocent triangulations.

I dropped the tarp and fled.

BY NEW Year's Eve, things were looking up: Simon's job was nearly done, the Halsey crime scene diorama now included both floors of one side of the house, and I had a new client, a ridiculous, and ridiculously wealthy, woman who dreamed of styling her pool house into a seraglio and wanted me to source a carved teak daybed from a women's furniture collective in

Bali. I had many better things to do than hang around Simon's office, finding reasons to mess with his stuff. Yet I could not stop.

The sticking point came when I decided to rehang his certificates. After an interior paint job, the client usually puts a room back together, including the pictures. But clients dislike this part of a renovation because it means puncturing the perfectly smooth surfaces that their painters have created at such expense. It's a melancholy business, a minor exercise in tolerating lost perfection. And Simon was already tolerating so much loss. It would be easy to hang his certs.

In this puffed-up mood, which even I knew was not exactly generosity, I arrived at Simon's office and opened a window to clear the air of the smell of paint. As I leaned over Simon's desk to hammer a nail into the wall above it, I knocked a pile of junk mail to the floor. A thick manila envelope, held shut by a rubber band, caught my eye. I picked it up. Apart from the band, the packet was unsealed. Inside was a document typed onto onionskin, which riffled on the cold breeze coming in from the window.

It was a case study of some sort, and its author was Benno Sanger.

I set down the envelope, I picked it up, I set it down again. A headache bloomed behind my eyes. I leaned out the window, sucked hard for air.

Kind of stuffy in here, isn't it?

I spun around. Harry Deluca loomed in the doorway. He was sooty to his fingernails; he must have come straight from work. High on his forehead, there was a bruise, as if he'd bumped his head on something. I closed the window, and from somewhere deep within the building, a door slammed shut.

What are you doing here, Harry?

I saw your car and thought I'd say hello. What are *you* doing here?

My job, I told him. Or at least I *was*, until you got here.

Harry eyed the gleaming crown moldings, the freshly repaired sill. He dragged a grimy finger along the doorway lintel, smudging it.

Now stop, I warned him, before you make a mess that will take me all night to clean up.

He trailed his finger along a muntin: Very pretty.

Why are you here, Harry?

I know I'm not your one and only, he said, giving me a significant glance. He wasn't a large guy, but I felt cornered in this small space.

Harry—

Lately I'm starting to think you're just not the one-and-only type.

I hope you're not following me around. I'm in the mood to take out restraining orders.

Your license plate says COOKIE. The whole *town* can follow you around.

He had a point, but I'd be damned if I was going to give him the satisfaction of letting him know.

Have you eaten?

This was the real offer: a meal, his company.

A body has to eat, he pressed.

Not hungry, I said, meaning: *Not tonight. Not with you.*

I stuffed the fat envelope into my purse.

Never figured you for the sticky-fingered type, he said as he leaned over Simon's desk and began leafing through his papers.

Leave those alone, I said. They're none of your business.

Abruptly he said: I heard from Phelps.

I'm sure he's calling everyone. He's running out of leads.

Damn straight, Cookie. He had the nerve to ask *again* where I was the night Chuck Halsey bought it. He thinks I put a mark on him, that I was sleeping with his snobby wife. What a moron. I don't pretend to know what goes on in his beetle-brain.

Harry kept talking, on and on, even as the hair on my arms stood up.

Listen, Harry. Phelps *had* to call you in. He had no choice. You had a site key. So did I, and he called me in, too. Besides, I've already vouched for your character.

He snorted.

Really, Harry, everything's fine. Now it's time for me to close up and get on with my evening. I was just heading out to see my mother.

The prospect of a distasteful family obligation was usually enough to disperse Harry. But he kept looking past me, as if there was something he needed to see on Simon's desk.

How is she anyway? Your mother?

I'm sure she'd love to see you, if you felt like stopping by.

Before I had finished the sentence, he was out the door.

WHEN YOU'VE gone down the wrong road, it's never too late to get off it. The problem is knowing whether the road you're on is the wrong one in the first place. Benno's case study bulged in my handbag: Was this the right road or the wrong one?

The wrong one, I suspected. If I didn't open the envelope, I could simply return it. I left the bag on a shelf and turned my attention to other matters. Or tried to, anyway. *Au travail.*

I was at my worktable. The hour was late, and my eyes stung with paint fumes. I was laying a fresh coat on a tiny replica of Chuck's bedroom, hoping to correct a subtle error. Perhaps the primer was not exactly the same as what I'd used on the site, or maybe the paint itself had been compounded differently. Whatever the source of the problem, the shade was wrong, and I could not get it right. Tamping my frustration, I mixed another batch and kept at it. The radiator clanked. My shoulder ached. Distantly, a car's alarm rang out and fell silent.

Simon's fat envelope peeked out of my handbag.

People don't usually reveal their inner worlds to me directly. I've always been able to glean what I needed from the way they arranged the stage sets of their lives, their choices in paper and paint, in knickknacks and furnishings. Yet I'd always felt like I was cheating. What would a direct confession be like?

I was on the wrong road. I could still turn around. But the envelope wasn't sealed.

Wasn't my curiosity a matter of professional interest, a way to get to know my client better?

Besides, I still didn't know what Chuck had told Benno about me, about us. What lies had he told, what gossip had he shared?

I wasn't a psychiatrist. Most likely I wouldn't understand the first thing about it. What was the harm?

Carefully I removed the case study from its wrapper. It felt like pulling a pin from a grenade. But this was no grenade. It was an original typescript, not even a photocopy, of a case study. Scanning the first line, I got snagged on details: *A small man of uneasy bearing. A surgeon's fingers. Dishpan hands.*

33

The Intake Interview

A small man of uneasy bearing, Dr. X arrives precisely on time, the day's chill clinging to his overcoat. It is late winter, a time that invariably finds me overwhelmed with new patients dispirited by nature's slow return to life, which always sits badly with their ongoing feelings of deadness, feelings I am hardly able to dispel even when the world is not about to burst into leaf and bloom. Psychiatry is an impossible profession, and this is an impossible time of year.

He offers his hand: long, thin fingers surmounted by chapped knuckles. He's a surgeon, he explains. He washes up a lot.

I am busy. My calendar is full. I can't take another patient. Not an ordinary one, anyway.

But Dr. X is not ordinary. He is that rare consolation, an exceptional person in need of a boost. They do exist--demoralized captains of industry, child prodigies gone stale, sad beauty queens. Or, as in this case, a brain surgeon of some local renown.

For all his fame, he presents as a forgettable all-business type--rumpled chinos, oxford shirt, tweed sports coat--but his beltful of beepers announces that he is someone special, one whom others cannot do without.

It may be clinically relevant that I feel discouraged in his presence, as if the beepers are not the self-propping theatrics that I know them so often to be--that years of clinical experience have taught me they are. Instead they seem to signify something real that casts my own work in shadow. This is not totally unrealistic. What specialists like Dr. X could do in moments with a knife, I struggle for months to accomplish with speech, gesture, and the several varieties of silence--and without the benefit of anesthesia for either party. I keep reminding myself that lobotomies went out of style decades ago, and for good reason.

Yet here he is, a neurosurgeon in a psychiatrist's office. He has come for help, which he clearly needs. My envy is not his problem. When I offer to take his coat, this simple inquiry undoes him. Unable to decide whether or not to give it over, he stands there slipping his hands in and out of his pockets like a magician conjuring rabbits. I invite him to take a seat. He selects the most distant one, an Eames chair beneath a Picasso print--the famous one from 1931, of the dreaming woman with the yellow hair.

I tilt my head, waiting. It's better if the patient begins.

His wedding ring flashes, gold with a fine patina. He's been married for some time.

My wife, he says tentatively.

Yes?

She is renovating our house.

This is among the stranger reasons to see a psychiatrist, but people do sometimes lead with trivialities, greasing the rails for the real work.

We can't afford it, he continues.

But you must make a good living, and your wife--she doesn't work?

She owns an import-export business. Textiles.

I scratch in my notepad because I can't bear to look at him. Fidgeting, prickly with electronics, he seems on the verge of an explosion.

Put the pen down!

Dr. X, I tell him, stilling my pen. I must be allowed to take notes. They will be useful in your treatment. I can assure you of complete confidentiality. Everything you tell me stays in this room.

He sets his mouth in a stubborn twist. He won't say a word so long as I'm threatening to record it.

It's only natural to be anxious, Dr. X.

I'm not, he retorts. I'm not anxious!

Right, I tell him. Let's try a different tack. What brings you?

My wife and I have retained an, uh, uh . . .

He's either lost the word, which would lead me to a presumptive dx of dementia, or he can't settle on the right one and he desperately wants to, which makes me think he's obsessional, a perfectionist.

I cut in: You've retained a lawyer? That does sound serious.

He scowls. I've irritated him.

We have retained an *interior decorator*.

In the consulting room, my irritation does bring some people--obsessionals mainly--into focus. He's one of those people. I drop the dementia possibility.

It seems to me that a decorator is no cause for alarm, I say mildly, hoping to irritate him more.

Right, he says. A beating only hurts.

For all its pathos, the phrase as he utters it sounds canned, rehearsed. I should call it out, so as not to avoid giving the impression that he can keep me at a distance with malarkey. But to follow this intuition now, when I've hardly met him, risks his trust, which I have not earned--and may not, for a while.

What's the problem with your renovation?

He replies as if I am a glitching EEG: Have *you* ever renovated a house?

Now I'm the one who's irritated. To quell the mood, I imagine its opposite. This is a bit of a trick. Feeling inflated? Imagine a pin. Blazing with anger? Starve the flame, suffocate it. Imagine a lead apron, the sort found in a dentist's office.

A wonderful substance, lead. Completely nonreactive substance, totally inert--until you make a bullet from it.

You don't want to waste your time on petty comforts, I say. These things enrage you.

My tone is mild, friendly, but I don't like the way I feel, how I'm pushing back a murderousness he has roused in me. No wonder his wife wants to kill him. Perhaps he is just that sort of person, a person you might want to kill.

You've made yourself comfortable, and look how you've been hurt.

I am most comfortable, he sneers, in a world without all this comfort-seeking. This clown, this *decorator* asked me five times what I wanted for my bedroom.

What did you tell her?

I told her to fuck off.

You actually said, Fuck off?

I *said*, Give me an oblivion of light.

Fuck off, in other words.

Out loud I say: Tell me about this

decorator. It sounds like she's under your skin.

She wears cowboy boots in New England. She carries important papers in a tote from Yankee Candle.

He goes on in this vein, listing various sins of wardrobe and bearing. Her name is something ostentatiously stupid, Candy or Fruity.

He continues: She asks stupid questions like "What color makes you feel happiest?" and "What are your associations to wallpaper?"

Her methods don't sound objectionable, Dr. X.

Her dogs have stupid names. She hires stupid contractors. She sits with my stupid wife in the stupid kitchen, stupidly debating the merits of fifteen indistinguishable shades of off-white until I want to scream.

Seems normal for a renovation, I say, stupidly.

I hate it.

Hate's a strong word.

"Hate's a strong word," he mimics me.

He's an excellent mimic.

I say: She's sloppy.

She could stand to lose a few, yeah.

I keep my face still, in order to avoid betraying my real feelings, which would surprise him. I admire those with the courage to flout ordinary, marketable conventions of sexiness. My wife was like this, too. And didn't I adore her. *And was it not enough?*

Without knowing it, he has touched my tenderest spot, as only the sickest patients know how to do. I suppress my scowl as best I can. This is important clinical data.

What does all this comfort-seeking bring to mind for you, Dr. X?

He says, You're seeking my history.

And so he gives it to me, dispassionately, as befits a neurosurgeon. He reports a chaotic childhood marked by early loss of both of his parents, a grave development further exacerbated by serial losses of parental figures as he was bounced from one foster home to the next.

He has virtually nothing to say about his early life beyond a few carefully manicured memories. His longest sojourn with a family--several years--involved foster parents who, despite their evident reliability, remained vague and distant figures--almost certainly a reflection of how vaguely and distantly he had himself been treated by them. In his presence, I, too, feel vague and distant, at a remove from him and from myself.

Despite his inauspicious beginning, his excellent scholastic performance enabled him to attend an elite private university followed by stints at an equally prestigious medical school and residency program. Although he now lives comfortably due to his successful surgical practice and his wife's considerable business interests, he feels burdened by domesticity. It is simply not exciting.

Of course you feel burdened, I tell him. You've come a long way without the usual supports--a normal family, a predictable home. How would you know how to handle domestic life? You've had no chance to learn.

Adroitly he changes the subject. His excellent social skills, honed over the course of his precarious childhood, are chiefly what stands in the way of his treatment, not to mention his happiness. This is the way of the orphan: Please, appease, be pleasant even to the god-awful. And lose yourself utterly.

Dr. X, I press. *Why are you here?*

His gaze drifts out the window. He sneers at something beyond the pane.

What is *beyond pain*? I ask, staring at his contorted face. There is no way this man is beyond pain.

I once had a trainee I worried about, a young man who allowed, or invited, his patients to provoke him. He was handsome in a Prince Valiant way, and teasing, too--a menace on a ward full of patients, mostly women, looking for a fight.

But he was great on that ward. The work gave him just what he liked: pushing, being pushed. Once I understood that, I didn't worry about him. He was going to make a fine psychiatrist. He had all the right equipment.

I glance at the clock and then I draw a line beneath my final note, my personal hieroglyph for *The session has ended.*

Beneath that, I scrawl: UNREALITY.

A Period of Fog

The next several sessions are devoted to his present circumstances, in particular his relationship with his wife--and her several avatars and substitutes. What follows is a summary of those sessions, which were filled with much similar material but less anxiety on Dr. X's part. I believe patient's repetitiveness belies a reliance on stereotyped behaviors; in novel situations, as in the first session, he is completely at sea.

In relationships, too, he behaves in patterned ways. He charms, and then he prompts doubt: Does he really care, or is his apparent empathy a defensive maneuver, a smoke screen concealing his antsy core, which is inevitably betrayed by the squirrelly moves he makes as he prepares his dash for the exit? He is aware--barely--that he compulsively stirs anxiety in his intimates, but he's a long way from seeing how keeping these women on tenterhooks and at the very margins of his life serves his deeper need to repeat, and so perhaps--for once--to master, the patterns of his history.

Closer examination of his social life reveals additional predictable entanglements. Put off by his glossy outward bearing, his colleagues also keep him at a distance. In his complete lack of self-awareness, he misattributes this distance to secret envy and hatred. Gripped by this fantasy, he has lately become obnoxious at work, and now he is ensnared in a serious dispute that is likely to eventuate in a malpractice lawsuit and perhaps the loss of his medical license.[1]

When I attempt to draw Dr. X back into stories of his childhood, he grips the armrests of his chair, whitening the skin around several dark pits that mar the backs of his hands.

What are those? I ask, as if I don't know.

Dermatological, he snaps. I told you. I wash up a lot.

We both know he's lying. The last time I saw that particular "dermatology," I was reviving an overdose. I'm doing more and more of that lately. Everyone is. Narcan in the medi-kit, that's the standard now.

The session ticks past the three-quarter mark. It's too late to be opening wounds. Now is the time to close them.

I don't think you're getting it, he continues.

---

1. I have not attempted to influence this outcome, as I believe the loss of his license would be a useful development, as it would at least increase his compliance with the requirement of First, do no harm.

Getting what?

My wife wants to kill me.

Well, Dr. X, it does sound like you don't trust her to arrange your environment. But isn't there always hash to settle in a marriage? It's hardly grounds for homicide.

Here's the problem, he insists. It's the damned oven.

An oven doesn't seem so problematic.

For my sin of minimizing, I receive a disquisition on ovens. Apparently his wife wanted to restore the house's original oven, something called a "beehive," which was in such disrepair, it could only be salvaged at great expense and apparently significant risk to life and limb. His, I mean.

And she made me--

Made you?

She absolutely insisted. I had to triple the death benefit on my insurance. You'd have to be a moron, he wound up, using a tone that suggested I might be among that class of persons, to fail to make the inference.

Surely you've heard of something called divorce? She might avail herself of that option and avoid a jail term.

He's shaking his head. Murder is real to him, but jail terms aren't. They rarely are, to middle-class people.

Besides, I add, the insurer won't pay out if you die under suspicious circumstances.

She'll make it look like an accident.

Have you taken precautions?

What should I do? Put a lock on the bedroom door?

I'm not in the business of advising on home security, Dr. X. Sometimes minor problems just seem more pressing when we don't want to deal with other, more disturbing things.

I've no idea what you're talking about, Dr. Sanger.

You're a surgeon, I say. Let me be plain and direct just as you are at your best, with the knife in your hand. Your relationships suffer from your actions, which are hasty, impulsive, and not always realistic. This acting out includes an affair with your decorator, with whom you have reversed the roles of your marriage so you can for once play the role of contemptuous superior, an attitude to which you were all too distressingly subject as a helpless orphaned child.

Abruptly he rises and quits the room. I've cut close to the bone, too close.

So that was how Chuck saw me. My clothes, my studio, my mutts—all had served only to reinforce his contempt. He hadn't even liked my boots.

Next I found a sheaf of notes typed on the reverse side of various documents. Some were expectable business correspondence addressed to Benno: utility bills, offers for discounted subscriptions to magazines like *Psychology Today*, *JAMA*, and *The Psychotherapist's Home Companion*. Others, though, were home-décor-related—and addressed to the CEO of Lana Pura.

Why was Benno reading Lana's junk mail?

Clinical notes (FOR FILE):

Altogether Dr. X strikes me as a competent person functioning at the limit of his capacities. He remains prey to the sadness of his lonely childhood, when he must have pined for a family to which he might securely belong.

It is well-known that feelings of boredom and emptiness are defensive responses to overwhelming fear. These defenses marked our sessions, which were excruciatingly boring and empty. To me, I mean. He himself seemed not to mind.

His defenses are durable. For instance: His array of beepers functions as an extension of his perceptual apparatus, a way to involve himself--remotely, therefore safely--in others' lives, and in this way, he can participate in intimacies from which he is otherwise painfully excluded. He makes a world around himself--but strangely, compulsively, haphazardly.

The beepers also ensure that he is never really alone, a prospect that, since he feels alive and substantial only in others' approving presence, must frighten him deeply.

When frightened, he flees--another defense. Once, when I was obliged to cancel a session at the last moment, after he had arrived in the office, he simply turned and left. The next session proceeded as if nothing had happened. Far from it: I fear I lost whatever small trust he had dared to place in me. He became increasingly polite, reserved, and considerate. He arrived and left on time; he paid his bill promptly. Once established, his distant coolness served to maintain this mysterious and strangely lulling homeostasis. I could not break through despite making numerous attempts.

Interpretations, when I felt bold enough to offer them, did not result in improvement. On the contrary, his paranoid anxieties only increased. He took to posting anonymous reviews of other doctors online.

Of me, he wrote nothing. I did check, compulsively, resenting the way his paranoia had infected me. I felt entirely at his mercy. I resented that, too.

I continued to urge him to renounce surgery. When I mentioned that I had a duty to warn the hospital if I thought he was a danger to anyone, he shrugged me off. My duties were not his concern. Having exhausted one approach, I tried others--flattery, persuasion. With his medical experience, I said, he would be in a unique position to participate in his wife's booming textile business. Why not get out of surgery, with its heavy responsibility for the lives of others, and apply his organizational talents in this other, less fraught arena?

At this point he missed a session. My calls transferred to voicemail, and the line went abruptly dead. I couldn't even reach his beeper.

I kept his hour open, though, just in case he changed his mind. For six weeks, as I waited for him to arrive, I observed myself and the effect his absence had on me. There was only one notable change: Ever since meeting Dr. X, I have been unusually haunted by my wife's death. I have dreamed of her repeatedly. I have relived, over and over, the day she died. With his departure he has trapped me in amber, this Dr. X.

What is this amber precisely? It was the Fourth of July. April had been visiting her brother in Connecticut, and I had gone to pick her up. I was pulling onto the road to the farmhouse when I saw them. Wearing a straw boater, Henry was riding beside April on a tractor. April, who must have heard the car, glanced over her shoulder and blessed me with her smile. Oh, that smile. What I wouldn't give to be so blessed just once more. There was a huge noise, a flash, and there my life ended, and someone else's began.

The last thing I saw was Henry's boater, its brim singed black, floating down to rest on the grass.

I grew confused in the wake of the accident. It was a long time before I could feel, again, the difference between holding a woman and healing her. It was years before I trusted myself to accept a woman for long-term treatment. I never remarried. Even now, I hardly date. The solitude suits me, as it turns out. I tend my practice and April's plot at Grove Point, and the marriage goes on, strangely enough, in imagination and memory.

With all this quiet work, I thought I had laid my ghosts to rest. Somehow Dr. X had brought them back. To be sure, they *were* my ghosts--but were they also yet another symptom of *his* problems, a message about the danger in which he believed himself to be? My fresh preoccupation with losing April could be a clinical indication, some clue relevant to Dr. X--but what?

In the seventh week of his absence, as I was about to assign his abandoned hour to a new patient, Dr. X called out of the blue and asked to have his hour back. I accepted his overture. I also gave up my rumination, thrusting April, the carbonized memory of her, into one of my psyche's dark outbuildings. As it turns out, there are quite a few on the property.

Come back, I urged him. But let's proceed differently. This time around, your treatment will include your wife.

Again the account broke off. But there was still one more document, a final set of notes.

Détournement

People sometimes call us "shrinks." It's derogatory--of us, our patients, the therapeutic project. We're denigrated as wielders of undue influence, professional gamers of the mind. Nothing could be further from the truth. As our patients will tell you, we are distinctly ridiculous in the clutch. There's a reason Freud sat behind the patient, kept himself out of view.

My orientation is different. I see myself as a creator--of dilemmas, contradictions, paradoxes. Situations. Breaks in what my patient perceives as reality. Patients struggling to reconcile a new perspective with their old ways can, and often do, discover opportunities to be different--more authentic, more real, more alive. At least that is the hope.

With Dr. X I had my work cut out for me. He'd arranged his life in such a way that opportunities for such reversals hardly ever arose. He was orderly and coherent. Dealing with him was like grappling up a sheer rock face.

Some of the resistance was familiar and expectable. A doctor in another doctor's office will naturally fight to avoid becoming a patient, sensing a lack of control, an unaccustomed loss of dominance. Metaphorically Dr. X wore his white coat all the time--a dangerous situation for anyone. It is a fact insufficiently acknowledged that people are routinely crushed by their wardrobes.

My task was to engineer his prison-break. But first I had to find him in his prison.

Let me be clear: I only wanted to help.

But to do this I broke a rule: *I left the consulting room.* I allowed myself to be drawn into a situation, hoping to create a therapeutic Situation.

An orthodox end--to effect a cure--sometimes does justify unorthodox means.

But I underestimated a great deal: my distractibility, my stupidity, and above all, my collaborator. I failed to grasp that my accomplice, Mrs. X--whom I hoped to make my dupe--not only shared my interest in Situations but was the better artist of them, at once bolder and sharper, more detail-oriented.

Her methods are opportunistic. People are often glad to give up the burden of agency, and so she hustles the world into the exact shape she wants. She does this so quietly, so naturally, that it is easy to lose control. As I write this, I fear lapsing into self-justification and excusing myself from responsibilities that were, in fact, mine.

But I am getting ahead of myself. Let me try to say simply what happened.

On the appointed day, the day on which I planned to stage my Situation, Mrs. X arrived in a black limousine with a driver doubly concealed, thanks to tinted sunglasses and the car's smoked-glass partition. She shoved the door open, leaned out, and beckoned me into the deep back seat. She had considered my comforts right down to the bottle of chilled mineral water in the holder, the shining glass full of ice that she had set out for my use. I would be lying if I did not admit that these luxuries felt good, as if I were being rewarded for having passed an obscure test. At the same time, I was uneasy. I kept thinking of that stupid child, Edmund, seduced into the wardrobe by Narnia's wicked White Witch or, more precisely, her ample supply of Turkish delight.

But I was at the top of my game, wasn't I? Too old and wise to fall for appeals to infantile impulses, wishes to eat or be fed? To be treated--with treats? Surely, I was beyond all that. After all, I'd been analyzed!

Pride goeth. It always does. In the interest of building up her trust, I even allowed myself to be injected with her--what to call them? *Serums*, I suppose, though I prefer the Burroughs-esque word for it, *junk*. Which is exactly what it was: a bit of manipulative theater that effected little beyond making me feel vaguely dizzy and unreal, and discoloring my skin at the injection sites, leaving me with the same spots I'd seen on her husband, my patient. Also in the name of trust, I permitted her to move a large sum of money from their joint account to one she opened in my name, which she intended for me to use after I helped her to execute him. That was her plan, to kill him. He'd been correct about that, and I'd failed in my first duty--to heed him, to listen.

Now my plan was to stop her.

We zipped past scraggly clumps of beach pine. The engine purred; her pricey fizzy water tickled my nose. Through the window the sun shone brightly, but the car's air conditioning ensured that the heat remained distant, abstract, theoretical. I thought of April, the explosion that took her, the heat of that July day--all of that was theoretical now, too.

Lana had shown me the revolver and allowed me to inspect the chamber. It was empty.

Our route was northward. I didn't recognize the road.

Eventually we pulled into a strip mall fronted by a weedy parking lot. The building was shut like a betrayed face, metal blinds rolled down over the large windows. A long-legged dog was stretched out half-asleep in the shade of an awning. She led me into one of the storefronts; there was a litterbox odor. She turned on the lights. Before me was a massive bank of refrigerators. I was startled by the sight of several millipedes hurtling across the floor.

Even bugs have to live somewhere, she teased me. Maybe you're not cut out for this.

Maybe, I said.

Better that she should underestimate me; she would not imagine that I intended to foil her.

I sank into a dilapidated office chair, one of several scattered around the room alongside plastic-topped worktables holding desktop computers. In the corner, a makeshift kitchenette--a sink, a microwave, cupboards, a dorm fridge. On one of the tables I set my briefcase containing the laptop on which I have been writing this file.

She placed an extension cord on the table.

In case you feel like working, she said.

I had told her I was writing up her story as a case study for publication. Narcissists like the idea that they're at the center of every story. She was no exception. Though they want to be exceptions everywhere else, no narcissist is ever an exception to that.

On the far side of the room was an air mattress. She flipped a switch and air hissed into the bladder, plumping it. Beside the bed was a large cupboard from which Lana retrieved an armful of bedding.

My very own, she said as she set it on the mattress. Lana Pura, Extra Plush Egyptian cotton with a pharaonic thread count. Make yourself at home.

Winking, she grasped at her shirt, slipping a shiny button from its hold, widening the stretch of visible flesh.

You haven't slept, she said, until you've slept with Lana Pura.

Would sex with Lana be part of the Situation? Or was she trying to unbalance me with desire, stoking it with glimpses?

I smiled, acknowledging the offer.

I'm joking, she said as she buttoned up. You don't need to wince.

Let me be honest: Deceiving Lana has been a strain. I'm losing track of everyday things--time, space, objects. From one of the fridges, she removed a silver shaker and two coupes. She poured clear liquid from the shaker into the coupes and handed one to me.

To blunt the edges, she said. This cold chain business is good for more than just my chemistry experiments.

Cheers, I told her. The drink was cold, strong, and redolent of juniper. What chemistry experiments? I asked.

With a little liquor in her, it was easy to get the story, though I confess I followed little of it. The gist: To synthesize her materials, which she sourced from all over, she needed to keep the constituent parts cold en route.

But enough of that, she said. She must have

seen my eyes glaze over. My chemistry days are long behind me, it's true.

Tonight, she said, rising, we'll have a light supper, and then in the morning, after you've had a good sleep, you can take a look at the files.

The files?

You think I am going to bring you all the way to Quarry Lake and not give you something to do? The factory is in desperate need of a general practitioner.

I imagine machine accidents, emergency amputations.

You must know I'm not trained for that. I'm a psychiatrist.

You'll have an assistant, a nurse who can take care of the basics. Most of what these people need, you really can provide. Advice, a guiding hand, the ability to do ordinary things like order tests and prescribe antibiotics and vitamins. You'll stay, build trust, lend stability.

Stand in as a father, I said.

Don't you do that anyway? This is just fathering with more than words and a prescription pad, though prescriptions will be part of it.

A manipulator's trick: playing to strengths I considered my own.

Lana--

She shushed me, pressing a cool hand to my cheek.

Dear Simon, I know how it looks from the outside. Here I was, parachuting into a therapeutic intervention far riskier than anything I've ever contrived and well beyond the risks that are commonly accepted in ordinary practice. But this was no ordinary Situation. Simon, I have always believed in your capacity to sense these things, to intuit the true history behind the mask. I trust that you, of all people, can see my good intentions. I know I've let you down, but I hope to atone with this report. Consider it a tribute to your trustworthiness and your skill. A belated tribute--for which I am sorry. My admiration was never as full-throated as it should have been.

34

New Year's Day, 2008

I wrestled the Halsey house diorama into the station wagon and set Simon's packet on the passenger seat. I turned the key in the ignition. The engine coughed and shuddered.

It was seven in the morning. Anyone with any sense was sleeping—so no one would notice my first stop: Simon's office. Where I intended to tuck his packet back where I found it, beneath the tarp. And then I'd go to Phelps, ask him to look at the diorama. He'd be at his desk, filling out forms and checking boxes, taking advantage of the holiday quiet.

Chuck had spilled the secret of our affair to Benno. I had recognized myself in that case history. Who else might do the same? Would Simon? *Had* he?

How well had I known Chuck anyway?

And then there was the question of how Benno went from being an ordinary therapist who held sessions in his office to a practitioner so unorthodox he not only made house calls but also rode in Lana's limousine, engaged her in unusual cash transactions, inspected her weapons, and involved himself in her plan to kill Chuck. He intended to outsmart Lana and somehow rescue Chuck—but he didn't seem at all like the right guy for *that* job. He was an armchair superhero at best, jumping at millipedes and dreaming of clinical *détournements* like Bobby French with a medical degree. He would be no match for worldly Lana.

That night of the pig party, what was Benno doing in that house?

I was panicked, full of questions. I'd finally scared myself, sliding that knife across my arm, letting the blood drip on the flokati swatch. My arm was still sore where I'd cut it, and I tugged my sleeve down over the wound. Whatever I was doing, I couldn't keep doing it alone. I needed familiar things—colleagues, an office, a water cooler, a glugging coffee pot. I needed someone to advise me on my mess before it got any messier.

I needed Phelps, goddamn it.

The engine's hum dropped to a lower register. *Allons-y.*

35

When I pulled up to the station, Owen and Fiona were standing in line at the Sleeping Dog, their bikes chained to the rack. Fiona's face was wan in the shadow cast by the awning. They both looked in need of strong coffee and greasy food. Bare-armed in a muscle shirt, Owen was sporting a tattoo so new, it was still flushed pink in the water margin. I waved at him, who waved back, the essential small-town pantomime that maintains ties, but loosely.

The bikes' orange safety flags fluttered.

Hey, I called out. Can I get a hand?

They hurried over, and I swiped us in with my access card. Together we wrestled the diorama into the deserted lobby, where I propped my unwieldy package on the counter and tried the card on the inside door. Nothing. I made a mental note to talk with Phelps about that and rang the bell. Then I rang it again. Had I misjudged Phelps in his workaholism? I had a vision of him asleep in his bed, tucked into starched white sheets beneath a little-boy-blue coverlet, dreaming the self-satisfied dreams of the too-clever-by-half.

Shit, I said.

Owen raised a hand: Wait.

Fiona said: You wouldn't still have them, would you?

Owen dug in his pockets until he came up with a clutch of keys on a ring.

I can't run into Norman today, Owen whispered as he handed the keys to Fiona. Just give them back when you're done.

Why doesn't he have them already?

He hasn't kept track of a single thing since his girlfriend had that accident.

Right. Wendy Teller was on Norman's mind. Security wasn't.

Fiona and I angled the diorama through the door and down the stairs. In the basement, everything was just as it usually was, badly lit and echoing, pervaded by a strong odor of carbolic. But the floor felt tacky, and a handful of plastic cups, evidence of the prior evening's celebration, littered the floor by the door.

The lights flicked on. Fiona gasped.

I suppose I should have warned her. The glass-fronted cabinets were filled with the usual things—instruments of bodily investigation, bottles of alcohol and trays of tools, thick reference books, microscopes, empty jars, specimen cups. In the corner a dirty rubber apron hung halfway out of a container marked BIOHAZARD. It's a lot to take in.

You get used to it, I said.

Maybe you do. Jesus, Cookie.

We plunked the Halsey diorama on a slate-topped table. I'd worked fast, and the model, now two stories high, came complete with bloodstains. Mine, of course. Added, as I've said, for verisimilitude.

Phelps materialized in the doorway, hands shoved deep in the pockets of his slacks. Norman loomed behind him, eyes rolling in their sockets. No wonder he hadn't chased Owen for the keys. He didn't look like he was chasing anything but personal demons, all night, every night.

Norm, I said. What are you doing here?

He shrugged. Phelps said: Protocol.

I opened my mouth to say something, but Phelps cautioned me with a discreet headshake.

I introduced them both to Fiona and talked them all through the details of the diorama. Inside I felt numb, as if I were talking to a group at the Roach, sipping box wine and contemplating symbols, not standing around in a place where dead human bodies were opened and explored in the name of justice. As if my lover hadn't been one of those corpses. As if the scale model in front of us were not a representation of that crime, about which I now knew quite a bit more than I had before.

As I spoke, Fiona, seated on a low wheeled stool, began rolling toward the cabinets.

The chimney seems more central than ever, Phelps observed, peering at the diorama.

You mean architecturally? I asked. Mentally I set myself beside him, trying to deepen his absorption by becoming absorbed myself.

Phelps pointed to a tiny figurine pasted to the dollhouse floor—my recreation of Chuck's shabti. He asked: What's this?

We found it in the wall, between the joists.

Between the joists?

Go ahead, I said, handing him a pair of tweezers. It's just tacked, it'll come right up.

Phelps took the tweezers and squinted at the diorama, muttering angrily as he attempted to pick up the tiny figurine.

Been a while since I've seen the eye doctor, he said.

While Phelps struggled, Fiona was quietly and systematically trying each of Owen's keys in every lock.

At last Phelps managed to seize the figurine with the tweezers. He lifted the tiny object and turned it in the light.

It's from ancient Egypt, I said. Or it's a pretty good fake.

You found this *in the wall*?

A larger version of it, yes. Why?

I have a theory, he said.

Let's hear it, Norman said.

Phelps jabbered on about forensics, paying special attention to the bloody footprint on the wall by the window. He included fresh details: a kicked-out screen, a ladder in the attic giving easy access to the roof. Behind me, I heard a file drawer sliding softly shut.

And the DNA analysis? Norman asked.

Inconclusive, Phelps said crisply. The victim's DNA was found in the room, of course. There was a lot of blood, even with the fire. But at least some of the blood belonged to someone else.

You can't burn a whole human body that fast without accelerant. It's impossible, said Norman, pinching the bridge of his nose under his glasses, which looked like they had not been cleaned in days.

You can if the fire burns hot enough, Phelps replied. You can get a really hot fire if you manage the physics right. Something burns in a tight space, it needs just enough oxygen, and if there's a way to route the heat, focus it, well, then you're cooking with gas, excuse the pun.

Phelps reminded me of Harry, his obsession with combustion. Behind me, Fiona was rustling papers. The two men, intent on developing their explanation of the crime scene, ignored us both. I felt like a child in the presence of conversing grown-ups: seen but not heard. Not even seen, really.

Don't forget about the dental records, Norman added. The

whole body did not get burned. Not quite. We even know the manufacturer of his false teeth.

False teeth?

I willed myself to look blank and dumb. Neutral. Nonreactive. *Ish.*

Here's the thing: Chuck didn't wear false teeth.

But if the dead man at the Halsey house wasn't Chuck, who was he? What happened to Chuck?

Phelps uncoiled from his chair, one hand pressed against the small of his back, and groaned: Isn't today supposed to be a holiday?

Auld lang syne, Norman said.

As we say in English, Phelps replied, that's enough for one day.

36

The New Year's sunshine didn't last. By noon, rain was clattering through the downspouts. Lulled by the noise, I was drowsing when the doorbell rang.

I heaved myself up and hustled to the peephole. Simon stood nervously on the steps, pressing himself beneath the flimsy awning, his hands stuffed into the pockets of his barn jacket. I buzzed him in. When he appeared in the hallway, the dogs rushed out to greet him.

I shouldn't be here, he mumbled, the dogs circling excitedly around his knees.

Yet here you are.

Twin pink spots appeared on his cheeks.

Sorry about the welcoming committee, I added, hauling the dogs back. Why don't you come inside? Since you're here. There's coffee. It's even fresh.

My tone was light, but I was uneasy, unsettled by the morning's revelations, and unprepared for a visitor. In the kitchen Simon took a seat at the counter. I looked at him sidelong and saw his frown. We were both tense, staring warily at each other as the coffee brewed. I found spoons, napkins. I brought out two clean mugs and filled them.

He reached into his pocket and withdrew an all-too-familiar envelope held shut by an all-too-familiar rubber band. As he set it on the counter, the band snapped.

Mindlessly I spooned sugar into my coffee, worried that I might snap, too.

Your pancreas must be in good shape, he said.

I set the spoon down. Outside, the rain was letting up. Sunshine arrived in the kitchen like a belatedly remembered name. I gestured toward the envelope.

So?

I'm breaking a silence I ought to keep. But it's not like it's top secret. The author was thinking about publication.

I waited. He didn't know that he was only arguing with himself. I wasn't sure I wanted to be the one to break it to him.

It's a case study of, basically, a home renovation, he continued. The patient's presentation suggested the pathology was expressed in the construction.

Well, that's rich, I said. I mean, given your Slocum sofa trauma.

You're not wrong, Cookie. I think you can sense that the wound is still fresh. But life goes on. In its messy way, he continued ruefully, life goes on.

His vulnerability showed up in the tilt of his head, the half-smile he gave me. Newly a widower, he was picking up the pieces, taking care of the dull and necessary tasks of bereavement, investing them with his particularity.

Au travail. I reached for the packet. What exactly had Benno written? Not that it mattered—the false teeth on the corpse were dispositive. We had the wrong victim, and also, most likely, the wrong perp. Someone had killed someone else in that white room—but the victim hadn't been Chuck, as much as I still grieved him, making the killer unlikely to have been Harry, which had been my bigger worry.

Cookie? Simon prompted, interrupting my tumbling thoughts.

I'm not sure what I can add. No one will be astonished to learn that a home renovation sent someone into therapy.

But you're an expert, he said.

Simon—

I do have an ulterior motive. You've probably already sensed that. I've been invited to a professional meeting next month. And I'm supposed to discuss this case material. When I proposed the topic, I was nowhere near prepared to comment, and with Wendy's death—well, it's been hard to focus. Partly I'm just tired. But what I really need is a specialist. Someone who knows about renovations and what they do to a marriage.

I thought, then, of Wendy, angrily slicing lamb in their cheerful Cinzano kitchen, throwing back mouthfuls of bad wine before hurrying out to meet her lover and leaving me with Simon as if he were a child in need of a babysitter.

She was—had been—holding their shared life together. I could see that now. But then the spider had dropped to the counter: She wasn't in control of everything. In fact she was spread thin. Too thin. An accident waiting to happen.

We should have stopped her, I said.

Cookie, please. There is—was—no stopping Wendy when she had a wild hair. When she had an idea of how the world should be.

I flashed on a memory of Chuck opining: *He who truly loves the world shapes himself to please it.* If he had tried that *Felix Krull* baloney on her, she would have laughed in his face, and rightly so. I wished I'd done as much.

Cookie, Simon prompted, hauling me back into the present. Earth to Cookie.

So where is this nerd conference? I asked.

North of Boston, at Quarry Lake.

Quarry Lake. In New Hampshire, just over the Massachusetts line: a place so remote, you could only get there by funicular, unless you were willing to brave the tangled mountain road—or if you had a friend like Harry, who had his own ways of getting up there on hot nights. A place full of secret histories, in the form of cars and other large objects rolled for decades into a pit filled with water to a depth too great for any retrievals by police. A place where evidence went to die.

Sounds lovely, I said. A local junket that won't break the bank, and no jet lag either. When are you scheduled to speak?

Two weeks. Time's tight—

Listen, I interrupted, pushing the envelope back to him. I don't need to read this.

I'm asking as a favor.

You don't understand. I don't need to read it.

But that's impossible. It's unpublished. No one has ever read it.

Look, I said. I found it when I painted your office. You left it out. You hadn't locked it up.

The way I locked up other things, like the supply cabinet? Perhaps you also felt free to peruse my confidential patient files?

Those files were locked away.

You checked the drawers, too?

Those were *locked*. They stayed that way. But the case study—

—was sitting out, on the desk.

Like an invitation, I said.

So much like, he muttered, as to be.

It would be easy to fight about this, I said.

But also, he sighed, a waste of time, which we don't have.

I nodded, relieved. He'd spoken my mind.

Since you've already done the reading, do you mind telling me what you think?

Once upon a time, a husband and a wife fell out over a home renovation. Happens all the time.

Yet for this patient, Simon replied, the prospect threatens. As if it would destroy a lot more than his marriage.

As if marriage alone weren't punishment enough.

Simon looked at me sharply.

Sorry, I said. That cut too close.

Tell me more about this troubled marriage, he said.

I cast myself back to that first meeting with the Halseys. In my imagination I was standing awkwardly once again in their cramped galley kitchen, buttoned up against the cold and wondering where all the appliances and countertops were supposed to go, imagining something where there was nothing. Or where nothing merely seemed to be. Where there was just a wall.

Explaining the house's weird layout to Simon, I said: It's unusual to find a building that has been constructed over an older structure, but it happens. It's like finding a medieval crypt beneath a sixteenth-century church. Such things exist, but they're rare. It's the sort of thing no one knows about until there's a gut renovation, which is a huge undertaking.

Stressful, Simon said.

It does have a certain logic. You have to go back to the studs to find the bones of the structure, the foundation.

You like your bones up front, he said quietly. You like to know where the supports are, how the loads are balanced. The renovation you're talking about—

I said: The clients *had* wanted to keep their old beehive oven, just like Benno wrote. I advised the couple to build around it. Otherwise they were just adding complexity and expense, with no real gains, functionally.

I'm surprised you'd recommend that.

I'm no purist, Simon. Authentic beehive ovens are also authentically inefficient. The heat flies up the chimney. Which was in terrible disrepair to begin with.

He tapped the case study: Just as it was in these pages. What happened next?

The husband saw no need to spend the money, but the wife wanted to restore it. It's a status thing. You could rise a few notches on the social ladder with an object like that.

She wanted the real thing.

As do we all. What are you driving at, Simon?

You don't understand what goes on in a marriage.

Here I had to bite my tongue: Wendy had condescended to tell me exactly the same thing.

Let me put it bluntly. These two people were a single unit, one big self. They shared one mind, one vitality—

That's ridiculous, I said. They didn't even share a bed.

How would you know that?

Besides, I rattled on, Chuck had asked *me* for oblivion, not Lana.

So the guy in the case study *is* your client.

Who got paid, I said, is all I want to know.

These enmeshments often end badly, he replied gently. I see it all the time. So let's go on, just for the sake of argument. The guy in the case study is your client, and one day, the poor guy's found dead. No sign of a struggle.

He was found dead, I said. But there had been plenty of struggle.

I saw the news reports. And the wife's whereabouts?

Currently unknown.

As are Benno's.

You don't imagine Benno and the wife rode off into the sunset together, do you? I asked.

Well, that's pretty much what Benno suggests. But the Benno I know—

He paused.

He's a *moral* person. Mostly.

Mostly?

Not everything in that case study is true.

I don't understand why you're telling me this, Simon.

Because sometimes we can't see important things about the people we think we're closest to, okay? These were your clients, Cookie. You worked for them. But how well did you *know* them?

I had asked myself the same question.

Why do you ask, Simon?

Haven't you figured it out? This guy, this Dr. X—

Chuck.

Right. Chuck. Or whatever his name was. Cookie, don't you see? He was a *fake*.

My head spun. I couldn't think. A fake what?

I said: Benno said the guy acted fake because he was an orphan. Is that what you mean?

We're talking about a medical practice, Cookie. People are licensed and even, occasionally, monitored. Did anyone check with the licensing board to make sure this Halsey character actually was who he claimed to be?

I wouldn't know what the police checked out. I did get a call, though, right after it happened. The caller was one of *your* patients. Martha Benton. She visits your office. I saw her there all the time while I was working.

Martha? Martha *Benton*?

She was pissed off about something.

What else is new.

Something to do *with Chuck*, I said.

Simon passed a hand over his face, as if clearing his mind.

Maybe she knew he was a fraud. Benno certainly thought he was. But nobody goes to a psychoanalyst to talk about a beehive oven. If his bizarre presenting issue means anything at all, it has to be symbolic. It has to stand for something else.

Like what? I asked.

Like the guy's problem with reality. You can't cook *actual* food in a three-hundred-year-old beehive oven. You can't do brain surgery—or any surgery at all—and be out of touch with reality either. Sooner or later, the lie comes back to bite you.

And someone gets hurt, I said. The insight stole my breath. I remembered riding with Chuck in his car, cresting the hill at speed with the lights off. He could have killed us both.

I still don't understand why Benno would send you the case study in the first place. Why write about *this* patient, and why send it to you?

Maybe the guilt had become unbearable.

But Benno had nothing to feel guilty about.

I wouldn't say that about Benno, or anyone else in this business. It's a rare practitioner, he added quietly, who doesn't have blood on their hands.

My head buzzed with my own unconfessed sins—my involvement with Chuck, my equally combustive history with Harry. In memory, BLAST FROM THE PAST! screamed by me, and even now, I felt the scorch.

37

Sometime between our last Facebook exchange and the arrival of the news in my feed this morning, Erica slipped away. I got the news through Facebook—where else? The facts were thin on the ground, but I could make out the broad outline of what had happened. All those little notes, and then all those weeks of silence—all that time, she'd been unraveling.

People whose names I didn't recognize posted to her page: *Dear Erica, To my Darling Lost Friend.* From their lamentations I gathered that whatever trouble she was in, she'd been in it for a while. Her friends wondered less about her than about those in her immediate circle, asking not *Why did you do it?* but *Why were you not more closely watched, when you were so deeply loved?*

Overdose, I concluded. Another one. Lately my feed was filled with such notices.

I remembered the questionnaire she'd forwarded, the one I'd failed to pass on. Should I have? Would that small gesture have prevented this outcome? The bad luck she'd promised me—it wasn't just mine. Hour after hour, new posts appeared on her wall. She'd had so many friends, a huge social circle. Online, anyway. And it had proven to be no protection at all.

~

I WAS still keeping secrets. I hadn't told Simon about what I'd discovered at the morgue—the news about the false teeth and what it meant—and I hadn't said a word, either, about the extent of my involvement with Chuck; nor had I come completely clean about my extracurricular activities in his office, since I still hadn't mentioned Harry's visit.

Harry. Somehow he was mixed up in this mess. Had Lana co-opted him, too? Had she convinced him to take out a hit on Chuck? And then, in the heat of the moment, had he become confused and killed the wrong guy?

While I was monitoring the posts on Erica's page, I got an alert: Someone had left a new review on Chuck's profile. But before I could read it, I was distracted by a clatter, pebbles from the sound of it, against the window by my desk. I shifted the curtain. Fiona dismounted from her bike, kicking her Doc Martens to keep the hems of her jeans free of the chain, and hoisted a tote bag over her shoulder. A long cardboard tube poked out from the bag.

I rose and stretched, listening for the noise of Fiona's key in the lock. After the news about Erica, I was keenly aware of how good it was to have her in my office, in my life. Owen, too, for all his faults, had his charms, which were not unrelated: He was a wild card in all ways, and that could be enlivening as well as infuriating.

Inside Fiona shrugged out of her jacket, extracted the tube from her tote, and set everything on the worktable. I reached to close my laptop, hoping she hadn't noticed that the browser was open to Chuck's MedGrade page.

Haven't you turned off that Google alert, Cookie? Never mind, come over here. Wait till you get a load of this.

My attention was caught by a swaying movement high in the trees outside the window. The woodchuck had climbed to the top of the pear tree, which was too young and spindly to support him. The tree swung wildly, back and forth. I held my breath, and the woodchuck tumbled from the tree, end over end. The woodchuck waddled off, an early pear gripped in his mouth.

Fiona pushed a sheaf of papers toward me.

She'd pinched a folder from Phelps's lab. Between the manila covers was a stack of documents related to Chuck's death: photocopies of statements, photographs of the crime scene, and the coroner's report, which I skipped over, my heart thudding. After that came a series of legal documents, *pertaining to the matter of Benton v. Halsey*.

Turns out that, at the time of Chuck Halsey's death, he was embroiled in a dispute with a business partner, Fiona said. A real doozy.

The partner? I said. Martha Benton certainly fits that bill.

No, the dispute. I was up all night reading. This Martha Benton was covering his ass and getting nothing but grief. Why wouldn't she be pissed? It isn't *me* leaving those comments about Halsey on MedGrade. But I think I know who *is*. Or *was*—since the comments stopped after he bought it.

Hmm, I said.

According to this document, Fiona continued, every time he screwed up a surgery, she had to drop everything and scrub in, just to save his bacon—and their business. It was a big job, that salvage operation. They're in a high-stakes profession. Every gig's a high-wire act.

She paused, pressing her palms flat on the table. I kept my face neutral. I still had no idea where this was going.

Cookie, don't you see? She's ambitious, she's educated—and she was getting exactly zero credit for all the work she did, even as he collected legions of adoring fans. Why *wouldn't* she resent him?

You're saying she killed him?

I'm saying they were in a serious mess. One that could have provided her with a motive. Plus, he was using *my name* to make horrible accusations about *her*.

But why would he use your name?

Why not? I'm just your flunky, right? Disposable.

You're not my flunky.

I know that. But to him, I was.

I remembered Benno's case study, what he'd said about Chuck's effect on other people. Perhaps Chuck really did inspire homicidal impulses in everyone he met. For what he'd done to Fiona, I wanted to kill him myself.

I said: Did you ever get that stuff from the Preservation Society?

Fiona tapped the cardboard tube.

I struck gold, she said. Here's the document you wanted. The map of the Halsey lot.

I slid the tube over and pulled off the cover. The document was an original, not a photocopy. Part of one edge flaked off as I handled it.

This thing looks ancient, I said. How did you convince them to let you take it?

Let's just say I have a talent for persuasion.

And free train tickets, and—

She settled back in her chair and folded her arms across her chest.

I've done my bit, Cookie. Now it's your turn.

What's that supposed to mean?

I'm not stupid, and I'm not blind, either. The Halsey job has ended. Ingloriously, yes—but it is over, apart from the dunning. It's over for everyone, Cookie—except you. You're still in it, with that stupid diorama, and you're letting yourself get dug in deeper every minute. You can't bring him back, she said.

A silence unfolded between us that might have lasted a moment or a thousand years. I could lose her if I didn't make room for her now, acknowledge her smarts and the fact that she actually cared enough about me to use them on my behalf.

There's more to it, I said.

And I talked. I opened up, sort of. I told her what I could about Chuck, Benno, the case study, the conference coming up at Quarry Lake. But I kept it light, and I left out many details, including the ones about Harry.

What about Teller?

I can't possibly be his concern. He's grieving.

He is also now completely free. And he is interested in *you*.

I don't think so, I said.

A death can release a lot of energy, like a dam breaking. He keeps showing up.

It's too soon, I said, thinking of that near-miss in his vestibule. It seemed like a lifetime ago. But he did keep showing up—and he'd invited me to join him at his nerd conference at Quarry Lake.

Surely you can handle a grieving psychiatrist.

I couldn't handle a controlling neurosurgeon.

The guy was a psychopath, she said quietly. You don't have to put your life on hold in his memory.

Teller irritates me.

Chuck did, too, at first. Don't you remember?

The atmosphere shifted: A cold, dry air seeped through the windowpanes.

Or maybe that was just me, mummifying.

Go on, she said. Get out there. Find the trouble that's looking for you.

38

So that's what I did. I *got out there*. I went to *find my trouble*. After Fiona left for the day, I picked up the phone and invited Simon on a shopping trip.

If I'm going to finish your office, I said, we need to see about some fixtures. I have a line on a shipment of some great old stuff that's absolutely appropriate for your needs.

My needs.

Your decorating needs.

He snorted. Well, I guess it's time I finally overcame my Slocum sofa trauma.

We took off the next day, skipping the freeway in favor of the beach road down the coast. The storm had blown through that morning, and Simon's face was in the same constant subtle motion as the open water I now and then glimpsed, silvery and dark, from the road. If he would just let me have my way, I'd do his whole office in those grays: quicksilver, fog, rain. All the noncolors of New Preston.

Our destination reared into view. Noisy, drafty, chaotic, and dirty, the Salvage God was everything the Pottery Barn was not, five thousand square feet of high industrial chic housed in a rehabbed red-brick warehouse. We would find no Slocum sofas here. What we would find, though, was anyone's guess: vintage claw-foot tubs, fireplace mantels, rescued millwork, encaustic tiles, old-time radiators, ancient hinges and doorknobs. My heart beat faster. My foot grew heavy on the gas. I fishtailed into the lot and screeched into the first empty space I could find.

Simon's complexion had gone chalky. I killed the engine.

Sorry. I got excited.

Your driving skills, while obviously terrible, are not the problem.

You're afraid. Is the Slocum sofa on your mind again?

Don't shrink me, he snapped.

You call this progress?

He folded his arms across his chest.

All I'm saying, Simon, is that it happened a long time ago.

So?

So let's not get hysterical.

Scowling, he reached for the door handle. I followed him as he made his way, huffing and puffing, across the parking lot.

What's wrong? I asked, though on some level, I knew.

Isn't that a bit rich, he snapped. You're accusing *me* of getting hysterical?

I had learned at least one useful thing from Benno's case history: Some people can be pushed to action if you irritate them enough. You just have to be willing to be irritating.

I was willing.

Inside the warehouse, a clerk handed me a clipboard and yammered about policies. The merchandise was heavy, cumbersome, often fragile. *You break it, you buy it.*

As we wove through the aisles, I handed Simon little things, porcelain doorknobs and brass hinges. He was polite, but he clearly didn't share my enthusiasm. I was starting to think our outing would not last long, or yield much, when his attention snagged on a box of vintage fireplace tiles. He pulled out a handful and began to arrange them on a nearby tabletop. He reminded me of Cinderella in the ashes, sorting her lentils. Maybe that's just what grief looks like, sometimes.

Benno let me down in the end, he said, his voice distant and detached, as if he were dreaming out loud. He continued: I'd asked him for a recommendation to support my application to the Institute for Depth Psychology.

The IDP!

You know it?

It's only housed in one of the most architecturally significant buildings in Boston.

Well, it *was*, he said.

Simon was speaking of recent history: This magnificent place had recently changed hands. The new owners had scandalized preservationists from Boston to Atlanta by eliminating the building's historic details, right down to the fireplace tiles, interior doors, and radiator covers, all of which were sold off to the highest bidders up and down the East Coast. Even the Salvage God was rumored to have acquired a box or two, but I didn't feel like sharing that with Simon. It might have traumatized him all over again.

The tiles on the table before Simon were several sets all jumbled up: dark-blue majolica tiles with songbirds in relief; deep-amber tiles with a fleur-de-lis pattern; and a celadon group, all polygons.

Once upon a time, Simon said, the IDP was *the* most prestigious place. Benno had trained there himself. I knew my application wasn't strong. I tended to put analysts off. You can imagine how hard it was to ask Benno for this favor. But I did, and he'd agreed. When my analysis with Benno ended,

I presented myself as a candidate. Strangely enough, it seems he never sent the letter.

I tried to imagine a younger version of Simon arriving at an imposing Boston brownstone with all his hopes pinned to a letter he'd trusted someone else to write. His pants would, of course, have been a touch too short; his hair, too long by a similarly awkward interval. He'd have loped down the neighborhood's broad avenues, peering into windows. Which were not so different from the dusty ones now hanging above us, tags dangling. Had he admired them, or had he sneered?

You didn't deliver the letter by hand?

Don't act so stunned. I was young. Trusting. Stupid.

As were we all, I said.

The possibility of finding a piece of Simon's history in this place of loss and ruin made me suddenly, vertiginously sad. I sank onto a tufted bench.

Maybe this was a bad idea, I said.

In my line of work, Cookie, there are no accidents. We're here for a reason.

How did it all end? I asked.

Instead of a teaching analyst, I was assigned a trainee no older than myself who was also a total rube and, by the way, an idiot. We spent the next six months debating whether I had delusionally imagined my analysis with Benno—a mystery that could have been resolved with a simple phone call, which my new analyst refused to make and would not allow me to make in his presence, either. He was absolutely sure *I* had an idée fixe.

Oh no. That's quite a bind.

Exactly. He believed we'd find the problem's roots in my childhood. Which I'd already gone through, pretty exhaustively, with Benno. At least I was on familiar ground. Sometimes we talked about a woman I was seeing. I'd had sex with her exactly twice, both times followed by cold luncheons at her place, where I always felt intensely inferior.

What was her name?

Cold Cuts, if memory serves.

He grinned. He was funny.

I said: Some things are better served cold.

Not that thing. Can you imagine how weird it was, opening up to a man whose presenting delusion—well, not that I was in a position to judge, but still—was that *I* was delusional?

He thought you were a faker. You wanted to be an analyst like him, but he was the one with the credentials.

Credentials were about all he had.

He stepped back from the tiles and wiped dust from his hands.

We were both young and insecure, he said.

Trusting, I said. Stupid.

He was a bit further along, that's all.

I hoisted myself off the sofa and took Simon by the elbow. We moved into the bathroom fixtures section, where porcelain tubs were laid out in orderly rows, like hospital patients tucked into beds.

Did you ever ask Benno about it?

By the time I felt ready to confront him, the conflict just seemed immature. The field was moving away from psychoanalysis. There were all these promising new drugs. With Benno, I decided to bury the hatchet.

In my mind's eye, Lizzie Borden raised her axe. She was wearing a nurse's uniform.

What in the world just crossed your mind?

Nothing, I said. Forget it. Go on.

We kept things cordial. But it's always hard to know where you stand with a guy like Benno.

With a guy like you.

Simon smiled, acknowledging my point in a way that was intuitive without being intrusive. I felt a rush of warmth toward him.

Well, obviously, there's a reason therapists wind up with certain patients. The distribution isn't random. Anyway, no one knows where Benno's gone. But he left me the case study. His notes *must* contain a clue. I'd still love to hear your opinion.

A phone rang somewhere in the warehouse. Two rings, three.

I'm a decorator. What would I know from psychology?

You play dumb, he said quietly. But you aren't.

What I don't understand is why the client didn't simply divorce his wife. Obviously the problem was not in the house. It was in the marriage.

Bog-standard family dynamics, he said. Someone always makes a favorite of someone else, usually by excluding a third.

Oedipus, schmoedipus.

There are other permutations. You're always saying renovations can go wrong, Cookie. Your last job went wrong in the worst possible way.

Worse than you know, I said.

Simon whistled.

I told you the bones of the house had been covered up. The chimney guy discovered a void behind a wall. A little room that had been erected years before, when they covered up the fireplace.

Your chimney guy.

He's just a guy, I said defensively. A guy by the name of Harry Deluca.

Simon gripped my arm. His face had gone white. *Did you just say Harry Deluca?*

Well, I wouldn't have, if I thought you would manhandle me!

What do you know about Harry Deluca?

I peeled his claws from my arm.

He's an old friend. No one special. Don't touch me like that again.

Simon drew back. Embarrassed, I stared down the line of ancient tubs. The light had shifted; they'd lost their hospital aspect. I thought of my mother, standing alone and flanked by sarcophagi in her imagined Valley of the Kings.

I had dealings, once, with a man by that name, he said.

What dealings? I asked, rubbing my arm.

Never mind. Tell me about this Harry and the chimney.

The chimney was a mess, but they wanted to keep it despite the trouble and expense. It needed an absurdly complex ventilation system. That was Harry's responsibility. As you know, the husband was a doctor, too. And he was in trouble—

Simon's phone rang. He looked at the screen.

Shit, he said. I have to take this.

But I haven't finished—

Next time, he told me.

I recognized the order in the promise: *Don't be a nuisance.*

Anyway, he said, without looking up, there is the small matter of patient confidentiality.

Outside the sky darkened. There was a long, low rumble, and then the sky emptied in a downpour. As I stepped out from beneath the dripping awning, Simon pulled me back so hard I cried out. A white truck rushed past. Our reflections widened in the dark windows. Behind us loomed a powerful, broad-shouldered figure, familiar right down to the tool belt at his waist. I'd recognize the silhouette anywhere. But when I turned, there was no one.

39

The storm followed us back to Simon's office. The car was stifling, the air heavy with the damp funk of Simon's wet wool sweater, and Simon was silent, tense. He parked. Before I could say anything, he popped out of the car. The last I saw of him, he was jogging toward the building, holding a circular from the Salvage God over his head to keep off the rain.

My phone flashed a message: *There's been some trouble with your mom*. The afternoon's prospects narrowed to a single point: across town, at Tomlins Manor.

On my way, I texted back.

I won't lie: I had no business on the road in my present state—confused by Simon, worried about Mom, distracted by the drama unfolding around Chuck's reputation and questions that had been raised about his death.

All I saw, at first, was a bump on the shoulder. As I approached, the bump took on shape and contour. It was a body, a human one.

I pulled over and reversed. I got out of the car. Drivers whizzed past, and I walked in a hot wind of exhaust. No one else stopped, but then I'd had enough experience of human callousness to recognize the ordinariness of that fact, the absence of noticing, of simple observation.

But then there was nothing to see, nothing but blacktop unrolling against a blue sky. Whatever I'd seen, it must have been a mirage.

I returned to the car. Nothing felt real. My mind had slipped a gear. My email pinged with a fresh alert. I thought: I really ought to turn these off. It was time to move on, to forget about the things I'd done in the grip of whatever had gripped me all those nights in the white room with Chuck. I knew this, and still I lingered, parked on the shoulder, loading Chuck's MedGrade page on my phone. I found three new reviews, each a single outraged line:

He nearly ran me over in his new white truck!

He nearly drove me off the road!

He nearly killed me in the parking lot!

Who complains about a neurosurgeon's *driving*?

Hadn't Harry just purchased a new white truck? And didn't Simon know something terrible about him?

As I read, a new entry appeared: *Stop it, Martha. —FD*

Cars blew past, one after the other. Anyone could come hurtling around the bend and smack me right into next week. My heart was pounding, and still I sat there, waiting. For what, I don't know, I'll never know. For someone to take care of me, once and for all—the scream of brakes, the thud of metal, the end of everything. Which I wanted and did not.

I dug in my purse until I found a vial and shook from it a small white tablet, the last candy the town druggist ever offered me. The label was so old the dot-matrix printing had nearly disappeared, but enough remained to know this was no sugar pill, no horehound drop.

I swallowed the pill. A warmth spread through me. My

breathing became slow and regular, my heartbeat settled back into my chest. I inched off the shoulder, signaling into traffic.

SHE'S BELLIGERENT, the nurse told me. I was at the front desk, trying to make sense of everything, or anything. Apparently she was manic, hurtling down corridors at excessive speeds, overusing her fragile joint while sweeping at the legs of other patients with her crutches. At lunch she'd insulted another patient, making her cry.

It seemed that my mother had been hiding her medications in a potted fig tree by the nurse's station. No one noticed until all the leaves fell off.

I stared at the denuded plant. How could anyone miss this?

Long story short, the nurse said, your mother has been under-medicated for a while.

We're considering chemical restraint, she said.

You're always considering that.

She stared at me.

Don't do it, I said. Not yet.

I signed myself in and rubbed my hands with instant soap from the dispenser. The ritual soothed me, or maybe it was just the pill I'd swallowed earlier. Floating down the corridor, I decided to keep the visit brief—no more than fifty minutes, like a therapy session.

Mom was sitting by the window, in the armchair, and picking at her lunch, a scoop of mashed potatoes and a bowl of pureed carrots. On television, a young woman was singing and strumming her guitar. The volume was painful. When she stopped, the talk show host said she was only eighteen.

Marketable youth, I mused, pulling the remote out of its wall socket.

Child exploitation, my mother corrected me.

I pressed a button, the noise diminished, and my mother snorted: Saints be praised.

She gestured at the girl on television, her mouth rounded into a silent O.

We all know what her mother is like, she said. Don't we, Cookie?

Don't feel bad, I said. Nobody here remembers much from day to day.

Some people are like mists, she said quietly, sending her gaze out the window. They form and re-form, and seem so real, and then like the mist, they just burn off and blow away.

I'm sorry I haven't visited.

I suppose you heard about the plant I killed? You know, I did other bad things, too.

The speed limit was unposted, I said.

Oh, Cookie. I knew you of all people would understand.

Mom, I said. Do you remember that little Egyptian thing I showed you?

Provenance is everything, as I suppose you know.

Is there anything else you can tell me about it?

The antiquities market has always been awash in fakes. But in the Gilded Age, you couldn't shake a witching stick around here without whacking an adherent of some form of . . .

She paused, searching for the words.

Of. *Of.* Shit, Cookie. Don't get old. Of—

Mom—

Occultism! That's it.

Did Russell Warren—

Give her forty whacks? Cackling, she slapped her good leg.

What? Mom, that's ridiculous.

Don't you get pissy with me, Cookie. It doesn't suit you.

Mom, listen. Did Russell Warren have Egyptological interests?

Oh, that Russell Warren. I remember him from high school. Used to iron his shirts, I did.

My heart sank. My mother was getting dotty. To hide her problems following our conversation, she had resorted to filling in the gaps, assuming Russell Warren was someone she used to know. An old flame.

You don't know him, Mom. He'd been dead for decades by the time you were born.

He liked them with a little starch, she said.

My father on a Sunday, buttoned into a shirt that smelled of ironing, of starch and laundry soap.

You want to iron his shirts? God help you, Cookie. Your father was *a married man.*

I said: You don't have to accept or understand.

She mimicked me: *You don't have to accept or understand.*

Her sharp, appraising glance reminded me of Lana.

AT HOME I cracked a window and rested it on one of my mother's shabtis, a sturdy Horus-headed bit of faience that made Simon's window-propping Rolodex look positively modern. I had the afternoon off, with nothing to distract me from my goal, which was to spend some quality time with the plans Fiona had unearthed.

When I'm doing my thing, when I'm comfortably *into it*, I look like I'm just holding a piece of old hardware—but I'm actually feeling my way into another world. These days the pace of life is faster, and we have more time-saving gizmos, but our basic motivations remain the same. We all want handles that turn, valves that open. There are only so many ways to vent a chimney, even one that's built into a strange little void in the wall. The plans had to contain some clue.

I unrolled the document a few crumbling inches at a time. The ancient paper was so fragile, whole strips of the top edge had already fallen away. I struggled to decipher the notes, which were written in a cramped eighteenth-century hand. Outside, thunderclouds were massing. I flicked on the lamp as a gust spattered rain against the screen. A folded square of paper slipped to the floor. As I unfolded it, a corner fell off. The rest was brittle but intact. It was a pamphlet advertising a series of religious tracts—works of "theosophy," which rang a bell, had my mother mentioned it?—issued in 1859 from a Boston publisher. On the inside back flap, there was an advertisement for a builder, one Jack Morse, who had a number of talents: masonry, carpentry, plumbing. "Jack of All Trades," he styled himself. Below that tag line were the letters JVM, set within a circle. The very same trademark I'd seen in the secret chamber of the Halsey house.

What had Mom told me about these people—the holly rollers, as she'd called them, with unintended wit? Theosophy was an offbeat religious movement based on the little that was known about ancient Egypt and filled out with fantasies that had grown around those kernels of understanding. To the theosophists ancient Egypt symbolized lost ancient wisdom whose authority could be used to subvert New England's buttoned-up ethos. This pamphlet trumpeted the discovery of a cache of figurines, whose secrets would be divulged at seven in the evening at an unfamiliar Boston address.

It must have been quite a party.

Had Warren counted himself a theosophist, too?

That's when it hit me: In colonial homes, the beehive oven was typically set in the largest chimney, which was almost always at the center of the house. The earliest New England settlers were frugal, especially with firewood; they kept the home fires burning in the heart of the residence. The Halsey place was no exception, despite the later expansion by Warren. In fact, the chimney was so central to the structure that it abutted a significant, load-bearing beam, a beam that could not be moved without threatening the whole. That tiny room must have been a leftover from the earliest history of the residence. The Egyptian-themed decoration may have come later. Perhaps it had been a ritual space, devoted to evenings of table-knocking, Ouija-boarding, séances. People have done many things in closets. But more to the point: Any weakness in that chamber would compromise the integrity of the whole house.

Any weakness. All that wire and Semtex. I grabbed the phone.

Listen, Simon. I have the Halsey plans. There's a—

I couldn't bring myself to say it.

—a flaw, a *structural* flaw, in the center of the Halsey house.

There was certainly a flaw in that marriage. Are we talking more than metaphor?

When your house burns down around your faulty chimney, which someone has constructed to burn as hot as possible within a secret recess lined with dry tinder, that's no metaphor. I can't believe I *missed* it.

I'll come to you, he said. But there's one more thing. While we were out gallivanting, I got a call. The cops found the tape.

The tape?

Of Wendy's accident. A traffic camera caught some footage of the vehicle that ran Wendy off the road. The police traced the plate to a vehicle belonging to someone whose name, unfortunately, I recognize. As will you.

40

I texted Phelps to say that I'd be at the station in an hour. Then Simon showed up at my door, and I texted again: *Make that two.*

Coffee?

Bourbon, he replied. Neat.

I set the bottle on the table with two glasses. He poured a finger into each of them, then topped his own: two fingers. And a half.

You got some news about Wendy's accident? I prompted.

He downed half his glass and refilled it. I can't talk about that, he said. It would prejudice the investigation. Which is something I should not be talking about, either.

Your secret, I told him, is safe with me.

Safe?

As houses.

He said: I'll drink to that.

We touched glasses.

I set the coroner's report—the file Fiona had nicked from the morgue—before him on the worktable. I still hadn't been able to bring myself to read it. Simon lifted the folder, sifted the papers. He pulled out a blurry photograph, a close-up of something.

You didn't tell me what was in his mouth. Do you know what this is?

Leaning in, I could just make out the image of a small round object that looked similar to my mother's gift from years before, the one I'd lost with Harry during the speed trials at Black Rock.

My breathing grew ragged.

That's an obol, I said, as casually as I could.

A second image showed the reverse side and, like the coin I lost, it was embossed with three netchers and a tiny bee.

What's an obol?

Grave goods. Survivors left coins in the mouths of their dead as payment for the ferryman, to get the deceased across the river of death in the afterlife.

How in the world do you know this?

Well, I went to school, I sneered. I took a class or two in art history.

He said: Seriously?

My mother was an art historian. Is, rather. With a specialty in grave goods. Though she herself is still alive.

Oh? He raised an eyebrow, but I sensed something practiced—professional—in his curiosity.

This isn't your consulting room. I'm not going to talk with you about my mother.

Guilty as charged, Simon said as he cast his eyes down the page. According to the report, he continued, reading, the coroner found the obol under Chuck Halsey's tongue. His false teeth not only survived the fire but also showed signs of blunt trauma. As if they were clamped shut and the obol had been pushed straight through them.

I flopped backward, letting the sofa absorb my shock.

So Harry had been the culprit after all. Even if whatever

he'd done to the chimney was merely a botch and not outright sabotage, only Harry could have been in possession of my obol; and only Harry would have known to leave it as a calling card, secure that his violent message would find me sooner or later. The stain from the aglet attested to the presence of heavily worn boots at the crime scene. Those decrepit boots in Lana's kitchen must have been his. He must have been hiding in the white bedroom that night, lying in wait.

But then how had he managed to kill the wrong guy?

There's something I should tell you, I said.

Simon swiveled to look me straight in the eye. Oh?

Chuck didn't wear false teeth.

What?

You heard me.

I couldn't bring myself to look at him, though I felt his eyes on me.

That's a pretty intimate thing to know about someone.

Yes, I said. It is.

If Chuck's not dead, where is he? And who went to the morgue?

Right, I said. These are my questions.

He ran a hand over his face.

Look, Cookie. There's something I should have told you, too. Benno's been in touch. He's going to that conference I told you about. The one at Quarry Lake.

WE WAITED at the station, in the lobby. The door crashed open, slamming against the opposite wall. Phelps shambled in, blinking at the bright light, his eyes wobbly as two indifferently boiled eggs. As he walked us downstairs to his office, I relayed as much as I could of what I knew about the conference and its link to Chuck Halsey. Phelps's head was spinning, literally spinning, as he strode ahead of us down the corridor, trying to take in everything I was saying. And then Simon chimed in, mentioned something about Benno.

Chuck's shrink, he said, nodding.

And possibly Lana Halsey's partner in crime, I said.

Or her friend, or her employee, Simon interrupted, catching my gaze in his.

Right, I said. Score one for Simon, who had just cured me of my habit of compulsively throwing shade on Lana.

We don't really know the precise nature of the relationship, I said.

Unlocking his office, Phelps said: You had to know the investigation would come back to Harry Deluca eventually, Cookie.

I shook my head, still unwilling—despite all the evidence—to believe it. Simon frowned at the mention of Harry's name.

This guy is all over the place, he said.

More than you know, Phelps said sadly, motioning us to take seats.

Does this have to do with the tape of Wendy's accident?

He nodded.

We traced the license plates, we found the truck, and all the signs point to Harry as its driver.

Harry?

Jesus, Bill, I shouldn't be hearing this—

Simon interrupted: Nor should I. Harry and I have a history.

You do?

Unconnected to Chuck's death, he said.

Phelps's eyebrows were, by this point, halfway to his hairline. We'll have to talk more about that, Simon. Privately, of course.

I burst out: Simon heard from Benno.

Phelps turned to Simon. You got a call?

Not exactly—

He's giving a talk at a meeting, I blurted. Next month. Up north, at Quarry Lake.

Quarry Lake?

It's a conference for psychiatrists. He's been missing for months, but now he seems to have come right out of the woodwork.

Phelps looked at each of us, nodding slowly, in a way that reminded me of my father when he hatched a plan my mother would hate.

He roused his laptop and rapidly punched the keys. I saw the conference website pop up on the screen, followed by the schedule.

I'll make arrangements on the ground, he said. Get the local boys involved. If Lana Halsey's implicated herself in any funny business—and I'm not saying she has or she hasn't—they'll want to know about it.

What are you saying, Bill?

It could go like this, he replied. You'll go to the conference with Simon. Enjoy yourself. Take the famous funicular. You could give a talk, provide us with some cover.

I'm going to give a talk?

Yes. About your crime scene dioramas.

The prospect of presenting my weird sideline to a room full of psychiatrists does not thrill me, I said.

Someone always cancels at the last minute, Simon cut in. It wouldn't be hard to get you on the program. You should present your *Acorn Studies*. They're very psychological.

Oh, for God's sake. You mean I'm going to be giving a talk on something like "Reading Rooms: What Forensic Miniatures Tell Us about the Psychology of Crime?"

That title is perfect, Simon said.

Perfectly awful, I said.

And while you're there, you can tail Benno, Phelps added. See what you can see.

As if I didn't have clients, a business to run, the dogs to look after. As if I could simply up and leave, like those women of grand action who sprouted like crabgrass all around me—Lana Halsey, Wendy Teller.

You want me to help you run your little sting operation.

Technically, yes.

I'm not a cop. Surely this is illegal.

On the contrary. Laypeople get themselves involved in stings all the time. Think of the honeypot who reveals the affair to the aggrieved party.

I would have preferred not to think of that, actually.

Phelps pulled out his phone and swiped at it with fierce concentration.

You just don't want to force anyone to commit a crime during the operation, he continued. Because then it's entrapment and the whole case gets thrown out on a technicality.

I'd forgotten that a trial was the desired endpoint. On TV, the bad guys go straight to jail; in my own life, they tended either to disappear or to die. Justice was a whole new world.

Simon interrupted: You've probably been over this a thousand times, Bill. But did you check the guy's history? Do his transcripts match his résumé?

Why do you ask?

Now and then, I see an impostor in my line of work. I wondered if you considered that possibility.

We've considered *all* the possibilities.

Simon nodded. He was working Phelps, giving him control, letting him know he wouldn't press.

May I remind you that this—I gestured at the diorama—is still an *open* investigation? We can't possibly present this work to anyone until we've figured out who was responsible for the murder.

Phelps said: The Halsey case is technically cold. We're about to close the books on it. We don't have to worry about compromising our work here.

It's an ill wind, I said, as sarcastically as I could manage.

You can make your own decision. No pressure.

You're going to arrange for me to make a presentation at an international conference, ask me to spy on a dead man's psychotherapist, threaten to end the Halsey investigation if I don't comply, and you call that no pressure?

Well, that's not all you'll be doing, Phelps said.

What else, then, will I be doing? Infiltrating a maple syrup smuggling ring? Eating pizzas with the hockey dads?

Phelps cocked an eyebrow. It was a look I knew—arrogant, self-assured. He had something on me. I grabbed my bag.

Forget it. Just forget this whole stupid business right now.

Not so fast, Cookie. We suspect Lana's with Benno. If you give a talk, the conference will publicize it, and that might be enough to lure Lana out of the woodwork.

Are you kidding?

The question erupted from me, and a corresponding fear played on both their faces. Neither of them could be brave in the face of an angry woman, not even a creampuff nonentity like me.

You'll be perfectly safe. You'll wear a wire, so you'll be in contact with me and my boys the whole time.

You're going fishing, I sputtered. And I'm the *bait.*

41

Where Simon was bold—he probed, he interrogated, he convinced people to act as decoys in cockamamie sting operations deep in the granite heart of Nowhere, New Hampshire—I held back. My mother, too, had found me guilty of passivity. Yet I'd made a living from precisely this quality, setting aside my preferences in order to make space for those of my clients. I was vulnerable to anyone who might want to put a ding in my psyche. If only people limited themselves to that.

At the same time, I had to admit to some posturing. Styling myself a domestically inclined variation of a hard-nosed businesswoman like Lana Halsey, I had convinced myself that I understood my own weaknesses. That for all my passivity, I was the last person who would find herself triangulated between a married man and his wife. In fact, I had become one of those easy-to-despise women, a perpetual third wheel who was always losing her self-respect along with the panties she'd kicked under the bed.

Something had to change. No, someone.

That's when I got the call: Somewhere on a cargo ship in the Pacific Ocean, six containers had slipped overboard and could not be recovered. One of them was holding the carved teak daybed I'd ordered for that difficult client with the dream of the pool-house seraglio, the one who would only be content with sustainably sourced furniture from a microloan-financed Balinese woodworking collective with ties to a Hollywood up-and-comer.

Gorgeous how reality conspired with my wishes. *Magnificent* to imagine that damned daybed at the bottom of the sea. *Astonishing* to think that, a year ago, I would have proposed a fifty-fifty split, but that was back when I had an interest in sustaining relationships. Now I knew: That way was for suckers. I made the call, and then I made *the call.*

My client tried to shift responsibility, to claim that technically, since I'd brokered the deal, I bore some responsibility for the loss.

Yet she was the one who declined to insure it, as I pointed out.

Who the hell do you think is going to eat the cost?

Her shout watered my eyes. She was still shouting as I hung up.

She could dun me for it, if she cared that much. I'd just put the bills in the shredder.

While we were fighting—okay, negotiating—I'd missed a call from Bobby.

I've got a line on a buyer for the Lizzie Borden dioramas, he said when I got him on the line.

He named their price. It was a lowball offer. Very low.

It takes some balls, I said, to insult me like that.

I've got bills to pay, Cookie.

Welcome to the club.

The exposure will be good for you.

I told Bobby I'd think about it, but we both knew I was just getting him off the phone. I took the dogs for a walk, trying not to think of the chance I'd just turned down. I didn't need to make a killing. But I didn't see why I had to keep taking one loss after another.

SIMON'S OFFICE was my next stop. In keeping with my new damn-the-torpedoes philosophy, I'd given no advance warning of my visit, but even so, I was already slipping back into my old ways. In my purse was a people-pleasing packet of biscotti, the fancy kind, from the hipster bakery in the old mill. Atonement, in other words, for my sins, including the one I was about to commit.

The waiting room gave an orderly impression, calm and open, like a mind at reasonable peace. If my paint color, those shades of *ish*, had this effect had on me, surely it worked a similar magic on everyone who passed through. For all my shortcomings, I'd done a good-enough job with this place. I felt myself relax.

Simon looked surprised to see me, but he didn't say a word. He ushered me into the consulting room, his expression shifting between surprise and concern. We'd come a long way from that first meeting—the limp handshake, the awkward flinch.

What are you doing here?

I handed over the biscotti.

Sorry, I said. For showing up unannounced.

I owe you one on that score. So we're even.

Simon extracted a biscotti from the packet and sank into the recliner. I smiled to hear it squeak.

One of these days we'll have to replace that, I said.

Somehow I doubt you're here to talk about furniture, Cookie.

I want to know why you think it's a good idea to undertake an international sting operation.

Don't you think someone should get to the bottom of this?

Someone should. I don't see why it has to be me.

Heedless of the carpet, he swept crumbs from his lap, asking: You don't want a free trip to Quarry Lake?

I stared at him.

You've lost your mind, I said.

I want to do this, he said. I admit it's not exactly a junket. But don't you think it's possible to be too rigid about the rules for this kind of thing?

Love blinds us, I informed him, thinking of Chuck.

Ah, he said, in psychotherapeutic fashion. You are reluctant.

Don't shrink me, Simon!

All I am trying to convey, he said, is that the phenomenon is well-known. I'm not sure I should say this—

I snapped: It's not too late!

He frowned.

Listen, Cookie. I wasn't at the job site with you and Chuck. I wasn't at your Friday night meetings. There are things I'm simply never going to understand. All I know is what you told me of the affair, and whatever I could glean from Benno's account, which was one-sided, to say the least. But my point is, it's not for me to judge you, Cookie. It never was.

He did look apologetic, I'll give him that. But I was wary of that guy—the easy apologist. Usually they'd had a lot of practice.

I'm sorry, he said, if I gave a different impression.

A truck charged past, rattling with equipment. The noise echoed in my mind's ear like one of Harry's mocking laughs. I smiled uneasily, not wanting to accept Simon's apology but not wanting to reject it, either. Wasn't I supposed to be stronger than this, more independent and assertive? And here I was letting Simon and Phelps call all the shots.

The door thumped downstairs. Simon scowled, riffling the pages of his AT-A-GLANCE.

A patient?

I haven't scheduled anyone. That I can remember, anyway.

Someone pounded up the stairs and crashed into the waiting room, slamming the door so hard that Simon's door also rattled in its frame.

With a sigh, Simon set the calendar aside, straightened his jacket, and opened the door.

HARRY LOOMED in the doorway, his hands shoved in his pockets, his hair sticking out in all directions. He looked at once both utterly vulnerable and exactly as bat-shit crazy as I'd always suspected him to be.

Simon immediately positioned himself between us, blocking my view so I could only see Harry's dusty work boots, the laces brand-new but untied as usual.

So you did your time, then? Simon began.

Don't fuck with me, Harry growled.

Harry, I called out. Harry!

Surely whatever bad blood was between them, we could talk it out, like in therapy. Who knows how well it might go in this newly redone room, with nicer furnishings and calming paint. I was losing myself in this self-congratulatory line of thought when Harry leaned around Simon, squinting at me, and whistled through his teeth.

Well, if it isn't Cookie Cooke.

Simon spun around, and, pale-faced, he made a quick gesture: I was not to speak. He was right to want my silence. The rage came off Harry like a heat, blurring his outline. Furnishings and fresh paint were not going to solve Harry's problem. Conversation wasn't going to do it, either.

You might as well come in, Simon muttered, since you're already making yourself at home. Though after what you've done, I'm not sure I can still promise to honor my therapeutic obligation.

Harry's mocking echo: Your therapeutic obligation!

He hiked his belt and stalked into the room, claiming as much space as possible with his wide stance, his work boots crushing the pile of the carpet. When he leaned against the lintel and lit a cigarette, Simon's face twisted in disgust. Harry didn't notice, didn't care. He seemed at ease, as if used to Simon's presence even if he didn't like him all that much. Simon cleared his throat as if to speak, and that was enough to set Harry off. Now Harry was talking and talking, sluicing Simon with speech while shutting him up, going on as if this were his personal therapy session, as if he were one of Simon's patients.

Had he been?

Harry's story reprised the broad outlines of what I knew, how he'd gone back into the family business, working as a mason and "all-around chimney maintenance guy," as he put it, before his life "went down the shitter." As familiar as Harry's story was, I had trouble following certain parts of it, as he recapped important talks with lawyers and judges in a way that suggested Simon knew the parties involved.

Simon listened, his head cocked. He seemed intent, but without giving any hint of his response.

Coming to the end of his story, Harry ground his spent cigarette under his boot heel. My nostrils prickled at the odor of burning wool.

Harry, I repeated. The carpet.

Oh, he repeated, mimicking me. The carpet!

He winked at me. The wink was a power play, an effort to establish, in Simon's presence, an intimacy that excluded him.

Simon, I said, let me explain. Harry often works on my jobs. He worked with me on the Halsey project.

Ah, Simon grunted. He knew all this, of course. We'd talked about Harry before. But I wanted to undo the exclusionary move Harry had just made, turn the two-way into a three-way.

That job was quite the oddity, Doc. We found an ancient Egyptian doll in the floor.

Simon turned to me: A doll? Like the ones in your office?

A muscle twitched where Harry's jaw met his neck. Simon winced.

What do *you* know about her office? Eh, Doc?

What *are* you here for, Harry? Simon asked quickly, as if sensing his misstep. If you need a referral, he continued, I have plenty of friends who need a handyman. How about that? Work is good therapy—for all of us.

I've got more work than I can manage, thanks very much—and I'm no one's handyman.

My mistake. I still don't know why you're here.

I'm collecting a debt.

I don't see how I can help you.

Harry gestured toward me with his cigarette.

Why *is* she here?

She's my decorator.

Your decorator! Harry hooted. Then again, maybe you need one. No one would ever mistake you for Mr. *Good Housekeeping*.

I see you remember something about my marriage. Perhaps you also remember my wife? The one who drives her minivan, sometimes, over the Chepinoxet Bridge?

Harry spewed a long stream of foul smoke.

She goes back and forth a lot for a person with no business on that side of town, he said. But I guess we already know what she was doing over there with Norman Sawyer. You're still pretty pussy-whipped, aren't you, Doc?

Given your experience with women, surely you understand, Simon said evenly.

Can't live with 'em, nor without. Ain't that what you always told me? And you were right. I never got married.

He glanced at me. I'm sure my face said everything.

Not exactly, anyhow.

Good man. Smart move. You don't want to get into that sort of thing. Take it from me. Getting out is expensive.

Simon had shifted to a different register—chummy, conspiratorial, as if they were just two guys dishing on women. I felt myself fade into the upholstery.

"Good man," Harry mimicked Simon. "Take it from me." What a load of bullshit. Let me tell *you* what's expensive, he snarled. Five years in the slammer, that's what I call an expense.

Did you get any time off? Simon asked. I mean, while you were inside.

Good behavior's never been my jam.

Well, there we agree. You're impulsive. Even when you're doing something that will land you in hot water you do it anyway. We've talked about it many times. Our old friend, impulsivity. It's unfortunate, this character trait, but it doesn't make you incompetent to stand trial. Which is more or less what I told the judge. Isn't that why you're here? Because I came to that conclusion about you?

Harry scowled. Simon was right, and Harry knew it. Simon turned to me.

Harry thinks his jail term was my fault, he said. I was hired to offer an opinion on his capacity to stand trial for attacking a woman who tried to leave him. You broke her nose, you gave her a shiner, and you dumped her by the side of the road! Poor

Erica crawled half a mile in that condition before someone picked her up.

Erica?

Erica ain't never been any of your business, Cookie-Puss.

As Harry and I glared at each other, it all came rushing back—the unspooling westbound highway, the dusty red desert, the dank hotel room.

I didn't give the opinion you wanted, did I, Harry? Simon cut in. In fact, I didn't give any opinion at all. What you have to understand, Harry, is that to tell the truth—that you're a manipulative jerk with an anger problem—would not have helped your cause. I wasn't going to lie on your behalf. Silence seemed the better option. Apparently you disagreed.

He paused before continuing softly: I know you lost part of your life, Harry.

Harry cupped his ear, a loose grin playing around his mouth. I knew that look: Simon was approaching a line he shouldn't cross. I felt sick.

What's that, Doc? About my wife?

Your wife! What's that about *my* wife?

Harry, I cut in. For God's sake, we're ancient history—

You can't fool me, Harry. I know it was you, with your anger and your grievance and your ruthlessness—and your fucking monster truck!

Weren't you supposed to *help* me, Doc?

I'll help you out the window if you like.

Simon looked so fierce at that moment that I thought he actually might do it—might pick Harry up bodily and toss him through the window. Instead he picked up the phone.

Or perhaps you'd prefer a squad car?

Harry shifted position, and as he did, a pencil stub slipped from behind his ear and fell to the floor. As he reached after it, I saw something—the stiffness in his musculature, the way he stretched toward me, the tendons straining at his neck. These details came into focus like a language I'd been trying to decipher, a message I should have understood from the first transmission, years ago, at the trailhead in Nevada.

The phone fell, clattering, from Simon's hand as he leapt up.

That's enough, Harry, he said, in a voice that was low and even. He raised his palms, a nonthreatening signal, but he kept himself between me and Harry, leaving a free path to the door.

Tell me where it is, Harry growled.

Your file contains nothing that would exonerate you.

Give me the file! I came here for the goddamned file!

Simon leapt, tackling him, and Harry's head smashed into the side table's glass top. I winced as it shattered. Grunting, Harry rolled to the floor. Simon heaved him up and levered him toward the threshold. Blood ran down one side of his face. He staggered out, throwing me a last, wild glance. His intentions, whatever they were, would not be changed by a mere flesh wound. Sooner or later he'd return, and he'd get what he wanted come hell or high water or shattered coffee tables. He stalked out, thumped down the stairs. The door slammed in the foyer.

The fire alarm began to whoop.

42

Simon yanked me to my feet and dragged me into the waiting room. Smoke curled around our ankles and was rising up the walls. I popped my collar and breathed through it. On my way out the door, I tripped on the damned kilim.

Get out, Simon hissed.

That rug, I choked. Will be. The death. Of me.

If you stand here arguing with me, Cookie, the cause of death will be smoke inhalation. And stubbornness, let's not forget that.

Simon crossed the room and flung open a window. Coughing, he grabbed my arm and pulled me with him out the door and down the stairs. Thick smoke was billowing from Lou's office. Lou was still inside, waving a throw pillow before an opened window. Flames licked at the drapes.

Simon rushed in and pushed past her, disappearing toward the back of the building, where the kitchen was. He returned carrying the tiny fire extinguisher that I'd stashed away for him all those weeks ago. He popped the safety and let the extinguisher rip. Lou rushed over, dragging one of her wing chairs. Simon moved to help her. There was a crash, and fresh air pushed into the stairwell; they must have thrown the chair right through the window.

I gripped the banister and felt my way down. A moment later, Lou was in the stairwell, too, reaching blindly through the smoke.

Come on, I told her, taking her elbow.

Simon shoved past us, swearing under his breath. Lou and I followed, Lou holding tightly onto me, her face ashen.

Outside we huddled in the parking lot beside Simon's minivan. The wing chair was shattered on the postage-stamp lawn. A fire truck arrived, and then another. As the firefighters made their way through the building, I watched their shadows through the windows.

Lou had a lot to answer for. The smoke-blackened shingling around her window would not be cheap or easy to fix. As for Lou herself, something was obviously very wrong. She was gaunt, and her pallor defied description. Foam from the fire extinguisher clung to her hair.

If you have another session scheduled, Simon said softly, you'll need to make a cancellation.

Simon spoke with the sort of anxious delicacy I associated with the investigation, sans anesthesia, of an abscessed tooth. This gentle shoptalk seemed intended to calm Lou. It did nothing of the sort. As she spoke, she only became more agitated.

I can't cancel, she said. The patient will kill me.

Surely you're overreacting?

No, she will. Kill me. You know she will. Don't pretend you don't. She was yours to begin with.

I remember. And I might still care how she's doing. How you're *both* doing, he said gently. What about you? How are *you* doing?

I'm fine, Lou snapped.

From a pocket she extracted a pack of cigarettes. She lit one and blew the smoke in Simon's face. He leaned back, letting the minivan take his weight.

Isn't it funny, Lou asked icily, how hostility begets more of the same?

He said: I don't want to fight.

May I remind you, Lou said, speaking in short smoky gasps. You turfed her to me. You turfed me your neurotic neurosurgeon.

Ah. This sounded familiar. I pretended fascination with the boxwoods.

Lou said: She comes to sessions and lectures me on the composition of cerebrospinal fluid and the proper way to train someone to remove another person's frontal lobe. Which is not with an ice pick, I'll have you know. Though the thought of a lobotomy occurred to me more than once—and not just for her.

Your countertransference is showing, Simon said.

So's yours, Mr. I Don't Want to Fight. Of course you want to fight. Good! Me too! And you contradict me to avoid the main point, which is that you could not deal with *her* emotional conflicts. Which says a lot about your own.

What should I know about her emotional conflicts? Simon asked.

A damn sight more than you do, Lou retorted. She's up to her eyeballs in trouble with her business partner. You know, the dashing neurosurgeon she's in love with? Whose mistakes she corrects? Whose messes she cleans up? Endlessly! Selflessly! Out of love, you see? And he doesn't love her back. He loves someone else. A person not his wife.

Sounds like your average telenovela to me, he said.

Out of "love," Lou went on, she covers his sorry, incompetent ass at work.

Simon frowned.

And now she's complicit.

In what?

In everything he did. Everyone he maimed. Killed.

Oh please. We both know she's trying to smear him. Hell hath no fury, and all that.

Lou smirked.

Your countertransference is showing, Lou said snidely. And now he's dead.

So: Lou's patient had a dead philandering neurosurgeon for a boss. Chuck—my philanderer, my neurosurgeon—was also someone's boss. Someone, as it turned out, who had plenty of reasons to resent him. And me.

Oh, Lou said, startled. She'd forgotten I was standing there.

Don't mind me, I choked, wiping my eyes on my sleeve. I'm just the decorator.

Lou stared at her watch, her pallor deepening.

She'll be here in five minutes, she said. I have to be upstairs when she arrives. But I can't handle her alone, not today.

You just had a fire in your office. You can't cancel her session?

Lou shook her head, a quick panicked refusal. No way, she said. I'm going back in.

She hurried back into the building and was stopped near the staircase by a fireman who was coming down. He enfolded her in his Kevlar-sleeved arms and shepherded her back out the door.

We pulled out fast, the minivan's small tires screeching, and the last thing I saw was Martha Benton in the rearview, mounting the stairs to the office.

43

Phelps's offer took on a shine. Recent events portended nothing good, at least in the near term. The longer term was not my concern. Not when I could still get out of town. Lay low.

Just before daybreak Phelps arranged a police escort to the New Hampshire border, where he was waiting in a squad car at a security checkpoint. He was brusque, all-business. His face expressionless, he hustled us down a flat-packed road until we reached an outpost, not much more than a trailer. As the sun rose, we followed him into a windowless room, where I was kitted out with everything I would need to present myself convincingly as a psychiatric conference participant, starting with a fake ID that identified me as Simon's wife.

In case anyone asks why you're sharing a room, Phelps said, handing me the card.

I stood there open-mouthed. Simon, looking pained, stared at the linoleum.

Next Phelps handed me a folder containing a set of printed remarks focused on the Lizzie Borden dioramas. These mostly historical comments, which he'd gleaned from the brochure from my exhibit at Bobby's gallery, were supplemented with a slide deck composed of stills of my work that he'd taken at the show. Phelps directed me to his laptop to walk me through the material. They weren't bad, these photos. Phelps had taken them to advantage, in tight focus with an artfully blurred background. In the photo of the diorama I'd made for "The Norwood Builder," even the tiny Penguin volume of stories by Conan Doyle looked crisp.

Looking at the pictures, my confidence surged. Maybe I was up for this adventure after all. I tucked the thumb drive in my hand luggage along with a ziplock bag full of additional gear, and then Phelps showed me the "wire" that he expected me to wear.

The receiver and transmitter were a single tiny unit that fit in a cavity under the inside sole of my right boot. The whole assemblage worked by a complex technology involving a satellite uplink and other bits and pieces that I didn't even begin to understand. We wouldn't be completely on our own, though. Phelps had assembled a crew of associates in local law enforcement, and they were standing by, ready to assist us. They had backup, Phelps added, from the feds.

Now don't look so shocked, he said. Lana Halsey's something of a known quantity around here, he announced. Turns out she's been making trouble for a while across the border, in New Hampshire, and she's come to the attention of the DEA. They're eager to move on her, but they don't have what they need. Yet.

He paused. Are you all right, Cookie?

The DEA? But she's a textile manufacturer.

Well, she has some extracurricular interests, Phelps said, pressing a fat envelope into my hand. Inside was a wad of cash.

To cover expenses, he said.

~

I HAD to close Ministry again. First up: paying the bills—or, as it turned out, arranging not to pay them. While Simon drove, I called the bank and convinced the manager to extend my line of credit, something he was glad to do in exchange for a promise, easily given, that I'd speak to his wife about designing their home theater.

Easy peasy, I lied, suspecting I'd be dead at the hands of some mobbed-up maple sugar mogul before I'd be required to make good on the promise. Just for kicks, I called the dunning service, too. As I listened to the phone ring, I was surprised to discover how little Lana Halsey's debt now meant to me. It was a nuisance, nothing more.

I called Fiona, who promised to take care of the Allǝns and check up on my mother, whose discharge date was looming.

You'll be back in time for that, won't you?

Oh yes. Wouldn't miss it.

But where will she live?

No idea, I replied. I guess we'll cross that bridge when we come to it.

Fiona sighed: Fail to plan, plan to fail. You can't just leave her housing situation unresolved.

She can bunk at my place, I said, if it comes to that. You've got the keys, you could get her in.

I suppose I could, but I'll tell you this, I don't think she'll be too happy about it.

On the contrary, I said. She'll be overjoyed to leave rehab. I doubt she cares very much about where she lands.

Did you ever look at those documents from the Preservation Office?

I sure did. You'll never guess who the mason was.

You mean the guy who did the chimneys in the Halsey house and left his monogram on the wall in that little hidden room?

And the beehive oven. Don't forget that.

Don't keep me in suspense, Cookie. Who was it?

Vinnicum Morse, that's who. Lizzie's uncle, her father's nemesis, who had possibly also been her lover.

Well, I'll be damned, Cookie. So he built the Halsey house, too. Small world.

Small town, I said. See you on the flip side, Fi.

Simon tuned the radio to the local news and turned it up. A journalist was speaking outside Mass General, reporting on a rash of post-op deaths connected to Boston-area hospitals. *The acute responses were suggestive of allergic reactions*. The radio voice crackled with static. Simon shook his head, disbelieving.

Allergic reactions to what? I wondered.

To whatever junk painkillers they're prescribed on discharge. Though "allergic" in this case is really more of a metaphor.

His phone rang. He glanced down, frowned, and then silenced it.

Harry? I asked.

Good guess. He wants more than I can give him.

He always wants that.

Phelps was sending instructions and yet more equipment via FedEx to our hotel. Someone from law enforcement would meet us there. Simon flicked the radio off, and we drove on in silence. There was no traffic. There never is, once you get past Boston, toward Lowell.

Simon grunted, pressing a hand on his lower back.

You all right?

Back spasm. Occupational hazard.

Let me drive a while.

He pulled over and we switched positions. My thoughts unspooled along with the highway. I couldn't stop thinking about Harry and his involvement with Erica. It was hard to square my memory of that daredevil girl behind the wheel of her race car with the horrifying image Simon had provided, of a badly injured woman dragging herself along a road.

The recognition broke over me all at once.

Harry's a menace! He *should* be behind bars.

My realization was entirely my own. Simon had checked out. Asleep, he was imposing as a mummy—eyes shut, earbuds stuck in his ears, hands folded over his buttoned cardigan. I felt a wave of sympathy for Wendy, who could never get his ear even though it was for rent by the hour to everyone in New Preston. Here I had whole hours with him, and I could not bring myself to interrupt the solitude into which he'd disappeared with so much authority. He was his own slammed door.

The road was empty, the car quiet. Simon wasn't Wendy's problem anymore. Was he mine? Did I want that?

As we shot north through the morning, I rehearsed an apology to Phelps, something simple that wouldn't provoke questions.

My phone flashed: a text from Bobby.

I have your next commission.

A sick feeling came over me. How could I leave Chuck's disappearance uninvestigated? I'd already missed so much. By focusing on Lana's failures as a wife, I'd blinded myself to her successes as a schemer—including her astute awareness that my preoccupation with Chuck kept me usefully uninterested in what she was actually doing with her industrial fridge, her cold chain operation, and her new warehouse in New Hampshire. *Au travail.* I silenced my notifications, dropped my phone in my bag, and forgot every word of my fantasied apology. I had a job to do. The art world would have to wait.

44

The conference hotel was new, large, and so posh that, arriving at the foot of the mountain, a uniformed hotel employee emerged from a thatched kiosk to relieve us of our luggage and usher us onto the shining glass funicular. After Simon stowed his briefcase, sheepishly struggling with the dodgy clasp, we chose our seats and buckled ourselves in. Despite being embarrassed by his own accessories, Simon seemed pleased with the arrangements—the quaint mode of conveyance, the fresh breeze that blew into the compartment from an opened window. It was as if he'd forgotten all about the nature of our errand, the reason we were here in the first place.

At the last minute, we were joined by another uniformed member of the hotel staff. He slipped aboard just as the doors were closing, took a seat across from us, and shifted uncomfortably in the seat as if he were unused to something, perhaps just being stuck in an enclosed space with the hotel's guests. As the funicular gained the air, he raised a finger as if he'd finally made up his mind about his role and how he would play it, and he launched into a monologue about local attractions. As he spoke, he waved his arms to gesture at a spot down in the valley, where large boxy buildings were arranged around a parking lot. Ant-size cars were speeding in and out: The place was hopping.

You'll want to check that out, he said, glancing at me. There's some good shopping. Factory outlets as far as the eye can see. J.Crew, Williams Sonoma, you name it.

To him I was yet another wealthy middle-aged woman with a wallet full of credit cards and a bad shopping habit.

Look at that, said Simon, pointing in the other direction.

The early mist had burned off, and the famous mountain ridge was rearing up, identifiable from a million postcards. The sky was the color of an interior ceiling, flat and white. But the driving approach to Quarry Lake was clogged with traffic, a long line of cars and trucks edging against rusting Jersey barriers, no protection at all against a rollover, and the old quarry now full of water shining silver far below. A gust rocked the carriage. As we continued to climb, I glimpsed a distant stone finishing facility where tall cranes were hoisting huge loads and setting them down on truck beds. One crane lurched to a stop, and a huge gray container swung freely in empty space. The funicular slowed, then stopped.

The man in the uniform grunted: What the hell's going on?

We're new here, Simon said. Why don't you tell us?

As we dangled in the air, one end of the distant container sprang open, and its contents spilled out like candy from a ruptured piñata. Gravel poured down, kicking up thick gray dust. Simon, coughing, retreated behind his shirt collar. I found a Kleenex in my bag and breathed through it.

Another item—large, long—slipped from the swinging container. At first I thought it was a mummy, unrolling from its bandages as it fell.

Oy, Maria! shouted the stranger. I saw him run through a gesture, touching fingers to forehead, lips, and heart.

No doubt in response to our shocked faces, we got the whole story. Or at least his version of it. Immigrants had swelled the population of the town and taken up all the jobs. The newcomers were exploited, and when they got sick, they strained the already-burdened hospital system. So many died that it became customary to reserve spaces in the containers, along with the granite, in order to ship themselves back home for burial, which was all anyone wanted from this life apparently. They'd paid hundreds, even thousands to secure this passage for their dead. What we'd seen was one such shipment.

The man fell silent. I tightened my seatbelt, as if that made a difference, as if being more tightly buckled into my seat would save me from certain death, now or later. My fear was absurd; but then everything was absurd. The world was upside down; everything seemed inverted; were there not now bodies, actual bodies, falling from the sky?

The funicular lurched, and I glimpsed the hotel's entrance, a large rotating glass door. There were no more unscheduled stops, and we arrived within minutes. We scrambled out, and our companion disappeared through a service door to one side of the entry. Simon headed up the walkway, spurred by some inward motor, his beat-up briefcase dangling from one hand. I dragged myself along in his wake, my heart heavy with what I'd just seen, my suitcase equally weighed down by Phelps's gear, the wheels bumping over the gravel.

The hotel was imposing, all modern angles and darkly reflective glass. Every inch of the cavernous travertine lobby was polished to a high shine, and the space was outfitted lavishly with sofas upholstered in dark velvet and lit by glittering chandeliers. A fresh pine fragrance wafted from diffusers. At the front desk, we relinquished our driver's licenses. When the concierge, smirking, called me Mrs. Teller, I blushed.

He tapped at his keyboard.

The room isn't ready, he said.

But a box had arrived for us—Phelps's matériel. It would be brought to our room with the luggage. Meanwhile, we were welcome to make ourselves at home in the lobby. The pleasant nattering continued; we mimed our understanding and slipped away, settling ourselves into one of the expansive sofas, by a large window that gave on a view of the valley, though there was not much to see since the air was so clogged with dust from the quarry.

I think I just blew our cover, I said. Those IDs were not convincing.

I wouldn't worry about it, Simon replied. That clerk has met many conference attendees who arrive with fake IDs proclaiming a fake marriage. All we need to do is keep up the theatricals—so let us now indulge in some fake small talk. Tell me what you learned from your conversation with Fiona.

A waiter arrived and set out the coffee service. The whole story spilled from me: the trademark in the Halsey house's Egyptian room and its reappearance in the house plans, and how Fiona's sleuthing at the Preservation Society had turned up evidence that at least part of the house had been built by John Vinnicum Morse. JVM.

Those were his initials in the trademark, I said. He was Lizzie's uncle. If local legend is to be believed, he was also her lover. He had been visiting when the Bordens were murdered. But they were killed midmorning, and apparently he had left before breakfast.

Apparently? Simon asked, spooning sugar into his coffee.

The coroner noted that the cuts that killed the parents were long and deep, I said. Only a woodsman or a butcher can use an axe with that kind of confidence. Before he got into the building trades, Morse had been apprenticed to a butcher. The first chronicler of the case, a reporter for the local paper, said the father had been killed "like an ox in a stall."

Was someone trying to frame Morse? Simon asked as he moved to fill my mug. I waved him away. My guts were all acid.

He may just have been reporting, I said. People knew a lot more about death in those days. The immense force required to kill something. Someone.

People still know plenty about death, Simon replied. We just don't hear as much about it, at least not outside of courtrooms and psychiatrists' offices. Could Lizzie really have summoned that strength?

In a rage, maybe. But Vinnicum Morse had the tools and the know-how. That morning, he ate two pears from the backyard tree—

The one that was in your diorama.

—while the Bordens bled out in the parlor.

That's a self-possessed person, Simon said.

A practical man, used to carcasses.

Fond of pears.

I remembered my own pear tree, and the woodchuck that had fallen from it, end over end.

I still don't understand his motive. Why would he risk such a huge mess?

Some say Lizzie's father had concluded a business deal to protect his considerable heritable wealth, including the Fall River homestead. Morse might have been close enough to him—to her father, I mean, Andrew Borden; some say he was Andrew's one friend in the world—to have felt he might have a claim to the place. There had been arguments. But Morse had an alibi, and he didn't fit the script.

The script?

Of the domestic drama.

It *is* familiar, isn't it? The oppressed young woman who acts out her rage by killing her oppressors, good old Mom and Dad. But, Cookie, plenty of young women grow up in straitlaced circumstances and manage to avoid becoming parricides.

Morse is a wild card, I replied. He was Andrew Borden's bosom friend and possibly the one person in the whole world on whom Lizzie could rely as well. I imagine him as a person of action, not given to reflection or remorse. He'd do another person's dirty work—Borden's, Lizzie's—so long as he stood to benefit materially.

Simon stroked his chin. So, he said, adolescent separation gone horribly wrong can't be the whole story. The fact that there was no single explanation for what happened—that's what stymied the investigation.

That's what I liked about your show, he continued. How you managed to convey that no single story could be the whole story.

Outside the dust had cleared. The valley stretched below, shadowy and ancient, unspoiled apart from one long stretch that had been eaten away in rectangular bites, exposing an inner surface of white stone. Granite, destined for kitchen renovations all over New England.

Simon hailed a waiter and asked for the check. While we waited for it, he kept looking over my shoulder.

The shrinks are arriving, he said. Like ants at a picnic.

I thought these were your friends.

They are my colleagues. They're not friends, no more than your therapist is a friend.

Your analyst?

Your analyst is definitely not your friend. Neither is your pill doctor, if that's the modality you prefer.

You sound so bitter.

Simon replied: You don't know this world.

It was true, I did not know this world—but it didn't look so bad to me. Spilling onto the terrace, Simon's colleagues clustered in cheerful, back-slapping clumps of two and three, men in navy jackets and chinos, women in dark suits and modest heels. Here and there, a bright scarf fluttered.

Simon picked up his phone: I still can't get a signal.

Who do you need to call?

Are you kidding? Everyone I know in psychiatry is here. Someone must know how to reach Benno.

Right. For Simon, this trip had always been essentially professional. He was among friends here, or at least colleagues, whereas I was an impostor acting more or less on my own.

I looked away, hiding my disappointment. It wasn't just that I didn't want to be reminded of the work to be done. Newly single and clearly coming out of his grief, with his slim build and full head of hair, Simon would be an object of desire, while I'd be just another person he had to deal with, another hand tugging on his white coat. I hadn't counted on this, and I didn't like it.

On the terrace, a pair of young women dressed in polo shirts and khakis had set up a large folding table and were piling tote bags on it. Everything, including the young women's attire, carried a different pharmaceutical company logo. I followed Simon to the table and stood silently by as he confirmed our registration. Clipping his nametag to his shirt pocket, he asked if Benno Sanger had checked in yet.

Who's Benno Sanger?

Simon did a double take. He's not on the list?

Across the terrace, a heavyset man rubbed his glasses with a handkerchief. He held my gaze for a beat longer than necessary before muttering something into his earpiece. The wind shifted, blowing dust into my face. I shivered.

The desk clerk hustled up, sneering: Your room is ready, Dr. and Mrs. Teller.

Simon leveled him with a glance, and the clerk retreated.

What a fool, Simon said. Is everyone here like this? Never mind, Benno has to show up eventually. If our plan is going to work, we should get ready.

Our plan. I wasn't sure we'd ever agreed on anything so concrete as a plan. Nevertheless, I nodded, content to let him decide, for now, what my reality was. We retired to our room to await developments, and Phelps's box.

45

The room was pleasant, sunlit. Mountains ringed the view, but half of the closest mountaintop had gone missing, another casualty of the quarry. There was a single queen-size bed. Simon took one look at it and disappeared into the closet. I couldn't blame him. I wasn't in the mood to negotiate sleeping arrangements, either.

Simon busied himself with small tasks, laying out towels and offering me the top drawers of the dresser. He showed me a folder of promotional material, mostly advertisements for local attractions—there were pictures of the lake itself and children swimming in it, coupons for discounts on meals and booze, tours to a local brewery and a candle-making shop, free rentals of inflatable beach toys, and directions to the high-end outlet stores I'd heard about already. He handed me an ad for the local Dress Barn outlet featuring a group of middle-aged women in brightly patterned caftans. On the flip side, a large infant delightedly shoved a nugget of maple sugar candy—the local specialty, I gathered—into its mouth.

Would you look at that, he said.

Around here everything revolves around eating, drinking,

swimming, and housework, I said. And shopping. Don't forget the shopping, I added.

Party pooper, Simon said. He gestured at the lake, visible through the window, a wide oval the color of a worksite tarp. The view's just like a postcard. Quarry Lake really *is* that blue.

I stared at the infant in the ad, dreaming up excuses to hightail it back to New Preston. *There's an emergency at the office*, I imagined myself saying. Or, acting the dutiful daughter: *My mother's health has taken a turn for the worse.*

Simon found the room service menu and called for lunch, ordering without consulting me—tuna sashimi, a summer salad, wine.

Sashimi? We're miles from the ocean.

It's not Topeka, Simon said. I'm sure it's fine.

Topeka, I muttered senselessly, is also fine.

I took a quick shower, as hot as I could stand. I hung a fresh dress off the shower rail, so the steam might loosen the wrinkles. I dried off, feeling slightly more human, and wrapped myself in a fluffy robe I found on a hook behind the door.

When the meal arrived, Simon lifted the domed lid, and I had to smile at the neat geometry of the plating: squared-off chunks of dark-red tuna surrounded by cubed pink melon and halved cherry tomatoes. Only a decorator would make a plate like that, all reds and pinks.

I could only manage a few bites.

Are you ill? You look ill.

I'm not sure, I said.

Simon's brow furrowed—with, I thought, concern. The clear light sharpened his features. His eyes had depths I had not noticed. But then so did Quarry Lake.

I shivered. Simon knew more than I did about stuff I

preferred not to face: violence, death, what people are capable of in relationships. The knowledge did not seem to faze him. I pushed myself up and watched as he threw himself around the room, preparing to join the conference. He was a sight to see, yanking clothes from his suitcase and hangers from the closet, his gold-buttoned navy-jacketed confidence falling into place before my eyes.

He shoved the plug of his portable clothes press into the wall socket.

Come on, Cookie. We have work to do.

I groaned, feeling lousy. But he was right: *au travail.* In the bathroom I exchanged the robe for my freshly steamed and only mildly creased dress. It wasn't perfect but it would have to do. I stuck a hand into my boot and felt for Phelps's transponder, still tucked beneath the insole. An ominous shifting in my gut was making me regret the fish. Fighting off nausea, I dabbed concealer on the dark circles beneath my eyes. It was hopeless. This lunatic foray into law enforcement had put me way beyond cosmetics.

I returned to find Simon seated on the bed, bouncing his foot. Other than that fidget, he was buttoned up in every way, right down to his shiny cufflinks. His intensity just made me feel worse. More than anything I wanted him out of the room.

He said: I should head back downstairs. Someone has to know where Benno is.

Great, I said. I'll meet you in the lobby in fifteen minutes.

You'll be all right on your own? You look a little peaked.

I'm fine.

He adjusted his tie and picked up his battered briefcase.

A new bag would do wonders for your look, I said.

I don't recall asking for fashion advice. See you downstairs.

The door shut behind him with a metallic click. The

conference guide was splayed on the coverlet. On the list of keynotes was a description of Benno's talk, something about memory and desire, which was accompanied by a pretentious headshot. Obviously coached for the photo, *this* Benno, so different from the one I remembered, smiled knowingly as he inclined his head. Here was a person of a remarkable sympathy tempered by wide experience, the photo seemed to say: a man who was at once consoling, impossible to surprise, and the smartest guy in the room. He didn't look like anyone who might be attached to a crime—of, say, drug dealing. Which was pretty funny since the last time I saw that face, it was attached to the arm of a guy lifting a bag of injectables from Lana Halsey's monster fridge.

The phone rang. When I answered, the woman on the other end asked if we were ready to return our room service items. I affirmed that was so, and she said she'd send someone right up. The fish, I thought, was also coming right up. My mouth filled with spit.

There was a knock on the door. *Housekeeping!* someone called.

The knock turned to hammering. *Is anybody home?*

I reached again for the phone, thinking to call the concierge, but my arm was refusing to cooperate with the rest of me. My whole body rebelled: I sank down, coming to rest half off the bed, and vomited onto the carpet.

Was. I. Dying.

The door popped off its hinges, and a cloth hood came down over my head. I felt myself being quite professionally manhandled, my arms and legs whirling as I was tossed into what had to be a laundry cart and wheeled away beneath a pile of hotel sheets.

46

I came to, twisted and squashed between boxes in the back of a utility van. At the front were two women dressed in bright flower-printed housedresses similar to the ones I'd seen in the shops, accessorized with pistols jammed into holsters at their hips. They were both trim, muscular. One set her feet, a sturdy pair shoved into flip-flops, on the dash, her toenails bright orange to match her dress.

The van took a corner fast, and I banged against one of the piles. It fell forward, emptying white powder all over the floor. My arms were caught behind me in rigid straps that cut. My legs had been zip-tied, too. The taste of vomit filled my mouth; the van reeked. I spat and retched.

They were bickering intently.

You should've taped the mouth, said one of them.

Tape your own mouth. I don't want to hear no sniveling from anyone. Not from you, not from her. No girly shit.

She doesn't look girly. Not with those hobnail boots.

Hobnail boots! You wouldn't know a hobnail boot if it kicked you in the ass.

As they bickered, I pushed myself into a corner, trying to find some kind of purchase. We headed steeply uphill, then quickly down again. We passed a town, where I caught glimpses of boxy retail shops, the factory outlets the driver had mentioned, and large bags depending from the shoulders of women pushing carts in gleaming chrome.

The van began a fresh ascent, steeper this time and even faster. Ancient pine trees clung to cliffs. Light filtered down, greened by the canopy. My ears popped, and I braced myself as we careened around a hairpin turn. Through the trees, an immense sky of powder blue; far below, the dark expanse of Quarry Lake.

My foot throbbed; the device Phelps had installed to track my movements had popped out of its socket and was now cutting into the flesh of my foot.

So long as it was still functioning, someone would know where I was.

But was it? Still functioning?

Simon should never have left me alone. I should never have come on this trip.

I took slow breaths to still myself. Out of the chaos came a single calm thought—of my mother, of a story she once told me.

The ancient Egyptians believed that the first person was created when a bumblebee stopped to rest on a leaf that was floating down the Nile. The bee was carrying a seed and a mantis that had achieved self-consciousness. The bee, who had achieved no consciousness at all, dumped its cargo, both the dumb seed and the clever mantis, and flew away. Although the mantis was too disheartened to move, the seed rolled into the water and washed up on the shore, where it germinated and grew into a person—the first one, human degree zero—a sprout from the Nile mud. No one knows what happened to the mantis. No one, as far as I know, has even wondered.

Trapped in the back of this foul van, veering around one hairpin turn after another, I just *was* that mantis, whose fate was not recorded, who never got the chance to set the record right.

The van shot down a steep slope, sending boxes flying as I lurched forward to bang against the front seat. Now it was the driver's turn to laugh, an ugly bark that took my measure and found it ridiculous. She was not wrong. I made myself snicker, composing my own epitaph: Here lies Hannah Cooke, the loyal—mostly—servant to the taste-making housewives of New Preston, finally outfoxed by the gun-toting ladies of Quarry Lake.

We pulled off the road and came to a stop beside a culvert. Water trickled through the bottom. The driver applied herself to parking the van. It wasn't easy. Every time she slipped the gears into PARK, they slipped right out again. She yanked the parking brake, and I felt the van come to rest against it. Her colleague pushed open the door and hopped out. She tried to slam the door behind her, but it wouldn't shut properly.

You pushed, said the driver, pulling at the door from the inside. And look what happened.

They managed to shut the door, at least enough to satisfy themselves that it was not going to pop open unexpectedly. I listened for the latch. *Fuggedabouddit*, one of the women said. I was still waiting for that click when the back doors creaked open and the driver reached in, her nose wrinkling with disgust, and yanked me out.

They frog-marched me downhill. Above me was a parking lot full of vans like the one in which I'd just been trapped. A cliff dropped off sharply to my right; water lapped the shore below. My captors dragged me around the back of a modern steel-and-glass building, a new construction out of keeping with the rugged natural landscape, with windows shuttered against the afternoon heat. A brass placard by the door informed visitors that this was a medical office. But on the building's far side, just visible around the corner, a truck backing up noisily caught my attention.

Two men stood on a loading dock preparing to shuttle pallets of white boxes, the same sort as the ones in the van, onto the truck. They were moving so furtively that I knew I was seeing something I wasn't supposed to.

I was yanked back around the corner to the front of the building, where we were met by a uniformed security guard. Her coral lipstick matched her lacquered nails, which looked wholly fake; at her hip was a semiautomatic pistol, which looked wholly authentic. I was taken roughly by the elbow and half-pushed, half-dragged down a long corridor and through a doorway into what looked for all the world like a general practitioner's consulting room.

What an afternoon. I had been drugged, kidnapped, and brought to the office of a doctor who apparently specialized in the ailments of people who required armed guards for their medical care.

The woman with the coral manicure relayed a few words via the intercom. After a moment, the door opened, and I was greeted by a man in clinical garb—white coat, clipboard, stethoscope looped around his neck. My doctor. The first one.

47

Chuck raised a hand toward me, a quick caution signal, before speaking to the guard in calm tones I remembered from when he took his patients' calls at the renovation site in New Preston. Sympathetic as he sounded, he was also projecting a lot of authority; she was listening closely and nodding, and then her features softened. She said something I couldn't hear, and then she left. He turned to me, his face all concern.

Cookie—

Don't *Cookie* me, I hissed. I went to your funeral!

Hush, he told me, as if I were on the verge of a tantrum, which only made me angrier.

All you have to do now is cooperate, he said. You'll be perfectly fine, I promise.

Are you kidding me? I've been poisoned, zip-tied, duct-taped, dumped in a van, and carted uphill to this charming hideaway. Don't tell me I'll be *perfectly fine*.

Something cold pressed against my wrist. I heard a snap as Chuck clipped the zip tie.

Easy, he said, and I flinched as the tie came away.

Stop it, I said. Stop. You have to stop. You have to explain.

He bent down and snipped the second zip tie from my ankles. From the cupboard he extracted a folded garment, which I thought at first was a johnny but which turned out to be yet another one of those loud housedresses.

It's awful, I know. But you can't stay in those clothes.

Shivering, I undressed and tugged the ugly frock over my head, trying not to think about how much I resembled a down-market sofa.

Sit still, please.

Chuck came around behind me and lifted the back of the dress I'd just donned. The room's chill pushed against my bare back, and I felt his hand, and a cold disk pressed against me, below my shoulder blade.

I know it's upsetting, but just play along, he said. Whatever you do, don't look over your left shoulder. There's a camera just behind me, hidden in the molding. We're being watched; there are cameras, shitty ones, all over. I don't think you'll be recognizable in this getup. Besides, Lana wants you alive. I intend to keep you that way.

Chuck continued his faux examination, pressing the stethoscope's disk, warmer now, to my back. His fingers brushed my skin, that instrument of memory.

I said: Stop it.

He sighed heavily, his breath taking over where his fingers left off.

I said, *stop*. What the hell are you doing here, anyway?

I guess you could say I got a new job. General practice. Lana's workers don't have health insurance, and since they're off the books, they also don't qualify for Medicare. They still get sick, though. Someone has to look after them. That's where I come in.

You're a company man, then?

Breathe, he ordered. We do this and that. Import-export. More or less. *Breathe.*

Freshly oxygenated, my inward gears began to creak: So this was the home office of Lana Pura.

Chuck came around again, back to where I could see him. From his pocket he extracted a penlight and aimed it at my mouth.

Open, he commanded.

Why? Are you looking for your obol?

Cookie—

I grabbed the penlight and flung it. It rebounded off a cabinet on the far side of the room.

I'm truly sorry about the obol, Cookie. Lana wanted to leave a message, and thanks to Harry, she'd happened on exactly the right means to that end.

Harry!

So Harry had given her the obol, and he'd probably explained its meaning, too.

Don't tell me you didn't see it coming. They both had bones to pick with you. Why *wouldn't* they team up?

Extracting a second penlight from his pocket, he shot me a triumphant glance.

Am I right? I am so right, aren't I. I *told* you I had reservations about your chimney guy.

Typical Chuck: Even now, he had to say *I told you so.*

You have to admit, he said, she has a gift for chaos.

You have a gift, too, I fumed, but don't ask me to tell you what for.

He tilted my chin to shine the light up my nostrils.

What do you export? I asked, thinking of what I'd seen on the funicular.

Textiles. Ceramics. Rugs. The occasional shipment of cut-rate medical supplies.

Painkillers?

Those, too, he said. Though that business has slowed down somewhat lately, no thanks to the too-clever types in pharmaceutical procurement.

I said: And you import the means of production.

Workers, you mean? Well, yes. Our workers. They come from as far away as China. Other labor, he sneered, we source closer to home.

He reached down and lifted his trouser leg. He was wearing expensive clothes and good, new loafers, but a hard plastic bracelet encircled his ankle.

I don't get out much anymore, as you see. My employer has noticed my, ah, tendency to wander.

So Lana finally put you under house arrest?

Ah, Lana. Haven't we always had better things to discuss, you and me?

Your wife's goons have just kidnapped me, and you're still thinking you'd like to take me to bed?

You could be here awhile, he said. You might want a diversion.

To my left, a window that opened onto the street. On the desk to my right, a Rolodex. Which gave me an idea.

What's up with that old thing? I asked, pointing to the Rolodex. You'd think you could do things by computer these days.

He snorted.

Do you see a single computer in this room? Lana prefers to keep me completely off the grid. Things are mostly still analog around here anyway. I can't say I mind it.

Fewer websites to monitor, fewer pages to troll?

Now you're just being silly. I'd never stoop so low as to—

As to use Fiona's name to throw shade on Martha Benton?

Lovely Fiona. That useful girl.

Dammit, Chuck!

I glared at him, thinking of all the trouble he'd caused her.

Never mind, I said. It's no good, trying to talk to you. I'm just giving myself a hot flash.

He looked at me strangely. Clinically.

You're not old enough for those.

Oh yes, I said, fanning myself with one hand, willing the blood to rise. I thought of embarrassments, the highlight reel of my history of shame: my mother's criticisms, the druggist's leer and his offers of candy, how hard I'd fallen for this unworthy man. The nape of my neck prickled with heat, followed by my chin, my cheeks. I was glowing all right.

Please, Cookie. Attacks of the vapors went out with the washboard and the pedal-pushed sewing machine.

Menopause starts early in my family. Just let me crack a window, I begged. I'll be fine, I promise.

Well, if you insist.

I crossed the room, pushed the window up, and shoved the Rolodex under it. It was just possible that Simon had noticed my absence and gone to look for me.

You don't need to do that, he said.

It won't stay up, I huffed. Trust me. That sash is as loose as . . . As loose as . . .

You've got some memory loss, too? Mostly nouns?

The humiliations of age, I replied. I try to be philosophical.

Chuck went to the sink and began to wash his hands. He turned them over and over, scrubbing with a small rectangular brush. It was a surgeon's washup: slow, practiced, methodical.

If he was really a fake, he was a deep one, fully lost in his clinician's role.

He threw me a backward glance, one that asked a question. He'd clipped the ties that kept me from running—so why was I still there?

I sprinted out and raced blindly down one dark corridor after another. When I hit a dead end, I backtracked, pushing on every door until I found one that opened into a high-ceilinged hall filled with stacked-up cages containing hundreds of mice. The animals were bleeding from their eyes and noses; the smell was indescribable. I sprinted between the rows, running hard for the door on the other side of the room. Someone stood beside one of the cages holding a squirming creature in one gloved hand and a syringe in the other. Catching sight of me, she dropped the mouse and with a shout went scrambling after it. I blew past her and out the door, which led to a staircase. I headed down, taking the stairs two at a time, and pushed through the door at the bottom.

The door opened onto a central courtyard that had been turned into a lush garden. Flowering vines shot from every crevice; the place hummed with bees. One of the women who had captured me earlier now stood before a row of glass globes that hung from freestanding wrought iron stands: hummingbird feeders. She was pouring a clear liquid into one of the glass globes.

Beside her stood Simon Teller, staring anxiously at the double doors across the courtyard and at the empty, cloudless sky.

I crept up behind them, staying in the shadow cast by the courtyard's colonnade.

Aren't you a doctor? For a person of substance, she said, you certainly have cheap taste in accessories.

She gestured toward Simon's briefcase, which of course was

gaping open; he'd never fixed the clasp. Smiling tightly, Simon pulled the briefcase shut.

What's that? he asked, gesturing to the decanter.

Sugar water, she said, shaking out the last drops. She dropped a tablet into the feeder. And a secret ingredient. It slows them down, she said. In this backwater we don't have so many ways to do proper quality control.

That was when I noticed the hummingbirds. There must have been a dozen of them, tiny and almost still, among the shrubbery. She picked one up, lifted a wing, and, after withdrawing a syringe from a pocket, shot the bird full of whatever the syringe contained. A bit farther down the path, bees swarmed small bodies, dead ones. My vision narrowed; the horizon tipped. Simon must have sensed me standing there, because he looked over and mouthed one word: *Steady.*

I slipped away, into the shadow of the portico, and ran until I reached a corridor that stretched away from the building. I turned the corner and followed it, keeping to the shadows, until I reached a loading dock where a thickset man stood shouting at a driver who was trying to shimmy his truck, open at the back, closer to the dock. A road stretched down and away from the building; in the distance was the cliff with its steep drop-off, and below it, the lake. The truck stopped, and from out of the truck's darkness emerged a woman holding a clipboard. It was Lana, of course—sporting the same expensively lightened hair, gleaming in the same damned white suit. She leapt from the truck to the dock, her lapels lifting in the breeze.

Lana! I shouted.

If everything went to hell, I wanted her to know exactly who set events in motion.

She turned to face me, reaching for something inside her jacket. I sprinted away, staying low, as she unloaded the clip.

Bullets whistled above my head as I scrambled down the terraces and finally crashed through a thick hedge of dragon-lady holly.

I WAS trapped. Downhill, the driveway ended in a locked iron gate that was too high to climb. Uphill, around the bend in the road, there was only the small lot where the van was still parked.

My arms were scratched to the elbows. I wiped my sticky face, and my palms came away smeared with blood. *Oh, it's just a flesh wound*, I remembered Harry saying, dismissing some pain I no longer recalled. It was a lesson: You could be casual about these things. And so I would be, for as long as I could.

I made my way uphill, toward the van. The driver's side door was open, and there was the parking brake, fully engaged, between the seats. I scooted over, getting myself to the passenger side where the door could be pushed open—if it came to that. Which it might. Best not to think of it. Gently I disengaged the brake. The van began to roll, picking up speed as it headed downhill. I grabbed the steering wheel and aimed for the gate. If I crashed it, I might just be able to spin the van through the first tight turn outside the compound. After that, my fate was anyone's guess. I would have to wing it.

Behind me, something rustled.

Stop the van, Cookie.

Chuck!

He must have sneaked in the back and been hiding among the boxes.

Stop the van this instant.

Keeping one hand on the wheel, I tightened the other around the parking brake. If he wanted control, he'd have to fight me for it.

Chuck pushed into the driver's seat and turned to me, his face arranged in something like openness, as if his charm might still work, as if he might still hold any sway over me.

Why are you driving from the passenger side, Cookie? You need to get into the driver's seat, you goose.

I leaned back, smiling.

You goose, he repeated, reaching for the wheel.

I lunged, connecting my head with his jaw. His head snapped back. I leaned again on the door that hadn't clicked shut.

Chuck's eyes locked on mine. The openness had disappeared, and so had the lower half of his face, now veiled in blood. Had I broken his nose?

Or maybe I was finally learning to love the world, by shaping it to please me.

Haw, I said. *Haw-haw*.

The gate approached, twenty feet away and closing. Suddenly the air was thick with white dust. A box must have opened in the back. I held my breath and leaned once more on the wonky door. One last push, and it gave way. I flew into a blue rectangle of sky—and landed on my face. Grit filled my mouth; blood washed it all out again. Pain ripped through my shoulder, and then my arm went numb. I rolled to the side of the road, toward the safety of the margin.

There was a crash as the van collided with the gate. The rear door popped open, releasing a cloud of white dust. The gate gave way with a metallic shriek. There was a muffled thump as the van landed somewhere far below.

Silence. Birdsong. Wind in the pines.

A burst of laughter echoed across the lake. *Lana*.

Blood was pooling in the gravel beneath me. The lake yawned below, one long stroke of blue. The transponder in my heel buzzed once, twice—a low power alert.

Footfalls crunched on the gravel. Louder now. Someone approaching.

Be near me when my light is low—

Simon's face rose above me, another moon. *Steady*, he said. He said something else, but it was drowned by the noise of helicopters. I leaned out, over the edge. In the distance, a loaded pickup truck struggled up a narrow incline, trailing twin lines of black smoke.

48

I woke up flat on my back in a hospital bed, with a clear view of a damp-mottled ceiling dotted with squashed bugs.

You sprained your shoulder, Simon said. You've torn a ligament, too.

Help me up, I said.

My right arm was folded across my chest, held in place by a sling. I rolled onto my undamaged side, tried to push up from my elbow. Fire shot through my clavicle. The room spun.

Simon positioned another pillow behind me. Hold on, he said. He went to the end of the bed and began, with difficulty, to turn what must have been a crank. The motor's out on this thing, he said.

So what happened? I asked.

You passed out and missed all the fun.

My shoulder throbbed.

I had plenty of fun, I said. I'm just glad I'm not dead.

You got lucky. You have a pretty good shiner, and you won't be lifting anything heavy for a while. But it could have been a lot worse.

How did you find me?

Phelps gave me your approximate coordinates. You were still

wearing the transponder. I found the factory building and happened to look up. Lo and behold, there was a window propped with, of all things, a Rolodex.

He chuckled: That was a nice touch.

What about Lana? Is she dead?

While you were passed out, six squad cars full of New Hampshire's finest attempted to swarm the compound and found themselves outgunned by a posse of women who, despite appearances, were packing quite a bit more than cookie guns. There was a shootout. Lana escaped in her helicopter.

And Chuck? I asked, not sure I wanted to hear the answer.

He's the one who's dead.

The news didn't grieve me as much I'd expected it to. The person I'd cared about had always been more or less a figment, someone Chuck had encouraged me to conjure up. He'd asked just the same of his patients, too. That was how he rolled. The only thing I'd really lost was my belief in an illusion.

Simon, I'm starving.

Well, you're hardly under house arrest, you know.

MY SHOULDER ached, but I didn't want the painkiller the nurse offered. Wiser to tough it out, I thought, given what I knew about the local hospitals and their pharmaceuticals. Besides, there would be wine with lunch, and I wasn't saying no to either wine or lunch.

Life, as they say, is short.

We drove through the valley to a restaurant that the nurse had recommended for its spectacular view of Stone Monument, a massive profile of a giant's face that had hung off the cliff for as long as anyone could remember, or so said the brochure. We parked in the lot below the restaurant and hiked up, the scent of mint rising as we trampled the brush. The path switched back, and the view widened. A long verdant ridge stretched out like a giant taking a nap. The ridge ended at the cliff, where I could just make out the giant's face in profile. It didn't look like much.

The pain in my shoulder was intensifying. I was glad to find the restaurant, happier still to take a seat by a window with a view of the ridge. A waitress brought a platter of specialties: corn bread studded with fat blueberries, marble-sized balls of butter to which the cream still clung, a maple-pumpkin chutney, a salad of cold shredded chicken dressed with a maple vinaigrette. Simon filled a plate and slid it toward me.

As I tucked in, Simon pulled something from his pocket. It was a vial of clear fluid like the one I saw a lifetime ago, in the Halseys' fridge.

Lana has a problem, he said, handing me the vial.

I peered at it, but I was just being polite. In fact, it was nothing new. Unless it was.

Do you have any idea what this is? I asked.

Yes, he said. It's a cut-rate precursor to a powerful new opiate. Lana was buying it in huge lots, relabeling it, and sending it to be reconstituted in plants all over the world.

So Chuck had told me: Lana Pura wasn't just exporting textiles.

How did you find out? I asked.

Wendy always had some idea of what was going on, because of her work.

He smeared butter thickly on a wedge of corn bread and took a bite, chewing thoughtfully.

And you know how nosy shrinks are, he went on. We have ways of getting people to talk. The guard told me a few things, too, and I pieced the story together.

The waitress arrived with a bottle of wine, an off-piste New

Zealand red, and Simon poured out two glasses. I sipped mine. It was drinkable, and I intended to drink quite a lot of it. Too much clarity of mind seemed distinctly undesirable.

I said: Tell me what they told you.

Her plan was ingenious, he said. She'd branched out, business-wise, and she needed a doctor's help with the technical details and to minister to her army of wage slaves, who occasionally had the temerity to get sick. Remember what she told Benno, the job she promised him?

I nodded.

She'd offered him a nice retirement, with a little clinical action to keep things interesting, and a nurse to do the real work. And so she and Chuck together lured Benno into a trap. They killed him so Chuck could take over Benno's identity and practice here, in the back of beyond where no one would know him, under Benno's name. He was even about to give Benno's talk.

Simon paused to swallow a mouthful of wine.

It's not good, he said, grimacing.

It's okay, I said, refilling my own glass. It's a very okay red.

Simon chuckled. I guess you're right, he said. Makes me homesick, a little.

So the man who had slipped away, I said, the night of the fire—the man in the gray suit—hadn't been Benno at all but Chuck, in Benno's clothes.

Chuck might have gotten away with it, Simon said. That Benno was a professional recluse didn't hurt. No one had seen him for months, and Chuck was protean. I've met a few of these guys. They're chameleons. It's rare to find one as functional as Chuck. I still don't know how he managed to fool the licensing board. Most of them wind up in prison.

But why kill Benno? I wondered.

Simon spread chutney on a cracker and offered it to me.

He knew too much, he said. Maybe he was threatening to go public.

This chutney's not half bad, I said. Do you think Chuck really did hurt his patients?

Some of his bad reviews may have been merited. If we dig, we're likely to discover more than one suspicious death. You know Martha Benton filed a lawsuit against him. Lou told me, though I had to apologize first, for not taking her seriously. But don't look at me that way, unless there's chutney on my chin?

You're fine, I said.

Listen: Martha had a real beef. Not only did he get credit for her work, but by cleaning up after him, she'd unwittingly acted as his accomplice.

I still don't understand why Benno sent you the case study.

I've wondered the same thing. At first I thought he was in real trouble and the case study was a call for help. But now I think it was just plain exhibitionism. He needed to tell someone, anyone, about what he'd done. How clever he'd been.

How clever could he have been? He wound up dead.

He missed his own cues. The bit about his wife, for instance.

I had barely registered it myself. Something about her dying, a farm explosion.

April Sanger didn't die young in a tractor explosion, Simon went on. She was alive and well through my residency.

But—but that was years ago.

Don't remind me, he said, downing another gulp of Okay Red.

But why lie?

Simon resettled his napkin on his lap.

He needed a story to fill a gap in his narrative about Chuck, and that's what he conjured up. Interestingly, the scene—a man, a woman, a third party, and an explosion—looked a lot like his own final moments.

You mean he knew what was coming.

He had a premonition. He just didn't recognize it.

Why send the case study to you, though? It wasn't like you had a close relationship.

True. It wasn't just the debacle with the IDP. It was the way he withheld everything.

Everything you ever needed—

In the dairy aisle, he said, grinning.

That night in your kitchen seems like a thousand years ago.

I wonder if Benno sent me that report, he went on, because he felt freer with me. He wanted my response, but he didn't have to take it seriously. He'd already established his dominance. He would always be the serious and respectable analyst. And I would be the unanalyzable lump on the sofa.

What Benno did to Chuck was unforgivable, I said. He was supposed to help.

To you, that will always be a sore spot.

Not to you?

I keep telling you. These down-and-out types are everywhere.

Maybe Benno was down-and-out, but I couldn't see Chuck that way. I flashed on a memory of him staring into his laptop screen, typing furiously. He was probably writing nasty reviews of Martha Benton's work and signing them with Fiona's name. That was pretty down-and-out behavior, actually.

I said: Canceled people—

Cancel people. Invalidation is their great talent. Don't feel too badly. We all get taken in, now and then. I idealized Benno, too, remember?

I nodded. So many miscues. Missed cues.

Some people do play on the self-destructiveness of others. They recruit it for their own ends. Behind his façade, Chuck was miserable.

Give me an oblivion of light.

You're saying he wanted to die? I asked. And he found someone to do his dirty work?

In a manner of speaking. Though I would say, knowing Benno, that as usual, he just wanted to help.

I stared out at the cliff, at the stone man's portrait emerging from an indistinct mass of rock. The giant's profile, just visible in the distance, appeared only about as large as one of my mother's shabti. So: Chuck had solicited Benno in what turned out to be a death-match; and Lana, in turn, had solicited me to provide the oblivion her husband required. Shabtis were everywhere. But what made her think that I was just the right sort of hired gun?

Well, I'd been shtupping her husband. Perhaps she'd seen in me a kindred spirit: another manipulator of loyalties and perceptions, deadlines and budgets, spreadsheets and *matériel*. Another artist of the long con.

Is something bothering you?

Everything is bothering me.

As a doctor, he said, I prescribe an excursion.

THEY COULDN'T outgun Lana's ladies, but even so, Phelps's people had moved in fast, shutting down operations at the factory and getting the message out: There would be no more work for now. The town went on holiday, and the locals took over the hotel pool, which was oddly constructed, a narrow rectangle of deep water, Olympic in its length, with no shallow end to speak of. They scattered on the lounges, anchored their claim on the space with big coolers full of beer. Two men and three teenaged boys, who all seemed related in the way of cousins and uncles, laid claim to the best spot, in the bright sun, near the ladder leading down into the water at the far end. While Simon settled us on a chaise, tucking away his shoes and his briefcase, I listened to the crack of cans opening. One of the kids seemed a little out of it, and the others kept punching him on the arm.

Simon wanted to swim. I followed him down the ladder and floated there, hanging on with my good arm. The water was icy, and the cold felt like a weight at my feet, threatening to drag me down. When I couldn't take it anymore, I pulled myself back up and stood dripping on the stone edge, trying to still my chattering teeth. When I felt like I could move again, I stretched out on the chaise, babying my bad shoulder and enjoying the sun's warmth, lazily eavesdropping on conversations about ordinary things—hours, schedules, kids and their school intrigues. All I could think of was the town, so like and yet so unlike New Preston, overflowing with cheap goods made under sweatshop conditions by desperate people, many of them employed by Lana. Not just cheap goods—cheap drugs, too. Powerful ones that could take you to the very edge, tip you out of life like water from a cup. As Erica, too, had been tipped—my old friend.

Simon's dark head bobbed in the water. One of the teenagers, the floppy one, had dropped, or been dropped, into the pool, and now something was wrong. The kid's head dipped once, twice. He turned over, tipped his head back. Enough New England summers had taught me: This was a bad sign. I held my breath. Around me rose a wild chatter. People flew into the water, sending up frightened shouts. The lifeguards had gone off somewhere, if they'd ever been there at all.

Simon swam hard for him, with an efficient four-beat crawl,

and as he came within reach, he looped an arm around the kid's torso and dragged him toward the ladder, where a group had assembled to pull him out. As Simon followed, dripping, out of the pool, a small man shoved to the front. Let me help, he said.

He knew CPR. He worked at the hospital. Behind his glasses, his eyes were ringed with dark circles like bruises. He looked exhausted. Simon told him: He needs more than CPR.

The boy was stretched on the concrete, unresponsive and blue around the mouth. Surely it was too late.

My bag, Simon shouted at me. *Quick!*

On the blanket, the briefcase gaped open. I gathered it up and ran it over to Simon, who pulled it from me without taking his eyes off the boy. The boy's mother stared at us both, her eyes hard as pebbles. Others stood around, hands on hips.

From the bag Simon withdrew and unfolded a small card-board box. Inside was a syringe and a vial. He uncapped the syringe, drew the contents of the vial into the syringe barrel, and plunged the needle into the boy's upper arm. When the syringe was empty, he cast it away and started CPR, pinching the kid's nostrils and breathing into his mouth, pushing on his chest at intervals. The other doctor held the kid's head and counted, keeping Simon's breathing on track. A mechanical wailing that had started up some distance away grew louder, closing in. By the time the ambulance arrived, the kid was conscious, flushed pink. The EMTs hustled over with their stretcher. One of the men came forward, gesturing angrily.

No hospital, he shouted. There was a chorus of agreement: *No hospital!*

Someone had pulled the kid up to a seat. He leaned forward, head on hands, blinking and dazed, a foil emergency blanket tented on his shoulders like a pair of useless wings. The EMT continued to argue with the man who didn't want to send the kid to the hospital. Eventually the EMT ran out of arguments, or else there were other emergencies to tend to. He slammed back into the ambulance, and it roared off. The family packed up in silence.

Why wouldn't they let him go to the hospital? I asked.

The stranger, the doctor, said: They always refuse us. I don't know why.

Simon turned to him: Sure you do.

The doctor raised his hand.

Please. We don't have all the facts.

That kid was OD'ing. That's a fact. With the mortality rate at your hospital, I don't think you can afford to wait for more of them.

The doctor allowed his sunglasses to slide down, shielding his eyes, and turned abruptly back toward the hotel. Simon and I watched him leave. I waved a bluebottle from Simon's neck, which was ringed with salt, white against his tan.

People are dying in hospitals here, too?

Quite a few bad reactions to Lana's pills, Simon said.

49

That evening I stayed at the hotel. I was done with the grim hospital, with its yellowing ceiling tiles and uncomfortable beds. It would be a relief to sleep between crisp hotel linens, in complete privacy—well, apart from Simon, who offered to take the couch.

I said: That's gallant.

Party noises drifted in from the courtyard, where a wedding reception was getting underway. Simon's breathing deepened. My mind wandered all over, from New Preston to the Nile. I hoped Fiona and Owen were doing all right. I worried about my mother, wondered what she was doing, if she was okay. With all my heart, I hoped that death, when it came, would be just like the Egyptians imagined, with a goddess at the scales, tweaking the knob of forgiveness. Meanwhile, I wouldn't go quietly.

Hey, Simon said, sitting up. You're talking.

Sorry, I replied. I got excited.

He came over, brought his face close to mine. I smelled mouthwash on his breath. What happened next did not surprise me, though I wondered if I'd regret it. Well, so what—regret was plentiful as joe-pye weed. No sense trying to uproot it all. Pristine lawns were for the suburbs.

In my purse, my phone rang once and went quiet.

FIONA'S VOICEMAIL was so garbled I could pick out just a few words—something about an explosion at the Halsey residence. It seemed that she'd fielded a call from the dunning service, too. No doubt they wanted to close the books on my case. While I was returning Fiona's call, another one came through. I recognized the number—of course I did.

I said: This better be good, Harry.

Come on, Cookie. I'm sorry about what happened in that stupid shrink's office. But if you think about it, you'll see it was all just a mix-up—

That's what you call a mix-up?

I am very sorry, Cookie.

As hard as he was hitting this apology, he couldn't eliminate the self-pity from his tone. Then again, apologies had never been his *métier*. My shoulder ached. I switched the phone from one ear to the other.

Besides, Cookie, I've already made it up to you.

Oh no. What have you done, Harry?

He said: Check your bank account.

I was only able to piece everything together later, after I'd called everyone I knew in New Preston who might have been able to corroborate the whole unlikely story. Which was this: Someone had blown the Halsey property to an uncountable number of historically and, now, forensically significant bits. The lab's results weren't complete, but the preliminary findings suggested a homemade bomb, a mass of wire and Semtex, the placement and mechanics of which I already knew too much about. My blueprints hadn't lied, as much as I wanted them to: The beams at the flashpoint had been load-bearing, and so the whole place had come down.

It was a total loss, and one I took personally. All that work, a season of my life—gone.

There was one silver lining. Lana, who of course still owned the property, also held the insurance policy on it. Here was the meaning of Harry's hint. I alerted my dunning service to these developments, and Lana sent what she owed down to the last plaster-dusted penny, a cool twenty thousand paid directly into my bank account. The payment arrived with a note, a final bit of nastiness: *For services rendered, contracted and otherwise—haw-haw.*

A month later the papers broke a story about a global ring of shady dealers who had been buying cheap opiates that had been diluted with dangerous filler materials and selling the stuff to hospitals all over the US according to a complex scheme involving multiple repackaging switch-points, warehouses, and small-time factories operating quietly in sleepy outposts like New Preston and Quarry Lake. The scheme might have worked, too, but a series of unexplained deaths at area hospitals had roused alarms, and an investigator had picked up the trail. I failed to find Lana's name among those nabbed in the sting. That didn't mean she wasn't in on it.

I did make one last move that was all my own: Along with those articles, I emailed Benno's case study to Phelps. If anyone could make the link, it was him. This fish was bigger than my frying pan, but it might just fit in his. There was something attractive, too, about the possibility that Chuck's case might actually be closed. Closure wasn't justice, but it beat the alternative. So long as I was flush, I was disinclined to quibble.

Phelps wrote back with his thanks and asked me to tell

Simon that Chuck's undergraduate and medical school transcripts were nowhere to be found.

Turns out Simon was right about that, Phelps wrote.

Benno had been right about Chuck, too. There was a lot of truth in his case report. And Martha Benton—she'd seen right through Chuck from the first. I'd underestimated her. We all had, except for Lou, but no one took her seriously, either.

50

Everyone had advice for me in the days and weeks that followed, as I parceled out my painkillers and waited for my bones to knit. Fiona was the first to call, reminding me to take the dogs for their shots and urging me on long walks for the exercise. As a get-well gift, she sent me a tiny black leatherette notebook with a card that said: *For your dreams.*

My dreams? I asked, when I called to thank her.

And your daydreams. You can do anything you want in fantasy.

She was well-intentioned, but privately I wondered if, out of school and feeling vulnerable, she'd been taken in by some huckster career coach who was making suggestions that she was only too relieved to pass along. As for me, I slept heavily, dreamlessly. Fantasy was nice, but Fiona's point had less to do with creative visualization than with freedom. Lana's payout meant I'd be comfortable for a while, perhaps a year if I was careful. But in New Preston, no one was returning my calls. I would need to make a fresh start somewhere else.

Boston beckoned, close but far. I found a subletter for my loft and a realtor who sent me listings from the still-ragged edge of a neighborhood near the city hospital. The night before the movers came, I invited Simon to dinner at my place. The meal was nothing fancy, just take-out boxes of garlic tofu and snow peas, disposable chopsticks, candlelight. The dogs dozed, piled at our feet. Shadows played on the moving boxes.

So you're getting out of town, he said, poling the last of the snow peas onto his plate.

I need to lay low. Let the dust settle.

Avoid reminders, he said.

You sound like you know what you're talking about, I said.

My practice was never busy, he said. Now it's even quieter. I still have patients, but not many, and I could make some real money if I worked as a locum in the city.

Enough to keep your office here?

And a bit more, to cover rent somewhere.

Somewhere. A tealight guttered.

You mean with me.

You have to admit, he said, speaking into the deepened dark, it would be convenient. We're adults. We can manage ourselves. If it doesn't work out, I'll find another place. I won't burden you.

Let's take it slow, I said as I moved to relight the candle. No commitments.

We can take it slow, he said. We can play it as it lays.

THE COURTYARD was desolate. As we pushed our way in, the iron gate swung heavily on its hinges and clanged against the far wall. The dogs ran ahead, pulling hard on their leashes. Simon glanced at me. I'm fine, I cried as they yanked me along. It's fine.

At the other side of the open space, a door creaked open, and a huge mastiff, gray as asphalt, emerged growling. I hauled on my dogs' leashes as the mastiff loped toward us, all teeth and slobber. The dogs erupted in a fury of barking, and I was shouting, too, straining to hold them back. A rangy woman came out, a thin leather lead dangling from one hand.

Max, Max—

Simon stretched out his hand.

The mastiff dropped to his stomach, growling.

Sorry-sorry-sorry, the woman panted as she leashed the enormous beast.

Her face had a familiar tautness, a subtle strain that I had learned—from Chuck—to associate with hungers beyond the physical. I sensed Simon move toward her, a tiny shift in posture that communicated openness and safety. She took a step back, dragging the dog, who didn't want to come. She glared at her dog and mine, at Simon, at me.

We might have remained at that standoff, but then another door opened, and a small stout man jogged out, his tie askew around his neck. Apologizing for his lateness, the landlord took firm hold of my arm, ushering me and the dogs past the mastiff, who growled as we passed. The woman hissed an imprecation, and Simon said kindly, Sorry to intrude. We'll just be on our way.

The apartment was serviceable, with overstuffed furniture upholstered in pale taupe—apparently other people also appreciated Simon's beloved *ish*—to match the manila-folder-colored walls and a kitchen, not too clean but well supplied with pots and gadgets, lit by a large window overlooking the alley behind the building. The day was overcast, but I liked the way the high north light slipped in. The walls were lined with old books, tripledeckers from the nineteenth century. The place felt like a refuge.

The owner teaches literature at one of the schools, said the landlord. He'll be gone through the spring semester. Meanwhile I'm managing the place.

Simon nosed among the volumes, hemming and hawing,

letting out an occasional happy *Ah!* He was already in deep. I liked the place, too, but then again, I would have liked anything in our price range so long as the building was pet friendly. There did, however, seem to be a shortage of friendly pets. Oh well, surely we could work it out.

We'll take it, I said.

I dealt with formalities, paying the first month's rent and deposit and showing my driver's license to prove I wasn't faking anything. Strange how often such questions need to be asked; strange, too, how often people fail to ask them. I watched as he entered the information in a small notebook. He slapped a loaded keyring on the counter and looked at me, his agitation evident on his face.

I need to warn you about that woman, he said. Your neighbor, Pina—she's a real problem. She shouldn't have that enormous dog. Her apartment is too small. She should not do what she does, spending all day smoking out the window and making messes on the stove.

There were many things, apparently, that Pina should neither do, nor have, nor be.

Was she always like this? Simon asked.

The man shrugged: Who knows? I'm just the landlord.

His phone rang then, the marimba racket that everyone's phone made in those days.

I have to take this, he said as he left, hugging his telephone to his ear.

THOSE FIRST weeks in Boston, Pina woke us repeatedly in the wee hours, screaming her side of some horrible conversation. Was all of this directed at another person, perhaps on the phone, or only at shadows, memories, herself? Simon worried as her shrieks knifed through the walls.

I bought a packet of foam earplugs and stored them in the nightstand drawer, resigned to bad sleep for the duration of the lease.

One night I started awake, and the cause wasn't Pina. It was the telephone that had begun to howl, a distant echo of the bomb that had gone off in New Preston. But it was only the desk clerk at Tomlins Manor. Had I seen my mother? Was she with me?

She is not, I said. It's three in the morning, why would she be with me?

If she is not with you, then I regret to tell you that we have no idea where she is.

She can't have gone far, I said, panicking. Not with her bad knee.

Ms. Cooke, she's an adult. Her knee is largely healed. We can't keep anyone who really wants to leave.

I tried to get more details from the clerk, but all I succeeded in prying from her was a hint about my mother's escape plan. She'd somehow managed to disarm the system that kept the front door locked at night. In my mind's eye, I saw her swinging down the cement front walk of Tomlins Manor, and at the last moment, turning back to wave her crutches in triumph, breathing deep drafts of cold night air.

Isn't that you, Simon asked when I told him about it.

I wanted out of New Preston, I sighed. It's true.

Simon said my restlessness meant that I was remembering something—or trying to.

Or trying not to, I said.

Simon grinned. You're catching on. Now if you'll excuse me, I have some business to take care of.

He left, a yellow legal pad tucked under one arm along with

a new AT-A-GLANCE. A moment later I heard Pina's voice, welcoming him into her apartment down the hall.

THE CALLS kept coming—so much advice, so much support, so little ready cash. I fretted on the phone to Bobby, who dismissed my fears. A little time away won't hurt you, he said. You need to rebrand anyway.

Rebrand! And how will I do that?

As usual he had a ready answer. He told me about a project called *BLOSSOM* that he was organizing with another Boston artist, a woman I'd never heard of, who did site-specific installations. She planned to take over an abandoned mental hospital and fill the place with flowers.

She has a site already?

Yes, Bobby replied. It's slated for demolition. We have the run of the entire space, and she just won a huge grant. Which means we really can do whatever we like. She needs someone on-site, he said. Someone who can organize a crew. Get shit done.

You need to do this, Bobby urged. It's a lot more significant than just spitting food into jars. Or making little scenes about dead people.

Touché, I said. I guess you haven't heard about Erica.

I heard, he said. Sad story.

I said: You don't know the half of it.

That afternoon he emailed me a photo they were using to promote the exhibit—a faded image of a 1950s-era wheeled desk chair, light-colored, powder-coated steel with cracked leather upholstery, in a small office room lit by a window. The chair was surrounded by a field of sepia-toned tulips. The image evoked something complex in me—a mixture of nostalgia, whimsy, sadness. *Behold*, I thought ruefully, *the magic of juxtaposition.*

She had a vision and a grant, and, in Bobby, she had an energetic collaborator. What the two of them needed now was organizational brains. Someone had to do the administrative heavy lifting: to order the flowers, arrange for delivery, figure out how to get hundreds of potted plants onto refrigerated trucks and off again, to lay down five thousand square feet of sod, enough to fill the basement.

As if it were a carpet, I said on the phone with Bobby the next day.

Exactly. What's needed is the art, and skill, of a general contractor.

I had to admit, he was speaking my language.

We made our arrangements: He measured the rooms at the old asylum, emailed me floor plans and lists of flowering plants that would be easy to ship in midwinter: deep-purple violets, cyclamens in pink and white, flame-colored tulips, camellias in every imaginable hue.

My first time on-site, I was surprised to find a swimming pool in the basement. It had been emptied years earlier, and now it was full of cast-off junk—broken furniture, empty boxes, a Shop-Vac.

She wants to fill it with bluebells, Bobby said, his voice echoing off the tiled walls. What do you think?

In that case, I'll order some violets, too, I said. For the deep end.

THE FLOWER orders were just about finalized when Fiona quit. She was going back to school at last, to get her degree in interior design. She'd found a place in Hyde Park, a cottage with a backyard garden and a second bedroom for Owen. The rent was reasonable, she could commute into the city on the train, and New Preston was on the same metro line.

Sounds perfect, I said.

She, shyly: It sure seems that way.

There was a silence, and I sensed a shadow in it, some cold edge lapping like an ocean at her happiness.

And you, what about you? Are you living with Simon now?

I am. But it's been hard for him. He still sees patients in New Preston, but not often enough to cover his office rent, so he's working shifts in Boston as a locum, too.

That doesn't sound like happily-ever-after.

There's always more to the after, I said. That's the part they never tell you about. But it could be worse.

It can always be worse, she said.

She promised to visit. I wondered if she would.

THE DAY before the show, a postcard arrived covered in foreign stamps. On the front was a wide-angle shot of an Egyptian temple, its broad stone columns painted to resemble a stand of reeds, as if the whole complex were in homage to the surrounding marsh; in the distance were palm trees and the broad silver ribbon of the Nile. On the back was a note in my mother's scrawl: PARADISE IS A WETLAND.

THE NIGHT before *BLOSSOM* opened, we hosted a soft launch for friends and family. Simon, of course, was eager to come and see what had been done with the hospital. As it turned out, he had worked there as a student. He called the place *my old stomping grounds*.

He met me there, in front of the building, at six, as we'd arranged. He was just off work, rumpled and a little fragrant in his navy jacket, his day-old button-down. As soon as we walked in, the sound system crackled—Bobby's touch, a soundscape. We heard distant conversations, footfalls approaching and receding, now and then a slamming door.

Astonishing, Simon said. That's just what it was like when I worked here.

I pointed to the clock high on the wall. Was that stopped, too?

Not at all, though the days sometimes felt that way. Frozen. Long.

That night, I had a task: to photograph every room where we'd installed flowers: the entryway full of enormous white chrysanthemums. The tiny office where flame-colored tulips crowded like children around a 1950s office chair. The dayroom filled with two-tone asters, each a ring of deep-orange petals orbiting a yellow sun. The pool in the basement, bluebells in the shallow end, dark violets where the water had once gotten deep. The long, dank corridor of bright-green grass, which I watered and raked while Simon lingered by the lockers. He seemed lost in remembrance. Nights of suffering and relieving suffering, of fights and hijinks, families ripped apart and reknitted—I could imagine it all so easily.

Where will the flowers go after the show closes? he asked.

To mental hospitals, I said, and halfway houses, and shelters. Isn't that sweet?

He passed a hand over his face, suddenly upset.

What is it, Simon?

No one ever sends flowers, he said. Not to people in mental hospitals.

AFTERWARD WE took a walk in the Common. The evening was gusty, the air thick with impending rain. Office workers hurried by, solo and in groups of two or three, overcoats flapping open, neckties loosened over day-worn button-downs. Dozens of saffron-colored flags rippled from upright posts across the park, cutting a bright path through the threadbare landscape.

Simon said: They're like a row of flames.

All I see is cloth and stitching. Do you remember the mummy who fell out of the sky at Quarry Lake?

Simon replied: We're talking about fate.

We're talking, I said, about what things cost.

We walked in silence for a while. I was thinking of my mother, wandering the corridors of ancient temples, making her dreams for herself come true at last. I was glad for her sake, but her solution wasn't going to be mine. Somewhere along the way, I'd lost my feeling for the past, for the historic part of historic preservation. If all that mattered were property values, the price tags that people could put on their immaculately restored historic homes, the past was just another commodity like everything else. I was starting to wonder if it were possible to live another way, closer to what I'd known as a child: What if being at home meant catching fish every night from the comfort of an old sofa positioned on a riverbank? To decide against rooms, in favor of living. To prioritize different things.

Still, I felt pulled toward transformation. *BLOSSOM* had shown me that part of myself, but in a new light, oriented toward the future rather than the past.

We paused outside the building that had once housed the Institute for Depth Psychology, and I thought I saw Simon wince, either from his memory of the place or from the decline into which it had fallen, the front steps overgrown and mossy, all the windows boarded up. But the night was dark, the way lit only by dim gas lamps. The expression on his face might have meant anything.

The cobbled sidewalk heaved up in places where the ice had got in, and I tripped over a lifted stone. Simon caught my elbow, and I leaned on the arm he offered. We made our way to a bench, where I sat down hard, landing practically in his lap, and unlaced my boots. My ankle was already swelling.

You can't blame that on my kilim, he teased.

The rug was never the problem, I said.

It was a cheap rug, Cookie.

I said: Not everything deserves curation.

My phone buzzed. Bobby's number lit up the screen. I'd missed his call, but he'd left a message. I hobbled to a bench under a streetlight and put him on speaker while Simon crouched down before me and pulled my foot into his lap. He turned my ankle gently, feeling the joint through my boot, and I bit the inside of my cheek, trying not to yelp.

Bobby was talking fast, the street was loud with nighttime traffic, and pain made everything around me seem a little removed and distant. But I caught enough to get the gist. A developer had at last found the money to restore the old powder mill on the banks of the Chepinoxet, and the historic district commission had, with uncharacteristic quickness, green-lighted the project. The city had weighed in, too: All the units would be rent-stabilized, with an option to buy in at a fair price, in exchange for control of the underground parking garage.

Was I available to consult, provide an estimate? Could I maybe come see the place—tonight?

Simon caught my eye as I ended the call.

A fresh opportunity, he said.

No way. I'm done with all that.

Bobby said it's zoned for mixed use. There'll be shops on the ground floor. It's what everyone wants. Your station wagon is parked across the street, Simon continued, and the meter is expiring.

I can't drive. Not with this ankle. I'd have to take the train.

You forget, he replied, that I, too, have a license.

It does sound like a pretty good deal. For everyone, I added.

I bet there's even space for a doctor's office.

You'd let your old place go?

The rent's due for a hike. I wouldn't mind getting out. I could design my own consulting room for once. Get it done my way. He added, very sly: I do know a good decorator.

You're sweet, I said.

And a little old-fashioned. Here, let me help you up.

I set my bad foot on the ground beside my good one. With one hand on Simon's shoulder, I pressed up and found that I could stand. Simon took my elbow, and I found that I could walk.

The old feeling shot through me. The job was mine if I wanted it. Did I want it?

Of course I wanted it. Wanting was one thing I knew how to do.

That night I returned to New Preston, Simon behind the wheel and me in the passenger seat, staring out the window as the countryside flew by, the lakes and fields and cranberry bogs, the streams and creeks that fed the Chepinoxet, that little place of departed spirits who flickered in the darkness as I scheduled my calls and sketched my plans, gripped by a rumor of development.

AUTHOR'S NOTE

This book began with an intuition: the more stuff we own, the more unreal we feel. This soon turned into an informal research project on imposture and possession.

The psychoanalyst Helene Deutsch's "The Impostor: A Contribution to Ego Psychology of a Type of Psychopath" (1955) informed my presentation of the clinical relationship between Benno and Chuck, as did the self-psychologist Heinz Kohut's exceedingly strange case study, "The Two Analyses of Mr. Z" (1979), in which Kohut seems to have posed as both himself and his patient, resulting in an epic game of autobiographical hide-and-seek. Charles Strozier's reflections, published in "Heinz Kohut and 'the two analyses of Mr. Z': the use (and abuse?) of case material in psychoanalysis" (1999) provided additional insight. Though Benno claims to be a Freudian, his methods are aligned less with Freud than with late-twentieth-century critics of consumer society, particularly the Belgian Situationist philosopher Raoul Vaneigem who, in his influential *The Revolution of Everyday Life* (1967), suggested that consumer culture, with its relentless focus on possessions, in the end possesses us, making impostors of us all.

Attentive readers will catch echoes of Chuck in Thomas

Mann's unfinished novel *Confessions of Felix Krull* (1955), Chuck's favorite book about a remarkably flexible con artist, and in the novels of Patricia Highsmith. At different places in the text, I have adapted lines from William Blake's "Auguries of Innocence" (1803) and Alfred Lord Tennyson's "In Memoriam" (1850).

I drew additional inspiration from Angela Carter's short story, "The Fall River Axe Murders," which explores Lizzie Borden's experiences as a child of unloving parents. As New England's oldest cold case, the Borden murders still inspire speculation. The nature of John Vinnicum Morse's involvement remains contentious.

For information about the work of Frances Glessner Lee, I am indebted to Corinne May Botz's *The Nutshell Studies of Unexplained Death* (2004) and to Linda Josefowicz for drawing my attention to it.

Cookie's closing art gig is based on Anna Schuleit's *Bloom* (2012), an installation of 28,000 potted flowering plants in a Massachusetts mental hospital slated for demolition. On the night the show opens, Simon and Cookie take a walk beneath an imaginary version of *The Gates* (2005) by Christo and Jeanne-Claude along Boston's Commonwealth Avenue.

New Preston does not exist, but its architecture resembles that of College Hill in Providence, Rhode Island. There is a real "Halsey House," but apart from the name, it bears no resemblance to the Halsey residence as I have imagined it. The architect Russell Warren (1780–1860) is a real historical figure whose distinctive buildings can still be seen in and around Providence.

In naming the places of New Preston, I took my cues from Rhode Island's most ancient human inhabitants, the Narragansett Indian Tribe, whose Algonquian poetry of place-names rings through the area's toponymy. Several place-names are derived from the invaluable scholarship of Dr. Frank Waabu O'Brien of the Aquidneck Indian Council, particularly *American Indian Place Names in Rhode Island: Past and Present* (2003) and *Understanding Indian Place Names in Southern New England* (2010). I wrote the book in Providence, Rhode Island, on the traditional, ancestral, unceded territory of the Narragansetts, whose ancestors stewarded these lands with great care, and who continue as a sovereign nation today.

Netchers are real hieroglyphic signs; these and scattered other Egyptological details are gleaned from Susan Brind Morrow's *The Dawning Moon of the Mind* (2016), a modern translation of the Pyramid Texts that is also a beautiful meditation on the nature and meaning of Egyptian hieroglyphic writing, which has been for too long burdened by the biases and projections of Western scholars.

ACKNOWLEDGMENTS

Like a renovation, a book is the work of many hands—and this book is no exception. For feedback on early drafts, I'm indebted to Martha Kempner, Robin Kirman, Felicia Sullivan, Rick Moody, Matthew Carnicelli, Laura Mamelok, Liz Parker, Jaclyn Gilbert, and Kirstin Allio. Aram Fox offered a key insight at a late stage; Danielle Trussoni provided a further nudge.

I'm grateful beyond measure to my Soho team, particularly Juliet Grames for her visionary leadership, and my brilliant editor, Alexa Wejko, whose keen eye and generous notes inspired me to fine-tune the manuscript. Abigail Colegrove Adam Ferraz, and Loren Ward deserve thanks for saving me from many gaffes. I'm grateful as well to Rachel Kowal and Lily DeTaeye for their dedication and advocacy.

Behind the scenes, Heather Brown kept me focused on the big picture. Thank you, Heather.

To my late friend, Julie Sloane: Thank you for keeping me company over coffee at four A.M., when you knew I was up and writing. I am so grateful to have known you and your glorious art.

Finally, I am grateful to my family for their patience, their good humor, and their excellent company during this long period of work. My husband, Matthew, and my daughter, Jane, bore the daily brunt of my commitment to this writing, and I thank them for their forbearance. Michael Josefowicz, my beloved late father-in-law, did not live to see this book reach publication, but his passion for print continues to nourish my faith in books and writing. This book is dedicated to my mother-in-law, Linda Josefowicz, who over many years has taught me much about homes and families, their making and remaking. Home is where my heart is, even when I'm writing, and they are the reason why.